A GANGSTA'S LAST KISS

KYIRIS ASHLEY

U.A.D PRESENTS

STAY UP TO DATE

To stay up to date on new releases, plus get information on contests, sneak peeks and more,

Click the link below...
https://mailchi.mp/6d21003686d1/subscribe

SOUNDTRACKS

Scan the QR Code below to listen to the Soundtracks/Singles of some of your favorite U.A.D titles:

Don't have Spotify or Apple Music?
No Sweat!
Visit your choice streaming platform and search URBAN AINT DEAD.

Currently on lock serving a bid?
JPay, iHeartRadio, WHATEVER!
We got you covered.
Simply log into your facility's kiosk or tablet, go to music and
search URBAN AINT DEAD.

U.A.D PRESENTS

Like & Follow us on social media:

FB - URBAN AINT DEAD

IG: @uadpresents

Tik Tok - @uadpresents

Submission Guidelines

Submit the first three chapters of your completed manuscript to urbanaintdead@gmail.com, subject line: Your book's title. The manuscript must be in a .doc file and sent as an attachment. The document should be in Times New Roman, double-spaced, and in size 12 font. Also, provide your synopsis and full contact information. If sending multiple submissions, they must each be in a separate email. Have a story but no way to submit it electronically? You can still submit to URBAN AINT DEAD. Send in the first three chapters, written or typed, of your completed manuscript to:

URBAN AINT DEAD
P.O Box 448
Maybrook, NY 12543

DO NOT send original manuscript. Must be a duplicate.
Provide your synopsis and a cover letter containing your full contact information.
Thanks for considering URBAN AINT DEAD.

Chapter One

"**K**iss, get yo' ass up right now. Yo' ass ain't bout to miss this bus for the second day in a row. You miss that shit today, and yo' ass gone be walkin' to school. Play with me if you want to."

Kiss' mother's voice sliced through the small room like a siren. Sade didn't need an alarm clock to get her daughter up for school. With Sade working nights, she liked the quiet time she had alone, while Kiss was at school. So, she made sure to wake her up on time every morning. The morning before, Sade had fallen asleep before she made sure Kiss had left the house. However, this morning would be different. Sade would be sure not to lay down until Kiss was out the house and heading to the bus stop.

Kiss groaned, dragging her fluffy pink comforter tighter around her slim frame. She hated mornings, especially these mornings, the last two weeks of school before summer vacation. The teachers had already checked out, and the students were restless, not giving a damn about the rules they'd followed all year. Kiss swore waking up this early for nothing was cruel and unusual punishment.

"I'm up," she lied, head still on the pillow.

The bedroom door creaked open, and Sade walked inside. Sade Johnson was thirty-four years old with caramel skin that was still flawless and beautiful, despite exhaustion. She'd just came home from her midnight shift at the nursing home where she worked, the curves of her body filling the light pink scrubs that she wore. Her hair was in tiny braids that stopped halfway down her back. Sade was a single mother and had been for the last twelve years. Kiss' father had never been in her life, leaving the moment Sade had told him that she was pregnant. Sade didn't let that stop her from having her child. She went to school to get her LPN license and had been working hard to provide for her daughter ever since.

"Kiss, don't play with me," she spoke, arms crossed. "I told you before I left for work last night not to stay up too late. You got one minute before I snatch that cover and drag you out this bed."

"I said I'm up," Kiss repeated, sitting up slow with a pout. Her long braids swung around her shoulders, the ends clicking with pink and white beads. She rubbed her almond-shaped eyes, blinking hard, then stood up.

Sade gave her a quick once-over before softening. "Thank you. Now take a shower, brush your teeth, and put on your uniform. Make it quick. The bus ain't gon' wait on you."

"Yes, ma'am."

Satisfied, Sade left her to it. Kiss rushed to the bathroom and took a quick shower before brushing her teeth. Kiss tugged on her uniform, a navy polo shirt tucked into a khaki skirt, then slid on her sneakers. She checked herself in the mirror, running her hands over her slim frame. Her light brown skin glowed under the natural light coming in from the window. Her big eyes flickered, as she looked at herself. At just twelve years old, Kiss wasn't into makeup, but she made sure never to leave the house without applying lip gloss.

Sade already had a bowl of cereal waiting on the table when Kiss came downstairs. Kiss ate fast, knowing that she didn't have a lot of time before the bus came. She'd just taken the last bite of her cereal when Sade handed Kiss her bookbag.

"Have a good day. I love you, Kiss."

"Love you too, Ma."

The screen door creaked, as Kiss stepped out into the cool morning air. The sun was high in the sky, and Kiss knew it was going to be another hot day. She walked down to the corner where kids gathered, waiting on the bus. Kiss smiled when she saw Omari and Onyx Blackwell.

At thirteen, the twins were already known across the block. Both were dark-skinned and tall for their age. Both had sharp cheekbones and matching brown eyes, but anyone paying attention could tell them apart instantly.

Omari stood straight, his uniform neat, bookbag strapped tight across his slim shoulders. He had a serious face, one that made him seem older than he actually was. However, Onyx was different – same dark skin but stockier, his shirt untucked, sneakers barely laced. He grinned wide, playing around with two boys from their class, laughing loud enough for everyone to hear. Between the twins, he was the trouble.

The moment Kiss walked up, Onyx spotted her. "There go Kiss!" he called out, grinning. "Thought you overslept again."

A few kids laughed. Kiss rolled her eyes but smiled, clutching her backpack strap tighter.

Omari glanced at his brother with annoyance before turning his steady gaze on Kiss. "You good?" he asked quietly, his voice low and calm.

Kiss nodded, heart skipping. "Yeah, just tired. I was up late last night again."

Omari gave the smallest nod. Onyx smirked, sliding closer. "You always tired, girl. Bet you stayed up late writing 'Mrs. Kiss Blackwell' all in your notebook."

The group of kids cracked up. Kiss' cheeks warmed, but she snapped back instantly. "Ain't nobody thinkin' about you, Onyx."

Omari shot his twin a look sharp enough to cut his laughter

short. The bus pulled up with a squeal, folding doors opening wide. Kiss climbed on with the twins following her. Kids in the back called out greetings, as Kiss and the twins made their way to their seats.

At school, the day passed in the same familiar blur the last two weeks of school had. Kiss sat two rows behind Omari in math, watching the back of his head, as he worked problems neatly on his paper. Onyx, meanwhile, spent half the class cracking jokes until the teacher snapped and made him stand in the hallway. For the twins to have the same face, they were like night and day when it came to their personalities.

At lunch, the three of them sat together, trays of pizza and chocolate milk between them. Omari quietly slid his extra fruit cup to Kiss without a word, knowing how much she liked them. Onyx noticed, smirked, and tossed his milk carton at another boy across the cafeteria, starting a playful food fight. The entire cafeteria began throwing food and drinks at one another. The teachers were so mad that they tried to give them all detention; however, with it being the last two weeks of school, nobody stayed.

By the time the final bell rang, Kiss felt lighter. Summer was just two weeks away, and freedom was almost here. She didn't take the bus. Instead, she walked home with the twins, the late afternoon sun blazing against cracked sidewalks. Omari carried her books without Kiss even asking. Onyx kicked a can down the street, teasing both of them. At the corner, they split ways, Omari and Onyx heading to their side of the block, while Kiss climbed her porch steps.

Inside, the house was quiet. Her mama was sleep, getting her rest before her midnight shift began. Kiss reheated leftovers, ate at the kitchen table, then walked to her room. She sprawled across her bed with her diary, doodling hearts around Omari's name before slamming it shut, embarrassed at herself. She really liked Omari, and she knew he liked her too, but he had yet to ask her to be his girlfriend. They had been talking for months, and she couldn't figure out what was taking him so long.

Around ten that night, Sade walked into Kiss' room. "I'm about to go to work. Don't stay up all night, Kiss. Take yo' butt to sleep at a decent hour."

"Yes, Mama."

The moment Sade's car pulled out the driveway, Kiss got up and went into the living room to watch TV. She'd heard what Sade said, but with her being gone all night, Kiss had the house all to herself, so she was able to do what she wanted to do. When the house phone rang, Kiss looked down at the caller ID. Seeing that it was Omari, she answered it.

"What you over there doing?" Omari asked.

"Nothing much, just watching a movie. What about you?"

"I'm just chilling, trying to see what's up with you. Did Ms. Sade leave for work yet?"

"Yeah, she gone."

"You want some company? I could watch the movie with you."

Kiss smiled before telling Omari that he could come over. She rushed into the hall closet to grab the air freshener. She sprayed the entire house, wanting to make sure it smelled good when Omari walked inside. Five minutes later, there was a knock at the back door, and Kiss knew it was Omari. He always came to the back when her mother was at work. She had told him about the nosy neighbor across the street. Kiss had warned him that she was always looking out of her window at all times of the day and night. The last thing either of them wanted was for her to see Omari and tell Sade he was there.

Omari walked in, and Kiss led him through the kitchen and into the living room. They took a seat on the couch.

"What you watchin'?" Omari asked, smoothly placing his arm over Kiss' shoulder.

"*Jason's Lyric*, but we can change it if you want to."

"Nah, this cool. Let's watch it."

They sat there, watching the movie and enjoying each other's company. Omari had never seen the movie before and was all in by the time Lyric was shot. When the credits started rolling, Omari looked over at Kiss.

"I really like you, Kiss."

Kiss blushed, smiling back at him. "I really like you too."

"Would you be my girlfriend?"

There it was, the words Kiss had been waiting on for months. The day was finally here. Kiss wanted to scream it from the mountaintop, tell everyone she was now Omari Blackwell's girl, but her voice felt like it was caught in her throat. She nodded her head yes, but when she opened her mouth to say the words, nothing came out. Kiss cleared her throat and was finally able to say the words.

"Yes, Omari, I would love to be your girlfriend."

Omari hugged Kiss tightly and planted a kiss on her cheek. He told Kiss to pick another movie, and they sat there, watching TV together for hours, before Omari decided to go back home.

"I'll see you at the bus stop tomorrow. Or do you want me to pick you up in the morning so that we can walk together?"

"Us walking together would be nice," Kiss replied.

"Cool, then I'll be here at seven twenty-five."

Kiss smiled and hugged Omari goodbye. She watched as he walked through her back yard and through the alleyway until he faded into the darkness. Kiss closed the door, still smiling. *He asked me to be his girlfriend,* she thought, as she walked up the stairs to her room. As she drifted to sleep, she heard the sirens in the distance, something she heard every night in Detroit. However, tonight, they didn't scare her. All that was on Kiss' mind was how she'd finally become Omari's girlfriend.

Chapter Two

Omari was at Kiss' house the next morning just as promised. He'd left early to ensure he was on time. Kiss stepped out, swinging her bookbag over her shoulder. She smiled when she saw him. He wore a white polo and a pair of navy-blue pants. He wore the same uniform that everyone that went to their school wore. However, to Kiss, Omari looked better in his than anyone else at the school did.

He didn't say much, but the way his eyes softened when he looked at her said everything. "You ready?" he asked.

Kiss nodded and without even thinking twice, slipped her hand into his. Omari's fingers tightened around hers – not too tight but firm enough for her to feel safe. For the first time, walking to the bus stop didn't feel like a chore to Kiss. It was the start of something new.

Onyx was already at the bus stop when they arrived, standing with a group of boys, talking loud enough for the entire block to hear. His uniform shirt was half untucked, his sneakers were barely tied, and he looked like he had just rolled out of bed and came to the bus stop. The second he spotted them, his eyebrow shot up.

"Look at y'all," Onyx said, grinning wide. "Holding hands like some married couple. Bro, that's why you left early, so that you could walk with Kiss? Nigga, you trippin'."

The group of boys Onyx was talking to cracked up laughing.

Kiss rolled her eyes and tried to let go of Omari's hand, but he squeezed tighter, his jaw flexing. "Mind your business," he spat, his deepening voice carrying just enough edge to quiet the laughter.

Onyx smirked, eyes flickering from his brother to Kiss. "Aight then, damn. You ain't even gotta be like that. I was just playin' with y'all."

Kiss pretended to look away, but inside, her stomach fluttered. She liked the way Omari stood up for her. It was different from Onyx, who always had something slick to say.

"You good?" Omari asked, looking over at Kiss.

"Yeah, I'm cool. Ain't nobody thinkin' bout Onyx."

The bus arrived with a squeal, and kids piled on in a rush of backpacks and chatter. Omari guided Kiss up the steps, their hands still linked together, while Onyx trailed behind, humming to himself like he was already planning his next joke. However, he was quiet during the bus ride, just sat there, looking out the window the entire ride.

The hallways buzzed with end-of-year energy, the air heavy with the scent of sweat, paper, and cafeteria food. Kiss walked with Omari by her side, trying not to grin too wide when people whispered. A girl in her class nudged her friend and whispered, "Omari goes with Kiss now?" Kiss pretended not to hear, but her cheeks warmed.

In math class, Omari sat right in front of Kiss, focused on his notebook. His handwriting was neat and precise with each number lined up like soldiers. Kiss admired the way he stayed calm even when other boys were cutting up. Onyx, for example, lasted all of fifteen minutes before the teacher had enough.

"Onyx Blackwell, hallway. Now!" Mr. Upshaw yelled.

The class erupted in muffled laughter, as Onyx dragged his feet to the door, smirking like he'd won something. He glanced at Kiss on his way out, giving her a wink. Kiss shook her head, but the truth was that Onyx's antics were funny, even when she didn't want to admit it.

By lunch, Omari and Onyx had reunited at the table where Kiss sat. Omari slid his untouched fruit cup across to her without a word. Kiss smiled, peeling back the lid. Onyx leaned back, watching with a smirk.

"See, that's why girls like my brother," he said. "He always giving away his food. You better enjoy that, Kiss, 'cause he gon' be broke one day, handing out all his money."

Kiss laughed despite herself. Omari gave his twin a look sharp enough to cut steel. "Shut up, Onyx. Maybe if you gave a little something, you would have a girl too."

"What? I don't need no girl if all they do is have they hand out. I'm stackin' my bread." Onyx shrugged, still grinning. "But for real, y'all cute, but don't get too cute."

The three of them sat in the same familiar triangle they always sat in, Omari and Onyx on one side and Kiss on the other. The cafeteria was loud and filled with children, but Omari was the only person Kiss saw. His dark chocolate skin gleamed in the lighting, and all Kiss could do was stare. When lunch was over and class started again, Kiss could barely pay attention because all she wanted to do was look at Omari.

The sun burned hotter by the time the final bell rang. Kids poured out of the school in waves, laughter and shouts carrying down the block. Kiss walked with Omari, their hands brushing, until he finally took hers again.

"You gon' come outside later?" he asked quietly.

"Maybe. I gotta ask my mama," Kiss replied, shy but smiling.

Onyx walked a few steps behind them, kicking a crushed pop can along the sidewalk. His usual chatter was gone, replaced by silence. Kiss glanced back once, catching the look on his face. He looked as though something was bothering him, but Kiss didn't ask. When they got to the end of the corner, Onyx continued to walk home, while Omari walked Kiss back to her house. When they got there, Omari stopped at the bottom of the porch steps. He shifted, scratching the back of his neck, suddenly awkward. Kiss tilted her head, waiting.

"See you tomorrow," he said finally then leaned down and pressed a quick kiss to her cheek. Her skin tingled where his lips touched, her heart racing.

"Bye, Omari," she whispered.

When Kiss walked into the house, it was quiet except for the hum of the refrigerator. Already knowing her mother was asleep, Kiss set her bag down, reheated the food her mother made, and sat at the table. When she was done, she washed her dish and went into the living room to watch TV. The TV played, but all she saw was Omari's face. She knew he'd told her that he would see her tomorrow, but Kiss couldn't wait. She called Omari and asked if he wanted to come over and watch movies when her mother went to work. She smiled when he agreed, saying he would be over around eleven.

Sade was dressed and ready for work around ten fifteen that night. She walked into the kitchen, grabbing the lunch she'd packed for herself, before walking into the living room.

"You eat?" she asked, looking down at Kiss on the couch.

"Yeah," Kiss replied, grinning without meaning to.

Sade narrowed her eyes. "What you cheesin' about?"

"Nothing, just something on TV."

"Mhm." Sade slid off her shoes and sat across from her. "That boy, Omari, walk you home again?"

Kiss' face gave her away before she could even say anything.

Sade chuckled, shaking her head. "Lord have mercy. You growing up faster than I thought." Her tone shifted, soft but serious. "Just remember, boys ain't nothing but a distraction unless you keep your head straight. You hear me?"

"Yes, ma'am."

Sade kissed her daughter on the forehead before walking out

the door. Knowing Omari would be over soon, Kiss started searching the TV, trying to find a movie for them to watch.

Omari sat in his bed, waiting for the clock to hit eleven. He couldn't wait to see Kiss and was happy when she called him and asked him to come over. Onyx walked into the room they shared and grabbed his sneakers out the closet.

"Where you bout to go?" Omari asked.

"Shit, I'm going to go make some money."

"Make some money? Onyx, what the hell are you talkin' about?"

"That nigga, Blue, saw me earlier when I was walking to the store. Told me if I wanted to make some real money, then I should come to his spot tonight. So, that's where I'm going. You wanna roll with me?"

Omari and Onyx didn't have a father in their life, so their mother, Tamika, worked two full time jobs to make sure her children had everything they needed. Because of that, Tamika was never home, and when she was, she was either sleeping or getting ready to go to another job. Because of this, her sons practically raised themselves.

"Nah, I'm good. And if you ask me, you shouldn't go either. Blue steals cars; that's how he makes his money. Do you know what would happen if you get caught doing that shit? Besides, I'm going to Kiss' house tonight."

"You would rather go to a broad house than go get some money? You sound crazy. Let me spit some game to you right quick. You will lose a lot of money chasing bitches, but you will never lose a bitch chasing money."

Omari looked at Onyx and shook his head. There was no way he was going to steal cars with him. As much as he wished his brother wouldn't go either, he knew there was nothing he could do to stop him. Omari watched as Onyx put on his shoes and walked out the door on his way to ruin his life. Omari got ready as well so that he could go to Kiss' house.

He walked out the house, walking down the street and through the alley, until he got to Kiss' back door. He knocked, and a few moments later, she answered the door. She was wearing a pair of purple sweatpants and a white tee shirt. When he looked at her, he saw the most beautiful girl in the world. They walked to her couch and watched movies with his arm wrapped around her. They sat there for hours, just enjoying each other's company. At about two, Omari finally decided he needed to go home and get some sleep. He placed a kiss on Kiss' cheek before walking out the back door. He walked back home with thoughts of Kiss on his mind. Kiss was his first girlfriend, and he hoped they would be together for a long time.

When Omari got home, Onyx still wasn't there. He laid out his clothes for school the next morning before putting on his pajamas and getting in the bed. Onyx walked in their room about ten minutes later. He turned on the light, not giving a damn that Omari was already in bed.

"You see this?" Onyx spoke, holding up a wad of money. "This what I made in one night. This like four hundred dollars, and you could be making it too."

Omari just shook his head before turning over and placing the cover back over his head. He couldn't believe that his brother was really out there running with street niggas. Even though they were identical twins, they were as different as oil and water. Where Onyx wanted to be in the streets, Omari wanted to be in the books. Omari didn't have anything to say, so instead, he just went to sleep.

Chapter Three

*E*very morning until the last day of school, Omari picked Kiss up to walk her to the bus stop and walked her home every afternoon. On the last day of school, Omari walked Kiss home. Kiss asked him if he wanted to come over after her mother went to work. When Omari agreed, Kiss smiled before going into the house. She was all smiles until she walked inside and saw her mother's boyfriend, Darren, sitting on the couch. He had his legs kicked up on the coffee table with a beer in his hand as he watched TV.

Kiss didn't like Darren and hated when he came over. He stood six feet tall with light skin and hazel eyes. He had long, curly hair down to his shoulders that he kept in two braids to the back. His skinny frame was filled with multiple tattoos across his chest and down both of his arms. Darren didn't have a job and wanted Sade to do everything for him while he was there. Kiss didn't say a word to him, as she walked directly to her room. She knew her mother would be going to work that night, so she went in her room to change her clothes before she went back outside. Kiss had just changed her clothes and walked back into the living room when her mother walked out the kitchen.

"Kiss, I was just coming to get you. We need to have a little family chat." Sade smiled. "Go head and sit on the couch. This won't take long."

Kiss nodded her head and walked over to the couch. She

looked over at Darren, wondering why he was still sitting there if this was supposed to be a family meeting. *His ass ain't family. He can leave,* Kiss thought.

"Kiss, Darren is moving in," Sade spoke.

Kiss' eyes widened in disbelief. "Moving in? Why?"

"Because we are together, and when you love each other and want to be together, that's the next step. I want my man here with me when I wake up and when I go to sleep, and he wants to be here."

"Me and yo' mama gon' get married one day. I feel that it's only right that we live together."

"We want to be a family, and the only way to do that is for Darren to move in. It's going to be fun, Kiss. We going to be a real family, and you will finally have a father figure in your life."

Kiss just looked at her mother, not believing what she was saying. How could she want him to be her father figure when he didn't even know the first thing about being a man? Kiss knew that nothing she said would change the fact that he was moving in, so she didn't say anything. She just nodded her head and stood from the couch.

"Can I go outside now?"

"Sure, just be back by the time the streetlights come on," Sade replied.

Kiss walked out the house and went down the street to see Omari. When she knocked on the door, Onyx answered.

"What up doe, Kiss? You here to see Omari, huh?"

"Yeah, he home?"

"He just walked to the store. Why you lookin' so sad?" Onyx asked.

Kiss looked up at him, ready for the joke she knew would follow. However, his face was surprisingly filled with concern. Before Kiss could say another word, Omari walked up.

"Hey, Kiss. I didn't even know you were here. I would have

bought you something from the store if I did. You want me to go back?" Omari asked with a smile.

"Nah, I'm okay."

"She ain't okay, bro. She look sad as hell and was just about to tell me what was wrong with her before you walked up," Onyx confirmed.

Kiss sat on the weathered steps, looking up at Omari. Her knees were drawn up, and her fingers were twisted tight together in her lap. The wood was warm beneath her thighs, and the evening sun poured over the neighborhood, but none of that mattered. Her stomach was heavy and knotted, and all she wanted to do was cry. She couldn't believe her mother was about to ruin their wonderful family by adding Darren to it. Omari and Onyx sat on either side of her in deep concern, as they waited for Kiss to tell them her problems.

"My mama told me something today," Kiss said finally, her voice smaller than she wanted.

Onyx cocked his head, brushing his hand over his head. "Well, what she say? You sound like you about to cry."

"I'm not crying," Kiss snapped, though her throat burned.

Omari's eyes softened, watching her closer. "What'd she say?"

Kiss pressed her palms against her skirt, wringing the fabric between her fingers. "She said Darren's moving in," Kiss whispered.

Onyx sat up straighter, his grin gone. "Moving in? Like in y'all house?"

Kiss nodded, her throat tight. "She said that they want us to be a family, and they love each other, so this was the next step. My mama sat me down to have a family meeting, so they could tell me. I don't even know why because it seemed to me that their minds were already made up when they told me. She didn't even ask me how I felt about it."

Omari's jaw flexed, his dark eyes narrowing. He'd always

been the quiet one, the thinker. But even now, Kiss could feel the anger building inside him. "And how do you feel about it?" he asked, his voice low, steady.

"I don't want him there. I don't want him there at all. It's bad enough that he spends the night when my mama's off. But to be there every day? I'm going to hate it." She swallowed, lowering her voice. "He gives me this feeling, and I don't know what it is, but I don't like it."

Omari's fist curled against his knee, knuckles pale against his dark skin. "Ain't nothing nice about Darren. I remember when my aunt dated him. He ain't do nothing but cheat on her. She was on the phone crying to my mama damn near every day."

Onyx leaned forward, elbows on his knees, shaking his head. "Man, this is crazy. Your mama really gon' let that dude move in?"

Kiss blinked fast, trying to keep the sting out of her eyes. "Yeah, and I guess I don't have a choice in the matter. But I want a choice. I want to tell my mama that I don't want him there, and I want her to listen to me. But I already know she won't."

The porch went quiet except for the hum of cicadas and the sound of kids yelling down the block. Omari's silence was thick, his chest rising and falling like he was holding in more than he could ever let out. Onyx, for once, didn't have a joke ready. He just muttered under his breath, "Man, hell nah, that's crazy."

Kiss finally looked up at them, her wide, almond-shaped eyes searching their faces. "I'm going to hate being at home now."

"You don't have to be there with him. Come over here when you wake up in the morning. You can stay here all day," Omari suggested.

Kiss nodded quickly, her heart beating fast. "Yeah, I can do that."

Omari leaned closer, his shoulder brushing hers, his voice dropping low so only she could hear. "Don't be scared to tell us if he do something, Kiss. Don't keep it inside. I don't care what your mama say. If he ever tries you in a way…" His jaw clenched again. "And don't even worry. He won't be around long. He moves from female to female. How long has he been with yo' mama?"

"A little over a year," Kiss replied.

"It's gon' be all good, Kiss. Don't even sweat that shit. We got you," Onyx spoke, looking at Kiss with a half-smile.

The promise sat heavy in the warm evening air. Kiss nodded, her chest loosening just a little. For now, with the twins on either side of her, she could almost believe she was safe. Onyx smiled at Kiss before standing to his feet. He walked inside the house, and the screen door slammed behind him. Omari wrapped his arm around Kiss, and she laid her head on his shoulder.

Kiss kept her eyes on her knees, twisting the hem of her skirt between her fingers. "You know what this means, right?" she whispered.

Omari tilted his head, watching her carefully. "What?"

She let out a shaky breath. "It means you probably can't come over at night no more. Not with him in the house. Darren ain't gonna let that happen." Her voice cracked. "I don't know how it's gon' work."

Omari didn't answer right away. He shifted closer instead, the wood groaning beneath his weight. His arm wrapped tighter around her.

"Then we'll find another way," he said simply.

Kiss finally looked up at him. His face was calm, as if he wasn't worried at all.

"You don't get it," Kiss said, shaking her head. "He gon' be there, Omari. Like in my house every day and night. You don't know how that feels. I can't even walk through my own living room comfortably because he's there now."

Omari's jaw tightened. "I know what you mean, Kiss, but he won't be there long. Knowing him, he probably cheating on yo' mama right now. Trust me, Kiss, he will be gon' before you know it."

"I sure hope you're right"

"And we still going to see each other. I don't care if I gotta climb the tree next to your house and crawl into your window."

Kiss laughed, but when she looked over at Omari, she saw that he didn't even crack a smile.

"You serious?" she asked.

Omari turned to her fully, his knees brushing hers. "Kiss, I been serious since the first day I told you I liked you. You think I'm just gon' sit around and let some dude make me not see you? Naw, if I can't be there the same way, then I'll find a new way. But either way, I'll be there."

Kiss smiled as she placed her hand into Omari's, her head still on his shoulder. "Thank you, Omari."

"You don't have to thank me, Kiss. I'm your man, so I'm going to always be there for you. That's something you can trust."

Kiss stared at him, her heart pounding in her ears. The truth was that Omari was the only person she totally trusted. Even when she felt like the whole world was turning against her, she knew he'd never switch up.

"I trust you," she whispered.

For a long moment, they just sat there, hands clasped, the quiet between them saying more than any words could. A car drove by slowly, its headlights sweeping across the porch, reminding her how late it was getting. She glanced at the corner of the block where the streetlights had just flickered on, casting the sidewalk in a pale-yellow glow.

"I should go home," she spoke reluctantly.

Omari didn't let go right away. His eyes searched hers, heavy with all the things they were too young to say out loud. Finally, he nodded. "Alright. But remember what I told you. I don't care what it takes, we'll find a way. Tonight will be the only night that I don't come over."

Kiss stood, her knees shaky. "Okay. I'll see you tomorrow, Omari."

"Come on. I'll walk you back home."

Omari took her hand, and they walked together, the streetlights glowing down on them. Kiss' chest tightened with each step she took closer to her house. She held Omari's hand tighter, as she breathed in and out. When they got to her house, Omari hugged Kiss tightly, and she melted into him. She walked up her steps slowly, not wanting to go inside. Sade's car was still in the driveway, so Kiss knew she was still home.

She rushed inside and went to the kitchen to wash her hands. She didn't see Darren and hoped that she wouldn't for the rest of the night. Kiss quickly fixed herself a plate of the dinner her mother had cooked that night and sat at the table to eat. Sade walked into the kitchen wearing a white tee and a pair of pink shorts.

"You not going to work tonight?" Kiss asked, looking up from her plate.

"Nah, I decided to take a vacation day so that Darren and I could celebrate his first night here together."

Kiss looked at her mother, relieved that she wouldn't be alone with Darren. She watched as Sade grabbed a bottle of cheap wine out the fridge and two glasses before walking out the kitchen and back to her room. Once Kiss finished her food, she walked into the living room to watch TV. Darren and Sade didn't leave the room for the rest of the night.

Over the next few weeks, Kiss would get up in the morning, get dressed, and go down to Omari's house. She wouldn't return until the streetlights came on. On the nights that her mother went to work, she would stay in her room until Darren went to sleep, then she would let Omari into the back door. Sometimes, they chilled in her room, and other times, they went into the basement. No matter where they were, Kiss was just happy to be with him.

One morning, Kiss woke up while the rest of the house was quiet. The sun hadn't fully climbed over the neighborhood yet, and the air inside still carried that heavy stillness of early morning. She lay in bed a moment, just listening. Sade was still knocked out, and Kiss couldn't understand how when she could hear Darren's snoring all the way in her room. Her stomach tightened as she listened. The reminder hit like a weight on her chest. Darren's stuff had already filled corners of the house, crowding out the familiarity she'd always known – his jacket slung over a chair, his cologne hanging in the air too heavy, his voice echoing from the back room every night. It was all too much for Kiss.

Kiss slipped out of bed and pulled her robe around her, careful not to let the floorboards creak. She hated how much effort it took to move quietly in her own house now. She walked to the kitchen and grabbed the cereal box from the counter and poured herself a bowl. The cereal falling into the bowl sounded too loud, and she winced, glancing toward the hall like Darren might come stomping out. She hated that feeling. It was like she was sneaking, even when she wasn't doing anything wrong.

She ate fast, barely tasting the food, her ears straining for every sound in the house. When she finished, she rinsed the bowl, set it in the sink, and padded toward the bathroom with her towel in hand. The hot shower helped. For a while, and she could almost trick herself into feeling normal. Steam fogged the mirror, and she closed her eyes under the spray, letting the water beat against her skin until her shoulders loosened. She turned off the water and stepped out, wrapping the towel tight around her body. Steam swirled around her, as she wiped at the mirror with her palm. Her reflection was blurry but enough to brush her teeth. She leaned over the sink, toothbrush in hand, still damp from the shower.

When the bathroom door opened, Kiss' head snapped up. Her eyes locked on the mirror just as the door creaked wider. Darren stood there, broad shoulders filling the frame, his eyes cutting straight to her. He froze like he was surprised, but Kiss knew better. She'd been in the bathroom long enough that anybody would've heard the water running. So, she knew he'd known she was in there.

"Oh, my bad," Darren spoke, dragging his words out slow, like he was taking his time to pull them together. His gaze flickered over her, too slow to be innocent. "Didn't know you was in here."

Kiss' heart thudded against her ribs. For a second, fear locked her in place. The towel felt thinner, her skin hotter under his stare. Then, anger flared, sharp and sudden, burning through the fear.

"Yes, you did," she snapped, her voice trembling but fierce. She clutched the towel tighter around her chest, toothbrush clattering into the sink.

Darren raised his hands, smirking faintly. "Chill, little girl. I ain't even see nothing."

Kiss' stomach twisted. That smile, slick and wrong, told her he'd done it on purpose.

"Get out," she hissed.

For a beat, he didn't move. His eyes lingered a second too long, and the tension stretched so thick she could hardly breathe. Then, finally, he chuckled under his breath and stepped back, pulling the door closed behind him. The second the door clicked, Kiss sagged against the sink, her knees weak. She pressed her forehead against the cool mirror, trying to steady her breath. Her hands shook as she yanked her clothes on, movements jerky and rushed. She couldn't shake the heat of his stare or the wrongness of his smirk. She rushed into her room, put on her sneakers, and walked out the front door.

The air outside hit her like a blessing, still cool from the early morning hours. Kiss didn't look back at her house. She walked fast, almost running, her arms wrapped tight across her chest like she was holding herself together. Omari's house wasn't far, just across the block, but the distance felt like miles with her thoughts pounding as loud as her footsteps. She didn't stop until she was at the Blackwell's porch, her hand banging against the screen door with more force than she meant. It was Omari who answered. He wore a plain tee shirt with black hoop shorts, and his eyes were still heavy with sleep. But the moment he saw her, his expression sharpened.

"Kiss? What's wrong?"

She opened her mouth, but the words tangled. Her throat was tight, her heart still racing. "Can I come in please?" she whispered.

He stepped aside without hesitation. She brushed past him, pacing the living room, while he shut the door.

"Kiss," he said again, his voice steady, calm but firm. "What happened?"

She stopped, turning to him, her chest heaving. "He came in the bathroom, while I was in there."

Omari froze. "What?"

"Darren." She spat the name like poison. "I had just got out the shower and was brushing my teeth when he just walked in like he didn't know I was there. But he knew." Her voice broke, and she pressed her hands to her face, fury and fear spilling out together. "He tried to act like it was an accident, but it wasn't. He was smiling, Omari. Smiling like it was funny or something."

Omari's jaw clenched so tight a muscle ticked in his cheek. He stepped closer, his presence steady and grounding. "Did he touch you?"

"No," Kiss whispered. Her hands dropped, fists balling at her sides. "But he wanted me to know he could. That's what it felt like. Like he was telling me without saying it." Her voice shook, but her eyes burned with anger. "I'm not crazy. I know what I saw."

Omari reached out, his hand brushing hers before taking it, holding her tight. "I believe you," he assured. "Don't ever think I don't."

Tears welled in her eyes, but anger kept them from falling. "Mama won't believe me. She'll say I made it up, or I'm overreacting. But I'm not."

"You still need to tell her."

Kiss shook her head, her lip trembling. "I hate him. I hate that he's in my house. I don't even feel safe in my own bathroom."

Omari's grip tightened. "Then you don't gotta be there by yourself. You hear me? If you need to get away, you come here. Any time. Day or night."

Her chest rose and fell, her heart still pounding, but his words wrapped around her like a shield. She nodded, clutching his hand tighter. "Thank you."

Kiss stayed at Omari's house all day. They sat on the couch, watching movies together. When Kiss got hungry, Omari made her a sandwich. For those hours she was with him, Kiss felt safe. But when the streetlights came on, her stomach tightened, as she realized it was time for her to go back home.

"Leave the back door unlocked for me tonight, and I'll be over once yo' mama leaves, and Darren goes to sleep."

Chapter Four

$\mathcal{K}$iss laid across her bed, watching the streetlight flicker through her curtains, as she waited for Darren to fall asleep. It had only been a few hours since she'd left Omari's house, but she missed him already and couldn't wait for him to come over. They had gotten their system down pat, and it had worked for them so far. Omari would come into the back door, and Kiss would meet him in the basement.

She hugged her pillow to her chest, rocking just a little, waiting. The waiting was the hardest part because she never knew when Darren would go to sleep. Her eyes flicked to the clock, and she saw it was nearly midnight. Kiss slid off her bed and slowly made her way to her bedroom door. She looked down the hall to see her mother's bedroom door closed. She knew that meant Darren was sleep.

She slipped into the hallway and could still smell Darren's cologne lingering in the air. Kiss' heart pounded in her chest, and she didn't understand why. She'd done this same routine every night for the past three weeks, but something about tonight felt different. She walked into the dark kitchen and over to the back door. Her fingers hovered over the lock, trembling. Kiss unlocked the door then headed back up to her room to call Omari.

The moment Omari told Kiss he was on his way, she felt better. She hung up the phone and grabbed two blankets for them to cuddle up under. She walked over to her drawer and grabbed the deck of Uno cards that was inside. Omari always brought snacks with him when he came, so she knew he had that part covered. With everything that she needed already in her hands, Kiss was ready to head to the basement. She smiled, knowing that in just a few minutes, she would be with Omari.

Kiss was just about to go down to the basement when her bedroom door slung open, and Darren appeared. He was standing there in a pair of red hoop shorts and a white tee. Sweat beaded off his light skin, and his tall frame towered over Kiss, as he stepped toward her.

"Darren, why are you in my room?" Kiss' voice carried throughout the small bedroom.

"Where do you think you're going is the real question." Darren looked down at the two blankets in Kiss' hands.

Darren took steps toward Kiss, as she stepped back. Her heart pounded in her chest, and she knew she'd just been caught.

"I'm just…"

"You just what?"

Before Kiss could say anything, Darren grabbed her. He pulled her so close that Kiss could smell the liquor on his breath.

"Darren, please let me go. I'm gonna tell my mama if you don't."

"Tell her. She not gon' believe you anyway. I see you and the way you look at me. I know you been waiting on this."

Omari jumped up the moment Kiss called and told him the back door was unlocked. He loved spending time with her, so every night when her mother went to work and Darren went to sleep, he made his way over and snuck in her back door. Omari walked into the bathroom to brush his teeth before putting on a pair of sneakers. Onyx was sitting on the couch, watching TV, when Omari walked into the living room.

"Where you 'bout to go?"

"Shoot to Kiss' crib real quick. Sade at work, and you know she hate being there with Darren alone."

"Hold up. You need to take this shit with you." Onyx left the room and returned a few moments later with a black .38 in his hand. The gun was just small enough for him to handle.

"Onyx, where the hell did you get this from?"

"Blue gave it to me. He gave me two actually and told me never to leave the house without at least one of them being on me. Now, I'm giving one to you. Just in case."

"Just in case what? I ain't trying to shoot nobody. Why would I even need this?" Omari looked down at the gun in his hand, ready to hand it back to Onyx.

"Shit, just in case anything happens. You never know what could happen. Darren is there, and if he catches you sneaking inside the house, anything could go down. So, you need to stay safe."

Omari nodded and tucked the gun into his waistline. He prayed that he would never have to use it, but he would much rather be safe than sorry. He grabbed the bag of snacks he got from the store earlier and walked out the door, smiling, as he made his way to Kiss' house. If there was one person that Omari loved spending time with, it was Kiss. She was easy to get along with, and he felt his best when he was with her.

He walked through the alley and up the steps to her back porch. Just as Kiss had told him, the back door was unlocked. Omari slowly walked through the dark kitchen, careful not to bump into anything. He'd just made his way to the basement door when he heard Kiss screaming from her room. Instinctively, Omari grabbed the gun from his waistline and ran through the house to Kiss' bedroom. His eyes widened in horror when he saw Darren trying to pull Kiss' pants down. Before he could think, Omari pulled the trigger and fired two shots into Darren's back. Omari dropped the gun, breathing heavy, as Darren's limp body fell onto Kiss.

The gunshots cracked through the house like lightning, and for a beat, everything froze. Kiss' scream never made it out of her throat as it locked. Her breath was stuck somewhere between her chest and her lips. She stared, wide-eyed, at the body slumped on top of her. The sound of the bullet hitting him still echoed in her ears. Omari stood over him, looking down at the gun, smoke curling from the barrel. His face was pale, his eyes wide, like he didn't recognize the weapon or himself. His chest rose and fell in quick, shallow bursts.

"Omari!" Kiss yelled, trembling underneath Darren's body. Tears streamed from her eyes, as she struggled to move Darren off of her.

Omari was so shaken up that it took him several seconds to register that Kiss was still underneath Darren. Once he snapped back, Omari rushed over to help her. Struggling with the dead weight, it took them several seconds to move Darren enough for Kiss to crawl from underneath him.

"Kiss, are you okay?" Omari asked frantically.

"He tried... He was gonna... Oh, my God. Omari, is he dead?"

"I..." His voice cracked, his lips trembling. "I didn't... Kiss, I didn't mean to... He was hurting you, so I..."

Kiss stumbled back until her legs hit the wall, her entire body trembling. "Oh, my God... Omari." Her voice was barely a whisper.

Darren didn't move. His chest didn't rise. Blood seeped across Kiss' pink comforter. All Omari could do was shake his head, as he looked at Darren's dead body.

"He was trying to hurt you," Omari spoke, voice trembling.

Kiss pressed both hands over her mouth, tears flowing down her cheeks. She couldn't look at Darren's body anymore. She couldn't look at the gun either. All she could see was Omari standing there like he'd shattered his whole world in one pull of the trigger.

"What do we do?" Kiss asked, voice cracking.

Omari turned to her, his eyes wild and lost. "I don't know."

The words scared her more than the gunshots had. Omari was supposed to be steady, calm, and unshakable. Seeing him like this, hands trembling, voice breaking, made everything unravel. She slid down the wall until she was sitting on the floor, her knees pulled to her chest. Her heartbeat thudded in her ears, too loud to shake. She wanted to throw up. She wanted to run. She wanted to rewind time and stop all of it from happening, but she knew she couldn't.

Omari paced the room, his hands clutching his hair, his breaths ragged. "They gon' lock me up. Kiss, they gon' put me away forever. I…" He stopped, his chest heaving.

Kiss shook her head violently, her tears spilling now. "No. No, you were protecting me. He was gonna…" Her words broke, sobs choking them down. She couldn't even finish the thought.

Omari's eyes met hers, pained and desperate. "Don't matter. They won't care why I did it. All they gon' see is me standing here with the gun."

His words hung heavy between them. Kiss knew he was right, and that clawed at her insides until she could barely breathe. Silence stretched again, broken only by the ticking clock on the wall. Each second felt like a countdown to something neither of them could name.

Kiss wiped at her face, her hands trembling. "We gotta do something. We can't just…" She glanced at Darren's still body and flinched. "We can't just leave him there."

Omari stopped pacing, his eyes darting to the body then away. He shook his head, biting his lip hard enough to draw blood. "If we call the cops, it's over. If we tell your mama, it's over. If we just run…" His voice cracked again. "Kiss, what do we do?"

Her chest tightened. She didn't have an answer. The truth was that she was just as lost as he was. She wanted to believe they could figure it out, that somehow they could fix this, but deep down, she knew nothing would ever be the same.

She crawled toward him on shaky knees, grabbing his trembling hands in hers. "Omari. Look at me."

His eyes flickered down, dark and frantic.

"You didn't mean to. You were trying to protect me. You saved me from the horrible things he was about to do to me." Her voice broke again, but she held on tighter. "We'll figure this out."

Omari stared at her, his jaw tight, tears gathering in his eyes though he fought to hold them back. Finally, he sank down onto the floor beside her, their hands still locked. The weight of what he'd done pressed down, heavy on his chest. Neither of them had the answers. Neither of them knew what tomorrow would bring. But in that moment, sitting on the floor together, they both knew that everything had just changed.

Chapter Five

Not even twenty minutes later, Kiss' street was filled with police cars. A few of the neighbors had heard the shots and called the police. The pounding at the door made Omari's chest tighten. He wanted to run but knew that if he did and they caught him, it would be worse. Tears were now falling from his eyes, as he looked over at Kiss. Before he could say anything, the police broke down the door.

"DPD! If anyone is in the home, identify yourself now!" the officer yelled.

Kiss looked at Omari and he nodded his head, already knowing what he had to do. He stood up, and Kiss grabbed him. She shook her head, not wanting Omari to give himself up. Omari gave a half smile before mouthing to Kiss that everything would be okay. He walked out of Kiss' room with his hands up, while Kiss stayed on the floor of her bedroom, crying uncontrollably.

The officers grabbed Omari, placing cuffs on him, and one took him outside. The other officers searched the rest of the house, finding both Kiss and Darren's body. Everything happened in slow motion as the officers grabbed her up. She saw his lips moving but didn't hear anything that was coming out of his mouth. She was placed into handcuffs as well, and they walked her out the house. She could hear the neighbors' chatter, as she was walked outside.

"That's Sade's house. Oh, my God, that's her little girl," were just some of the things she heard.

The female officer placed Kiss into the car, cuffs tight around her small wrists. As she looked through the window, she saw Omari sitting inside the car next to her with his head hung low. Kiss couldn't stop shaking. Her hands were ice cold, even though sweat dripped down her back. Tears rolled down her face, as she wished she could rewind time. The street was filled with police cars and nosy neighbors, and all Kiss wanted was her mother.

<hr>

At the station, the fluorescent lights buzzed overhead, cold and merciless. They sat Kiss in a hard, plastic chair, cuffs still digging into her wrists. Omari was led down another hall, out of sight, but she could still hear him shouting her name.

"Call my mama!" Kiss cried, her voice cracking. "Please somebody call my mama!"

The officer at the desk barely looked up. "We already did."

Time blurred, every second stretching until it felt like hours. The smell of stale coffee and disinfectant made her stomach churn. She stared at her knees, fighting the urge to throw up. Her stomach had been in knots since the moment Darren had walked into her room, and it wouldn't go away. Finally, after what seemed like hours, the door burst open.

"Kiss!" Sade's voice, sharp and panicked, cut through the station.

She rushed forward. She wore a pair of black scrubs, and her tiny braids were placed into a ponytail on the top of her head. Her eyes locked on her daughter, wide and disbelieving.

"Oh, my God, baby, what happened? What's going on?" Sade dropped to her knees, her hands trembling, as they reached for Kiss. She hugged her tightly, but the cuffs on Kiss' hands stopped her from hugging Sade back.

Kiss broke when she realized she couldn't hug Sade, tears falling from her eyes faster than before. "Mama, Darren, he… Omari was trying…" She choked, unable to get the words out.

Behind Sade, another woman stormed in – Ms. Blackwell, the twins' mother. She was tall, dark skinned, with a fire in her eyes that could burn a hole through stone. "Where's my son?" she demanded. "Where's Omari?"

Two officers walked out, trying to calm the situation, but neither Sade nor Tamika were calming down until they knew exactly what was going on.

"Tell me what happened," Sade snapped, her eyes wild, darting between the officers and her daughter.

The officer cleared his throat, his voice detached. "There was a shooting at your home. Darren Merriweather was found deceased at the scene. Your daughter and Omari Blackwell were found with the body," he informed.

The words hit like a sledgehammer. Sade staggered back, her hand flying to her mouth. "Deceased?" she repeated, her voice breaking. "No, no, no…" She shook her head violently, tears springing to her eyes. "You lyin'. Darren can't be dead. I just saw him before I left for work tonight."

"Mama." Kiss sobbed.

Sade's eyes snapped to her daughter, wide with shock, confusion, and hurt written all over her face. "What did you do?" Her voice trembled. "Kiss, tell me you didn't do that."

"She didn't!" Omari's voice thundered from the hallway, as an officer pushed him forward in cuffs. His chest heaved, and his eyes were red. "It was me! She didn't do nothing!"

"Omari!" Tamika cried, rushing to him. She cupped his face in her hands, tears spilling down her cheeks. "What did you do, baby?"

"I had to," Omari choked out. His voice cracked, and he

looked at Kiss, his gaze steady despite the tears. "I couldn't let him hurt her."

Sade's knees gave out, and she sank into a chair, her face pale. Her world was unraveling too fast for her to keep up. Darren was gone, her daughter was in cuffs, and a boy that was barely thirteen was confessing to the murder.

"Mama, Darren, he came into my bedroom tonight. He been looking at me funny for weeks. Ever since that day he walked into the bathroom when I was in there. He been weird. And I wanted to tell you, but he said you wouldn't believe nothing I said." The words spilled out, sharp and desperate. "Omari saved me! Darren would have hurt me if it wasn't for him."

Sade's face twisted, pain etched deep. She shook her head, covering her ears like the words themselves were knives. "No! No, no, no," was all she could say.

Tamika turned, her eyes blazing. "You hear your daughter, Sade? You hear what that man was doing in your house? My son had to step in because you didn't protect her! Now look at this shit. This is yo' fuckin' fault!"

Sade flinched, her tears spilling freely now. "Don't put this on me," she whispered hoarsely. "Don't you dare."

"Then who else is it on?" Tamika fired back. "Your daughter was crying for help, and you let that man move in anyway!"

The station rang with their voices, a mixture of fear, anger, and grief, all colliding at once. The officers watched, silent, as the two women faced off, their children caught in the middle.

Omari shook his head, his voice raw. "It don't matter now. Darren's dead. And I'm the one who pulled the trigger. If y'all locking me up, do it. I would have did anything to make sure he didn't hurt Kiss."

Kiss sobbed harder, her chest aching like it might cave in. "No! No, they can't take you, Omari. You were saving me. They gotta understand that!"

Kiss knew this wasn't right, but deep down, she knew the

truth. The law didn't care about saving or protecting. The law only saw blood and a boy with a gun. Kiss could only pray that everything would work out.

One of the officers grabbed Omari, while another grabbed Kiss and walked them down the hall with Tamika and Sade following close behind. The interrogation room was cold, and the walls were bare except for a buzzing light overhead. The officers removed Kiss' cuffs the moment they walked inside the room but left Omari's on. Kiss sat with her arms wrapped around herself, the oversized chair swallowing her small frame. Every second felt heavier than the last, every sound from the hall making her flinch.

Omari sat across the table from two officers. His eyes were red from crying, but he still never took them off the officers. Kiss could see the tremor in his hands from where she sat, even though he tried to hide it. Tamika was pacing behind him, her hand pressed to her forehead. Sade sat rigid near Kiss, staring at the tabletop, her eyes glassy.

Finally, one of the officers leaned forward. "Omari, we need to know exactly what happened. You understand the seriousness of this situation, right?"

Omari's jaw clenched. His voice was hoarse but steady. "I pulled the trigger."

Kiss' breath hitched. "Omari!"

He glanced at her then, just for a second, but his eyes told her everything. "I pulled the trigger," he repeated, louder this time. "Kiss didn't do nothing. She was in the room, but she had nothing to do with it. I'm the one who shot Darren."

The words seemed to suck all the air out of the room. Kiss shook her head violently, tears spilling. "No, no, you don't understand. He was trying to protect me! He was trying…"

"Enough." Tamika's voice cracked, thick with grief and fury. She touched her son's shoulder, squeezing it tight. She looked down at him, and Omari nodded his head.

The officer scribbled notes, his expression unreadable. He turned to Kiss. "Is that true? You had no part in this?"

Kiss' voice trembled, but she forced it out. "He's telling the truth. It was Omari. I didn't touch the gun. But he only did it because he wanted to save me." Her chest heaved, each word stabbing her deeper.

The officer nodded. "Then you're free to go."

Kiss launched forward, wrapping her arms around him before anyone could stop her. Tears soaked his shirt as she whispered, "I'm sorry. I'm so sorry."

Omari leaned into her, his voice low and steady. "Don't be. I told you I'd protect you. This is what that means."

Tamika pulled her son back gently, her own tears slipping down her face. "Come on, baby. You gotta be strong now."

The officers moved to lead him away. Kiss reached out, her fingers brushing his one last time, before he disappeared through the door. The sound of the lock clicking shut behind him was the loudest sound Kiss had ever heard. She collapsed into her chair, her whole body shaking. Sade reached for her, but Kiss pulled away, her voice breaking.

"Mama, I knew Darren wasn't right. And now Omari's gone because of it."

Sade's lips trembled, her face pale. She had no words, just sobs. She didn't understand how she'd let something like this happen under her own roof. As sad as she was that Darren was gone, she was more hurt by what her daughter had revealed.

Chapter Six

The clang of the heavy iron door echoed in Omari's chest long after it closed. He sat on the narrow cot, his knees pulled up, his back pressed against the cold wall of the detention cell. The mattress beneath him was thin and lumpy, and the sheet was scratchy against his skin. It didn't feel like a bed. It didn't feel like anything meant for people. It was his first night inside, and he was more nervous now than he was when he shot Darren.

The guards hadn't said much after they booked him, just took his fingerprints, snapped his picture, stripped him of his shoelaces and anything sharp enough to cut. They gave him a set of gray sweats, two sizes too big, and led him to this room with nothing but a cot, a metal toilet, and a window too small to see out of. Omari couldn't sleep. Every time he closed his eyes, he saw Darren's face. The way he slumped when the bullet hit him. The way the blood spread fast across Kiss' comforter. The sound of Kiss' sobs in the background. The weight of the gun in his hand. His stomach churned, and he pressed his fists to his temples, wishing he could turn his brain off.

Across the hall, a boy cried out in his sleep. Somewhere farther down, someone cursed, their voice echoing off the cinderblock walls. Doors slammed and metal scraped, and Omari lay back, just staring at the ceiling, trying to steady his breath. He wasn't scared of the other boys. What scared him was the unknown. The not knowing what tomorrow looked like, what court would bring, how long they planned to keep him here.

He couldn't stop thinking about Kiss. How scared she looked when the cops took her away in cuffs. How her tears had cut him deeper than any cell bars could. He'd promised her she wouldn't have to go through this alone, and now there she was, out there, and he was trapped in here. The thought clawed at his chest, more painful than anything he'd ever felt.

The next morning, a guard banged on the door. "Get up! Breakfast!"

Omari slid off the cot, his body stiff from a night of restlessness. He shuffled down the hall with the other boys, their gray uniforms blending them into one. Some were his age, barely teenagers. Others were older and taller, with eyes hard as stone. The cafeteria smelled faintly of bleach and something unfamiliar. He sat at a long, metal table, the tray in front of him carrying a scoop of powdered eggs, a slice of toast, and a carton of milk. He poked at the food, but his stomach turned.

"Yo, that the boy?"

Omari lifted his head. Two boys at the end of the table stared at him. One was short and wiry, his eyes sharp. The other was bigger, a smirk tugging at his lips.

"Heard he shot a grown man," the short one whispered.

The bigger boy leaned forward. "That true?"

Omari stared back, his jaw tight. His heart thudded in his chest, but he didn't flinch. "Yeah." His voice was steady, even though his insides shook.

The bigger boy's smirk widened. "Damn. You crazy as hell."

Omari dropped his eyes to his tray, unwilling to give them more. He didn't need friends here. He just needed to survive long enough to make it to court. He felt that as long as he stayed to himself, then he would be okay.

The days blended together. He woke up, lined up, ate, sat, and waited every single day. Sometimes, the guards marched them into a rec room with nothing but a TV bolted to the wall and plastic chairs. Other times, they sat in silence in their cells, listening to the hum of the building. Omari kept to himself, speaking only when he had to. At night, he lay awake on his cot, staring at the ceiling. The boy across the hall still cried sometimes. Another one banged on his door until the guards threatened to take away his privileges. Omari listened, quiet, his mind looping the same questions over and over. *What will the judge say? How much time will they give me? Will Kiss hate me for leaving her alone?*

He thought about her every night. The way she'd whispered his name, the way her eyes had begged him not to take the blame. But he'd already made that choice. He'd rather lose everything than let her carry even a piece of it.

On the third night, he rolled onto his side, clutching the thin pillow. The air was thick with the stench of sweat and disinfectant, the walls pressing in tighter than ever. He pressed his eyes shut, forcing the tears back, whispering into the silence, as he told himself it had to be done. The words echoed in his own ears, but no one answered.

Omari shuffled into the courtroom, the cuffs around his wrists cold and heavy, linked to the chain at his waist. His sneakers squeaked against the floor, as the guard guided him down the aisle. His gray detention uniform felt too thin, exposing every inch of his shame to the rows of people watching. He kept his head low, but when he looked up, his eyes immediately scanned the benches.

His mother sat stiff against the bench, her hands clutching a tissue that was already twisted and torn. Tears shimmered in her eyes, but her chin was high, like she was daring the whole court to see her pain. Beside her, Onyx leaned forward on the bench with his elbows on his knees. The sight of them nearly undid him.

Omari swallowed hard, as he was guided to the defense table, the weight of every stare pressing down on him. He sat, the chair creaking beneath him, the chain rattling when he shifted. His lawyer whispered something about staying calm, but Omari barely heard him. His focus was locked across the room. Onyx caught his eye first. The twins shared that look they'd always had, the one that didn't need words.

Omari tilted his chin, his lips parting just enough to mouth, *Where is Kiss?*

Onyx's eyes flickered, a shadow passing over his face. He glanced at their mother then back at Omari. Slowly, he mouthed, *Sade wouldn't let her come.*

The words hit like a punch to the gut. Omari's chest tightened, his throat burning. He tore his eyes away, staring down at the scratched surface of the table. His cuffs rattled, as his fists clenched. *Sade wouldn't let her come* was all that played in his mind. Of course she wouldn't. He'd killed Sade's boyfriend, so he knew she wouldn't allow Kiss to come and show her support for him.

He closed his eyes, his jaw grinding so hard it ached. It wasn't fair. He hadn't done this for himself; he'd done it for Kiss. To protect her and stop Darren from ever putting his hands on her, from ever crossing that line. And now, she wasn't here. She wasn't allowed to see him. He opened his eyes again, searching the room one last time, desperate for a glimpse of her. But all he saw were strangers.

Onyx shifted, his lips parting again. This time, he mouthed the words, *Stay strong.* Omari nodded slightly, even though the knot in his throat nearly choked him. The judge entered the courtroom, and the proceedings began. Voices rose and fell, charges were read, lawyers argued, and words like manslaughter and juvenile court echoed through the air. But Omari barely heard any of it. All he could hear was the absence, the empty space, where Kiss should've been.

The trial stretched on for weeks, each day bleeding into the next, until Omari lost track of time. The walls of the detention center were one kind of prison, but the courtroom was another. It was sterile, cold, and heavy with eyes that never left him. He sat in the same gray uniform at the same scratched wooden table, chained at the waist, his lawyer whispering instructions that barely sank in.

Every morning when the bailiff brought him in, Omari searched the benches first. His mother never missed a day. She sat with her hands twisted tight around a tissue, her back rigid, her eyes red and wet with tears. Onyx was always there beside her, restless, his jaw clenched, his gaze locked on his twin with a loyalty so fierce it steadied Omari when nothing else could. But Kiss was never there, not even once. That emptiness was a wound that reopened every time he glanced toward the crowd. Each day without her was another reminder of what he'd lost, what he'd done, and what he was left to face alone.

The prosecution painted him as a violent boy with no control, reckless enough to take a man's life. They called him dangerous and a threat. "He may only be thirteen," one prosecutor had said, his voice ringing through the courtroom, "but his actions were deliberate. He chose to pull that trigger."

Omari sat still, his fists clenched in his lap, forcing himself not to react. His heart hammered with every word. His lawyer pushed back, arguing self-defense, protection, and circumstance. "He acted out of fear," he told the jury. "He acted to protect a young girl who was vulnerable and alone in her own home. He's not a killer; he's a child forced into an impossible situation."

Some days, Omari felt hope flicker when she spoke. Other days, the prosecutor's words drowned everything out. Witnesses came and went. Neighbors who had seen the police that night. Teachers who said Omari was quiet, bright, and not the type to pick fights. Even kids from the block who whispered about what they'd heard about Darren. That he had been "creepy" around Kiss, that Omari was always the one stepping up to defend her. But none of it seemed to matter. The weight of Darren's absence hung heavier than any words of defense.

It was in the third week of trial when they finally called Kiss to testify. Omari's breath caught the second she walked into the courtroom. For the first time since that night, since the flashing lights and the cuffs, he saw her. She looked smaller than he remembered, her shoulders hunched, her hands twisting nervously in her lap, as she took the oath. Her hair was pulled back, her eyes wide, glistening under the courtroom lights.

He wanted to run to her, to hold her, to tell her he was sorry for everything. But all he could do was sit, chained to his chair, and watch.

Kiss' voice shook at first. "Darren, he made me uncomfortable. He looked at me in ways that weren't right. I told my mama that I didn't like him, but she didn't seem to care. I wanted to tell her how uncomfortable he made me, but I felt like she wouldn't care about that either. Then, he walked in on me in the bathroom when I'd just got out the shower. I know he knew I was in there. I know he did it on purpose."

Gasps rippled through the courtroom. Sade, sitting stiff on the bench, covered her mouth with trembling hands. Kiss' tears spilled, as she continued. "I was scared. I didn't know what he was gonna do. Omari, he was the only one who believed me. Him and his brother, Onyx. He only wanted to protect me. He told me I wasn't alone." Her voice cracked. "That night, when it happened, I'd unlocked the back door for Omari to sneak in. I hated being alone with Darren when my mama went to work, so Omari came over every night so that I wouldn't have to be.

When I came back into my room, Darren walked in, and he tried to force himself on me. Omari didn't mean to shoot him. He just… He was trying to keep me safe."

Omari's chest ached, as he listened. Every word she spoke was a knife and a bomb at the same time – painful because she had to relive it, healing because finally, finally someone was saying the truth out loud. The prosecutor tried to twist her words, pressing her to admit she'd exaggerated, that Omari had acted out of anger, not fear. Kiss held firm, her chin trembling but lifted. "No. He saved me."

Omari's vision blurred. He blinked fast, swallowing the lump in his throat. Pride swelled in him, fierce and sharp, but it mixed with guilt. She shouldn't have had to sit there, shouldn't have had to carry this weight, shouldn't have had to cry in front of strangers just to make them believe her. When they finally dismissed her, she glanced at him as she left the stand. Their eyes locked. Just for a moment, it was like no one else was in the room. Then, she was gone again, and the emptiness slammed back into him.

By the final week, Omari's nerves were frayed. Every night in detention, he lay awake on his cot, staring at the ceiling, wondering how many years of his life the judge would steal from him. On the morning of sentencing, the courtroom was packed. His mother sat in the front row, gripping Onyx's hand so tight he winced. Sade sat farther back, her face drawn, her eyes hollow. Kiss wasn't there; Omari had stopped expecting her, but the absence still burned.

The judge's voice was calm, measured, as he recounted the case, the evidence, the testimonies, and the arguments. Omari barely heard the words. His heart was pounding so loud it drowned out everything else. Finally, the gavel came down.

"Omari Blackwell," the judge intoned, "this court finds that while you are a juvenile, your actions had irreversible consequences. A man is dead, and a family has lost a loved one. After reviewing the case, this court sentences you to remain in custody until your twenty-first birthday."

The words slammed into him like a physical blow. *Until twenty-one? That is seven years away.* Omari's breath caught, and his vision blurred. He barely felt the cuffs tighten around his wrists again, as the bailiff moved him to stand. His mother wailed, her body shaking, as she cried out his name. Onyx jumped to his feet, shouting, "That's not fair! He was protecting her! He ain't no killer!" The guard held him back, but his voice rang out, fierce and desperate.

Sade bowed her head, silent tears slipping down her cheeks. Omari forced himself to look up, to meet his mother's eyes. Her face was twisted in grief, but when she saw him looking, she nodded through her tears. He straightened his shoulders, trying to be strong for her, for Onyx, and for Kiss, even though she wasn't there to see him damn near breaking down. But inside, his chest was hollow. His future, his freedom, and his childhood were all gone. As the bailiff led him out, the sound of the chains dragging on the floor echoed louder than anything else.

Chapter Seven

The streets of Detroit glittered with snow. It clung to the curbs in gray piles, but inside the Blackwell house, the heat was blasting, and Christmas break meant late nights and lazy mornings. Kiss sat cross-legged on the living room rug, sipping hot chocolate, while Onyx flipped through channels with the remote, never stopping long enough to let anything play.

"You ever gon' pick something?" she teased, her voice soft but edged with laughter.

Onyx smirked, leaning back into the couch. "You know I don't watch nothin' straight through. Gotta keep my options open."

Kiss rolled her eyes, but her smile lingered. A knock sounded at the front door. Onyx rose, stretching, and opened it. The winter air swept in along with the thud of boots on the porch. The mailman handed over a thin stack, and Onyx flipped through it quickly. When his eyes landed on one envelope, his whole body stilled for a heartbeat before he slid the rest of the mail onto the counter.

"You got somethin' for me?" Kiss asked, trying to sound nonchalant.

Onyx didn't answer right away. He just turned, the envelope pinched between his fingers. He stretched out his hand and handed it to her without a word. Kiss' hands trembled as she took it. The return address was burned into her memory, Wayne County Juvenile Detention Center. She stared at it a long moment before sliding her finger under the flap. Onyx didn't press. He just sank back into the couch, eyes on the muted TV. He always gave her that privacy when Omari sent letters to her. Omari knew that Sade would never give Kiss any letter he sent to her house. So, he sent them to his house, and Onyx made sure she got them.

The paper inside was lined notebook paper, folded twice. Omari's handwriting filled every space, words pressed hard into the page like he needed them to last.

Kiss,

Two years gone by, and it feel like forever. Some nights, I close my eyes, and I can still see that porch, the streetlight buzzing, you sitting there like time wasn't movin'. That's the picture I keep in my head to get me through these walls. I won't lie to you. It's hard in here. The days all run together. Boys talk tough, guards don't care, and sometimes, the silence gets so heavy it feels like it's choking me. But then, I think of you. You laughing, you holdin' my hand when you scared. That's what keeps me steady.

But I gotta be real with you. I don't want you to spend all these years waitin' on me. I can't ask you to put your life on pause while mine stuck in here. You deserve more than letters from behind a wall. You deserve the world. If we meant to be, then when I get out, we'll find our way back to each other. But for now, live your life, Kiss. Don't chain yourself to my mistakes. I love you. Always. But I love you enough to let you go if that's what it takes for you to be happy.

Omari

. . .

Kiss folded the letter carefully, pressing it to her chest. Her tears fell hot and silent, soaking into her sweater. Onyx glanced at her finally, his expression unreadable.

"You good?" he asked quietly.

She nodded, unable to find her voice. She loved Omari and was thankful for everything that he'd done for her. She wanted nothing more than to be with him, but if he didn't want her to wait for him, then she wouldn't.

"He told me not to wait on him. That if we were meant to be, then we would be."

Onyx leaned forward, elbows on his knees. His eyes, so much like his twin's yet somehow sharper, locked on Kiss. "You know he only sayin' that 'cause he don't want you hurt. That's Omari. Always tryna take care of everybody but himself."

Kiss wiped her eyes, her voice hoarse. "But he's all I think about. Even when I try not to. Even when I tell myself to move on. I can't just let go."

Onyx's jaw flexed, and for a long moment, he didn't respond. Then, he sighed, leaning back. "That's between you and him. But whatever you decide, you got me here. Don't forget that."

Kiss looked down at the letter again, her heart torn in two. Omari's words had been heavy with love but also with finality. He was giving her freedom, but all she wanted was him. Snow tapped against the window. The Christmas lights outside glowed faintly in the early dusk. Inside, the air hummed with the unspoken truth that time was moving forward, with or without Omari. And for Kiss, that was the cruelest part of all. She sat in Onyx's living room for a few more hours, as they watched TV together.

The house was too quiet on New Year's Eve. Kiss sat on the couch, knees tucked under her, flipping through channels without really seeing what was on the screen. Outside, faint pops of early fireworks cracked through the cold Detroit night. Sade had left for work hours ago, her scrubs rustling as she grabbed her coat by the door.

"Lock up, Kiss," she'd said, tired eyes soft. "Don't be up too late."

"I won't," Kiss promised, though she already knew she couldn't sleep. Not tonight. Not when the year was ending and Omari still wasn't with her.

She tried not to think about his last letter. She kept it folded neatly in her dresser upstairs. *Don't wait for me,* he had written. *If we meant to be, we'll find our way back.* His words echoed in her chest, heavy and hollow. She missed him so much it hurt, but he had pushed her away in the only way he knew how, out of love. Her phone buzzed, and she looked down, seeing it was Onyx.

"What up doe? You at home?"

Kiss chewed her lip before replying. "Yeah, I'm here. What's up?"

"Come through. My mama having a party."

She hesitated. It felt wrong somehow, spending New Year's with Onyx when Omari was locked away. But she also didn't want to spend the night alone, counting down with the silence. So, she agreed, telling him that she would be there in ten minutes.

The Blackwell house was alive with noise when she arrived. Music thumped through the walls, and laughter spilled out of the open window. The smell of fried chicken and macaroni filled the air, mixing with the crisp bite of winter.

Tamika greeted her warmly, pulling her into a hug. "Kiss! You look beautiful, baby. Come on in."

Inside, the living room was packed – neighbors, cousins, and friends of their family. People danced in the cramped space, plates piled high with food, cups raised in cheers. The warmth and energy wrapped around Kiss like a blanket, chasing away the loneliness she'd carried from home.

Onyx found her quickly, weaving through the crowd with his easy grin. "Hey, Kiss, I'm glad you came."

Kiss rolled her eyes, but she couldn't hide her smile. "You didn't give me much choice."

He laughed, handing her a cup of punch. "Just didn't want you missin' out. It's New Year's, so we gotta celebrate."

And celebrate was exactly what she did. For hours, she let herself be pulled into the rhythm of the night. She danced with the other girls, laughed at the jokes flying around the room, even let Onyx drag her into a game of spades at the kitchen table. For a while, she forgot about Omari, about the weight pressing down on her every day. For a while, she just felt like a teenager again.

As midnight drew closer, the energy in the house shifted. People grabbed fresh drinks, voices raising as the countdown neared. Someone turned up the music then switched it off suddenly, laughter filling the pause.

"Ten… nine… eight…"

The entire room shouted together, bodies swaying, smiles wide. Kiss found herself shoulder to shoulder with Onyx, their eyes meeting in the flicker of Christmas lights still strung along the walls.

"…five… four… three…"

Kiss' heart pounded. The noise around her blurred. All she could feel was the heat of Onyx beside her, the way his gaze lingered just a little too long.

"…two… one! Happy New Year!"

The room exploded – cheers, laughter, and fireworks popping outside. People hugged, kissed, raised their glasses. Kiss turned, and Onyx was right there. For a moment, neither moved. Then, almost like it happened without thought, their lips met. It was soft at first, tentative but real. The room roared around them, but Kiss felt only the warmth of him, the steadying grip of his hand brushing hers. The kiss lingered, long enough to mean something, short enough to leave her breathless when they pulled apart.

Chapter Eight

The morning after the New Year's party, Kiss woke up with the weight of confusion pressing down on her chest. The house was quiet except for the faint hum of the furnace, the chill of January creeping through the thin walls. She lay in bed, staring at the ceiling, the memory of midnight running on repeat in her head – Onyx's kiss, gentle and warm against her lips. She touched her fingers lightly to her mouth, half in disbelief. Guilt coiled in her stomach, fighting with something softer, something she wasn't ready to name.

Oh, my God. Omari. His name was always the first thought in her head when she woke. For two years, she'd clung to his letters, his promises, and his words that made her feel seen even when he was behind bars. He'd told her not to wait on him, and even with that, she knew kissing his brother last night was wrong. She didn't want to let go. But she also couldn't deny the way her heart had raced when Onyx leaned close, when the entire room around them erupted in cheers and fireworks outside, and somehow, it was just them in that moment.

A knock at the front door startled her. She pushed herself up, tugging a hoodie over the tank top she'd slept in, before shuffling down the hall. When she opened it, Onyx stood there, hands shoved in his pockets, his breath puffing white in the cold air.

"You up?" he asked, his usual smirk tugging at the corner of his mouth.

Kiss nodded, stepping aside, so he could come in. "Barely."

He kicked off his boots and flopped onto the couch. "You disappeared after the party last night. Thought you was mad at me or something."

Her stomach tightened. She sat on the arm of the couch, crossing her arms. "Why would I be mad?"

He shrugged, eyes on the TV remote he'd already picked up. "I don't know. Thought maybe you didn't like it."

Kiss' heart skipped. He was talking about the kiss. She swallowed, her throat already dry. "It was fine."

Onyx looked up at her then, his eyes sharp and unreadable. "Just fine?"

Heat rushed to her cheeks. "I mean, it wasn't bad or nothing."

For a moment, silence stretched between them. Then, Onyx chuckled, shaking his head. "You always got a way with words, Kiss."

She rolled her eyes, but her smile betrayed her. The truth was that Kiss enjoyed the kiss, maybe a little too much. She knew she wasn't supposed to have these feelings for Onyx, but she couldn't deny them. He was the closest thing to Omari, which made it both right and wrong all at the same time.

The days that followed carried a new rhythm. At school, Onyx walked Kiss to class, his presence steady beside her. At lunch, they sat at the same table, his jokes pulling laughter from her even on the hardest days. After school, they sometimes ended up at his house, the hum of video games and the smell of whatever Tamika was cooking filling the air. People whispered, of course, but this time, Kiss didn't care. She held her head high when she walked with Onyx, proud to be with him.

One cold February afternoon, they sat in Onyx's room, music

low on the speakers, the faint sound of kids playing in the snow outside. Kiss lay sprawled across his bed with a notebook, doodling absentmindedly. Onyx sat at his desk, spinning slowly in his chair.

"Can I ask you something?" he said suddenly, his tone now more serious.

Kiss looked up. "What's up?"

He spun to face her, his expression rawer than she'd ever seen it. "You ever think about how it's always been him first?"

Kiss frowned. "What you mean?"

Onyx's jaw flexed. "Omari. He always the one people looked at. Teachers, girls, even you. I was just the other twin. The loud one, the one that was always in trouble." He shook his head. "Even now, he in there, and I'm out here, and I still feel like I'm second."

Kiss sat up, her chest tightening. She'd never heard him say anything like this before, never seen the way his shoulders slumped when he let the words out.

"You're not second, Onyx," she said softly. "Not to me."

He searched her face, eyes dark and searching. "Then what am I?"

Her lips parted, but no answer came. Because she didn't know what to say just yet.

The silence stretched until Onyx looked away, rubbing his hand over his hair. "Forget it. I just was talking shit."

Kiss looked at Onyx. She wanted to say so much but didn't have a clue where to start. Onyx was nothing like Omari and everything like him all at the same time. She knew that was what attracted her to him in the first place, but now, she saw things differently. She saw him differently and could only wonder what they could be.

The weeks turned to months as the seasons changed. The gray slushy snow had melted, and green grass lined the sidewalks. The trees were starting to grow leaves, and April showers were coming down to bring May flowers. Even though the seasons had changed, Onyx and Kiss' relationship was getting stronger.

It was in the small things at first. The way he carried her books between classes without Kiss asking. The way he leaned against her locker, always waiting, even when she swore she didn't need him to. The way he noticed when her mood slipped low, sliding her a piece of gum or cracking a dumb joke to make her smile. Kiss couldn't ignore it anymore. He wasn't just Omari's twin. He was Onyx – louder, bolder, and reckless at times, but wonderful. And the truth was that he was there, and Omari wasn't.

One Friday afternoon, Kiss found herself at Onyx's house once again. Tamika had fried chicken, the smell curling through the air. Onyx had dragged Kiss into his room with a grin.

"Come on. I wanna show you something," he said, digging through a shoebox under his bed.

Kiss perched on the edge of his mattress, watching him with curiosity. "If this is one of your dumb mixtapes, I swear."

Onyx shot her a mock glare. "You got no faith." He pulled out a stack of notebooks, their covers battered and bent. "I've been writing."

Kiss raised her eyebrows. "You been writing what?"

"Don't sound so surprised," he muttered, flipping one open. "Not like poetry or nothing, but I been writing lyrics."

He hesitated then handed her the notebook. Kiss took it carefully, her eyes scanning the words scrawled across the page. They were raw, full of anger and pain, but also rhythm. She could hear the beat in her head as she read the words.

"This is actually good," she admitted, looking up at him.

Onyx shrugged, trying to play it cool, but he cracked a small smile. "It's just something I do when I can't sleep. Helps me think."

Kiss smiled, flipping to another page. "You ever gonna let somebody hear this?"

He smirked. "Maybe one day but for now, just you."

They started hanging out more outside of school. Onyx walked her home almost every day, even when she insisted that he didn't have to. He'd sit with her on her porch and talk to her for hours, and Kiss enjoyed every moment.

One night, as they sat on Kiss' porch in the cool night air, Onyx nudged her with his shoulder. "You ever feel like people already decided who we supposed to be? Like, no matter what, I'm always gon' be the troublemaking twin. Even with Omari sitting in jail, my mama still fusses at me, wondering why I can't be more like him."

Kiss glanced at him, the bitterness in his tone heavy. She thought of Omari in his cell, writing letters full of love and sacrifice, and she thought of Onyx here beside her, carrying his own burdens no one seemed to see.

"You're not him," she said softly. "And that's not a bad thing. You don't gotta be like Omari. You just gotta be you."

Onyx stared at her, his breath fogging the air. "And what if being me ain't good enough?"

Kiss reached out before she could stop herself, her fingers brushing his hand. "What do you mean? Being yourself is always good enough."

Kiss needed for Onyx to know that he never had to be anyone else except for himself. She liked him just as he was, no matter what anyone else thought of him. She wanted him to know that no matter what, he was enough.

By May, the whispers at school had faded into background noise. People found new gossip and new scandals to talk about. Kiss was grateful for the quiet, but her relationship with Onyx was growing. One Saturday, he surprised her with an invitation.

"Let's go out," he said, leaning against her porch rail.

She frowned. "Out where?"

"Anywhere. Movies, skating, doesn't matter. Just out, like on a real date."

Her heart jumped. "A date?"

He smirked. "Yeah. Unless you scared."

Kiss rolled her eyes, but her cheeks warmed. "Why would I be scared of a date?"

"Okay. Then, this Saturday, we going to the movies."

Saturday came quick. Onyx told Kiss the night before that he would be at her house at three that afternoon. She woke up around noon and took a shower. She made her way to her room and slipped on the outfit she'd picked out the night before, a pair of light washed jeans and a pink cropped tee. Her braids were freshly done, and once she laid her baby hairs and slid on some lip gloss, she was ready. She put on her fresh pink and white Air Force Ones and was ready to go. Just as he'd said, he was there to pick Kiss up at three.

She walked outside to see Onyx standing next to a white Toyota Camry. His dark skin was flawless, and his lineup up was fresh. He wore a pair of black jeans, a white shirt, and a pair of black and white Jordans.

"Whose car is this?" Kiss asked, walking over to him.

"It's ours for the day."

Onyx opened the passenger door for her, and Kiss slid inside. They ended up at the movies, the theater buzzing with teenagers wanting to have fun on a Saturday afternoon. Kiss sat with a bucket of popcorn in her lap, the glow of the screen painting her face. Onyx leaned back in his seat, one arm draped casually along the back of hers. She tried to focus on the movie, but her attention kept slipping. His hand brushed hers when they reached for popcorn at the same time. His laugh rumbled low when something on the screen was funny. And when their eyes met in the dark, something unspoken passed between them.

"So, how was it? Did I do good?" he asked.

Kiss smiled. "Yeah, it was nice."

"Nice?" he teased. "That's it?"

She laughed softly. "Okay, it was fun. Better?"

He grinned then grew serious. "I like being with you, Kiss. Not just 'cause you Omari's girl – or was – but 'cause you see me. The real me."

Her chest tightened. She stopped walking, turning to face him. "Onyx…"

But he didn't let her finish. He stepped closer, his eyes locked on hers, and kissed her. It wasn't like the quick and surprising peck she received on New Year's. This was deliberate, slow, and full of meaning. Kiss melted into it before she could think, her hands clutching his shirt. When they finally pulled apart, her breath hitched.

Onyx searched her face. "That feel wrong to you?"

Kiss swallowed hard, her heart pounding. "No."

Kiss meant what she said. It felt terrifying, maybe even dangerous. But it also felt right. They got back into the car and went to a park. It was a nice day outside with the sun sitting high in the sky. They sat and talked for hours, neither one of them wanting to stop. By nine, it was time for Onyx to take Kiss home.

One Saturday, a few weeks before school let out for the summer, Onyx showed up at her door with two bikes.

"Get dressed," he said, grinning wide.

Kiss blinked. "Bikes, really? What we bout to do with these?"

"Yeah, bikes. We ridin' to Belle Isle. You always talkin' about how you never go nowhere, so come on."

She laughed, shaking her head. "You crazy."

He leaned on the handlebars, raising an eyebrow. "What? You scared or something?"

That word always got her. Ten minutes later, she was pedaling beside him, the wind in her face, her laughter mixing with his, as they wove through the streets. By the time they reached the island, her legs ached, but her chest felt lighter than it had in years. They sat on the riverbank, Detroit's skyline rising behind them. Onyx tossed pebbles into the water, watching the ripples spread.

"You ever think about the future?" he asked suddenly.

Kiss hugged her knees, staring at the skyline. "Sometimes, but it scares me."

"Why?"

She shrugged. "'Cause nothing ever stays the same. People leave, and things change."

Onyx was quiet a moment then said, "What if change ain't always bad?"

She turned to him, her heart tripping at the way he looked at her. And in that moment, under the fading sun, she let herself believe him. She laid her head on his shoulder, as she watched the water move. When Onyx grabbed her hand and held it tightly, she smiled. Kiss felt safe with Onyx, the same as she did when she was with Omari.

"I like spending time with you," Onyx spoke.

"Me too."

They stayed on the island for hours before finally taking the bike ride back home. When they got back to Kiss' house, Onyx told her she could keep the bike for the next time they took a ride to the island. She smiled, thanking him, before hugging him goodbye. She pulled the bike inside before closing the door behind her.

"You spending a lot of time with that boy," Sade said, walking into the living room and startling Kiss.

"Oh, um, we took a bike ride to Belle Isle."

"I don't know how I feel about you hanging with him. Them twins are trouble. One of them already had you testifying at his trial, and he wasn't even the bad twin. That family has already done enough."

Kiss just looked at her mother, not saying a word. Nothing she said would make a difference anyway. Even after all this time, Sade still hated talking about what happened that night. It was mainly because she had a hard time believing the things Kiss said about Darren. She wanted to believe her daughter, but the Darren she knew would never do anything like that. In the back of Sade's mind, she wanted to believe that Omari had shot Darren for no reason – as much as she knew that wasn't true.

Kiss took the bike to the basement before walking into her room. She had nothing left to say to Sade. If she didn't believe her, then that was Sade's problem, not Kiss'. That night, she went to sleep with thoughts of Onyx on her mind.

On the last day of school before summer vacation, Onyx walked Kiss home, holding her bookbag the way he always did. He walked her to her front door and gave her a hug. Before he pulled away, he whispered to her that he wanted her to be his girlfriend.

"Really?" Kiss asked as though she was surprised.

"Yes, I'm serious. I want nothing more than for you to be mine." Onyx took her hands into his. "I know that Omari is going to feel a type of way, but you let me worry about that. I'll handle him."

Kiss looked into his eyes and knew he was serious. She couldn't lie. She wanted to be his girl just as much as he wanted her to be. She knew it would hurt Omari, but he'd told her not to wait on him. He said that he wanted her to live her life, and she wanted Onyx to be a part of it. So, she told him yes and agreed to be his girlfriend. And just like that, they were official.

Chapter Nine

The sound of the doors was what got to him every time. They slammed shut with a finality that echoed in his bones. Even after years inside, Omari couldn't shake the trapped feeling he felt every time the doors closed.

Mornings started the same. A guard banged on the bars, his voice sharp and bored at the same time. "Get up! Count time!"

Omari would sit up on his cot, rubbing his face with both hands, the scratchy sheet sliding off his shoulders. The air was always cold, heavy with the smell of bleach and sweat. Breakfast came next. The boys shuffled down the hall in two lines, gray sweats hanging loose on their small frames, shoes dragging against the concrete. Some were loud, cracking jokes, trying to prove they weren't scared. Others stayed silent, their eyes darting, shoulders hunched. Omari stayed in the middle. He was quiet but alert, never being too soft or loud. The food was always the same, rubbery eggs, toast that crumbled like cardboard, and milk that tasted faintly sour. Omari ate just enough to keep going.

The days blurred together. School inside wasn't like school outside. It was worksheets handed out at long tables, guards watching from the corner, boys either scribbling answers or passing notes when the guards weren't looking. Omari did the work, more out of habit than anything else. He knew he was smart, teachers back home used to tell him that all the time, but in here, being smart didn't matter. Being tough was the only thing that mattered here.

Fights broke out all the time. One small shove in line would turn into fists flying. An insult muttered under breath became two boys rolling across the floor until guards dragged them apart. Omari kept his head down, but he knew the unspoken rule. Sooner or later, somebody was going to test him, and he would need to be ready. It had taken years for it to happen, but the day was finally here. He was in the rec room, sitting on a plastic chair, flipping through a beat-up magazine someone had left behind. A taller boy, maybe sixteen, sauntered over and knocked the magazine out of his hands. He was light skinned with a low haircut and a few tattoos on his face.

"What you think you doin', pretty boy?" The kid sneered. "Heard you shot a man. But you don't look like no killer to me."

Omari looked up slowly, his heart pounding, but he kept his face steady. He didn't say anything.

The boy shoved his shoulder. Hard. "Say somethin'."

Around them, the room quieted. Other boys leaned in, waiting to see what Omari would do. Omari stood, his fists tight at his sides. His chest burned, fear and anger mixing hot. Even though he was labeled a killer behind the wall, none of them knew why he'd done it. Nobody knew that he would do it again if it meant protecting Kiss. The sound of the gunshot played in his head, as he looked at the boy.

"I don't gotta prove nothin' to you," Omari uttered, his voice low.

The boy laughed. "That mean yo' ass scared."

Omari didn't move. His fists stayed clenched, but he forced his body still. He knew if he swung first, the guards would have him on the floor in seconds. He knew if he backed down, the other boys would smell weakness. So, he had to make the right choice at the right time.

Finally, the guard barked, "Break it up!" and shoved the taller boy back. The moment passed, but Omari knew it wouldn't be the last time. That night, laying on his cot, staring at the ceiling, he whispered to himself, "I ain't scared of shit!" and he knew it was the truth. The detention center was changing him, and he could feel it.

Letters were the only thing that kept him connected to the outside world. Every week, he received one from his mother, brother, and Kiss, and each week, he wrote one to each of them. He wrote with a stub of a pencil, pressing hard, so the words etched deep, like he needed them to last beyond the walls.

Kiss,

I don't know how to tell you what it's like in here. Every day feels the same. The food nasty as hell, the walls close in on you, and at night, it's loud. Boys be in here cryin', fightin', and all these guards do is yell. Sometimes, I close my eyes and pretend I'm back on the block, sittin' with you on the porch until the streetlights come on. That's the only thing that feels real anymore. I hope you enjoyin' life out there. And Kiss, I hope you not holdin' onto old shit and is movin' on with yo' life. Trust me, if we meant to be, we will be.

Love, Omari

He folded the letters neat, pressing the creases straight, then handed them off to be mailed. He always sent them to the Blackwell house. Onyx would make sure Kiss got them. It was the only way he knew she would be able to read them. Some letters were full of hope. Others were heavy with regret. But the one that had hurt him the most to write was the one where he told her not to wait. As much as he meant what he said, deep down, he hoped that Kiss wouldn't fall in love with anyone else.

At night, when the lights went out and the walls hummed with the sound of boys shifting restlessly in their bunks, Omari thought of Onyx. He wondered how his brother was handling things out there. He missed him, their inside jokes, their arguments, the way they always had each other's backs. But sometimes, in the quiet, jealousy pricked at him. Onyx was free to do anything he wanted. Onyx was the one handing Kiss his letters, the one seeing her face when she read them, the one standing beside her, while Omari was stuck behind bars. Everyone thought that Onyx would be the one to go to jail, but it turned out that Omari was the bad twin.

One night, laying in his bunk, Omari pressed his hands together, his lips moving in a whisper.

"God, please just let me make it out. Let me see her again. Let me fix the mistakes I made. In Jesus' name I pray. Amen."

The cell was cold, the mattress was thin, and the sounds of the detention center echoed all around. But Omari clung to that prayer like a lifeline. He had five more years to serve, five years until freedom, until he would finally be able to see Kiss. And he promised himself that no matter what it took, he'd survive them.

Days turned into weeks. Weeks bled into months, and months turned to years. Time inside didn't move the way it did on the outside. Out there, people had clocks, schedules, weekends to look forward to. In here, time was counted by head checks, by the rotation of the food cart, by the way the sun shifted through the tiny square window high on the wall. Omari learned to live in rhythms of what went on around him. Waking up to the guards yelling. Eat the same bland breakfast every morning. Go to school where a tired-looking instructor handed out worksheets and collected them without ever looking up. Yard time twice a week – if there weren't too many fights. Lights out at nine sharp, no matter what.

When Omari first got there, he'd counted days in his head, scratching tallies on a scrap of paper until the guard caught him and tore it away. After that, he stopped keeping track. It was easier not to know how long he'd been in. Easier to just focus on surviving the day in front of him.

He learned the boys inside had their own hierarchy. There were the loud ones, always talking tough, puffing their chests out, like they were grown men. They picked fights quick, just to remind everybody they weren't weak. Then, there were the quiet ones, the ones who sat back and watched, calculating and waiting. There also were the ones like Omari, stuck in between, trying not to draw attention but knowing eventually someone would test them anyway.

It happened often. Shoves in the lunch line or trash talk in the rec room. Omari didn't go looking for fights, but when they came to him, he stood his ground. A busted lip here, a bruise on his knuckles there. Enough to earn him a sliver of respect and let others know that he wasn't backing down. Still, every fight left him shaking inside – not from fear but from the weight of it. He hadn't wanted this life. He hadn't wanted to be here at all. But one night, one decision, had changed his entire life.

There were moments of connection too. A boy named Uno, skinny and dark skinned with a quick laugh, started sitting next to Omari during meals. "Man, you quiet as hell," Uno said one day, stabbing at his eggs with a plastic fork. "What's your story?"

Omari shrugged. "Nothin' to tell."

Uno smirked. "You think you the only one killed somebody in here? You better learn to talk, or this place gon' eat you alive."

Omari's chest tightened. "I didn't mean to. It's not like I went over there to kill him," he muttered.

"Don't none of us mean to," Uno spoke, his voice softening for just a second. "But we still here."

After that, the two boys became friends. They played cards together sometimes, passing long hours with spades or tonk. Uno cracked jokes that made Omari laugh despite himself, though the laughter always felt strange in his chest. He felt like he shouldn't be able to laugh when he was locked away.

Nights were the hardest for him. That was when he thought about what life would be like if he was with Kiss instead of in jail. How in love they would be and the dates he would take her on. He prayed that God would make it all better, and he had faith that he would.

Chapter Ten

Snow drifted lazily outside the window, soft flakes settling on the sidewalks like powdered sugar. Kiss sat cross-legged on her bed, staring at the ceiling, her headphones buzzing faintly with an R&B playlist. It had been almost a year since she and Onyx had made things official. A year of hallway hand holding, of late-night porch talks with just the two of them. An entire year of feeling like she could finally breathe. She was now in her junior year, and Kiss couldn't be more excited.

She thought about Onyx constantly – not just when they were together but when she was supposed to be studying, when she was supposed to be sleeping, when she was brushing her teeth or tying her shoes. He was there, filling every corner of her mind. The way he smiled with that half-cocked grin, the way his laugh rumbled deep in his chest, the way his eyes softened when he looked at her like she was something precious to him.

She loved him. She hadn't said it out loud yet, but she knew she did. And more and more, she found herself thinking about the one thing they hadn't done. Her stomach fluttered at the thought, equal parts excitement and nerves. She'd never gone that far before, not with anyone. With Omari, everything had been cut short, stolen by sirens and cuffs before they ever had the chance. And now here she was, a year into something real with Onyx, and she was wondering if she was ready to take that step.

The guilt clawed at her whenever the thought came. Omari's

face still haunted her dreams sometimes, his letters folded neatly and tucked safely inside her dresser drawer. She could still hear his words: *If we meant to be, we'll find each other when I'm out.* But Omari was gone right now, locked away, living a life she couldn't touch, while Onyx was here. Onyx was the one that had been here every day. He'd been patient with her. He'd never pushed or pressured her to do anything. But the way he touched her now was different. The way his fingers lingered at the small of her back, the way his lips brushed just a little slower against hers. It made her ache in a way she couldn't ignore anymore. She closed her eyes, her chest rising with a slow, shaky breath. She wasn't sure if she was ready, but she was sure she wanted him.

That Saturday, Kiss found herself at Onyx's. Tamika was working a double shift, and the house was quiet except for the hum of the heater and the faint bass of music playing from Onyx's speakers. They were sprawled across his bed, half-watching a movie neither of them cared about. Kiss leaned against him, her head resting on his shoulder, his arm draped casually around her waist.

"You ever think about the future?" Onyx asked suddenly, his voice low.

This was the second time Onyx had asked her something like this, and she couldn't help but to think he had more to say. *Was he asking me this because he sees a future with me?* Kiss thought to herself.

Kiss tilted her head up at him. "What you mean?"

He shrugged, his fingers tracing absent circles against her hip. "Like what we gon' be in a couple years. Where we gon' end up."

Kiss smiled faintly. "You sound grown."

"I am grown," he teased. "I just... I want somethin' real, Kiss. With you."

Her heart thudded hard against her ribs. She searched his

face, the seriousness in his eyes and the warmth in his touch. He wasn't playing. Kiss could tell he meant every word.

She sat up a little, turning toward him fully. "You already got somethin' real with me."

"Yeah," he said, his hand sliding up to cup her cheek. "But I want all of it."

The kiss that followed was slow and deep, full of a heat that left Kiss breathless. Kiss' fingers curled in his shirt, pulling him closer, her body answering before her mind could catch up. When they pulled apart, her chest was heaving, and her lips were tingling. In that moment, she realized that she was ready to give him more.

The movie still played in the background, but neither of them were paying attention. Kiss sat there with her pulse racing, as she still felt Onyx's lips on hers. Onyx's hand still rested against her cheek, his thumb brushing slow against her skin. He looked at her like he was memorizing her, like she was the only thing in the world that mattered to him, and in that moment, Kiss felt like she was. It made her chest ache and her breath catch all at once.

For a long moment, she said nothing. Her mind fought with itself – guilt, fear, longing, and curiosity all colliding in her chest. Omari's face flickered in her memory, his letters folded inside her dresser. *Don't wait for me.* The words that had once cut her open now came back softer, almost like permission. Her gaze drifted back to Onyx, to his steady brown eyes, to the warmth of his palm against her face.

She swallowed hard, her voice coming out barely above a whisper. "Onyx, I think I'm ready."

He froze, his hand still cupping her cheek, his breath hitching. "You mean?"

Kiss nodded, heat flooding her face. "Yeah. I mean."

For a second, the air between them held still, thick with meaning. Then, Onyx's expression softened, almost reverent. He leaned forward, pressing his forehead against hers.

"You sure?" he whispered. "'Cause I don't ever wanna make you do somethin' you don't want to do."

Kiss' throat tightened, but she nodded again, firmer this time. "I'm sure. I want you."

Her words broke the last of the distance between them. The rest of the night unfolded in slow-motion. They didn't rush. Instead, Kiss found herself watching him more closely than ever, every careful movement, every lingering glance, every question in his eyes, as he touched her like she was something fragile and precious. Her nerves buzzed, but underneath them was a surprising calm. Because this wasn't about just the act. It was about trust. It was about choosing him, fully, for the first time.

Every kiss lingered longer than the last. Every touch told Kiss that Onyx wanted only her. And when she finally gave herself over to the moment, it wasn't fear that filled her chest. It was warmth and safety. It was knowing that after everything they had been through, they had built something real together.

Later, they lay tangled together in the soft quiet of his room, the music still humming low in the background. Kiss rested her head against his chest, listening to the steady beat of his heart beneath her ear. She thought about all the years that had brought them here. About the little girl sitting on her porch with Omari that had now grown into a young woman that was now with Onyx. She thought about how she had fought the guilt, how she had resisted the pull, how she had finally let herself see Onyx for who he truly was.

Her fingers curled against him, her eyes fluttering shut. For the first time in what felt like forever, she wasn't haunted by the past. She was here with Onyx, the one who had been her anchor, her laughter, and her safe place since the moment Omari went to jail. And in her heart, she knew this was only the beginning.

By his fourth year inside, Omari had hardened – not in his heart but in the way he carried himself. He'd stopped flinching at the sound of doors slamming. He learned how to move in the cafeteria line, so no one bumped him on purpose. He kept his answers short with guards, long enough to avoid punishment but never enough to give them anything. He started working out in his cell, doing push-ups, sit-ups and squats until his muscles ached. It gave him something to control, something that was his. He allowed the sweat to replace the fear, and it had washed it away.

When new kids came in, eyes wide with terror, Omari recognized it instantly. He'd been that boy once. Sometimes, he'd nod at them, let them sit near him at meals, give them quiet advice about how to survive while they were inside – all the things he wished someone had done for him when he first got there. Still, no matter what he did, the guilt never left. Every time he closed his eyes, Darren's face was there.

Time passed differently in lockup. A week felt like a month, and a year felt like it stretched forever. Seasons only showed through the small square window at the top of his cell with the snowflakes swirling past in winter and bright sun in the summer. Omari grew taller, his shoulders broader with muscles that carved from hours of push-ups and pull-ups against the bars. He wasn't the boy who went in anymore. He was becoming a man, whether he was ready for it or not.

On Omari's seventeenth birthday, Tamika and Onyx came to see him. He was excited because he knew he was one year closer to getting out and being with Kiss again. He walked down the hallway, smiling hard, as he was led to the visitation room. When he walked inside, the first face he saw was his mother's. He walked over to her and hugged her tightly.

"Happy birthday, son," Tamika greeted.

"Thank you, Ma."

Onyx walked up next, hugging his brother, happy to see him. "Happy birthday, bro."

"Happy birthday."

The three of them took their seats. Omari was so happy to see his family that he couldn't stop smiling. It wasn't that they didn't come to visit him because they did. Tamika was there twice a month, and Onyx came every month. However, something about today felt different. Tamika talked to him about everything that had happened since the last time she visited, and Omari listened to every word. However, Onyx was quiet, and Omari wondered why.

"Ma, why don't you go and get us something to eat?" Omari suggested.

Tamika agreed before standing to her feet and walking off, leaving Omari and Onyx alone at the table.

"Okay, what's up, bro? I can tell by the look on your face that something is wrong, so what is it?" Omari asked, looking Onyx directly in the eyes.

Onyx took a deep breath before speaking. "I don't know how to tell you this, so I'm just going to come out and say it. Kiss is pregnant."

Omari closed his eyes and took a deep breath. He knew he'd told Kiss not to wait on him. He didn't want her to stop her life for him. He wanted her to be happy, needed her to be. But finding out she was now pregnant wasn't something that he wanted to hear. Not on his birthday.

"Damn, man, who she fuckin' with now?"

Onyx dropped his head before lifting it back up again. "Me. The baby is mine, and Kiss is my girl."

Omari's brows deepened. He'd heard the words when they left Onyx's lips, but they didn't register. *There's no way he just said what I think he said,* Omari thought.

"What you just say?" Omari asked, wanting to be sure he'd heard everything correctly.

"It's my baby, Omari. Me and Kiss are together now and have been for a while. I know it's fucked up, and I'm sorry, but I love her."

Omari looked at his brother but didn't see his twin that he'd loved all his life. He didn't see his first best friend. Instead, he saw a person that had betrayed him in the deepest way. He wanted to jump up and put hands on Onyx, but he knew the guards would break it up before he could do any real damage.

"Fuck you just say to me?" Omari asked through clenched teeth.

"I said me and Kiss is going to have a baby. We in love and been together for a while." Onyx's voice never wavered, and his eyes never left Omari's. As bad as what he did was, he knew he had to stand on what he'd done. "I didn't know this would happen, but I can't say that I'm sorry because we're happy. I really love her, and she loves me too. We're going to be a family."

The visitation room was loud with overlapping voices and chairs scraping against the floor. However, the only thing Omari heard was the words Onyx spoke. He sat at the small, plastic table, his hands folded in front of him, trying to keep his body steady and his voice calm. For a long moment, Omari felt like he couldn't breathe. *My baby, Kiss, is havin' a fucking baby with Onyx, my own fucking brother? My fucking twin? This is too much,* Omari thought.

His chest burned hot then cold. A thousand images flashed through his mind all at once. Kiss laughing on his porch, Kiss crying in the station, the way she'd whispered *I'll wait for you* in her eyes even when her lips couldn't say it. He thought of the letters, each one soaked with his hope, his promises, and his love for her. He thought of all the nights he whispered her name into the dark, vowing to make it back to her, and now this. Omari's fists clenched on the table, knuckles aching against the cuffs. Jealousy clawed at him and rage sparked hot. He knew he told her not to wait on him, but her being with Onyx was the last thing he thought would happen.

Omari leaned back, his chest heaving, trying to hold himself together. Inside, though, he was unraveling. The girl he loved and the brother he trusted had built a life without him. They were about to be a family, and that was something that was supposed to be his. Part of him wanted to shout, to curse. He wanted to flip the table and let the anger tear free. But another part of him was completely broken.

Before Omari could say anything else, his mother came back to the table, snacks in hand, still smiling. For the rest of the visit, Omari barely spoke. He couldn't. His words would've betrayed the storm in his chest. Instead, he stared at his brother across the table, the weight of the news pressing down on his chest. When the guards called time, Omari stood slowly, his body heavy. As he walked back toward the barred door, he could only shake his head. That night when Omari got back to his cell, he cried himself to sleep.

Chapter Eleven

"**I** told him. I told Omari about us. And about the baby." Onyx spoke the moment he walked into Kiss' living room.

Kiss sat there on the edge of the couch, her body stiff. Her mind was spinning. For a second, she thought she'd misheard him, that maybe her brain had twisted his words into something she feared. But when she looked up and saw the tightness in his jaw and the guilt flickering across his face, she knew she'd heard him correctly.

"You what?" Her voice cracked, sharper than she intended.

Onyx rubbed the back of his neck, refusing to meet her eyes. "I couldn't keep it from him, Kiss. He's my brother. He deserved to know. Plus, neither our love or our baby needs to be a secret."

Her throat went dry, and her heart pounded so loud she could hear it in her own ears. Omari knew she was pregnant. He knew about her and Onyx. She knew this would be the end of their friendship and anything else they could have had. A sharp pang of grief punched through her chest. It was so strong it almost knocked the breath out of her. She imagined Omari sitting in that cold, gray visitation room, hearing the words spill from his brother's mouth. She pictured the look in his eyes. All the betrayal and hurt that he must be feeling. The way his face must have fallen when he realized the two people he trusted most had moved on together and done him wrong in the process.

Tears welled in her eyes before she could stop them. She turned away, covering her face with her hands. "Onyx, how could you? That wasn't your choice to make."

"I know you mad," Onyx spoke quietly, taking a seat on the couch next to Kiss, "but I couldn't keep lying to him. That's my twin. If I ain't man enough to tell him, then what does that make me?"

"It makes you selfish," Kiss snapped, her hands dropping from her face, tears rolling down her cheeks. "You didn't think about me or how it would hit him. You just…" She broke off, pressing a fist against her mouth.

Onyx leaned forward, his voice firmer now. "You think it would've hurt less comin' from somebody else? From rumors he might hear inside? He needed to hear it from me. From us."

Her head shook slowly, the weight of it pressing heavy against her shoulders. "You don't know what you just did to him. You don't know how much he loved me."

Onyx flinched at the words, his jaw tightening. For a long moment, neither of them spoke. The silence hung between them like a blade.

It had only been a week since she found out. She hadn't even told her mother yet. Kiss' mind drifted back to that night, standing alone in the bathroom with the test clutched in her shaking hands.

Her heart had pounded, as the little pink plus sign appeared, sharp and undeniable. Her knees went weak, and she sank down onto the edge of the tub, staring at it, tears stinging her eyes.

"I'm pregnant."

The words had rolled through her chest like thunder. Fear hit her first. The fear of Sade's reaction, the fear of whispers at school, the fear of all the ways her life was about to change. She wasn't ready. At just sixteen, she was still a girl herself, still trying to figure out how to survive her own world. And now, she would be responsible for another life.

But as she sat there, staring at that tiny stick, something else bloomed beneath the fear. A warmth. A fragile, flicker of joy. She placed a trembling hand on her stomach and whispered, "It's real."

When Kiss told Onyx, his eyes had widened, shock flickering across his face. For a moment, she thought he might panic, that he'd bolt, that he'd leave her holding this truth alone – the same way her father had done to her mother. But then, his hand had pressed against her stomach, his voice soft and certain.

"That's our baby. We really 'bout to have a baby."

Kiss wiped at her cheeks angrily. "You should've let me tell him. He's in jail, Onyx. And he's alone. Now, he knows the truth in the worst way possible. You think he's just gonna accept that?"

Onyx's eyes softened, but his tone stayed steady. "He'll have to. This ain't about him no more. This about us and our family."

Her hand drifted to her stomach unconsciously, pressing lightly against it. The guilt tangled with the love she already felt for the life inside her, pulling her heart in two directions.

"I don't want to hurt him," she whispered.

Onyx leaned closer, tilting her chin up, so their eyes met. "I know you don't. But you can't save him from this, Kiss. What we got, it's real, and so is that baby growing inside you. That's where our focus gotta be now."

Kiss' eyes blurred with fresh tears. She wanted to believe him. She wanted to hold onto the hope, the joy, the future she and Onyx were building. But in her heart, Omari lingered, and she didn't know if it would ever let her go.

The silence between them was heavy. Kiss pulled away from Onyx's touch, standing up and pacing across the living room. Her arms wrapped around herself, as if holding her own body together was the only way to keep from falling apart.

"You don't understand," she finally spoke, her voice sharp but trembling underneath. "Omari was my first everything. My first kiss, my first love, my first promise. And now he's sitting in that place because he wanted to save me. And you just..." Her throat closed as tears burned her eyes. "You just ripped it away from him."

Onyx sat on the couch, his elbows braced on his knees, his hands clasped together. His head was bowed, as if he was in deep thought. For once, he didn't fire back right away. He just let her words sink in. When he finally looked up, his voice was low.

"You think I don't feel that too? You think it don't kill me knowing I took somethin' that used to be his? You don't think that makes me feel like I'm second best? Every day, I wake up with that weight on me, Kiss. But I'd rather live with the truth than a lie."

Kiss pressed a hand to her forehead, wiping at her wet cheeks. "You didn't give me a choice. You didn't even let me decide how to tell him."

Onyx stood, walking over to Kiss slowly. He stopped just in front of her, his voice steady even though his eyes were red. "You right. I should've told you that I was going to tell him. But I couldn't stomach the thought of him finding out from anyone else. I told you that I would handle it, and that was me handling it. He's my twin, Kiss. That bond… people born alone won't know. I owed him that much, Kiss."

Kiss stared at him, not saying anything. Anger flared inside her, but beneath it, she completely understood what Onyx was saying. As much as it hurt her to know Omari was hurting, she knew that lying would have only hurt him worse. Her hand drifted again to her stomach, a subconscious gesture she couldn't stop. The thought of the life that she and Onyx had created growing inside her softened the edges of her fury.

"This baby is ours, Kiss. That's somethin' Omari can't change, no matter how he feels. And I ain't sayin' it to be fucked up. It's just the truth. We can't live our life apologizin' forever. We got a family to think about now."

Onyx guided Kiss to the couch, and they sat back down. For a long while, neither spoke, their thoughts filling the space like background music. Kiss wiped her tears with her hand before finally looking up at Onyx.

"I'm scared," she whispered.

"Of what?"

She gave a short, humorless laugh. "Of everything. Of bein' a mama when I'm still tryin' to figure out myself. Of tellin' my mama that I'm pregnant. Of people lookin' at me different, whisperin' and shit. Of Omari hatin' me forever. Of not bein' enough for this baby. I'm just scared, Onyx."

Onyx reached for her hand, threading his fingers through hers. "You ain't gotta be enough by yourself. You got me, and we gon' be enough together."

Her throat tightened, her eyes stinging again. She wanted to believe him. She wanted to lean into that promise, to let it hold her steady. But the doubts clawed at her still.

"You say that now," she whispered, "but what if you get tired? What if it's too much?"

Onyx squeezed her hand tighter. "Then I'll get stronger. 'Cause I ain't walkin' away. Not from you and not from this baby. I don't care how hard it gets; I'm here."

Kiss' heart softened with those words. When she looked into Onyx's eyes, she knew he was telling the truth. Onyx wrapped both arms around Kiss, pulling her closer to him.

"You ain't alone, Kiss," he whispered softly, "and you never will be."

That night, when Onyx left, Kiss went to her room, closed the door behind her, and leaned against it, her body heavy with exhaustion. She could still hear Onyx's voice in her head, still feel the warmth of his hand against hers. But when she glanced at her bed, she remembered the shoebox filed with the letters that she'd removed from her dresser drawer. A fresh wave of guilt washed over her. She crossed the room slowly, pulling the box out and lifting the lid. The letters were all there, folded neatly, his handwriting jagged but familiar. She picked one up, the paper soft from being read too many times. Unfolding it, she sat on her bed and read it again.

Kiss, you the only thing that keep me sane in here. I close my eyes and see you, and it reminds me why I gotta survive this. I love you. Always have and always will.

Her tears blurred the words. She pressed the paper to her chest, her heart aching.

"I'm sorry," she whispered into the quiet room. "I'm so sorry."

She set the letter back gently, slid the box back under her bed, and sat down. Her hand drifted to her stomach, her palm resting flat against it. A fragile smile touched her lips through the tears. "I promise Mommy is going to give you the best life possible." She spoke the words softly, and her voice was shaky, but she meant what she'd said. The fear was still there, but in that moment, none of it mattered as much as the tiny flicker of life inside her. For the first time in years, she felt like she had something that was hers.

***

Kiss sat on the edge of her bed, knees bouncing, her hands folded tight in her lap. The house was quiet, the hum of the old heater filling the silence. Her stomach churned, not from morning sickness this time but from nerves. For days, she'd been carrying the secret, the weight pressing heavier with each sunrise. Tonight, she couldn't hold it anymore. Her hand drifted to her stomach, palm pressing lightly against the still-flat curve. She didn't even know how far along she was yet, but the test hadn't lied. She was carrying Onyx's child. The thought made her heart flutter and ache at the same time.

She imagined Sade's face when she told her. Her mother had

worked double shifts for years, sacrificing everything to make sure Kiss had clothes on her back and food on the table. Sade wanted better for Kiss. She wanted her to go to college, get a career, and not get sucked into the streets of Detroit. So, Kiss knew she wouldn't be happy about a teenage pregnancy.

The front door opened, and Kiss jolted. Sade's voice floated down the hallway, heavy with exhaustion. "Kiss, you home?"

"Yeah, Mama," Kiss called, her throat tight.

She heard the shuffle of Sade's shoes hitting the floor, the clatter of keys dropping on the living room table. The smell of fried chicken from some takeout place drifted in, as her mother walked into the living room, still in her scrubs, hair pulled back, face shining with sweat from a long day. Kiss got up from her bed and walked into the living room to greet her mother.

"You eat?" Sade asked automatically, digging into the bag.

"Yeah," Kiss lied. Her stomach was too knotted for food.

Sade sank onto the couch, kicking off her shoes. She sighed, leaning her head back, her eyes closed for a moment. Kiss stared at her, her chest pounding. She opened her mouth then shut it again. The words tangled in her throat.

Sade's eyes snapped open. "Alright, what is it? You standin' there lookin' like you done stole somethin'."

Kiss swallowed hard, stepping into the room. Her voice came out smaller than she wanted. "Mama, I gotta tell you somethin'."

Sade frowned, sitting up straighter. "What happened? You in trouble?"

"No," Kiss whispered, twisting her fingers together. "It's not that."

"Then what is it?"

Kiss' chest rose and fell in a shaky breath. "I'm pregnant."

The words hung in the air like smoke, thick and choking. For a moment, Sade didn't move. Her eyes blinked once, and her face froze in shock. Then, she stood, pacing the room like she was trying to outrun the truth.

"Pregnant? You… Lord, Jesus, no. Please tell me you're just playing." Her hands went to her head, gripping her braids tight.

Kiss' eyes blurred with tears. "Mama, I…"

"Don't 'Mama' me right now," Sade snapped, her voice sharp with disbelief. "You sixteen years old, Kiss. Sixteen. I worked my hands raw, so you wouldn't be like them girls out here with babies on they hips and no future. And now you tellin' me you pregnant?"

Kiss' tears slipped hot down her cheeks. "I didn't plan this, Mama."

"Oh, I know you ain't plan it," Sade cut in, her tone bitter. "But you sure laid down and let it happen."

Kiss flinched, wrapping her arms around herself. "Mama, please."

Sade's voice rose, her anger spilling out. "And don't tell me it's by that boy."

Kiss froze. Her silence was the only answer.

Sade laughed, but it was a hollow, bitter sound. "Onyx? Of all people, Kiss? That family done already brought enough pain into this house. His brother sittin' in juvie for murder, and you got the nerve to lay up with the other one? Are you tryin' to kill me, or you just that fuckin' stupid?"

Kiss shook her head, sobbing now. "No, Mama, it's not like that. He loves me, and he loves our baby."

Sade stopped pacing, her chest heaving, her eyes sharp and wet at the same time. "Love don't pay bills. Love don't raise a child. Love don't keep you safe when the world already set against you." Her voice cracked, but her anger didn't waver. "I gave up my whole life for you, Kiss. Every dream I ever had, I put it on hold, so you could have better. And this is what you do? This is what you bring home to me?"

Kiss' legs trembled beneath her, but she forced herself to speak through the tears. "Mama, I'm scared too. I don't know how to do this. But I love this baby already. And Onyx, he's not like what you think. He's been there for me when nobody else was. He's all I have."

Sade's lips pressed together tight, her shoulders shaking with restrained fury and heartbreak. She turned away, pressing a hand to her mouth, her breaths ragged.

"You don't know what you're doin'," she finally spoke, her voice breaking. "You think love gon' fix this? You think a boy who don't know how to be a man gon' raise a child? You a baby yourself."

Kiss stepped forward, her hand on her stomach. "Then I'll grow up. I don't got a choice no more. I'm gon' be a mama, and I'm gon' do whatever it takes."

Sade turned then, her eyes glistening. For the first time, Kiss saw not just anger but fear. The fear of a mother watching her daughter step onto a road she couldn't pull her back from.

"You breakin' my heart, Kiss," Sade whispered. "You breakin' it wide open."

Kiss' tears fell harder. "I'm sorry. But I can't be sorry about this baby."

Chapter Twelve

The morning of the appointment, Kiss woke up with a knot in her stomach. She sat on the edge of her bed, staring at the floor, one hand resting gently over her belly. It was still flat, but she was starting to feel a difference in her body. Today would be the day the doctor confirmed just how far along she was. She heard her mother moving around in the kitchen, the rattle of pans and the scrape of a chair against the floor. Kiss pulled on a hoodie and jeans, her heart thudding with each step down the hallway.

Sade was already dressed, her scrubs crisp, her hair pulled into a tight bun. Her face was as hard as stone, and the bags under her eyes showed her lack of sleep.

"You ready?" Sade asked without looking up from the cup of coffee she was sipping.

Kiss nodded, her throat tight. "Yeah."

Sade grabbed her keys and purse, heading for the door. Kiss followed, her palms sweaty. As she stepped outside, Onyx was leaning against the car, his hands shoved into the pockets of his hoodie. Sade's jaw tightened the second she saw him.

"What's he doing here?"

Kiss' voice wavered, but she held her ground. "He's coming with us, Mama."

Sade turned, her eyes flashing. "Not in my car he's not."

"Mama," Kiss' voice cracked, but she stood firm, "this is his baby too. You might not like him, but he's part of this."

The air went sharp with silence. For a moment, Kiss thought her mother might make a scene right there in the driveway. But finally, Sade muttered under her breath and unlocked the doors. "Fine. Just get in the damn car."

Onyx shot Kiss a quick, steady look, as they climbed in, like he was telling her without words that he could handle it. Kiss slid in beside him, her heart heavy and grateful all at once. The car ride was suffocating and quiet. Sade's hands gripped the steering wheel tight, her eyes fixed on the road. She didn't speak, didn't even glance at the two of them in the backseat. Kiss sat stiffly, her fingers intertwined with Onyx's beneath the fold of her hoodie where Sade couldn't see.

Onyx stayed quiet. His jaw set, he gazed out the window. Kiss knew he wanted to say something, maybe to lighten the tension, but he didn't. And that restraint made her chest ache. Sade's silence was louder than any shouting she could have ever done. By the time they pulled into the clinic parking lot, Kiss' stomach was in knots. She pressed her hand against it, as she climbed out of the car.

The waiting room was crowded, the faint hum of voices mixing with the rustle of magazines and the occasional calls of the last names of the patients waiting. Kiss signed in at the desk, her palms clammy, then sat between Sade and Onyx. It felt like sitting between fire and water. Sade's body was stiff, her arms crossed tight over her chest, her lips pressed into a thin line. Onyx leaned forward, elbows on his knees, his hand resting just close enough to Kiss' that she could feel his warmth.

Kiss kept her eyes on the floor, not saying a word. Every so often, Sade's eyes flickered toward Onyx, sharp and full of judgment. Kiss caught one of those looks and shook her head.

"Mama," she whispered, "please don't."

Sade didn't answer, just looked away. A nurse finally walked out the door, looking down at the chart.

"Johnson?" she called out.

Relief flooded Kiss' chest. She stood quickly, Onyx rising beside her. Sade hesitated then followed, her disapproval trailing behind her. The doctor's office was small but bright, posters of smiling mothers and infants decorating the walls. The doctor, a middle-aged woman with kind eyes, greeted them warmly.

"Congratulations," she spoke, shaking Kiss' hand. "My name is Dr. Hampton. Is this your first pregnancy?"

Sade's face hardened at the word *congratulations*. Kiss felt it like a slap, but she managed a small nod.

"Yes, it is."

The doctor's smile was gentle. "Well, we'll start with some questions and then do an ultrasound to see how far along you are."

Kiss sat on the exam table, her hands folded tight in her lap. Onyx stood beside her, his presence solid and reassuring. Sade perched stiffly in the chair, her eyes narrowed, letting everyone in the room know that she wasn't happy about this.

The doctor asked about her last cycle, about symptoms, and about family medical history. Kiss answered as best she could, her voice quiet. Finally, the doctor wheeled over the ultrasound machine.

"Go ahead and lie back, sweetheart."

Kiss obeyed, her heart hammering with anticipation. Cold gel spread across her stomach, making her flinch. The wand pressed lightly against her skin, and then the room filled with a sound that made everything stop. It was the baby's heartbeat.

Kiss' breath caught, her eyes flooding with tears. She turned her head, meeting Onyx's wide-eyed stare. His hand found hers, gripping tight, his eyes shining. Even Sade froze. For the first time, her anger faltered. Her eyes softened, just a little, as the sound of her grandchild's heartbeat filled the room.

"That's your baby," the doctor said softly.

Kiss cried then, silent tears slipping down her cheeks. She had imagined this moment, dreamed it and feared it all at once. But hearing it was different. It was proof of the life growing inside her.

Onyx leaned down, pressing his forehead to hers. "That's ours," he whispered.

Kiss smiled as she looked over at the screen. She couldn't believe she was really hearing her child's heartbeat for the first time. She grabbed Onyx's hand, as they watched the screen together.

"Well, it looks like you are about six weeks along." Dr. Hampton smiled.

Chapter Thirteen

Onyx sat on the edge of his bed, elbows braced against his knees, his hands clasped together so tightly his knuckles ached. The house was quiet except for the faint hum of the heater and the creak of pipes in the walls. In his head, the sound was still there, louder than everything else. The rapid, steady beat of his baby's heart. It hadn't been real before. He'd believed Kiss, believed the test, believed the way her body was already shifting, but hearing it with his own ears was different. That sound had punched straight through him, fierce and raw, like a lightning bolt to the chest.

He hadn't even cared that Sade was in the corner with her arms crossed, looking like she'd rather be anywhere else. For one second, nothing else in the world mattered but that sound. However, the moment they left the clinic, the weight came back. Sade hadn't said much, but the look on her face had said it all. She didn't believe in him. She didn't believe he could take care of her daughter or raise a child. She looked at him the same way she had since he met her – like he was a problem, a mistake, a shadow standing in the space Omari had left behind.

Onyx scrubbed his hand over his face, frustration burning hot under his skin. He wasn't perfect, and he knew it. He'd made mistakes, gotten into trouble, ran the streets when he was younger. But he wasn't that kid anymore. He had Kiss and now a baby on the way. So, he knew he needed to do more.

As much as he loved Kiss, he knew it would take more than love to take care of her and the baby. That was the one thing Sade had been right about.

Onyx stood, pacing the small room he used to share with his brother. His phone sat on the dresser, screen cracked from being dropped one too many times. He stared at it, jaw clenched. There was one person he hadn't called in a long time, someone he swore he was done with when he decided to change. But now, he wasn't so sure.

Onyx grabbed the phone, scrolled through his contacts until he saw Blue's name. His thumb hovered over it for a moment, doubt creeping through him. He knew Blue's game, fast and dirty money. He knew calling meant stepping back into the kind of life he'd promised himself he'd leave behind once him and Kiss became serious. However, Onyx didn't see another choice being seventeen with a child on the way.

The line rang twice before Blue's voice came through. "Well, well. Look who decided to remember my number. Lil Blackwell. What's good, Onyx?"

Onyx swallowed hard, steadying his voice. "I need work."

Blue chuckled. "Work, huh? Thought you was done with me. Thought you was tryna play house with that girl."

Onyx's jaw tightened. "I'm serious, Blue. I got responsibilities now. I got a baby on the way. I need money and fast."

There was silence on the other end for a beat then a low whistle. "Damn. Didn't think I'd see the day Onyx Blackwell talkin' about bein' a daddy. Congratulations, lil' man. Guess that explains why you crawlin' back."

Onyx's grip tightened on the phone. "You got somethin' or not?"

Blue laughed again. "Relax. I got somethin'. Nothin' too heavy for a first job back. Couple cars sittin' downtown. High-end with clean plates. It's an easy snatch. You bring 'em to me, I'll cut you a stack for each."

Onyx closed his eyes for a second, the weight of the decision pressing down on him. He could already picture Sade's face if she ever found out. Hell, he could picture Kiss' too. But then he thought about that heartbeat, about the life growing inside Kiss. He had to make sure he could provide for them. He couldn't let them down.

"When?" he asked finally.

"Tonight," Blue said smoothly. "Meet me at the old garage on Jefferson at midnight. Don't be late."

Onyx hung up, staring at the phone in his hand. His stomach twisted, nerves sparking through him, but underneath it all was determination. Sade might think he wasn't good enough, but he was about to prove her wrong. He was going to show her that he could provide everything his family would need and more.

The rest of the day moved slow. Onyx tried to keep himself busy, but his mind kept circling back to the heartbeat. That sound was carved into him, like it had branded his soul. For the first time in his life, he understood what it meant to live for someone other than yourself. That was the reason he was going to do everything he could to ensure he provided a good life. Sade might not believe in him, and that was okay because Kiss did. And that was all that mattered to him.

Twenty minutes before midnight, Onyx was slipping out of the house, hoodie pulled low over his face. The city was quiet and the streets empty. The streetlights buzzed faintly, and the wind carried scraps of paper across cracked sidewalks. The old garage on Jefferson looked abandoned from the outside, rusted doors and graffiti on the walls. Several huge weeds pushed through the concrete, and the grass looked like it hadn't been cut in months. But when Onyx knocked twice and slid the panel back, Blue's voice cut through the tall grass.

"'Bout time yo' ass got here."

Inside, the garage was filled with life. A couple of young dudes leaned against a stripped-down Impala, smoking a blunt.

Tools clattered in the background where somebody worked under the hood of another car. The smell of oil, rubber, and smoke clung to the air. Blue stood in the middle, tall with broad shoulders. His dark skin glowed under the light. It was how he got the nickname Blue because his skin was so dark it looked blue. His huge chain glinting in the dim light. His grin widened when he saw Onyx.

"Damn, lil' Blackwell. Thought you wasn't gon' show up."

Onyx kept his face steady. "I told you that I need money."

Blue's grin turned sharp. "Yeah, I hear you."

Blue handed Onyx a paper that he looked over. Two cars, both luxury, both parked in spots Blue had already mapped out. He knew the work. He used to boost cars for Blue all the time back when he was fourteen. He still remembered the adrenaline rush of sliding behind the wheel, the hot pulse of knowing one wrong move could end in cuffs or worse.

"You in or not?" Blue asked, watching him closely.

Onyx folded the paper and slipped it into his pocket. "I'm in."

He walked home under the cold streetlights, his breath fogging in the night air. His mind replayed the doctor's appointment and the heartbeat. Then, he saw the disapproving look on Sade's face. He couldn't let her be right about him. If that meant risking everything, then so be it. Onyx shoved his hands into his pockets, the paper crinkling against his fingers.

"Don't worry, lil' one," he whispered under his breath, picturing the baby that was still no bigger than a grape inside Kiss. "Daddy gon' make sure you straight no matter what it takes."

Onyx's nights blurred into motion. The first job with Blue came easy. He'd slid into the driver's seat like muscle memory, his fingers dancing over wires the way they used to. The engine roared to life, and the rush hit him hard – heart pounding, hands steady, adrenaline washing away doubt. That first night, he brought the cars back to the garage, and Blue clapped him on the back, laughing. He knew he could do it over and over again.

That night, Onyx walked away with a stack of cash so thick he had to shove it deep into his pocket to keep it from spilling. It was two thousand dollars for the two cars he'd stolen. That meant he could stock up on diapers, wipes, and maybe even get a crib for the baby. He told himself it was worth it. Any wrong he had to do was to make sure his family had what they needed.

So, night after night, he hit cars – a Lexus one night, a Charger the next. Sometimes, he worked alone, sometimes with one of Blue's other boys. He hit the streets like he'd never left, and it had become second nature to him. Each car he boosted felt like another brick laid in the foundation he was building for his child.

The money piled up fast. He stashed it in a shoebox under his bed at first then graduated to a duffel bag he hid in the back of his closet. Every time he opened it, the sight of those stacks filled him with pride. He'd fan the bills out, counting them slow. He imagined baby bottles lined up on the counter, soft clothes folded in drawers, and Kiss smiling with relief when she realized he could provide. Sometimes, late at night, he'd pull the duffel out and sit on the floor with it, pulling out wad after wad, stacking them neatly just to see what he had. It wasn't millions, not even close, but it was something – more than he'd ever had in his life, enough to make him believe he could do this.

One afternoon, he walked into a baby store with his hood pulled low, feeling awkward as hell among the pastel colors and soft music. He wandered the aisles until a pack of onesies caught his eye. They were tiny and white cotton with little animals stitched on the front. He picked them up, fingers tracing the fabric. They were so small, and he couldn't help but smile. He bought them along with a pack of bottles and a blanket with yellow ducks on it. The cashier smiled, congratulating him, as she bagged his items.

Onyx just nodded, his chest swelling. He tucked the bag under his arm and walked out with his head high. When he gave the bag to Kiss later that night, her eyes filled with tears. She pulled the blanket out, pressed it to her cheek.

"Onyx, this is perfect."

He held her tightly, the weight of his choices burning his heart. However, when she looked at him, he knew it was all worth it.

One night, after boosting a Range Rover, he sat in the driver's seat for a long moment before pulling off. His reflection stared back at him in the rearview mirror. He was no longer the scared little boy but a man determined to have a better life.

Chapter Fourteen

The waiting room was bright, all pale walls and glossy magazines that no one ever read. Kiss sat in a plastic chair, her hands folded tightly in her lap, her hoodie stretched just slightly across the small curve of her stomach. It wasn't much yet but enough that she caught herself running her hands over it absentmindedly, protective and proud. Beside her, Onyx bounced his knee, his arm draped loosely across the back of her chair. Kiss bit her lip, trying to hold back her own smile. She was nervous, yes, but underneath it was excitement. Today, they'd know what they were having. Which meant they would finally be able to give their child a name.

Sade hadn't come this time. She'd been civil since the first appointment, but her disapproval still hung thick around everything. Kiss didn't mind her absence. This moment belonged to her and Onyx. When the nurse finally called her name, Onyx jumped to his feet before Kiss could even stand. He took her hand, squeezing it, as they walked back together.

The exam room was small and cool, the air smelling faintly of antiseptic. Kiss climbed onto the table, the crinkling paper loud beneath her. Onyx stood close, his hand still gripping hers like it was an anchor.

Dr. Hampton smiled warmly, as she wheeled the ultrasound machine closer. "Alright, Kiss. We're going to take another look today. And if the baby's in the right position, we should be able to tell the sex."

Kiss' heart thudded hard against her ribs. She looked at Onyx, whose eyes went wide.

"You ready?" she whispered.

He swallowed, his Adam's apple bobbing. "Been ready."

The gel was cold against her skin, making her shiver, but then, the wand pressed down, and the screen flickered to life. The grainy black-and-white image appeared. Their baby.

Kiss' breath caught, tears springing instantly to her eyes. The small body was more formed now, arms and legs visible, tiny but perfect. The heartbeat thrummed through the speakers again, steady and strong. Onyx squeezed her hand so tight it almost hurt, his other hand pressed against his mouth like he couldn't believe what he was seeing. Dr. Hampton moved the wand slightly, her smile widening.

"Well, looks like congratulations are in order. You're having a boy."

The words hit Kiss like sunlight breaking through clouds. They were about to have a son. She laughed through her tears, her free hand flying to her mouth.

"A boy," she whispered, her chest swelling so big it felt like it might burst.

Onyx's eyes glistened as he leaned down, pressing his forehead to hers. "That's my son," he whispered, voice breaking. "Kiss, we havin' a son."

Kiss nodded, tears streaming, laughter and sobs mixing in her throat. She'd never seen Onyx like this, so open and unguarded. His tough edges melted away, as he stared at the screen, his chest rising heavy with pride. Kiss smiled, as she watched him watching the screen.

When the doctor left them alone to clean up, Kiss lay there for a moment, her hand still on her belly.

Onyx bent down, pressing a kiss against her stomach. "Lil'

man," he murmured, his voice rough with emotion. "Daddy gon' take care of you. I promise."

Kiss smiled, believing every word Onyx spoke. She knew he would do everything he could to make sure their son had what he needed.

The ride home was different than the first appointment. Instead of silence, there was laughter. Onyx kept talking about the future – teaching their son to throw a ball, about what kind of sneakers he'd buy him, about how he'd make sure the boy never had to question if he was loved. Kiss leaned against the window, one hand on her belly, smiling through every word. She didn't know what the world had in store for them, didn't know how much struggle they'd face. But right then, she felt happy.

"You wanna come over when my mama goes to work tonight?" Kiss asked, as she looked over at Onyx.

"You already know I'll be over, baby. The moment she pulls off, I'm coming in."

Kiss kissed Onyx before getting out the car and going into the house. Sade was sleeping when she walked inside, so she went into her room and hung her ultrasound picture on her vanity mirror. She wanted it to be the very first thing she saw when she opened her eyes, a reminder of why she had to be better than she was the day before. That night as promised, Onyx came over and stayed the night, not leaving until it was time for Sade to get off work.

Onyx stood outside on the porch, the wind cutting sharp against his hoodie. It was early April in the city, but the air was still cold at night. Inside, he could hear Kiss moving around, singing to herself, as she folded tiny clothes that hadn't even been worn yet. She was now seven months pregnant, and he knew that in just a few short months, he'd be somebody's father. He lit a cigarette, taking a deep pull before blowing smoke through his lips. The crib was still set up in Kiss' room at Sade's house, the baby clothes stacked neatly on a shelf, and packs of diapers piled in the corner. But every time he saw them, he felt the same weight pressing down – him living with his mother while Kiss and the baby lived with Sade. He couldn't have his family living under separate roofs. He needed more money and fast.

Onyx pulled out his phone and scrolled through the contacts until he landed on Blue's number. It had been weeks since the last car job, and while the money was stacked up in the duffel in his closet, it still wasn't enough – not for rent, not for furniture, and not for the kind of life he wanted for Kiss and their son. Blue picked up on the first ring.

"What up doe, lil Blackwell?"

"I need more work," Onyx said flatly.

Blue chuckled. "Already? Thought you was sittin' on a nice lil' pile."

"It's not enough," Onyx muttered, taking a pull of his cigarette. "Baby comin' soon. I need real money, steady money."

Blue went quiet for a second then said, "You talkin' like you ready to level up."

Onyx's jaw tightened. "Shit, that's what I'm saying. I'm ready."

That night, he met Blue at the same garage, the smell of oil and smoke thick in the air. But this time, Blue didn't hand him a paper with parked cars. Instead, he leaned back against a stripped-down frame, grinning slow.

"Alright then. If you say you ready, I got somethin' bigger. Not just cars, product. It's real money in this shit if you ready to get it."

Onyx's stomach tightened. He knew that meant drugs – the same thing that had swallowed half the dudes he grew up with. Half of them were either on it or selling it. But he thought about Kiss and their baby boy and knew he needed that money.

He nodded once. "I'm in."

Blue smirked. "Knew you had it in you."

The work came fast. At first, it was just running packages across town – drop-offs, pick-ups, and no questions. Onyx kept his head down, moved quiet, making sure every handoff was clean. Blue watched him close, testing him, but Onyx didn't fold. The money was better and faster. Every night, he came home with more cash stuffed into his pockets, the duffel bag growing heavier by the day.

He started buying more things, not just baby clothes this time but furniture. Changing table, rocking chair, and everything else they needed to put into the baby's new room. He bought Kiss a stroller one evening, setting it in the living room of his mother's house with a small, proud smile. It was a black Mockingbird stroller that could be used for infants and toddlers.

Her eyes lit up, her hand flying to her mouth. "Onyx, it's perfect."

He kissed her forehead, his hand resting over her belly. "Nothin's too good for our boy."

"You're already a great dad, and our son isn't even here yet."

"I'm going to be an even better one once he gets here." Onyx kissed Kiss softly on her lips.

After Kiss went back home and Onyx was alone, he pulled the duffle bag from his closet. He began counting the money out, placing it in different piles for everything he needed. He didn't know how Sade would feel about Kiss and the baby moving in with him, but he didn't care. They were his family, so they belonged with him.

The streets were pulling him in deeper, and he wasn't doing it for nothing. Blue started giving him more responsibility, managing other runners, collecting payments, and handling disputes. Onyx's name started to carry weight in the streets. Dudes on the block nodded at him now and stepped aside when he walked past. Onyx now had respect in the streets, and he felt it every day.

One night, after stacking another wad of bills in the duffel, Onyx sat back on the bed, staring at the growing pile. He pulled out one of the tiny onesies Kiss had folded earlier that day, laying it gently on top of the money. He used it as a reminder that everything he was doing was for his son.

He whispered into the empty room, "I'm gon' get us out, lil' man. I swear it. I don't care what I gotta do."

The vow burned hot in his chest, sharper than the fear he tried to push down. Because deep inside, he knew there were only two ways this could end. He'd either rise high enough to give his son the life he deserved or the streets would swallow him whole. Either way, it was a chance he was willing to take.

Chapter Fifteen

Kiss was in Onyx's room, folding the clothes Tamika had gotten for the baby. Unlike Sade, Tamika was happy about the baby. She liked Kiss, no matter which one of her sons she was with. When Onyx walked into the room, she didn't look up, too focused on smoothing the creases from a pair of newborn onesies. But she felt him standing there, watching her, and it made her smile.

Finally, she glanced up. "Why you just standing there?" she asked softly.

Onyx sat down on the bed. He grabbed her hand and pulled her down on his lap. He rubbed her chin softly, as he looked into her eyes. "I got some news."

Her heart fluttered. "Good news?"

"The best news," he said, his grin widening. "We don't gotta stay with our mothers no more. We got our own place now."

Kiss froze, the onesie slipping from her hands. "What?"

He nodded, excitement flickering in his eyes. "One of Blue's people rents houses. Said he'd hook me up with somethin'. I already put money down. We movin' in next week."

"Onyx, are you serious?"

"Told you I'd take care of us. We gon' have our own space to raise our family in. No more side-eyes from your mama. No more of our family being separated."

Kiss pressed her face into his chest, the tears spilling freely now. Relief, joy, and hope all rushed through her at once, washing away months of fear. She pictured it instantly, a living room filled with baby toys, a kitchen that smelled like late-night meals, a nursery where their son would sleep.

"We really gon' have our own place?"

Onyx nodded firmly. "Yeah. It ain't fancy, but it's ours. And that's all that matters."

Kiss laughed through her tears, the sound shaky but bright. She kissed him then, slow and soft, tasting the promise of a new beginning. For the first time in a long time, she believed they might actually make it, and everything would be alright.

The ride through Detroit was quiet, but Kiss' heart wasn't. It beat fast as she stared out the window, her hand resting against the swell of her belly. They passed by rows of old brick houses, some boarded up, others still alive with kids running on porches and the faint thump of music spilling from cracked windows. Onyx's hand rested on the steering wheel, his other arm draped out the window.

"You gon' like it," he spoke finally, glancing at her with the faintest grin. "It ain't no mansion, but it's solid. And it's ours."

Kiss smiled, her chest warm. "Long as it's ours, it's enough."

They pulled onto a quiet block on the west side, not too far from Grand River. The street was lined with old two-story homes with huge porches, some with chipped paint, others kept neat with trimmed lawns and flowerpots. It wasn't fancy, but it wasn't the worst neighborhood either. Onyx slowed in front of a small brick house with white trim and a wide porch. The paint on the porch railings was peeling, and the steps could use a coat of fresh paint, but the yard was clean. The grass was cut low, a lone tree standing guard in the front. A for-rent sign leaned against the porch, and a tall, light skinned man with a low cut stood on the porch, waiting on them. He wore a pair of jeans, a black button up, and a pair of black leather loafers.

Onyx parked, hopped out, and came around to help Kiss out of the passenger side. She leaned into him, as they walked up, her eyes scanning every detail. The front door was painted a faded red, and the roof was newer than most houses on the block.

"This is it, y'all new home," the man on the porch spoke with a nod. "Three bedrooms with a full basement. Rent is due on the first." The man handed Onyx the keys to the home.

Onyx shook his hand quickly then turned to Kiss. "You ready to see the inside of our house?"

Kiss nodded, as they walked to the door together. The door creaked as it opened, and a faint smell of fresh paint mixed with old wood drifted out. Kiss stepped inside, her eyes sweeping over the living room. The hardwood floors were worn but polished, and the walls were freshly painted a soft cream. A wide window faced the street, sunlight streaming through sheer curtains. Kiss could already picture a couch against the far wall and a huge rug spread across the floor.

The kitchen was small but clean, with white cabinets and black countertops that shone under the overhead light. A gas stove sat in the corner, and she could already see herself cooking their first meal.

Upstairs, there were three bedrooms. The largest had a slanted ceiling and a small walk-in closet. Kiss' mind leapt ahead instantly, imagining their bed pushed against the far wall, Onyx's sneakers lined up neatly in the closet, her clothes hanging neatly from wooden hangers. The second room was smaller but perfect for the baby. The sunlight spilled in through the window, making the pale walls glow. Kiss pressed her hand to her stomach, smiling through the tears stinging her eyes. She pictured a crib against the wall, a rocking chair by the window, and shelves lined with books and stuffed animals.

"This gon' be his room," she whispered, her voice trembling.

Onyx stepped behind her, wrapping his arms around her belly. "Yeah. Lil' man gon' have his own space. Ain't gon' want for nothin'."

The third bedroom was small, almost more of an office than a real room, but Kiss didn't care. The house already felt like a dream. They went back down, the man leading them to the basement. The stairs creaked, but the space was solid. There were cement floors and white walls with laundry hookups in the corner. It had plenty of space for storage, maybe even a little workout spot for Onyx. Out back, the yard was fenced in, patchy grass mixed with dirt, but it was theirs. A rusted swing set leaned in one corner, and Kiss' heart tugged at the thought of their son running across the yard someday.

She turned in a slow circle, her smile wide, tears slipping free now. "Onyx, I can't believe this is real."

He pulled her close, his lips brushing her forehead. "I told you. We got a place of our own now, and this is just the start."

By the time they locked up and headed back to the car, Kiss' cheeks ached from smiling. For the first time since finding out she was pregnant, the fear wasn't louder than the hope.

She leaned against Onyx as they walked, her hand resting over her belly. Kiss had never been happier, and she knew she owed it all to Onyx. She was happy that he was keeping his word and doing everything he had to do to take care of their family.

The whole ride back, her mind was running ahead of her. She pictured curtains swaying in the kitchen window, a crib tucked against the wall in their son's room, late nights when the baby cried and she'd pad through the house barefoot with Onyx right behind her. For once, the future didn't feel scary; it felt close enough to touch. She wanted her mother to see that. She wanted to share the good news, even if Sade was hard sometimes.

The house smelled faintly of bleach when Kiss walked in, letting her know that her mother had been cleaning. Sade sat at the table, sorting bills. A cigarette burned low in the ashtray, while smoke curled into the air. The frown on her mother's face deepened, as she shuffled envelopes, muttering under her breath. Kiss' heart pounded. She smoothed her hoodie down over her belly and stepped into the kitchen.

"Mama?" she uttered softly.

Sade didn't look up. "Yeah?"

"I gotta tell you somethin'."

Finally, Sade glanced at her, one eyebrow raised, already suspicious. "What now?"

Kiss smiled. "Onyx got us a house. Three bedrooms with a backyard. We went to see it today, and it's perfect. We can move in as early as next week."

For a moment, there was nothing but silence. Sade just stared, Kiss' words hanging in the air. Then, her eyes sharpened, as her jaw tightened. She slammed her palm down on the table so hard the envelopes jumped.

"He got y'all a what?"

"A house," Kiss repeated, voice softer now. "It's not too far from here. And it's nice, Mama. We…"

"You not movin' in with that boy." Sade's voice cracked through the air like a whip, interrupting Kiss' sentence.

Kiss blinked, stunned. "What? Mama, yes, I am."

"I said no!" Sade shot to her feet, her chair scraping back. "You think you grown? Well, you're not. You sixteen, Kiss. You think havin' his baby mean you ready to play house? Let me tell you somethin', girl, you ain't ready for none of this."

Tears burned in Kiss' eyes, but she shook her head, her voice shaking. "Mama, please listen to me."

"I am listenin'," Sade snapped. "I been listenin' since the day you told me you was pregnant. You think I don't know what's goin' on? You think I don't see it? Onyx ain't no provider, Kiss. He ain't steady. He runnin' them streets same as always, and you blind if you can't see where that ends. He either gon' be in jail in a cell next to his brother or dead. Either way, yo' ass gon' be left to pick up the pieces."

Kiss' breath hitched. She thought of the duffel bag in Onyx's closet, the stacks of cash he never explained. She pushed the image away, her voice rising. "He's doin' what he gotta do! For me, for this baby. He loves us, Mama."

Sade laughed, sharp and bitter. "Love? Love don't mean shit when the light bill is due. Love don't mean shit when you need food on the table. And love damn sure ain't gonna stop him from getting tired of playing house. And you will see that when he walks out on you and that baby."

Kiss' tears flowed freely now. "Why can't you just believe in him? Believe in us? This house, it's our chance, Mama. You want me to be you so bad, but I'm not. It's not my fault your child's father left you and mine didn't. You would think you would want better for your daughter. But I guess not."

But Sade's face only hardened. "Ain't no boy draggin' my daughter and my grandbaby into a trap house on some block I don't know shit about. You stayin' here where I can keep an eye on you and that baby. It's not about you being me. It's about you being better than me. This is me making sure you are better."

Something in Kiss broke then. She straightened, wiping her cheeks, her voice steady despite the tears. "You don't get to choose for me anymore. I'm not a little girl. I'm about to be somebody's mother. And I want my son to grow up in a home that's his – with his father. So, I'm movin' in with Onyx whether you like it or not."

Sade's chest rose and fell in anger. "You gon' regret this, Kiss. Mark my words. That boy gon' break you. And when he does, don't come runnin' back here. You wanna go be grown, go ahead, but don't bring your ass back here."

Kiss swallowed hard, her hand moving instinctively to her belly. Her voice trembled but didn't waver. "I'll never regret choosin' my family. I'll never regret choosin' Onyx."

She turned then, leaving her mother standing in the kitchen, the cigarette smoke curling between them like a wall. She walked to her room and collapsed onto her bed, sobs wracking her body. She'd stood strong in front of her mother, but inside, she was breaking. However, even through the problems, she knew that everything would be okay.

Two weeks later, Kiss stood in the doorway of their new house, the keys still warm in her hand. For the first time, the rooms weren't empty. Boxes were broken down and stacked in the corner, new furniture glowed with fresh polish, and the faint smell of fabric and cardboard still lingered in the air. She let the door close softly behind her, her palm resting against her belly, as she turned in a slow circle, taking it all in. This wasn't Sade's cramped kitchen or the small bedroom she'd had all her life. This was an entire house, and it belonged to her and Onyx.

The first thing Kiss noticed was the couch, a plush sectional in a deep charcoal gray, wide enough for her to stretch out on. It was so soft that she already pictured curling up with the baby against her chest. A sleek black coffee table sat in front of it, its surface shining beneath the soft glow of the new floor lamp. The TV stand was modern, black with glass shelves, and Onyx had already hooked up the flat screen, wires tucked neatly behind it. A shag rug lay beneath the table, thick and cream-colored, warm against her feet when she kicked off her sneakers. Kiss smiled through tears, her hand brushing over the back of the couch.

She walked through the wide doorway into the kitchen. The white cabinets gleamed, newly painted, and Onyx had added silver handles that caught the light. A round dining table sat in the corner with four chairs, the wood dark and smooth. In the center was a vase of fake blue and white flowers. Onyx had stocked the counters with new appliances – a stainless-steel toaster, a shiny microwave, even a blender still smelling faintly of plastic wrap. The fridge hummed low, its surface covered with magnets and a notepad where Kiss had already scribbled a grocery list. She opened the cabinets and saw rows of clean plates, bowls, and cups – all brand new.

Her favorite part waited upstairs. She climbed the steps slowly, her hand on the railing, Onyx trailing close behind her with a smile tugging at his lips. The master bedroom took her breath away. A queen bed with a gray tufted headboard stood against the wall, covered in crisp white sheets and a soft white comforter. Two nightstands framed it, each with matching lamps. A dresser stood beneath the window, sunlight spilling across its surface. Onyx had even bought a mirror, leaning tall against the wall, its edges trimmed in black wood.

Kiss pressed her hand to her chest, tears pricking her eyes again. "It's so beautiful."

Onyx wrapped his arm around her waist, his hand resting on her belly. "Not as beautiful as you."

She laughed softly, burying her face against his shoulder.

But it was the second bedroom that made her cry for real. The baby's room. A crib stood against the far wall, painted white, its rails gleaming under the afternoon light. A small dresser doubled as a changing table, and a rocking chair sat by the window. Onyx had even rolled out a pale blue rug with little stars across it and placed it in the middle of the floor. On the shelf, stuffed animals sat in a neat row – soft bears, a floppy-eared dog, and a lion with a crooked mane. Above the crib, Onyx had hung wooden letters spelling out one word 'son'. Kiss' tears slipped free, as she pressed both hands to her belly.

Later, she wandered into the backyard. The grass was patchy but open, the fence sturdy enough to keep them private. She couldn't wait until her son got older, so they could play on the swing set together. Kiss smiled, as the thought crossed her mind.

That night, as the sun sank behind the houses on the block

and the city hummed faint in the distance, Kiss sat on the new couch, her legs tucked beneath her, her hands resting on her stomach. Onyx sprawled beside her, one arm around her shoulders, the other scrolling through his phone. She leaned against him, eyes drifting over the living room, the warm glow of the lamps, the rug soft under her toes.

"This feels like home," she whispered.

Onyx kissed her hair. "That's 'cause it is."

Kiss smiled, knowing it was true. Everything that she'd gone through in her life had led her to this moment, and she knew it had all been worth it.

Chapter Sixteen

The night was quiet, and the room was dark. Their new house was still strange to Kiss in some ways, the walls too bare, and she couldn't wait to hang pictures on them. As she lay curled against Onyx in their bed, she felt a peace she hadn't known in months. Onyx's arm draped heavy across her waist, his breathing slow and even against her neck. She smiled in the dark, her hand resting over her belly, tracing slow circles over the curve that had now grown big. She was now nine months, and it seemed like all she did was blink. Sleep tugged at her, but her body had other plans. A pressure built low in her stomach, the same kind of ache she'd been feeling for days. She sighed, easing out from under Onyx's arm.

"Where you goin'?" he mumbled, half asleep.

"Bathroom," she whispered, kissing his shoulder before slipping off the bed.

She padded down the short hall, her bare feet whispering against the floor. The bathroom light buzzed to life, as she flicked the switch, the mirror catching her reflection. Her eyes were tired, and her hair wild from the pillow. She laughed, thinking about how crazy she looked. She rubbed her hands over her head, trying to lay her hair flat. A sudden warmth spilled down her legs, shocking her into stillness. She gasped, clutching the edge of the sink, as the liquid pooled on the tiles beneath her feet. For a heartbeat, she froze, her mind blank. Then, the realization hit her like a lightning bolt. Her water had broken.

Her heart leaped into her throat. She pressed a trembling hand to her stomach, panic and awe colliding in her chest. "Oh, God," she whispered, her voice shaking. "It's time." The baby kicked as if he was answering her.

She grabbed a towel from the rack, fumbling as she tried to clean herself, but her hands wouldn't stop trembling. A sharp wave of fear washed over her. This was it. She was about to meet her baby boy.

"Kiss?" Onyx's voice came groggy from the bedroom. The mattress creaked as he sat up. "You good?"

She swallowed hard, her voice breaking. "Onyx!"

Seconds later, he was at the doorway, eyes wide, panic flashing across his face when he saw her clutching the sink, water still pooling at her feet.

"My water broke."

For a moment, he just stared, frozen, not knowing what to do. Then, he sprang into action, grabbing Kiss' arms to steady her. "Alright. Alright, just breathe, baby. We gotta get you to the hospital."

Kiss nodded, her body already trembling with the first hints of contractions. She leaned into him, fear and joy clashing together. It was finally happening. Their son was on his way. And Kiss knew nothing would ever be the same again.

The ride to the hospital was a blur, nothing but headlights and panic. Kiss clutched her belly in the passenger seat, sweat dampening her forehead, as another contraction tore through her. Onyx's knuckles were white on the wheel, his voice low but urgent every few seconds.

"Breathe, Kiss. Just breathe. We almost there."

She nodded, tears stinging her eyes, though she wasn't sure if they were from fear or the sheer force of her body taking over. The seatbelt cut across her chest, pressing against the round of her belly. By the time they rushed through the hospital doors, everything moved fast. Nurses with calm, firm voices told Kiss everything was going to be alright, as they wheeled her through the hall. Another nurse handed Onyx some paperwork for him to fill out, and all Kiss could do was breathe.

They wheeled her into a room with pale blue walls and machines that beeped steadily, ready to record every heartbeat. Kiss tried to focus on her breathing, gripping the edge of the bed, as another wave of pain seized through her. Onyx hovered beside her, his eyes wide. One hand rubbed her back, while the other was in a fist at his side like he couldn't decide what to do with it.

"I got you, Kiss. I'm right here, and I ain't goin' nowhere."

Kiss nodded, as she breathed through the pain. The nurse walked in to check Kiss and smiled.

"She's progressing fast. This baby is on his way."

The door swung open, and there was her mother. Sade's face was tight with worry, but her eyes softened the moment they landed on Kiss in the bed. She crossed the room quickly, taking her daughter's hand.

"Oh, baby," she whispered, brushing sweaty hair back from Kiss' face. "You gon' be alright. I'm right here."

Tears slipped from Kiss' eyes. "Mama."

Behind Sade, another familiar figure entered. It was Tamika rushing inside. Her face carried lines of hard years, but her eyes glistened with pride. She went straight to Onyx, placing both hands on his shoulders.

"You got this, son. Just know from here on out, you're not a boy anymore. This right here makes you a man."

Onyx nodded, swallowing hard, his jaw tight. The room was crowded, but Kiss wanted them all to be there. Hours blurred together in waves of pain. Contractions came harder and faster, each one pulling a cry from Kiss' throat. Sweat drenched her skin, her hands clutching the rails of the bed so tightly her knuckles ached. Onyx stayed by her side through it all. He wiped her forehead with a cool cloth and whispered encouragement in her ear. He kissed her hand when she whimpered. His face was pale, his eyes frantic, but his voice stayed steady.

"You got this, Kiss. You the strongest person I know. Just a little longer."

Sade held her other hand, squeezing each time a contraction hit. "Breathe, baby. Push when they tell you. You can do this."

The doctor's voice was calm but firm. "It's time to push. With the next contraction, we will count down from ten."

Kiss bore down, a scream tearing from her throat. Pain split through her body, raw and searing, but she pushed again, as everyone in the room counted down. She pushed hard until relief finally came. A cry split the air, sharp and high. Kiss collapsed back against the bed, tears streaming down her cheeks, her chest heaving. The nurse lifted the tiny, wailing baby, his skin flushed, his fists clenched tight. For a beat, Kiss couldn't move. She just stared, her world narrowing to the sound of her son's first breath.

Onyx made a choked sound beside her, his hand clutching hers tightly. Then, the nurse placed the baby on her chest. Warmth spread through her instantly, tears blinding her, as she wrapped trembling arms around the tiny body.

"My baby," she sobbed, kissing his damp forehead, "I've waited nine months to meet you."

Onyx leaned over, his hand shaking, as he touched his son's tiny back. His voice broke, as he whispered, "We got a son now, Kiss."

Sade stood at the foot of the bed, her own tears falling freely now. She covered her mouth, shaking her head in awe. "He's beautiful, Kiss."

Tamika moved closer, her eyes shining. "Look at him, another Blackwell boy." She touched Onyx's shoulder again, pride heavy in her voice. "Congratulations, son. You did that."

Onyx nodded, wiping his face quickly, though the tears kept coming. He bent down and kissed Kiss' temple, his lips lingering. "You did it, Kiss. You brought him into this world for us. He's happy and healthy with all ten fingers and toes."

The chaos slowly faded. The nurses began cleaning, and the machines quieted. The baby was swaddled tight in a blanket before being placed back into Kiss' arms. The room dimmed, soft and hushed now. Kiss held her son close, her heart swelling until it hurt. His tiny face scrunched, his little lips parting. She traced his cheek with her finger, whispering, "Welcome, baby boy. Welcome to the world."

Onyx sat beside her on the bed, one arm around her shoulders, the other hand gently stroking his son's head. He didn't speak, but his eyes said everything his mouth didn't. Sade sat quietly in the chair, watching, her face softer than Kiss had ever seen it, while Tamika prayed and thanked God for her healthy grandson.

Kiss was exhausted but still glowing. As she looked down at her son, she felt as though her family was complete, and everything she'd been waiting on was now in her arms. Kiss lay, propped up against pillows, exhaustion heavy in her bones, but her arms were full. She cradled the tiny bundle close to her chest, his face smooth and soft. He was so small that it almost frightened her but holding him felt like the most natural thing she'd ever done. Onyx sat at her side, close enough that their shoulders touched, his arm stretched protectively along the back of her bed. His eyes hadn't left the baby since the moment he'd been placed in Kiss' arms.

"He looks just like you," Kiss whispered, her voice raspy.

Onyx shook his head, a slow grin breaking across his face. "Nah. He got your nose. That little button nose, that's all you."

Kiss smiled through the tears gathering in her eyes. She pressed her lips against her son's forehead, inhaling the new baby scent that already felt addictive. The nurse had asked earlier what they wanted to name him. Kiss and Onyx had shared a look, the decision already written between them.

Onyx leaned closer, his lips brushing Kiss' temple, as he whispered, "Onyx Jr."

Kiss let the name roll off her tongue, soft and reverent. "Onyx Jr." She looked down at her son again, her chest swelling. "Welcome to the world, baby boy."

Their son stirred, letting out a tiny whimper, before settling again. Onyx placed his hand gently over Kiss', both of them holding their child together. Sade sat quietly in the corner, watching, her expression unreadable but her eyes shimmering with unshed tears. Tamika had left a little while ago to call family, her pride overflowing, but Sade stayed. For once, she didn't argue or have anything bad to say. She just looked at her daughter and her grandson like she was seeing them both for the first time.

Kiss caught her mother's gaze and offered a small, tired smile. Sade gave the faintest nod back. It wasn't forgiveness, not yet, but it was something. Kiss leaned her head against Onyx's shoulder, her eyes closing briefly, as the weight of the moment settled over her. They were parents now. The world outside was still rough, full of challenges, but in this room, with her son in her arms and Onyx by her side, she felt whole.

"Onyx Jr.," Onyx whispered again, his voice thick with pride. "My lil' man. I have a legacy now."

Chapter Seventeen

Omari had learned to live with the silence. In juvie, silence pressed in on you, thick and heavy, because you were only left with your thoughts. Nights were the worst. When the lights dimmed and all he had was the hard mattress beneath him, his thoughts began to spin. He'd been counting down the days, months, and years since he'd been there. Counting letters that stopped coming. Counting the ways life outside kept moving without him. He hadn't received a letter from Kiss in almost a year, and something told him that he wouldn't be getting one any time soon.

When the guard came to his cell and told him he had a visitor, his chest tightened. It had been weeks since his mother last came. He tried not to hope, but hope bloomed anyway. Maybe it would be Kiss. Maybe this time, she'd finally come to see him. But when he stepped into the visitation room, he saw Tamika sitting there, her purse clutched tight in her lap.

"Ma," he said, sliding into the chair across from her, "why you look like something's wrong?"

Tamika pressed her lips together, her hands twisting around the strap of her bag. "Baby, I need to tell you somethin'."

Omari's chest went cold. "What happened?"

Her eyes met his, soft and sad. "Kiss had the baby."

The words hit him like a punch to the gut. For a moment, he

couldn't breathe. He gripped the edge of the table, his knuckles whitening. "She what?"

Omari knew Kiss was pregnant; he knew a baby was coming. However, to know that it was here already hit different. His heart dropped in his stomach, as his world crashed around him.

"They had a son, and he's perfect. Named him Onyx Jr."

The name slammed into him harder than anything else. His twin's name. His twin's child that Kiss had given birth to. Omari's jaw clenched, his teeth grinding, as anger burned hot through his chest. His vision blurred, not from tears but from the fury boiling up, thick and sharp.

"She gave him my son?" he spat, voice trembling with rage. "She named him after him?"

Tamika reached for his hand, but he pulled away. "Baby, listen to me…"

"No!" His voice rose, drawing a few glances from the guards. He forced it lower, but the venom stayed. "That's supposed to be my life. She was supposed to wait for me. I told her if we was meant to be, we'd get back together when I got out." His fists pounded against the table, the sound echoing. "And now she givin' my brother what was supposed to be mine."

Tamika's eyes watered. "Omari, you can't keep holdin' on to somethin' that's gone. Kiss made her choice. And as heartbreaking as it is, that choice wasn't you."

He laughed bitterly, the sound hollow. "Her choice? What choice did she have? I been locked in here, rottin', while he been out there whisperin' in her ear. He stole her from me, Ma. My own brother."

Tamika shook her head. "Onyx is steppin' up. He's tryin' to take care of her, of that baby. You gotta let it go, son."

"I ain't lettin' nothin' go," Omari snapped. His voice shook, rage twisting deep in his gut. "Every night I close my eyes, I see her face. Every letter I wrote, I poured my heart out, and she…"

His voice cracked, and he slammed his fist against the table again, chest heaving.

Tamika's tears slipped free. "Baby, please. Don't let this anger eat you alive."

He leaned forward, his eyes blazing. "When I get outta here, Ma, it's gon' be different. He think he can take my girl and start a family with her? Nah. Onyx better enjoy it while he can 'cause I'm not gon' just let this shit happen."

The guard called time, and Tamika stood slowly, her hands shaking. She bent down, kissing her son's forehead, but he didn't move, his eyes fixed on the wall behind her. When she left, Omari sat back, his fists still trembling, his chest burning with rage. Kiss had a baby with his brother, and no matter what he'd gone through, nothing was worse than that. When Omari got back into his cell, he cried like never before. His heart was completely broken, and he knew that nothing but Kiss could fix it.

Chapter
Eighteen

The morning sun streamed through the living room windows, casting a golden light over balloons scattered across the floor. Kiss knelt by the coffee table, taping down the last corner of a blue-and-gold tablecloth, while Onyx tied the strings of balloons to the back of chairs. Their home smelled of barbecue already. Meat was outside sizzling on the grill, while trays of macaroni and cheese and baked beans were warming in the kitchen.

It was Onyx Jr.'s first birthday, and Kiss had been planning for weeks. The living room had been transformed. Blue, gold, and white balloons floated everywhere, clustered into bunches that bobbed against the ceiling. A banner stretched across the wall above the couch that read, *Happy First Birthday, OJ!* Glittered letters caught the light, sparkling each time the fan turned overhead. The coffee table was covered with treats — cupcakes frosted in pale blue, bowls of candy, and little bags of party favors decorated with cartoon lions.

The dining table was stacked with food: foil pans of macaroni and cheese, fried chicken, baked beans, cornbread, and collard greens. Onyx had insisted on grilling the ribs himself, while they got everything else catered. A three-tier cake sat on the kitchen counter, frosted in smooth buttercream, decorated with tiny fondant stars, and a crown on top. Across the bottom tier, written in perfect icing, it said, King Onyx Jr.

By early afternoon, the house was buzzing with voices and laughter. Family filtered in first – Sade, carrying a wrapped box almost as big as she was, then Tamika came next, her arms full of grocery bags she insisted on bringing. There were cousins, aunts, uncles, the whole nine. Soon after came neighbors and friends, everyone dressed in their best, smiling as they walked through the decorated front door.

Music poured from the speakers, old-school R&B, mixed with the latest Detroit hits, kept the energy alive. The kids ran wild, chasing each other with balloons, while the adults crowded the kitchen, piling plates high and trading stories. Kiss moved through it all like she was glowing. Every time someone bent over Onyx Jr.'s stroller to coo at him, her chest swelled with pride.

He was the star of the day, dressed in a tiny outfit Onyx had picked out – tiny blue jeans, a white button-up shirt with suspenders, and soft baby sneakers that looked like miniature versions of the ones Onyx wore. A small gold paper crown rested on his curly head, slightly crooked, but he didn't seem to mind.

Kiss scooped him into her arms, the warmth of his tiny body both familiar and comforting. "Look at you, birthday boy," she whispered, kissing his cheek. He giggled, grabbing at her necklace with chubby hands. Guests lined up to hold him, cousins snapping pictures, aunts passing him gently from arm to arm. Each time he laughed, the whole room seemed to brighten. Onyx stayed close, keeping an eye out, his expression proud but protective. He'd spent days making sure the house was spotless and the food handled, so the party would be perfect. Now, he leaned against the wall, watching his son with a smile that softened all the hardness in his face.

"That's my lil' man," he said when someone commented on how much the baby looked like him. "Onyx Jr. all the way."

Kiss caught his eye across the room, and he winked at her.

She smiled back at him, letting him know that everything was wonderful. The afternoon unfolded in waves of joy. Plates clattered as people filled them with food, laughter rang loud over the music, and Kiss moved from group to group, thanking everyone for coming. She was so happy that her little boy was so loved.

Children crowded the backyard, shrieking with joy on the swing set and chasing bubbles that floated high into the air. Onyx had rented a bounce house, and soon, half the neighborhood kids were bouncing inside it, squeals echoing across the yard. Inside, grown folks played spades at the dining table, the sharp smack of cards punctuating their trash talk. Sade laughed harder than Kiss had heard her in months, her earlier anger forgotten for the moment, as she showed her hand to her partner.

Kiss carried Onyx Jr. around, showing him off. People commented on his curls, his bright eyes, and his laugh. Each compliment filled her with warmth. She smiled, knowing her baby boy was the star of the show.

Finally, it was time for cake. Kiss placed her son in the highchair they'd decorated with streamers and a banner that read, "ONE." Everyone crowded around, phones ready to capture the moment. The big cake was brought out, candles glowing. Kiss leaned close, her hand on her son's small back.

"Ready, baby?" she whispered.

The room burst into song. "I wanna sayyy happy birthday to you…" The voices rose and clapped, echoing through the house. Onyx Jr. clapped his hands too, squealing in delight at the noise.

"Make a wish," Onyx spoke, his arm around Kiss' shoulders.

She leaned down with her son, blowing out the candle for him, as cheers erupted. Frosting smeared across her lips, and she laughed, wiping it away as Onyx Jr. dove headfirst into his own smash cake. His tiny fists dug into blue frosting, cheeks smeared, his giggles setting off more laughter around the room. Phones flashed, and guests cheered. Sade wiped tears from her eyes.

"Look at my grandson," she murmured, shaking her head with pride.

As the party stretched into evening, guests drifted out, leaving the house quiet again. Kiss sat on the couch, her son asleep in her arms, frosting still on his shirt. The balloons floated lazily above. Onyx sat beside her, his arm draped across the back of the couch, his other hand resting gently on their son's tiny foot. His eyes were tired but content.

Kiss looked around at the decorations, the gifts stacked neatly in the corner, the photos people had sent buzzing into her phone. For a moment, she thought about how far they had come. How she had gone from sneaking glances at Onyx across a porch to sitting here in their own home with a family. Her throat tightened with gratitude. She leaned her head against Onyx's shoulder, whispering softly. "We did good. Our son had a wonderful time."

Onyx kissed the top of her head, his voice low. "We just gettin' started."

Kiss smiled down at her son, her heart swelling in her chest. Onyx Jr. had no idea how much he was loved, how much had been sacrificed to bring him here. But someday, he would. And Kiss knew, as she held him close, that no matter what came next, this moment would be forever.

Over the next few years, Kiss and Onyx grew more in love than ever. They were talking about marriage and even having another baby. Onyx had even started to grow on Sade, and she came over to their house more often. One Saturday afternoon, Tamika came over to see Onyx Jr. She'd gotten him a few outfits, and Kiss was eager to see what she'd picked up. She walked inside and sat on the couch, smiling from ear to ear.

"I tried not to buy too much, but I couldn't resist," Tamika cooed. "Saw these little outfits at the store and thought about my grandbaby."

"Thank you. You didn't have to do that."

"I know." Tamika set the bag on the couch as she looked around the room. 'Where is OJ?"

"He upstairs in his room, playing with his toys. I'll go get him."

Kiss walked up the steps and returned a few moments later with Onyx Jr. on her hip. Tamika's smile grew wider as she scooped OJ into her arms.

"Oh, my goodness. Look at Grandma's big man. I swear you get bigger and bigger every time I see you."

"I'm a growing boy, Grandma." OJ giggled.

"That's right, baby. You sure are. But you growin' too fast. How 'bout you slow down for Grandma. How old are you now, ten?"

"Grandma, I'm these many." OJ laughed, holding up three fingers.

"I know you are." Tamika laughed, tickling OJ on the stomach.

Kiss watched, a mix of gratitude and unease stirring in her chest. Tamika had every right to love her grandson, but every time she came around, Omari hung heavy between them, unspoken but always present. Kiss knew Tamika genuinely liked her, but she knew the fact that she'd been with both of her sons couldn't sit right with her. After a while, Tamika set Onyx Jr. back down, smoothing the curls on his head, before turning to Kiss.

"Kiss," she spoke quietly, "I need to tell you somethin'."

Kiss' stomach dipped. She nodded slowly. "What is it?"

Tamika hesitated, her fingers twisting around the strap of her purse. "It's Omari. He's gettin' out this week."

The words hit like ice water pouring over Kiss' head. Her breath caught, her body going still. "What?"

"I'm so glad my baby is finally coming home. It's been a long time comin', but it's here. He'll be home before the week's over."

Kiss sat down hard on the couch, her hands trembling against her knees. The room felt smaller suddenly, pressing in around her. She heard Onyx Jr. giggling in the background, as he played with his action figures on the couch, but the sound felt far away. Omari was finally coming home, and she knew she would have to face him. Her chest tightened, emotions colliding inside her. Memories flooded her like they'd just happened yesterday. The way he'd asked her to be his girl when they were kids, the way he'd defended her, the way his letters had once been her lifeline.

She pressed her hands to her face, trying to steady her breathing. "End of the week?" she whispered.

Tamika nodded, her eyes soft but searching. "I thought you should know. He gon' want to see you. Gon' want to meet OJ."

The mention of Onyx Jr. made Kiss' stomach twist. The thought of him meeting Omari hadn't crossed her mind. *Damn, Onyx Jr. is his nephew,* Kiss thought.

Kiss swallowed hard, her voice trembling. "Tamika, I don't know what to say."

"You don't gotta say nothin' right now," Tamika spoke gently. "But you gotta be ready. Omari still loves you, Kiss. He always did. At the very least, you owe him a conversation."

The words stung. Kiss shook her head, tears burning her eyes. "But I'm with Onyx. We have a life now, a family. How am I supposed to…" She broke off, her throat closing.

Tamika sighed, sitting beside her. "I'm not sayin' it's simple. I'm just tellin' you what's comin'. Omari comin' home, and he ain't the same boy you remember. He's been waitin' a long time to see you."

Kiss stared at her hands, her mind racing. She thought about the house Onyx had gotten for them, the way he'd stayed by her side through her pregnancy, the way he'd cried when their son was born. She thought about how proud he was at Onyx Jr.'s first birthday, how much he loved their little family. Then, she thought about Omari, the boy who'd once promised her forever. The boy who had gone to jail because of her – because he'd tried to protect her. The boy who had written letter after letter, begging her not to forget about him but not to wait on him. She'd never forgotten what he'd done for her, and she never would. However, she was now in love with Onyx. The very thought made tears come to her eyes.

"I can't do this," she whispered. "I can't face him."

"You won't have a choice," Tamika enforced. "He'll come lookin' for you. And you gotta decide what you gon' say when he does."

Kiss shook her head, clutching her stomach like it could anchor her. She looked over at OJ, who was playing on the couch, not paying them any attention. She didn't know how Omari would feel meeting him for the first time – a child that she'd had by his brother. She once thought about having his children, but instead, she'd had his nephew.

Chapter Nineteen

The last morning inside seemed surreal. Omari lay awake long before the counts, eyes open to the hairline crack in the ceiling he'd memorized over the years. The dorm was quieter than usual, or maybe the quiet felt different because his mind wouldn't stop running. It had been years since he'd seen the outside. He'd grown into a man behind the wall, and he didn't know how the outside world would treat him. The building hummed with its same old noises – the vent that banged every forty seconds, the drip in the bathroom no one could fix, the cart's squeak that announced breakfast before it arrived. But this time, everything sounded like it was happening to somebody else. He sat up when the keys whispered down the hall.

"Blackwell," the CO called out, leaning his elbow against the frame. He was the same man who'd been there his first week. "You know the drill."

Omari set his shoes on the concrete and laced them slowly. He folded his blanket without thinking about it. He left nothing in the locker because there was nothing to leave. After all this time, his whole life fit into a drawstring nylon bag. Two state tee shirts, a notebook with bent corners, full of rhyme skeletons and ink-thick pages that got him through the nights he couldn't breathe, a handful of letters he hadn't thrown away, even when it hurt to look at them. He slung the bag over his shoulder, nodded to the boys who lifted chins from bunks as he passed. Uno tapped his fist against the metal railing.

"Be safe," Uno spoke, voice low. "Don't let the world trick you out your day."

Omari nodded again, not trusting his mouth. He kept his eyes ahead, down the fluorescent hallway that had swallowed him as a kid and was spitting him back out older than he felt inside. Release was paperwork that blurred. It was a pile of clothes in a property bin that smelled like closet dust and old soap. None of the clothes he came in with fit, so he was given a pair of gray sweats to leave in.

"Sign here," the desk officer said. "And here." The pen scratched. "Good luck out there, Blackwell."

Luck, he thought, *is for people who didn't know what waiting felt like*. He opened the door, blinking rapidly at the morning sun. For a moment, the world seemed bigger than what he'd remembered. He stood there, breathing deeply, as he felt the warm air hit his skin.

"Oh, my God, my baby is finally out."

Tamika's voice cracked before her eyes did. She stood, just beyond the line, in a yellow summer dress and matching yellow sandals. Omari's body folded into hers without thinking. He hadn't cried in years, and he didn't now, but something loosened between his ribs that had been knotted so long he'd forgotten it could hurt to let go.

"My baby," she spoke again, rocking him like he was twelve. "Look at you."

He stepped back, taking in the small differences in her face, the way grief and hard work added years to her appearance. She kissed his cheek, wiped it with her thumb like he was still small enough to let her. He could smell the lotion she used and the coffee on her breath.

"You hungry, baby?" she asked, already reaching for the bag. "I bought you that breakfast sandwich from the spot you like."

"I'm good," he said, though his stomach burned from nerves and not hunger. Omari looked around, hoping that Kiss would have been with Tamika. "Ma, did…"

Tamika shook her head slightly, already knowing what Omari was going to ask. "Let's get you in the car."

The first thing he noticed on the ride was that Detroit hadn't changed much since he'd been gone. Tamika's old Buick rattled at forty like it always had. He rode with his window down, feeling the wind against his face. They passed the stretch near the strip mall that used to be a block party every summer; now, half the storefronts were vape shops and cellphone stores.

"You quiet," Tamika spoke, looking over at Omari. "I know you got a million thoughts bumpin' around."

"I'm just takin' it all in," he replied, taking a deep breath. "I need to see her – today."

"Omari," she spoke softly, "you gotta breathe first. I'll take you to get a fresh cut. You'll get some clothes that ain't from 2014. We'll get food. Then, if you still want to see her and she…"

"Ma." He turned finally, eyes steady, voice firm, letting Tamika know he was serious. "I need to see Kiss today."

She held his gaze. She had always been the only person who could stand in the middle of his storm. After a beat, she nodded.

"Aight. But you gon' hear me when I say this. She got a life now. She built it while you was gone. There's a baby in the middle of it. Don't go in there like you can pull history over the present like a blanket, and it's just gon' fit. Because it may not."

"I ain't stupid, Ma. I know what this is."

"Angry people do stupid shit," Tamika informed, turning the corner onto a side street where the barber still put a "cash only" sign in the window.

The cut made him look like himself again – or like the version of himself he remembered when his reflection belonged to him. The chair still wobbled when you leaned too far left. The barber still dragged the blade with a flourish, the way old heads did when they wanted you to feel like the mirror was a stage. He paid with the money his mother had tucked in his palm before they'd walked in.

When they left the barbershop, they stopped and picked up jeans and fresh white and black t-shirts from the mall. Tamika insisted that he stay with her until he got back on his feet, and that was exactly what he was going to do. They ate in the car, while they watched the cars pass by – the same way they used to do when Omari was little. When they were done eating, Tamika pulled off.

Tamika parked halfway down Kiss' street and pointed the house out to Omari.

"You sure you want to do this?" Tamika asked, one hand suspended over the keys like she could freeze time with the ignition.

He pushed the door open before he lost nerve. "Stay in the car," he spoke, not looking back. "I won't be long."

He walked up the sidewalk, looking at the bright red door. Omari walked up the steps slowly, not knowing what he was going to say. He knocked on the door firmly and waited for her to answer. Kiss opened the door with a smile on her face. Omari saw it when she froze, not expecting it to be him on the other side.

"Omari?"

His name on her lips was a bell rung underwater. He could hear it and not hear it at the same time. She had changed, like life had added to her instead of simply aging her. Her face had softened and sharpened in different places. She had grown into the beautiful woman that he knew she would be. He opened his mouth, and nothing came. His throat had been sanded smooth by a thousand things he hadn't said.

"Kiss. Man, I missed you."

She blinked fast, as if she was trying to make sure he was really standing there. Then, she glanced over her shoulder into the living room before telling Omari to come inside. He stepped across the threshold and felt it like a line drawn on his chest. The house smelled like vanilla baby lotion. He could hear the cartoons playing in another room. It felt like someone's home. And it was, just not his.

He looked over, and his heart sank. OJ sat on the floor, playing with a pile of toys in front of him. He looked just like Onyx – headful of curls and big, wide eyes. He smiled half-heartedly. He wanted to meet his nephew but resented the fact that this child wasn't his son. OJ looked up from his toys when the door shut then right back down again.

Omari's heart went sideways. He hadn't thought the air could hurt to breathe. "That's..." He couldn't say the name. It hurt to even think about.

Kiss looked over toward OJ with a smile. "That's my son. His name is Onyx Junior."

Omari felt the swell of blood in his ears. *Out of all of the things she could have named him, she just had to make him a junior,* Omari thought. He stared at the child and could see his brother. He knew any thought he had that the baby just might not be Onyx's was gone the moment he saw him. Omari took half a step closer to him without even realizing it then stopped once he did.

"Omari," Kiss spoke, voice gentle. "Can we sit and talk please?

He followed her into the kitchen, and they took a seat at the table. Omari folded his arms on the table, as he looked over at Kiss. He waited for her to say something, but when she didn't, he began to speak.

"How long you been with Onyx?" he asked, getting straight to the point.

"We been together for a few years now. But Omari, I promise

you I was never with him while I was with you. I didn't plan this. It was just something that happened."

He nodded once like a judge who'd already made a ruling. "So, out of all the people you could have built a life with, you chose my brother?"

Her chin lifted a fraction. "I didn't build it to spite you. If that's what you think, you're wrong. I would never want to hurt you, Omari, especially after everything you did for me. I won't lie. I'm in love with Onyx, but I will always have love for you, Omari."

"Love for me?" He couldn't stop the laugh that came after that. "Then why would you be fucking my brother if you had so much love for me?"

"Omari, I know this is hard for you to understand, but neither of us did this to hurt you. I truly love Onyx, and he loves me too. I'm sorry, Omari."

He leaned back in the chair. "You sorry for being with my brother, huh?"

"I can't lie and say I'm sorry that I'm with him because I'm not. He gave me a beautiful son that we both love dearly. Without Onyx, Onyx Jr. wouldn't be here. I can't apologize for that. What I will apologize for is hurting you. Those were never my intentions. I was so hurt when you told me not to wait on you, and I was already spending time with Onyx. It just happened, Omari, even though neither of us meant for it to."

Omari's fingers curled into his palms until the short nails bit skin. He took slow, deep breaths, in through his nose and out through his mouth, trying to calm down. Kiss was right. He'd told her not to wait, but he never thought she would move on with his brother.

"You keep sayin' that you didn't mean to do it, but I don't see how this was a mistake, Kiss. I gave up years of my life for you, and you repay me by having a baby with my brother? Don't you see how fucked up this is?" Omari took another deep breath, calming himself before speaking again. "Like there wasn't another man you could have moved on with? You know how many niggas in the city?"

Her face softened. "I never wanted you to pull that trigger," she voiced in a low tone. "I never asked you to do that. You did it because you are who you are."

"And who's that?" The heat in his chest rose to his throat then into his eyes. He blinked it down, refusing to allow his emotions to get the best of him in front of her.

"Someone who loved me and didn't know any other way to show it." She folded her hands then unfolded them. "I loved you. You know that. You were my first love. But you had to go away, and Onyx was all I had. He's been there through everything, and as hard as that is for you to understand, you have to."

"So, you gave my place to him because his feet could find a porch?" Omari's words cut like a blade.

Kiss flinched. "I gave my future to the life that existed. Not the one I had to dream about every night."

Silence pooled inside the room. The sounds of cartoons and OJ laughing in the background was the only thing to breach silence. He thought about what it would be like to wake up to a son and Kiss every morning the way his brother did. It was a life he wanted badly but knew he would never have.

"You still coulda. You coulda looked me in my eyes in that visitation room and said, 'I fucked your brother, 'Mari.' But you didn't. You let Onyx tell me alone. It was like you didn't want to face me because you knew that shit was fucked up, Kiss."

"I didn't know how to tell you," Kiss admitted, eyes steady.

He looked at her fully then, let himself see the parts of her that had nothing to do with him – a girl who'd now grown into a woman and a mother. As much as it pained Omari, he knew Kiss and Onyx were now a family.

"Do you love him?" he asked, genuinely wanting to know the truth.

She didn't hesitate when she looked Omari directly in the eyes. "Yes, I do," she replied. "I love him so much, and he loves me. But overall, we both love OJ."

The words settled. He nodded once before speaking again. "Do you love me still?"

She closed her eyes, just for a second. When she opened them again, they were wet but not weak. "I love the boy that sacrificed years of his life to protect me. I love the boy that loved me more than he loved himself. I love what we were because it made me who I am. But I can't live in the past."

He sat back like the answer had pushed him. OJ still laughed in the background, as he played with his toys. It was a reminder to Omari that this was truly happening. Kiss stood, telling Omari she was going to check on OJ. She left the kitchen for a few moments before returning, taking her seat at the table.

"Can I…" he started then stopped because the words he was about to say felt like it belonged to someone else. He took a deep breath before speaking again. "Can I meet him?"

Kiss stiffened, a flinch almost invisible, but Omari caught it. She turned half toward the living room as if she was thinking about it. The fact that she had to think pained him even more.

"Maybe not today," she finally spoke, voice careful but honest. "He's different with new people, and I don't want him to get too overwhelmed. It's not you. It's…"

"It is me," he admitted, as he nodded his head. "It's me, and it's okay. You don't want me to meet him. I'm his uncle, not his father, so I respect it."

"You could come back," she offered. "When Onyx is here. That way, we can figure something out together so that it won't be so much chaos."

Her words hit him like a ton of bricks. He tasted his brother's name like a mouthful of coins. He pictured Onyx standing there with his nose turned up, letting Omari know that he'd taken everything that was supposed to belong to him. The one person he'd wanted his entire life now belonged to his brother.

"Maybe," he replied.

Kiss dropped her head, eyes looking down at her feet.

"You mad at me?" she asked, finally meeting his gaze again.

"I am," he admitted. "And I'm mad at the way shit worked out. I'm mad at myself for not being the version of me that wanted to ask you to wait. And I'm mad at Onyx for taking everything that was supposed to belong to me."

She ran her hand over her head and took a deep breath. "I'm sorry, Omari."

He shook his head, eyes dropping to the floor. "Ain't no need to be. You did what you wanted to do. Y'all both did."

Kiss couldn't say anything, and Omari didn't want her to because they both knew it was true.

"Omari," she finally spoke, voice steadying. "I know what you need is a villain. It's easier to be angry at a person than at a season or at a system that took chunks out of all of us. I can be that if it makes you move through your day. But when you breathe later, I need you to remember I had nobody when you left. My own mother looked at me like she hated me and blamed me for what Darren did to me. Onyx was that person for me. I hope you can understand that."

His throat clenched. He knew what she was saying was true. He did need a villain, and in his story, he had two. It saddened him that one of them was his twin brother – the person he was born with. The one person that shared his face and his DNA now shared love for the same woman. That was a grief too loud for him to process.

"I would've been a good father and a good man for you."

"I believe you," she replied honestly. "But we can only be good at the lives we get. So, we can't dwell on what ifs."

He pressed his hands together so tight his knuckles turned white. "What do you want from me now?" he asked.

"I want you to build a great life for yourself. I want you to be a man your mama can rest around. I want you to be an uncle who doesn't make our son a battleground for old stories. And if you can't be any of that today, I want you to work toward it."

He looked up and let her words sink in. She had always been the only one who could hand him a mirror for him to really look in.

"You think I'm him," he said quietly. "You think I'm gonna come through here tearing shit up 'cause y'all wronged me?"

"I think you're in pain, and men in pain set fires. I just want to make sure this isn't one starting."

He stood because sitting still had become impossible. The room felt too small for his body, or maybe his anger had grown a size he couldn't disguise anymore. He slid a hand down his face and blew a breath out toward the ceiling. His eyes burned, but he refused to allow one tear to fall in front of her.

"I'm not him," he assured, not sure which him he meant – the man who had pointed a gun because a girl he loved needed a door to stay shut or the man his brother had learned to be in the street to feed mouths Omari had believed he would feed one day. "And I ain't…" He stopped because the next sentence was a threat, and he had promised himself in a cold bed he wouldn't be a man who made women flinch the way Darren had.

Kiss rose too, like the room needed both their heights to recalibrate. They stood at the kitchen door, just looking at each other. They both had things to say, but neither of them said anything.

"You can see him," she said, nodding toward the living room. "You can come over any time Onyx is here to see your nephew. He needs to get to know his Uncle Omari."

He nodded, knowing that wasn't what he wanted to hear. He didn't understand why Onyx had to be home for him to see his nephew – or Kiss for that matter. They were both supposed to be his. Kiss was supposed to be his woman. He'd sacrificed his entire life for her, and he just wanted her to see that. The love Onyx had for her was nothing compared to his love, and he needed her to know that. But instead of saying those words, he just nodded his head.

He paused before he said anything else then turned to look at Kiss. "I'ma get outta here. I'll come back another time. You know, when Onyx is home."

Omari walked to the door, feet moving slowly as if he wanted Kiss to stop him. Deep down, he did. He wanted Kiss to look at him and see all the things they could have been – the things he still wanted to be.

"Omari," she called from behind. He smiled, pausing with his hand on the knob.

"Yeah?"

"I really am sorry. I never meant to hurt you."

He nodded his head, not wanting her to say anymore. There was no need for her sorry because the damage was already done. She couldn't take anything back, so Omari knew he would just have to deal with it. He walked outside, closing the door behind him. He stood on the porch for a moment, still holding the door-knob as if it had the power to change what had already been done. He took in a deep breath and looked up at the sky and just shook his head. The truth was just far too bitter for him to swallow. He walked to Tamika's car and got inside, leaning back in the seat before closing his eyes.

Tamika looked over at him and shook her head. She could tell that her son was hurting, and she wished there was something she could do. There was no way she could choose sides between her children, so she didn't. No matter who Tamika thought was right or wrong, she listened and didn't speak much.

"Well?" she asked.

He rested his forearm across his eyes for a second and took a deep breath. Then, he lowered his arm and stared straight ahead at nothing, trying to gather his thoughts.

"She happy," he finally said, and it was the hardest sentence he had said all day. "He… looks like them. Both of 'em together." He swallowed. "Looks like me too but he not mine."

Tamika nodded, hand reaching over to squeeze his wrist quick. "I'm proud of you."

"For what? Not flippin' her table the fuck over?"

"For bein' a man in a room you coulda been a boy in," Tamika replied. "That's how it starts."

He watched the house in the side mirror shrink as they pulled away. He clenched and unclenched his jaw until the popping felt like a clock. Time had moved on, she had moved on, and there was nothing Omari could do about it.

"You want me to take you by my place?" Tamika asked. "Or you want some time to walk it off?"

"Drop me two blocks over. I just need to walk this shit off for a minute."

"Okay, well, I'll be at the house if you want to talk when you get back. I'm here for you, Omari, just as much as I'm here for Onyx."

He got out at the corner store he used to walk to as a kid. The air smelled like fried food from the chicken and fish spot across the street. Omari walked with his hands in his hoodie pocket. He counted cracks in the sidewalk with each step he took – anything to get his mind off of Kiss and her baby. His brother's baby. At the corner, he stopped to watch two boys shoot a basketball at a bent rim with no net. The boys looked to be about fifteen, and Omari remembered back to when he was that young. He wasn't as carefree as those boys seemed to be. When he was that age, he was serving a sentence because he was trying to protect the girl he loved. The same girl that was now in love with his twin brother.

He watched until one of the boys called him over and asked him if he played. Omari shrugged, holding his hands up for the boy to toss him the ball. He drippled the ball for a moment before tossing it up and landing it into the hoop from where he stood. The boys cheered, and he smiled before walking off.

As he walked, he thought about his life and what would happen next. The life he once thought he would come home to was no longer his. He stopped and stared at his reflection in a storefront as a bus drove past. He saw a man whose anger he couldn't hide. He'd kept it together in front of Kiss, but now, he thought he would break down. *Come on, Mari. Keep it together. She made her choice, and it wasn't you.*

He turned back the way he'd come and put his head down as he walked. When he got back to Tamika's house, he walked upstairs to his old bedroom. His side of the room was untouched. His clothes were still hanging in the closet and folded in the drawers. He couldn't even fit any of them anymore, but Tamika had kept everything the way he'd left it.

The bags of items Tamika had bought for him were already laying on his bed. He pulled out a t-shirt and a pair of basketball shorts before grabbing a towel from the linen closet. He made his way to the bathroom and took the longest, hottest shower he'd taken in years.

Chapter Twenty

Onyx stood on the back steps behind the old brick building he ran. Blue had made him lieutenant over his Eastside spots, and Onyx was making more money than he'd ever seen. He tucked his hands into his hoodie pockets before checking the alley, making sure everything was clear. A car pulled up, and Onyx already knew who was in it. Marv, Blue's righthand, stepped out the car, holding two duffle bags that Onyx knew was full of product.

"Morning, Blackwell," Marv greeted, following Onyx into the building

"What up doe? I'm glad to see you 'cause we ain't have no work to start the day off with."

They walked into the garage where a stripped Monte Carlo sat in the middle. They walked into Onyx's office, and Marv sat the duffle bags on his desk. Onyx opened them, looking at the bricks of white powder that was inside. He took the bricks out the duffle bags and placed each brick onto his desk before refilling the duffle bags with money. He zipped them up and handed them back to Marv.

Onyx's team had been running through product left and right, so the re-up was much needed. Once Marv left, Onyx started breaking the weight down and passed it out to his crew. He'd just finished when his phone rang. He looked down at it to see it was Blue, and he walked into his office before he answered.

"What up doe?"

"Yo, I need you to meet me at the spot off Mack. I'll let you know what's up once you get there."

Onyx agreed, grabbed his keys, and made his way to meet Blue. He had no clue what Blue wanted to talk to him about, but whatever it was, Onyx knew it was going to make him some money. He rode through the city with the windows down, feeling the breeze. His radio was bumping Meek Mills' *Dreams and Nightmares,* as he rapped along. When he pulled up to the spot, Blue was standing outside, leaning against his car, waiting for him. Onyx got out the car and greeted Blue. He dapped him up before they walked into the old brick house.

"So, what's good, Blue? I know you didn't just call me over here, so you could see my face."

Blue motioned for Onyx to follow him, as they walked through the home. Blue took a seat before pulling an envelope from his pocket and handing it to Onyx. Onyx opened it and pulled out several pictures of a chubby, dark-skinned man in a white tee shirt. Onyx looked over at Blue, confused.

"Who is this?"

"His name is Ralow. That nigga been on bullshit ever since he got to the city. He thinks he can just come in and take over, but you know I ain't bout to let that happen."

"Okay. So, what's the plan?" Onyx asked.

"You gon' kill him. I was gon' put twenty-five racks on his head, but I need to make sure this shit is done right. So, I need you to take him out, and I'll just give the twenty-five racks to you once it's done."

Onyx froze. He'd done a lot of things for Blue. He'd moved weight and stole cars, but killing someone was a different ball game, and Onyx wasn't sure it was something he could even do. He leaned back on the couch as if he was in deep thought. Blue looked over at Onyx and saw the hesitation on his face.

"How 'bout this? I can give you half up front today and then the other half when the job is done. This an easy hit, Blackwell. I can tell you exactly where he gon' be and everything. All I need you to do is pull the trigger and make sure that nigga never breathes again."

Hearing that he would get half up front changed everything. Although Onyx was still scared, he agreed, knowing his family needed the money. Blue reached into his other pocket and pulled out another envelope. He counted out twelve thousand dollars and handed it to Onyx along with the picture of Ralow. Onyx nodded his head, letting Blue know that he would handle it.

"He be over there off Joy Road. He run with a couple niggas, so watch yo' back if you hit him on the block. If I were you, I would follow him and wait til he's alone to do it. Once it's done, just send me conformation, and the other half of the money is yours."

Onyx nodded, taking the money and putting it in his pocket, before standing to his feet. He'd never killed anyone before, but for twenty-five bands, he was about to become the killer that everyone already thought he was.

On Sunday afternoon, Onyx, Kiss, and OJ all pulled up to Tamika's house. She was having a welcome home dinner for Omari and made Onyx promise to be there. They hadn't spoken since Omari had come home, but Onyx knew that a conversation was well overdue. They walked in to find balloons and streamers through the living room and dining room. A huge, gold, welcome home sign hung from the wall, and a few gifts sat on the small table in the corner. A pot of greens simmered on the stove. Macaroni that had baked until the edges crisped sat in the middle of the table. There were ribs she would not disclose the secrets of and her sweet honey cornbread that Onyx loved. On the counter, there was a sheet cake with the words 'Welcome Home, Omari' written in gold icing.

Tamika smiled as they entered, rushing over to see OJ.

"How's Grandma's big man?" Tamika asked, as she kissed OJ's cheek.

"I'm good, Grandma. Just hungry. Mommy wouldn't let me eat before we left because she said we were eating here."

"And you are. Grandma cooked up a big meal for your Uncle Omari."

"My Uncle Omari?" OJ frowned.

"Dang, you don't see me standing here too, Ma?" Onyx joked.

Tamika laughed, opening her arms, and pulled her son in for a hug. Kiss asked Tamika if she needed help with anything before walking into the kitchen. She tied an apron around her waist and checked on the chicken that was in the deep fryer.

"Girl, what you doing? I asked you to come over to eat and celebrate, not to put you to work. Go in there and get yourself something to drink. I got this covered already," Tamika ordered, motioning for Kiss to get out the kitchen.

Kiss laughed and made her way to the living room to join Onyx. She'd just sat on the couch when Omari made his way down the stairs. Kiss paused when she saw him, her breath caught in her throat. Even though she'd seen him the day he'd gotten out, it was like she was seeing him for the first time. His dark chocolate skin was smooth and flawless. He was buff from the years he spent working out behind the wall. He smiled when he saw her, and Kiss smiled back. Then, she saw his expression harden when he looked over and saw Onyx sitting next to her.

Instead of speaking, Omari turned and walked into the kitchen. "Damn, Ma, you got it smelling good as hell in here."

"Good, because I made all your favorites. Ribs, fried chicken, macaroni and cheese, yams, greens, potato salad, cornbread, and spaghetti. I even got some cake and some pecan pie."

"That's what I'm talkin' bout, Ma. Hook that shit up."

Omari walked over to the stove and opened the pot of greens. He smiled as he inhaled the scent. Tamika had been going above and beyond since Omari had come home, trying to make sure he was comfortable, and it was greatly appreciated. Tamika walked over to him slowly, leaning in before she spoke.

"Maybe you and Onyx should go have a talk before everyone else gets here. Your Auntie Dot and your cousins are coming over, and you already know how nosy they are. I don't want them all in y'all business before y'all even get a chance to get into it."

"We can talk after dinner. Right now, I just want to enjoy myself. That shit gon' ruin my whole mood, and I ain't got time for that right now."

Tamika nodded, not wanting to push. A few moments later, Auntie Dot arrived along with her two daughters, Jessica and Dominque. They came in loud, happy to see Omari after all this time. Auntie Dot was the first to hug Omari, welcoming him back. His cousin, Peanut, was the next to arrive with his new girlfriend, Tabitha. Peanut and Omari were close as kids, but while Omari was locked away, Peanut didn't write him once. So, he was surprised to see him at his welcome home dinner.

"What up doe, cousin? You lookin' good, all buff and shit. I bought you a bottle of Henny, so we can get faded, and I can catch you up on everything that you missed."

Omari smiled and dapped his cousin up. "Put it in the kitchen along with the rest of the drinks. We can crack that open after dinner."

Peanut nodded, and they all went into the kitchen. Tamika had laid out the food on the counters and allowed everyone to help themselves. Omari was the first to grab a plate. Tamika wanted to make sure he got everything he wanted before everyone else made their plates.

Everyone sat down to eat, sharing old stories of Omari and

remembering the good times they had. Omari looked over at his twin, who was sitting beside Kiss with OJ sitting next to her. Onyx must have felt Omari looking because their eyes met. They stared at each other for a beat. It was like looking in the mirror. Onyx gave him a look, silently letting Omari know that they were good, but Omari just looked.

He looked down at OJ then back up at Onyx without saying a word. Omari continued to eat his food, every now and then glancing at the child that was supposed to be his. Tamika noticed him looking at OJ.

"Why you lookin' at him like that? Say something. He's your nephew, Mari."

Omari stiffened, glancing at Kiss then at Onyx, as if to ask permission. Kiss nodded her head softly. Onyx gave a smaller nod, letting Omari know it was okay. Before Omari could say anything, OJ looked up at him.

"You look like my daddy. Why?"

"Because we twins, lil man. I just had to go away for a while. But I'm back now, and I'm not going anywhere."

"Y'all got the same face. That's cool. But I can tell y'all apart. My daddy's eyes are different."

"That's right, nephew. They are." Omari smiled. "How old are you, lil man?"

"I'm three, but I'm almost four," OJ replied with a smile.

Once everyone was done eating, it was time for the cake. Tamika added candles to the cake and lit them. She told everyone to sing happy birthday to Omari in celebration of every birthday they missed while he was locked up. Omari laughed but made a wish and blew out the candles anyway.

"What you wish for, cuzzo?" Peanut asked, looking up at Omari.

"He can't tell you. It's not gon' come true that way," Tamika joked.

Omari chuckled before looking over at Kiss. He didn't speak

a word, but his eyes told Kiss that he'd wished for her. Once everyone had cake and poured drinks, they all spread around the house. Auntie Dot and her daughters had started a spades game in the kitchen, and Peanut was already cussing her out for cheating. Omari was on the couch with a drink in his hand, watching OJ play with his toys, while Kiss walked around the kitchen, covering the food with foil. Onyx walked into the kitchen to refill his drink, but before he could, Tamika grabbed his arm.

"You and your brother," she spoke, nodding toward the back door. "Y'all need to go talk. Outside and away from everyone else. But words only, Onyx. No hands."

"We grown, Ma," Onyx replied.

"That's what I'm afraid of."

Onyx nodded his head, walking into the kitchen to refresh his drink, before going to get Omari. They walked outside together, each one of them holding a red plastic cup with brown liquor inside. The warm sun beamed down on them, as they stood on the porch. For a moment, they were both quiet before Onyx finally spoke.

"I know this shit gotta be fucked up for you. I ain't trying to hurt you, bro."

"Shit, could have fooled me."

"You told her to move on and not to wait on you."

"I did, but I for damn sure didn't think she would pick my brother. And even if she did, a muthafucka couldn't have paid me enough to believe that you would go along with it. Where is yo' loyalty?" Omari asked, looking Onyx directly in his eyes. "Look, I ain't here to make Kiss choose between her past and her present. I just feel like it's fucked up, and I need for at least one of y'all to tell me why y'all would do something like this."

"I love her. She's the mother of my child, and she's going to be my wife one day. Neither of us planned this. It just happened. I know that's hard for you, but you're going to have to get over it because we gon' be together. I want you to be an uncle to OJ. I want you to be the best man at my wedding. I want the brother I had before you got locked up. But for any of that to happen, you're gon' to have to get over this. Kiss and I been together for years, Mari. Neither of us are going anywhere."

Omari flinched at Onyx's words. "It ain't been years to me. And I don't know how long it's going to take for me to get over the fact that my own twin stole my first love."

"I didn't steal anything. Kiss is not a possession. She's a woman, and she made a choice. I just need for you to respect it."

Omari's breath caught, more so because he knew what Onyx was saying was the truth. Kiss had indeed made a choice, and the choice wasn't him. As much as that pained him, he knew he would have to get over it. He'd told Kiss that if they were meant to be, then they would be. She was now with his brother, so they were clearly not meant to be together.

"It's like I came home and you got my life. Everything that was supposed to be mine is yours."

"And that's the thing, Omari. I don't have your life. I have mine. I just need you to understand that."

Omari nodded his head in understanding. "I forgive you and Kiss. We were all young when I went inside, and whatever happened already happened. Y'all got a family, and I'll respect that. I want to be the best uncle to OJ because that's what he deserves. So, we good."

Onyx smiled and pulled Omari in for a hug. "I just want my brother back. And if this is the start of that, then I'm all for it."

Without a word, Onyx reached into his pocket and pulled out an envelope and handed it to Omari. He watched as Omari opened it, his eyes widening when he saw the hundreds that were stacked inside.

"Yo, what's…"

"It's seven racks. It ain't much, but it's what I got right now. If you want, I could hook you up with a few jobs so that you can start getting you some real money," Onyx spoke, cutting Omari off mid-sentence.

"Damn, you still runnin' with Blue, huh? I don't know, bro. I think I want to stay on the straight and narrow after all those years inside. I'ma just get me a real nine to five and call it a day."

"If that's what you want, cool. But if you change yo' mind, I got you."

Omari nodded, taking a sip from his cup. He tucked the envelope into his back pocket, and the twins continued to talk. They stayed outside for hours, catching up on everything that had taken place over the past seven years, only coming into the house to refill their cups. By the end of the night, the twins had come back together like nothing had ever tried to break them apart.

When Onyx got home, he carried a sleeping OJ inside, while Kiss walked in front of them. He took off his son's shoes before placing him into his bed. He felt Kiss' eyes on him and turned around, smiling.

"So, everything is good?" she asked.

"Yeah, we had a long talk, and he seems to understand. I'm glad because I missed my brother."

Kiss smiled, walking over to Onyx and kissing him passionately. He wrapped his arms around her waist, holding her close to him. They were both pleased with the way the night had turned out. They spent the rest of the night in bed, making love, until they fell asleep wrapped in each other's arms.

Chapter Twenty-One

The air had turned sharp again, as November came to the city. Summer was long gone, and the air was cold. The trees were bare, and all the leaves had now fallen to the ground. As cold as it was, it hadn't snowed yet, but in Michigan, it could happen at any time. With the holidays right around the corner, Onyx knew he needed to hustle twice as hard. A few months had passed since Omari's welcome home dinner, and life had found its rhythm again. Omari had stayed around Tamika's place mostly, taking odd jobs because he still wasn't able to find a nine to five. Onyx had told him that he could work for him, but Omari still refused. Onyx knew he couldn't force him, but he told him that he was there if he needed anything.

For Onyx though, time wasn't slowing. His world spun faster now, like he was running on a treadmill that only went one speed. His hustle never stopped. What started as late-night moves and quick pick-ups for Blue had blossomed into something heavier and more lucrative. He'd graduated from a duffle bag full of money to a hidden safe. Every envelope got thicker, and every night stretched longer.

Onyx was working toward a bigger house for his family. He wanted to have more children with Kiss but knew they would need a bigger house before that happened – one that he'd bought with his own money and wasn't just renting, one in a nicer neighborhood where his children could play in the yard without them having to worry. Onyx had been stacking for months, but to him, it still wasn't enough.

The more money stacked, the less time he seemed to spend at home. Kiss didn't nag because she wasn't the type. She never asked what time he would be home, and she always left a plate of whatever she'd made for dinner inside the microwave for when he did come home. He told himself he did it for her and their son. He told himself that they deserved a better life, and his long nights were going to provide that. Although it wasn't a lie, it wasn't the entire truth either.

Because when the nights stretched too long and the work bled into hours where sleep didn't, Onyx found something else – a distraction, the company of a woman that wasn't Kiss but felt just as good. Her name was Aaliyah, a beautiful woman that he'd been spending time with over the past few months. She stood about five foot one, thick and light skinned, with a sleeve of tattoos on her right arm.

Onyx had met her one night after a run. Blue had thrown a gathering at one of his usual spots, a lowkey lounge on the Eastside that not too many people knew about. Onyx wasn't supposed to stay long, but Aaliyah made it impossible to leave, her eyes and smile calling him to stay.

"Why don't you have one more drink with me before you leave?" Aaliyah suggested.

"You just don't quit, huh?"

"Not when I see something I like."

That night, Onyx and Aaliyah left the bar together and went to a hotel room. That was about three months ago, and they'd been seeing each other a couple times a week ever since. Aaliyah knew her role and how to play her position. Onyx had been honest with her from the beginning, letting her know about his family and how he would never leave them. Aaliyah agreed and played the side, knowing that everything would be good as long as Kiss never found out.

A few days before Thanksgiving, the safe was stacked to Onyx's liking. He counted it all late one night when the house was quiet. With OJ and Kiss both asleep, he'd spread the bands of cash across the table, eyes glinting in the low light. Tens of thousands of dollars sat in front of him. Enough to start looking at houses outside the neighborhood they currently lived in. Enough to give Kiss the life he promised her when they first found out she was pregnant.

The Macy's Thanksgiving Day Parade played on the TV, while the smell of the meal being cooked in the kitchen filled the entire house. Kiss had chosen to host Thanksgiving dinner and had been cooking since the night before. Sade had come over earlier that morning to help Kiss cook, and Tamika and Omari would be over later for dinner. Onyx walked into the kitchen, wrapping his arm around Kiss' waist before kissing her on the temple.

Sade sat in a chair at the kitchen table, peeling sweet potatoes. Kiss had the counters crowded with seasonings lined up. The turkey was in the oven, and a small chicken sat thawing in the sink. Greens were soaking in a huge pot on the counter, almost ready to go on the stove.

"Morning, baby. You got it smellin' good as fuck in here," Onyx spoke in a soft tone.

"You gon' stand there or help?" Sade asked, not even looking up from the knife moving swiftly against the cutting board.

"Come on, Ma. It's Thanksgiving, so please don't start that. He don't need to help in here. He needs to help out there, keeping OJ while we cook." Kiss smiled over at Onyx and motioned for him to leave the kitchen.

Onyx grinned before nodding his head and walking out. He picked OJ up from the floor and sat on the couch with him. They watched the parade together with OJ smiling when his favorite characters ran across the screen.

By two, Tamika arrived with her famous macaroni and cheese, golden and ready to eat. Everyone loved her macaroni and cheese, knowing none of theirs even came close. Omari came with her, holding a pie in a box from the bakery down the street. He looked different than he had months ago at the welcome home dinner. He appeared to be much calmer, and Onyx could tell he was getting used to his life on the outside. Even though he was still living with Tamika, Omari had gotten himself a car and was one step closer to getting back on his feet.

They sat down to eat, the table crowded with both food and love. Onyx took it in, smiling at the first Thanksgiving dinner they'd hosted. It was a success so far, and he was happy about it. He bowed his head when Kiss said grace, the words rolling steady and heavy with gratitude. They had a lot to be thankful for, and today was the day they showed it.

Dinner was filled with family and laughter. Omari swearing he still made the best cornbread, even though he hadn't made it since he was thirteen. Sade telling OJ that one day, he'd eat three plates just like his daddy, while Kiss shook her head at all of them with mock exasperation. Onyx ate slow, savoring it, but his mind kept drifting back to the stacks of money hidden away. He couldn't wait to drop it on a down payment on his family's dream house.

After dinner, Omari helped Onyx take out the trash, and they stood on the porch for a minute, smoking a cigarette.

"This was real dope. I never thought I'd see the day that you hosted a Thanksgiving dinner," Omari joked.

"Yeah, this was all Kiss, and it turned out great. She really got an eye for stuff like this. But what's up with you? You still over there acting like you don't need this money?"

Omari looked around, making sure nobody was listening,

before he spoke. "I can't lie. I need some money. You think you can get me something? But no drugs or stolen cars."

Onyx thought for a minute, trying to figure out a way for Omari to make money that didn't involve those things. When he didn't come up with anything, he told Omari that he would have a meeting with Blue and try to come up with a job for him. Omari agreed, and they both went back inside.

The next morning, Onyx woke up restless, as if he hadn't just gotten a full night of sleep. Kiss was still sleeping soundly next to him, as he slowly got out of bed. He walked into OJ's room to find that he was still sleeping as well. It was just after eight in the morning. He walked into the kitchen and warmed up a plate of leftovers. When he was done, he placed his plate into the sink and went to take a shower.

"Where you on yo' way to?" Kiss asked the moment Onyx stepped out the bathroom.

She was wearing one of his white tee shirts that stopped just under her round backside. A smiling OJ was at her side, as she looked up at Onyx, waiting on an answer.

"Gotta run some errands. You know how it is, baby. It's the day after the holiday, so you know it's money to be made."

Kiss nodded. "Okay but remember that OJ has a doctor's appointment on Monday. He has to get his shots, so he can't miss it. It's at one in the afternoon, so please don't be late."

"I got it, baby. I remember. One o'clock on Monday afternoon, we will be in the doctor's office with our son."

Onyx kissed Kiss' forehead before getting dressed to leave, the cold Detroit air hitting his face the moment he stepped outside. He saw Kiss and OJ watching him from the window as he pulled out the driveway.

Aaliyah's place was across town in Dearborn Heights in an

apartment complex ducked off behind several trees. Onyx parked in his usual parking spot before using his key to open the front door. He walked into her bedroom to find her still fast asleep under her covers. Her apartment always smelled of vanilla, and he welcomed the scent as he undressed. He crawled into bed, cuddling up next to Aaliyah, as he wrapped his arms around her waist.

"Damn, baby, I thought you was going to come last night after yo' family dinner. I stayed up late waiting for you," Aaliyah whispered sleepily.

"I know. I was tryin', but they stayed over way too late, and my girl would have been asking all kinds of questions if I would have walked out the house that late. I'm here now though, and that's all that matters."

"You always worry about what she gon' think. Yet you come get in my bed and fuck me like I belong to you." Aaliyah turned on her side and faced Onyx, waiting on him to answer.

"You do belong to me. But you already know I ain't leaving my wifey. That was something I told you from the beginning. Shit been good, baby. So, don't fuck it up with this conversation that neither of us needs to have."

Aaliyah smiled, scooting closer to Onyx, closing the small gap between them. He grabbed a handful of her plump ass before kissing her deeply. The truth was that although Onyx would never leave his family, he had really deep feelings for Aaliyah. He knew it was wrong when he had Kiss at home waiting on him, but his feelings for Aaliyah wouldn't allow him to stop.

"I can't get too mad because you always come back to me."

"And I always will."

Onyx rolled on top of Aaliyah, as she opened up for him. He slid into her tight wetness and growled when he entered her. He moved to the rhythm of her moans, as he let the world around him fade. Nothing else mattered when he was inside of Aaliyah. At that moment, only the two of them existed. When it was over,

Onyx lay there in the quiet, staring at the ceiling, Aaliyah's head on his chest. His phone buzzed once on the nightstand, and he knew it was a text from Kiss. He didn't even look at it. Instead, he closed his eyes, guilt and desire battling in his chest all at once.

He was truly in love with Kiss, and the fact that he had sex with Aaliyah didn't change that. However, he had feelings for Aaliyah as well, so much so that he didn't want to give her up. He just hoped Kiss never found out. That way, he would be able to keep them both the way he wanted to.

Chapter Twenty - Two

Kiss' alarm went off at ten o'clock Monday morning. She rolled over, opening her eyes to see the morning sun shining in through her half open curtains. She heard OJ already up in his room, playing with his toys, and she smiled. The sound of him in the morning always made her smile. She rolled over in bed, stretching her arms wide, before reaching instinctively to the other side. The sheets there were cool, and Onyx was already gone.

She sighed, remembering the brush of his lips against her forehead. His voice was so low she'd thought she was dreaming when he told her that he would be back in time for OJ's appointment. Now, seeing that he was indeed gone, she knew that she wasn't dreaming. Kiss swung her legs over the side of the bed and pushed herself up, tying her robe around her waist. She walked into her son's room, all smiles.

"Good morning, Mommy. You wanna play with me?" OJ asked, looking up at her.

"Good morning, my little man. How about we play later? Right now, we need to get you some breakfast, so we can start getting ready to go."

"Where we going?"

"You have to go to the doctor's. Remember I told you?"

"But Mommy, you said I have to get a shot, and I told you I didn't want to go. I hate shots. They hurt." OJ pouted.

"I know, baby, but we have to go. And I promise when we get back, you can have all the ice cream you want."

OJ looked up at Kiss skeptically. "But what if I want two bowls?"

"Then you'll get two bowls."

OJ smiled before standing to his feet. He walked into the kitchen with Kiss leading the way. She connected her phone to the speaker and allowed her playlist to play, as she grabbed eggs and sausage from the refrigerator.

The clock on the wall ticked steadily, reading eleven o'clock by the time they were done eating. OJ's appointment was at one, and it was thirty minutes away. She had plenty of time to shower and get both her and OJ dressed. By twelve, they were both dressed and ready. She put on a pair of black leggings and an oversized gray sweater. She had OJ matching her fly with a pair of black jeans and a gray sweater. Kiss walked with OJ to the living room and put on cartoons, as they waited on Onyx to return.

When twelve-fifteen rolled around and Onyx still wasn't there, Kiss called his phone and got the voicemail. Thinking that he was probably driving, she put her phone down and continued to watch cartoons with OJ. By twelve twenty, Kiss was checking her phone again, only to see there were no text messages.

"Where you at?" she muttered under her breath, pacing the living room, while OJ continued to watch cartoons. "Why would you leave this morning when you knew he had an appointment to go to?"

Onyx had promised her that he'd be back in time, and now here he was, already late. She called him once more, and this time, the phone went directly to voicemail, making Kiss even angrier. For the past few months, Onyx had been slacking when it came to her and OJ. She hadn't said anything because she knew he was out there trying to make money for their family. However, today, when OJ had an appointment, it was too much.

By twelve-thirty, her patience was gone. She couldn't do anything but shake her head when she thought about how she didn't even have a car to get her son to the doctor's.

"Damn it." She pressed her forehead against the doorframe, closing her eyes.

There was only one option because they couldn't miss the appointment. She grabbed her phone, scrolled, and pressed Omari's name. He answered on the second ring, his voice steady.

"Kiss? Everything good?"

Her throat tightened. "No. OJ has a doctor's appointment at one that he can't miss. I don't know where Onyx is. He promised me he would be back in time, and now, he's not even answering the phone. The car seat is inside his car, and I don't have a way to get him to the doctor's."

"I got you," Omari spoke without hesitation. "Where you at?"

"We at the house."

"I'll be there in ten."

Relief and frustration tangled in her chest. She thanked him before ending the call. Just as he'd said, Omari was there within ten minutes to get them. He walked up on the porch and rang the doorbell before Kiss opened the door.

"Uncle Mari," OJ squealed the moment Omari walked through the door. OJ jumped up from the couch and ran over to him. Omari leaned down, hugging his nephew.

"What up doe, lil man? You all ready for your doctor's appointment?"

"No. I don't like shots, and I told Mommy I didn't want to go, but she says I have to."

"It's gon' be all good, lil man. Them little needles ain't nothing. You can take that. You my nephew. That means you stronger than any other three-year-old around."

OJ smiled before slapping Omari five. Kiss smiled as well,

thinking about how cute the little pep talk was. She grabbed her purse before turning to Onyx once they were in the car.

"Thank you," Kiss said finally, her voice soft.

"You don't gotta thank me," Omari replied, eyes on the road. "That's my nephew. You call, I come."

The pediatrician's office was bright and noisy, filled with murals of cartoon animals and kids running circles around their parents. Kiss signed in, while Omari and OJ took their seats.

The nurse smiled when she called them back. "Dad, you can come too."

Kiss froze, but Omari didn't correct her. He just nodded and followed, OJ giggling at Omari's side. Kiss walked behind them, her stomach twisting. She should say something. Tell the nurse that Omari was his uncle and not his father. But she didn't.

Inside the exam room, the doctor came in, cheerful and chatty. She looked at OJ then at Omari. "He's growing so well! Got his daddy's eyes, doesn't he?"

Kiss' breath caught. She wanted to scream, *No. He's not his daddy. His daddy didn't even show up.* But the words stayed locked in her throat. Omari shifted slightly, cleared his throat, but didn't correct her either.

"See, y'all got the same face. Even she thinks you Daddy," OJ whispered, still giggling.

Kiss watched as Omari held OJ's hand, while he got his shots and hugged him up when he cried just a little. It warmed Kiss' heart to see what a good uncle Omari was to OJ, but he wasn't his daddy. Kiss checked her phone once more while inside the office, and there was still no missed calls or texts from Onyx.

When they got back to the car, Omari buckled OJ into the backseat before double-checking the seat belt. Kiss stood with her arms crossed, the November wind biting at her skin.

"You mad?" Omari asked, glancing over at her.

She laughed bitterly. "Of course I'm mad. He promised me that he would be back in time, and he didn't even so much as call. And I know he got my missed calls and still didn't call back. This the bullshit I be talking about."

Omari leaned against the car, watching her. "You know I don't mind stepping in when you need me. This is what family does. We might not be a family in the most traditional way, but we still family, and I got you."

Her eyes met his. For a moment, she just looked at him as if she was searching for something. Then, she spoke. "Thank you, Omari, but you shouldn't have to do this. You're not his father. Onyx is."

OJ sat in the backseat, singing loudly and breaking the moment. Omari opened the door and slid in behind the wheel. "C'mon. Let's get y'all home."

Kiss got into the car with her arms folded. She was so mad at Onyx that she didn't know what to do. She didn't even notice that Omari hadn't pulled off yet until she finally felt him staring at her.

"Calm down, Kiss. I'm sure something came up. I can't see him missing OJ's appointment for any other reason. How bout we go get something to eat before I drop y'all off at home?"

Kiss thought for a split second before nodding her head. About fifteen minutes later, they were pulling up into the parking lot of Chuck E. Cheese. Kiss laughed before looking over at Omari.

"What is this? I thought you said we were going to get something to eat?"

"Yayyy, Chuck E. Cheese!" OJ squealed from the backseat.

"What you mean? It's Chuck E. Cheese. You heard my nephew. They got pizza and a salad bar here. We gon' eat good, and OJ can play all he wants."

Kiss shook her head but got out the car anyway. They walked

into the building with Omari holding OJ's hand. He paid for their tokens and food before they found a table to sit at. They ate and played for a couple of hours, which OJ seemed to love. They had so much fun together that Kiss had forgotten she was mad. That was until they got back into the car, and Omari took them home.

Kiss shook her head when they pulled into her driveway, and Onyx still wasn't home. It was a little after six that evening, and the sun had already gone down. Omari helped Kiss take OJ into the house, letting her know to call him if she needed anything else, before he walked out the door.

Kiss stood in her doorway, watching Omari walk back to his car. She waited until he pulled out the driveway before she closed the door. Seeing how her and OJ had already eaten, she didn't make anything for dinner. *If that nigga want something to eat, he can get it from whatever kept him from going to our son's doctor's appointment,* she thought.

So, instead, she ran OJ a bath and put him to bed before taking a shower herself. She'd just gotten in bed and turned the TV on when her phone buzzed, letting her know that she had a text. Looking down, she saw it was Onyx telling her how sorry he was and that he would be home soon. Kiss didn't even bother texting back. Instead, she put her phone on the nightstand and picked out a movie to watch.

Chapter Twenty-Three

It was seven in the morning when Onyx received the text from Aaliyah letting him know that they needed to talk face to face. Onyx sighed when he read the text, already knowing that whatever the conversation was about, he could do without having it. When a woman sent a text saying they needed to talk face to face, it was never good.

He knew it was Monday and that OJ had a doctor's appointment that Kiss had forced him to clear his schedule for. He couldn't miss it, so although he was going to Aaliyah's house, he kissed Kiss on her forehead and promised her that he'd be back. Before he left, he checked on OJ, who was still fast asleep under his covers. Onyx smiled, closing OJ's bedroom door softly before making his way out the house.

As he steered his car through the morning traffic, his mind wasn't on the pediatrician's office or on how mad Kiss would be when she woke up and he wasn't there. His mind was on Aaliyah and the text that he'd read several times before he'd even gotten out of bed. She wasn't the type to ask him to get out of bed to come see her for nothing, and he knew this wasn't a booty call this early in the morning. Whatever she needed to talk about was important, and Onyx needed to know what it was.

He told himself it would be a quick in and out. He'd see what she needed, shut it down if it was drama, and be back before Kiss had even gotten dressed. Still, the knot in his stomach tightened with every block he drove. Something felt off to him. He just wasn't sure what it was and prayed that whatever it was, it wasn't bad news. *Hell, if the bitch want to stop fuckin' wit me, she could have sent that shit in a text message,* Onyx thought.

When he got to Aaliyah's apartment complex, he parked in his usual spot before cutting his car off. He scanned the parking lot like always, trying to make sure that nobody who knew Kiss saw him. He climbed the stairs two at a time, his hoodie pulled low. Onyx pulled his key from his pocket just as the door swung open. Aaliyah stood on the other side, clearly waiting on him.

"Bout time," Aaliyah spoke, stepping back to let him in.

Her place smelled like vanilla just as it always did. Soft R&B music played low from a speaker in the corner as if she was trying to set a mood. She wore a pair of tight-fitting gray sweatpants and a fitted white tee. Her jet-black lace frontal was tucked underneath a purple bonnet, and her face was bare. That alone told Onyx something was wrong. He'd never seen Aaliyah in sweats. She was either fully glammed up or naked. There was no in-between for her.

"What's going on?" he asked, cutting straight to the point.

She closed the door and crossed her arms over her chest. "I'm pregnant. That's what's going on."

The words hit harder than a fist. For a second, the room tilted, and Onyx had to steady himself against the wall. He prayed he hadn't heard what he thought he'd heard. Aaliyah getting pregnant was never in his plans, so he hoped she was either playing or mistaken.

"You what?" His voice came out harsher than he intended, but he needed her to know that now was not the time for games.

"You heard me. I said I'm pregnant." Her chin lifted, daring him to deny it. "I was seven days late, so I took a test this morning. I'm pregnant, Onyx, and it's yours."

Onyx shook his head, pacing a short line across her living

room. His pulse roared in his ears. "Hell nah, you playing games."

Aaliyah's eyes narrowed. "Why would I play about somethin' like this?"

He didn't answer; he couldn't. His chest tightened like a vice. He knew that Aaliyah wasn't one to play games, not like this. But he hoped that just this one time, she was playing some type of cruel joke on him. *Fuck, how could I have been so stupid and fucked her without a condom? Fuck!* Onyx thought, as he continued to shake his head.

"Where's the test?" he snapped, finally opening his mouth to speak.

"In the trash. Where else would it be?"

"Show it to me."

She blinked at him then huffed, shaking her head. Aaliyah marched into the bathroom, as she mumbled something under her breath. A moment later, she came back with the white stick, the faint pink lines still visible. She held it out, handing it to Onyx.

Onyx stared, but his head shook before his eyes could catch up. "That don't mean shit. You could have had anybody piss on that stick. I need to see it myself."

Aaliyah recoiled. "You think I'm lying?"

"I think I need to know for myself," Onyx spoke through clenched teeth.

They stared at each other, the silence as thick as smoke. Finally, Aaliyah snatched her keys off the counter. "Fine. Let's go to the store."

The ride to the corner store was quiet. Onyx drove like the steering wheel was the only thing keeping his world from falling apart. Aaliyah sat stiff in the passenger seat, arms folded, staring out the window like she couldn't believe she was here, proving herself to him. In his heart, Onyx knew Aaliyah was telling the truth, but her being pregnant would ruin the family he'd already started with Kiss, and that was something he didn't want to lose.

When they got to the store, Aaliyah chose to stay in the car and let Onyx go in. He grabbed two boxes, both with two tests in each. He got two different brands, wanting to make sure they got the most accurate results. He paid cash at the counter and walked back to the car, pulling off down the street.

They rode back to Aaliyah's apartment in the same unusual silence they'd rode to the store in. Onyx went to hand her the bag of tests the moment they walked inside.

"Take them in front of me."

Her glare could've cut steel, but she didn't argue. She snatched the bag from his hands and walked into the bathroom with Onyx following right behind. She opened her cabinet and pulled out a paper cup. She cut her eyes at him again when she pulled down her pants and peed in the cup. She set it on the counter before wiping herself and pulling her pants up. Onyx watched as she dipped each test into the cup one by one before placing them onto the counter.

Minutes stretched like hours as he waited for the results. He thought about Kiss at home, who was probably up and fixing breakfast for OJ. He could see her smiling face singing along to whatever music she was listening to while she cooked. He couldn't imagine not being with Kiss anymore. But he knew that was exactly what was going to happen if these tests came back positive.

He didn't have to wait too long for the results because they all came back the same way within minutes, positive. And he knew that the life he'd known was now over. For a moment, he just stood there, not saying anything. He couldn't say a word, only shake his head at his own stupid mistake. Onyx's knees went weak, and he thought he would fall to the floor. He leaned against the wall to steady himself.

It wasn't supposed to be like this. Aaliyah was supposed to

be a secret, a distraction from his everyday life – something he could just walk away from if shit ever got too heavy. Kiss was his home and his forever. She was the mother of his child, the woman he wanted to marry and have other children with. But now, this was going to stop all of that, and Onyx knew it. His mind spun with different scenarios. Kiss finding out from the streets instead of him and taking his son and leaving him. Or her tears when he had to sit her down and tell her he was having a child with another woman. She would surely hate him, curse him out, and never speak to him again.

Fear crawled up his throat. He looked over at Aaliyah, who was still standing there with her arms folded. When Onyx didn't say anything, Aaliyah sucked her teeth and walked out the bathroom. Onyx followed her to the living room, sitting on the couch next to her.

"So, what you gon' do now? Because I'm having my baby."

Aaliyah's tone was clear, and Onyx knew she meant every word. His chest tightened as he tried to breathe through it. His phone buzzed, and he knew it was Kiss, but he couldn't answer right now. He feared she would sense his guilt over the phone and leave him before he even made it home. So, instead, he let it ring.

"Yeah, I figured you would want to keep it," Onyx finally uttered.

"You damn right I want to keep my baby. Children are a blessing, and we just got blessed."

"Blessing? Kids with my girl is a blessin'. This shit right here, this is about to ruin my entire life. Ain't no blessin' in this for me."

"You knew you had a girl when you was fuckin' me raw. So, I don't want to hear that shit."

Onyx nodded his head, knowing that her words were true. He knew what happened when you had sex raw, and he'd done it anyway. Now, he would have to suffer the consequences. He sat there for a long time, thinking about his son. He knew that one day, he would have to sit him down and tell him how he was the one that ruined their family. Just the thought of that made a tear come to his eye. He loved his family more than anything in this world, but he knew that his actions as of late had not reflected that.

For the first time in a long time, Onyx was scared. His phone buzzed again, and he saw that it was Kiss. Instead of answering, he turned it off, knowing that he couldn't face her. There was no way he could tell her about Aaliyah, and he knew that if he went home right now, he would have to tell her. So, with that, he stayed at Aaliyah's house.

Chapter Twenty-Four

The house was dark when Onyx pulled into the driveway, headlights shining into the living room window before he killed the engine. For a long moment, he just sat there, hands gripping the steering wheel, his pulse thrumming against his neck. He could see the soft glow of a lamp through the upstairs window, and he knew Kiss was still awake, probably waiting for him to return home.

He shut his eyes, a low curse sliding past his teeth. He'd told her he'd be back in time to take OJ to his appointment, and now it was hours later. Another promise broken, another lie folded into the stack of things he kept hidden from her. He sat there with the car off until the cold started to creep through his jacket, then he finally forced himself out of the car. Every step toward the door felt heavier than the last. The key slid into the lock too loud, the hinges squeaking like they were telling on him.

The house smelled faintly of lavender, and he knew that Kiss had been cleaning – something she always did when she was angry. He paused at the bottom of the stairs, his throat tight. Onyx took a deep breath before walking up. The bedroom door was cracked open. Inside, Kiss was propped against the pillows, her hair tied up, eyes trained on the doorway. She didn't say a word at first, just watched as Onyx stepped inside.

"You missed it," she spoke, her voice low and tight.

Onyx swallowed. "I know, and I'm sorry."

"You promised, Onyx." Her arms were crossed, her body turned slightly away, but her eyes burned into him. "You swore you'd be there. You promised me before you left this morning that you would be back in time."

"I got caught up." The lie came easy, as if he'd practiced it. His chest ached as soon as he said it.

Kiss laughed, short and humorless. "You always get caught up. Always something more important than us." She shook her head, pulling the blanket tighter around herself. "Your son had a doctor's appointment today, and you wasn't even there."

Onyx sat on the edge of the bed, his hands on his knees. He couldn't look at her, not with the image of those two pink lines still burned into his memory. His stomach twisted. "I'm sorry, baby."

"Sorry don't fix it." Her voice cracked, softer now, and that hurt worse than the anger. He could take her yelling, but disappointment? That gutted him.

He wanted to tell her the truth. The words itched at his tongue, begging to spill out. But he couldn't. The second he spoke the words, he knew that he'd lose her and OJ. They were the only things that mattered in his life, and he couldn't let them go. So, he stayed quiet, staring at the floorboards, feeling like they were swallowing him whole.

Kiss turned away, her back to him now. "Omari took us," she said after a long silence. "He didn't even hesitate. Came as soon as I called."

Those words cut deeper than any curse she could've thrown. His own brother stepped into the space Onyx had left empty. He could picture it clearly – Omari buckling OJ into his booster seat and driving them to the doctor's office with a smile on his face. *This nigga probably been waiting on this, waiting on me to fuck up so that he could step in. This what we ain't gon' do*, Onyx thought.

A wave of jealousy and shame crashed over him. He

clenched his fists, nails biting into his palms. He wanted to rage, to tell her she shouldn't have called Omari. But he knew she'd been left with no choice. He'd left her with no choice.

"I'll make it right," he muttered, his voice thick.

Kiss gave no response, just shifted farther toward the wall, leaving him staring at her back. Onyx leaned forward, elbows on his knees, dragging both hands down his face. The guilt pressed on him from every side, and he felt as though he would drown in it. He was about to have two children by two different women that he would have to take care of. Two households that would need him equally. He'd have to hustle twice as hard now, keep the stacks coming in steady to make sure no one went without. He couldn't let Kiss suspect a thing if he wanted to keep her in his life.

He couldn't lose her or his son. So, he made the choice, right there in the dark, with Kiss' silence thick in the room. He would keep Aaliyah a secret. He'd take care of her and the baby on the side, keep money flowing their way, but he would never let it touch his life with Kiss. It was the only way he knew everyone would stay happy. The weight of having a double life settled heavy in his chest. He knew it wasn't right, but it was the only way he could keep both families.

He shifted onto the bed, lying down beside her. She stayed stiff, her back pressed against the wall, her body a barrier he couldn't cross. He stared at the ceiling, his jaw tight, his heart pounding like a drum in a war he didn't know how to win. The silence stretched, broken only by the hum of the heater. Onyx closed his eyes, but sleep felt a million miles away.

He thought of Kiss, of the future they'd dreamed about. The bigger house, the yard, and all the children they wanted to have together. Him asking her to marry him and the beautiful wedding they would have. Then, he thought about Aaliyah, the way she'd looked at him when she told him that she was keeping the baby.

He knew he was trapped, and there was nothing he could do about it.

The only way forward was to carry it. To hustle harder than he'd ever hustled in his life. He would need to be two men at once – a loving partner and father at home and the secret provider on the side. He knew this would probably eat him alive, but he saw no other way. Onyx stared at the ceiling long after Kiss' breathing had evened out. He knew she was sleeping, but sleep wouldn't come easy for him, not tonight and probably not ever again. His eyes stared into the darkness as if he were searching for the answer to why he'd been so stupid, but he came up with anything. He knew this was on him, and he would have to be the one to fix it.

Every time he blinked, he saw those pink lines, and his chest tightened. He turned his head toward Kiss, and her back was to him. He mouthed the words I'm sorry, and he wished he could say them out loud. He wished he could tell her exactly what he was sorry for, but he knew that he couldn't. Guilt chewed at him, sharp and relentless. He knew that Kiss deserved better. She deserved a man who kept his word, who showed up when it mattered, and who didn't bring babies home. He wanted to be that man, God knew he did, but he hadn't been, and now he didn't know if he would ever be.

He pressed the palms of his hands to his eyes, swallowing against the pressure in his throat. He thought of his own father, a ghost of a man who'd left Tamika to raise two boys on her own. How many times had he sworn he wouldn't be like that? That he wouldn't disappear on his children like his daddy did? He needed to be better than him; he had to be. But now, it was as if he was standing on the edge of becoming the very thing he hated. The only difference was that he wasn't planning to walk away, only hide one. Which was probably worse.

Taking care of them both would mean more nights out away from Kiss. More runs with Blue and more risks. He'd already been stacking heavy, but that wasn't going to cut it anymore. Kiss wanted a house with a yard and more space for OJ to grow. Aaliyah would need rent money, doctor visits, and baby clothes. And both of them would expect him to provide without question. The thought made his stomach knot tighter. He couldn't afford a single mistake, not with the cops, not with rivals, not with Blue, and sure as hell not with either of the women in his life.

He turned onto his side, studying the curve of Kiss' back under the blanket. He thought of the first time he kissed her when they were just kids – when their love was simple and clean. He thought of the night OJ was born, the way Kiss had clutched his hand, sweat and tears shining on her face, the relief in her eyes when she heard their son cry. She had given him everything – her trust, her heart, and a family. And he was ruining it all.

His throat ached. He wanted to reach for her, to press his face into her shoulder and promise he'd do better, that he'd be there next time. But his arms felt too heavy, weighed down by guilt. He stayed still, the distance between them feeling like they were miles apart. Kiss shifted slightly, pulling the comforter tighter around her. She was asleep, but even then, her body told him what her mouth hadn't – that she was tired of being let down.

By the time dawn began to bleed in through the curtains, Onyx still hadn't slept. His mind spun fast and frantic – like wheels on ice. He heard OJ's little feet running across the floor of his bedroom, and Onyx got out of bed, heading to his son's room. He stood in the doorway, watching him play with his toys. Onyx smiled, looking at the little boy that looked just like him.

"Hey, Daddy," OJ greeted, as he turned around to see Onyx watching him.

"Good morning, lil man. You hungry?"

"Yeah, can I have pancakes?"

"If that's what you want to eat, we can make that happen. You wanna help cook them?"

"Yeah, let's go. Is Mommy up?"

"Not yet. So, how about we surprise her with breakfast?"

OJ smiled, standing up from the floor and walking over to Onyx. "Come on, Daddy. Let's go make Mommy the best breakfast she's ever had."

They went down to the kitchen, and Onyx pulled out the pancake mix, and OJ chose chocolate chips to mix in. On the side, they made cheese eggs, hash browns, and turkey bacon. When it was done, Onyx plated it and let OJ pour apple juice into a glass before they took it up to Kiss. She smiled at OJ, thanking him for the breakfast. She looked at Onyx and rolled her eyes, still upset with him. He knew she was and probably would be for a moment. And that was fine with him. He would rather her be mad at him for that than the fact that he'd gotten another woman pregnant.

Omari laid in bed, thinking about Kiss. The time they spent together the day before had been on his mind all night. For those few short hours, he pretended that things were the way they should be and that Kiss and OJ were his and not his brother's. He knew it was wrong, but he didn't care. If Onyx had been with his family instead of running the streets, then yesterday wouldn't have had a chance to happen.

He got out of bed and walked into the bathroom to take a shower. Onyx had hooked him up with Blue, and although he didn't want to be in the streets, it was hard for him to find a job after being in prison for so long. Today was the day he found out exactly what he would be doing. When he got dressed, he walked into the kitchen to find Tamika cooking breakfast.

"Morning, Ma. What you in here cooking?" Omari asked.

"Just some eggs, bacon, and hash browns. You want some?"

"You already know I do."

"You up and dressed early. Where you on yo' way to?"

"I got a job interview," Omari replied, taking a seat at the table.

"Oh, that's good. Well, let's start yo' day off on a full stomach."

Tamika placed a plate of food in front of Omari before making her own plate. They sat at the table and ate before Omari left out, ready to meet Blue. When he pulled up to the two family flat on 12th Street, he parked and got out the car. The wind was cold as it hit his face, and he placed his hood over his head before jogging up the walkway and knocking on the door. Blue opened it, and Omari walked inside.

The living room was bare, with only a small, dark blue couch, a dark wood table, and a seventy-five-inch flat screen that was mounted on the wall. Blue told Omari to take a seat and then walked to the back before returning moments later, holding a silver briefcase. He set the case on the couch before lighting a cigar and sitting down himself.

"I usually start new niggas off with small jobs, but yo' brother vouched for you, so I'ma let you get some real money. But that's only if you tell me you ready for this type of job. He said you didn't want to move no weight, so this would be the next best thing."

"As long as it's not weight or bodyin' no niggas, then I'm down. I need some money, and a nigga like me can't get no job with my record."

Omari leaned back on the couch, eyes tracing the smoke curling up from Blue's cigar. He waited for Blue to tell him what the job actually was. His heart beat fast in his chest, knowing that he was somewhere that he shouldn't be.

Blue smirked and popped the latches on the briefcase. The lid opened with a click that seemed too loud in the quiet room. Inside, stacked neatly, were a handful of glossy photographs. Blue spread them across the coffee table like cards in a winning hand. Omari leaned forward. The images showed paintings with bold colors inside frames that looked like they cost more than a house. He didn't know the artists, but he didn't need to. The way Blue handled the photos told him everything.

"This is where the money is," Blue announced, tapping one of the pictures with a thick finger. "These ain't just pictures for somebody's living room. These are investments, assets. People pay more for these than they would for diamonds."

Omari studied the photo closest to him, a piece splashed with reds and blacks placed neatly inside a gold frame. It was chaotic but somehow balanced. He could already picture it hanging in a gallery somewhere, guarded by alarms and glass.

"What you want me to do with these?" Omari asked carefully.

Blue grinned, sharp and easy. "I want you to bring me these. Each photo has an address on the back where the painting is being held. Some are in the same place; others are in different places. It's ten paintings here, and there will be more coming by the day. For every painting you bring me, I'll pay you five grand."

"Five grand? Per painting?"

"That's right. The risk is yours to take. You gotta figure out how to get the painting back to me without getting caught, so you need to make sure you come up with a system."

Omari thought for a beat before placing the pictures back into the briefcase. "I can start tonight."

"You sure about that?" Blue asked, looking over at Omari skeptically.

"I'm sure."

With that, Blue nodded his head and took another puff of his cigar. Omari took the briefcase and stood to his feet. "I'll see you later tonight," he spoke, walking out the door and back to his car.

Chapter Twenty-Five

The wind from the Detroit winter was cold, and the snow had finally fallen. Kiss slid into her mother's car, tugging her coat tighter around her shoulders. Frost clung stubbornly to the edges of the windshield, even though she'd already scraped it twice before she got into the car. She blew into her cupped hands, as she waited for the car to warm up.

It was a week before Christmas, and the city wore the season like it always did. Strings of colored lights wrapped around tired lampposts, wreaths hung in shop windows, and inflatable Santas swayed in the wind on porches. For once, Sade had pressed the keys to her car into Kiss' palm without hesitation.

"Go on, baby, get your shopping done," she'd said, taking OJ by the hand. "I'll keep him for a few hours. You need to shop without little hands pulling everything off the shelves."

Kiss pulled out onto the street, the heater rattling. Music played low from the radio, a holiday playlist caught between carols and R&B classics. Mariah Carey's voice soared over the speakers, and Kiss found herself humming, her mind already spinning through the list of things she needed to buy. The first store she went in was packed, carts bumping into one another like traffic on the freeway. Parents wore the same tired but determined expressions, scanning shelves for toys that seemed to disappear the moment they were restocked.

Kiss grabbed a cart and wove her way through the aisles, her eyes catching on bright boxes stacked high. She paused in front of a row of action figures that she knew OJ loved. She picked up one of each, not wanting to leave any of them behind. At three years old, OJ loved his action figures, and Kiss knew it. She then moved on to the race car section. She grabbed a huge Hot Wheels track and dozens of cars for him to play with. Her phone buzzed in her pocket. She pulled it out, half-hoping it was Onyx. But it was just a message from Sade asking Kiss to bring her some cooking oil when she came back.

Kiss smiled faintly, slipping the phone back into her purse. She wished Onyx had been with her, carrying bags and helping pick out gifts, but he wasn't. Lately, he'd been gone more than home, and she told herself it was the hustle, that he was just stacking money for their future. She knew it was the holidays and more money was being spent than usual, but Kiss still wished he was home more.

Her next stop was a department store, warm and over-decorated with garland strung along every aisle. The smell of cinnamon-scented candles mixed with the smell of leather and new clothes. Kiss made her way through racks of toddler clothes, pausing at a red sweater with reindeer stitched across the chest. She held it up, imagining OJ in it for Christmas morning photos. Into the cart it went, followed by a pair of soft pajamas and a winter hat with a pom-pom on top.

She drifted toward the women's section, running her fingers along a rack of dresses. She didn't have anywhere to wear them, but for a moment, she let herself imagine slipping into something new and sleek, Onyx taking her out somewhere fancy, his hand steady at the small of her back. She sighed, shaking the image away. He hadn't taken her out in months. The streets always came first for him, and as hard as Kiss tried to understand he was doing it for their family, she couldn't help but want him home more.

She picked up two dresses that she liked because she didn't

know which one she wanted to wear to Christmas dinner. She walked to the men's section to see what she could pick up for Onyx. They really didn't have much that he would like, so she just grabbed a dark green hoodie and a few white tee shirts.

As she made her way toward the checkout, a glimmer caught her eye. The jewelry counter sparkled under bright lights, rings and chains glittering against velvet displays. Kiss slowed, her gaze snagging on a delicate gold bracelet, thin but strong, a single diamond catching the light. She traced the glass with her fingertip, imagining it on her wrist. When the woman came to the counter, Kiss pointed to the bracelet, letting her know that she wanted to try it on. The clerk smiled, pulling it out of the display case, and placed it around Kiss' wrist. She smiled, admiring the way it looked on her, before telling the clerk she would take it.

Happy about the gift she'd just purchased for herself, she made her way to the register. A woman stood two registers down with bone straight, dark hair that was parted down the middle. She wore a pair of light washed, fitted jeans, black boots, and a black bubble coat. Kiss had never seen the woman in her life and had no clue why she was staring at her so hard. At first, Kiss thought she was imagining it. She thought that maybe the woman was looking at someone behind her, so she tried not to pay attention. But the woman kept looking. Every move Kiss made, the woman's eyes followed her.

What the hell? Kiss thought, turning her nose up. Kiss lifted her chin slightly, meeting the woman's eyes head-on. She expected her to look away, embarrassed, but she didn't. She just kept watching, lips pressed into the faintest hint of a smile, like she knew something Kiss didn't. Unease prickled along Kiss' spine. She turned back to the cashier, swiping her card, trying to shake it off. Detroit was full of people with attitudes, people who stared just to start something, so maybe this was what it was. Kiss grabbed her shopping bags and made her way to the car.

The car was packed by the time Kiss finished going into every store on her list. Bags were stacked in the trunk, backseat, and the front. She was glad she was done because she had no room left to fit anything else. She sat there for a moment with her hand on the steering wheel, staring at the glitter of snowflakes drifting under the parking lot lights. She didn't know why, but for a moment, the face of the woman who'd been staring at her in the store flashed through her mind. Kiss couldn't help but think that the stare wasn't as innocent as she had thought.

The first sound Kiss heard on Christmas morning was OJ's feet hitting the floor with a thud, followed by the rapid patter of him sprinting down the hall. She blinked awake, groggy, and before she could even sit up, he was tugging at the blankets, his voice high with excitement.

"Mommy, Daddy! It's Christmas!"

The clock on the nightstand glowed 6:03 a.m. Kiss groaned, pulling the comforter tighter around her shoulders. She'd barely slept, staying up late to set gifts under the tree, wrapping until her fingers ached. But OJ's wide-eyed smile was impossible to resist.

Onyx stretched beside her, rubbing at his face. "Boy, it's still early." His voice was rough with sleep.

OJ bounced on his toes, his little pajamas patterned with candy canes. "Santa came! The presents are under the tree! Can we open them now please?"

Kiss chuckled softly, shaking her head, as she swung her legs out of bed. "Alright, alright. Let's go see what Santa brought."

OJ dashed ahead, his small feet thumping down the stairs, his laughter echoing through the house. Kiss and Onyx followed slower, the scent of pine growing stronger, as they neared the living room. The tree glowed against the window, strings of lights twinkling like stars, ornaments catching the glow in reds, golds, and greens. Beneath it, piles of wrapped gifts waited, ribbons curling around them.

OJ froze at the sight, his mouth dropping open. "Whoa…" His voice was barely more than a whisper.

Kiss' heart swelled, as she watched her son's reaction. "Go on, baby," she said gently. "They're all for you."

OJ didn't need to be told twice. He dropped to his knees, tearing into the first present. Shreds of wrapping paper flew across the rug, as he revealed a remote-control car. His squeal filled the room.

"Aww, cool!" He pressed the wheels, watching them spin.

Onyx grinned, sitting back on the couch. "That's all you right there, lil' man."

Kiss laughed, grabbing her phone to record. She wanted to capture every second – the way OJ's eyes sparkled, the way his small hands fought stubborn tape, and the joy in his eyes each time he opened a gift. Each present brought a new round of squeals. A stack of building blocks tumbled out of bright paper, and OJ immediately began piecing them together into a wobbly tower. A firetruck with flashing lights made him clap his hands. A soft teddy bear earned a hug before being tossed aside for the next gift.

"Thank you, Mommy! Thank you, Daddy!" His voice rose between each new surprise, genuine gratitude mixing with excitement.

Kiss' eyes blurred with tears she didn't bother hiding. She glanced at Onyx, who sat watching their son with a small smile. For a fleeting second, Kiss wished time could freeze, that life could always feel this simple. Holiday cheer filled the house, as they sat next to each other, both watching their son. OJ's biggest gift leaned against the wall, wrapped in silver paper with a giant red bow. When he finally tore it open, his jaw dropped. A shiny red bicycle, complete with training wheels, was underneath.

"My bike!" he shouted, rushing to it, his little hands gripping the handlebars. "It's mine!"

Kiss laughed, clapping her hands. "You better not ride it in the house."

He giggled, climbing onto the seat anyway, his legs too short to pedal properly.

Onyx stood, steadying the bike. "We'll take it outside once the snow melts and teach you how to ride."

OJ beamed up at him. "Okay, Daddy!"

The living room was chaotic now – paper crumpled into mountains, empty boxes stacked in corners, and toys scattered across the rug. The smell of pine needles mixed with the cinnamon candles Kiss had lit the night before filled the room. A Christmas cartoon played softly on the TV, but OJ's laughter was louder than anything else. Kiss sat back on the couch, soaking it all in. Her son was happy, the house was warm, and the tree sparkled.

When OJ finally slowed down, distracted by assembling blocks, Kiss nudged Onyx. "Your turn."

He raised an eyebrow. "My turn?"

She grinned, pulling a wrapped box from under the tree and setting it in his lap. "Merry Christmas."

Onyx peeled the paper slowly, a smirk tugging at his lips. Inside was a sleek watch, silver with a black face. He held it up, the light catching on the metal.

"Damn, Kiss," he murmured. "This is nice."

"You're always running around, never on time," she teased lightly. "Now you don't have an excuse."

He chuckled, sliding it onto his wrist. "Fits perfect. Thank you."

Then, he reached under the tree, retrieving a small velvet box. He handed it to her without a word.

Kiss' heart flickered. She opened it slowly, breath catching when she saw the delicate gold necklace nestled inside, a tiny diamond heart gleaming at the center.

"Oh, Onyx, it's beautiful." Her fingers trembled as she lifted it.

"Put it on," he whispered.

She turned, sweeping her hair aside, as he fastened it around her neck. The metal was cool against her skin, but it warmed quickly, settling just above her heart.

Kiss touched it gently, her throat tight. "I love it, and I love you."

"I love you too," Onyx replied before kissing Kiss softly on her lips.

The sky was already dark when Kiss, Onyx, and OJ pulled up in front of Tamika's house. Christmas lights framed the porch in blinking red and green, the bulbs old but glowing strong. Kiss could smell the cooked food as she walked up to the door, and she smiled.

"Yayyyy, we at Grandma's house. I wonder if Santa brought gifts here for me too?" OJ asked, looking up at Kiss.

Onyx chuckled. "Yeah, boy, Santa came here too."

Inside, the warmth wrapped around them instantly. Tamika swept OJ into her arms the second they crossed the threshold. "There's my big man!" she crooned, peppering his cheeks with kisses. OJ giggled, squirming but smiling wide.

The living room was cozy, cluttered with holiday decorations – a small artificial tree glittering in the corner with gifts underneath and stockings pinned unevenly on the wall. The table was already set in the dining room, platters covering every inch of space. Kiss' eyes roamed over the spread, as they all sat down. There was macaroni and cheese with a golden crust, collard greens seasoned to perfection, a honey glazed ham shining under the light, fried chicken piled high, candied yams, dressing, and cornbread muffins stacked in a basket. A dessert table was off to the left, filled with cakes, pies, and peach cobbler. Omari walked in, and Tamika asked him to bless the food before they sat down to eat.

"You better slow down, lil' man," Onyx teased, passing OJ a napkin. He was putting forkfuls of macaroni and cheese into his mouth like it was going out of style.

Kiss smiled, watching her son's joy. He'd spent the morning surrounded by toys and wrapping paper, and now, he was just as thrilled to be stuffing his belly.

Tamika looked around the table, her eyes lingering on her sons. "This is what I love," she spoke, lifting her glass. "Having all of us together."

Omari nodded, leaning back in his chair. He looked different, much happier than he had in months, and everyone seemed to notice. Midway through the meal, Omari set his fork down and cleared his throat. The chatter eased, as everyone turned toward him.

"I got some news," he spoke, his voice steady. "I signed the lease on a townhouse yesterday."

A beat of silence filled the room, then Tamika clapped her hands together, her face splitting into a grin. "That's my baby! A whole townhouse? Look at you! That new job must really be paying you good."

Onyx raised an eyebrow but nodded, a hint of pride in his eyes. "That's big, bro. Congratulations."

Kiss smiled, genuine warmth blooming in her chest. "Congratulations, Omari. That's huge."

OJ, not fully understanding but catching the excitement, clapped his little hands too. "Uncle O got a new house!"

Omari chuckled, rubbing the back of his neck. "Yeah, something like that. It's nice though. It's a lot of space, and it has a little yard. I been working for it, and it feels good to finally have my own spot." He paused, eyes sweeping the table. "So, I want y'all to come over for New Year's Eve. Break it in right with me."

Tamika's eyes shone with pride. "You hear that? My son wants us to celebrate the new year in his new place."

Kiss caught the flicker of determination in Omari's eyes as he spoke. He wasn't just inviting them to a party; he was showing them that he'd built something, that he was moving forward, and she admired that. He was turning his life around, and Kiss was more than happy for him. If anyone deserved to be happy, it was Omari. Kiss sat back, smiling, as she admired Omari's growth since his return home.

After dinner, they all went into the living room so that OJ could open the gifts that Tamika and Omari had gotten him. They all sat on the couch with OJ in the middle of the floor, screaming each time he unwrapped a gift. When he was done, Kiss helped Tamika with the dishes. By the end of the night, OJ was on the couch, sleep, with his toys around him. Onyx picked him up, and they said their goodbyes before walking to the car, ready to head home.

Chapter Twenty-Six

Kiss stepped out the shower, steam curling around her, as she walked to the sink and brushed her teeth. It was New Year's Eve, and they were all getting dressed to go to Omari's new place. OJ was already dressed and sitting in the living room, watching TV. She walked into her bedroom and stood in front of her vanity mirror. R&B played through the speaker on her nightstand, and she sang along.

She slipped into a form-fitting, black, sequined dress that shimmered every time she moved, the hem stopping just above her knees. The neckline dipped low but tastefully, showing off the gold heart necklace Onyx had given her for Christmas. Her hair was styled into loose, glossy waves that brushed her shoulders, and her nails gleamed a rich wine-red. On her feet, she strapped on strappy, black heels that went well with her dress.

She grabbed the perfume she'd planned to wear tonight, Valentino Donna Born in Roma, and sprayed it on her pulse points before spraying some onto her dress. She looked at herself once more in the mirror, smiling at how beautiful she looked. The bedroom door opened, and Onyx stepped in, already dressed. Kiss' eyes traveled over him automatically. He wore a crisp, white, button-up shirt, tailored close to his frame, the top two buttons undone to reveal the glint of a thin gold chain resting against his chest. Over it, he'd thrown on a black designer blazer, paired with dark slim cut jeans, and fresh, white Air Force Ones. On his wrist was the watch that Kiss had given him for Christmas.

"Oh, you look good." Kiss smiled.

"Nah, baby. You look good. Like, good as hell. You got me wanting to skip the party altogether and take that dress off you right now."

"Boy, stop playing. We going to this party. But you can take the dress off me when we get back."

"Then let's get the fuck outta here, so we can get back."

Kiss laughed and grabbed her purse and fur coat, ready to go. OJ was sitting on the couch in a pair of black jeans and a tan Gucci sweater. Kiss smiled at how handsome her son looked. She put on his coat, and they all made their way to the car. Onyx put Omari's address into the GPS, and they pulled off.

They pulled up to Omari's brand-new townhouse about twenty minutes later. Tamika's car was already parked in the driveway beside Omari's, and Onyx pulled in right behind them. The brick exterior was clean, lights glowing warmly through the windows. A small porch with fresh paint and two black iron railings framed the front steps. From the car, Kiss could see a string of white lights in the front windows, subtle but festive.

Inside, the living room opened wide, freshly painted walls in a soft cream shade, hardwood floors that were polished smooth. A cream-colored sectional sofa sat against one wall, sleek and modern, with accent pillows in navy and gray. A glass coffee table gleamed under a chandelier that threw warm light across the room. Omari had set a few framed photos on a console table near the entry, pictures of him with Tamika, one with Onyx from years ago, and even one of OJ sitting on his shoulders at the park. The dining area opened into the kitchen where platters of food covered every inch of counter space.

Omari hadn't cooked; he'd gone big and had the night

catered. Silver chafing dishes lined the counter, lids pulled back to reveal barbecue ribs, fried chicken, macaroni and cheese, collard greens, Cajun shrimp pasta, cornbread muffins, and potato salad. On another table sat red velvet cupcakes, banana pudding cups, and peach cobbler. Omari didn't miss a beat and had everything set up so nicely. From the living room speaker, a playlist of 90's and early 2000's R&B filled the air. Kiss sang along to Mary J. Blige as she admired the home.

Tamika wore a deep burgundy sweater dress and gold hoop earrings, her laughter warm, as she helped Omari set up. She hugged Kiss and scooped OJ into her arms like always, planting kisses across his cheeks until he squirmed.

"Grandma, you gonna get lipstick all over my face." OJ laughed. But Tamika didn't care as she continued to kiss his cheeks and forehead.

Omari stood by the counter, dressed in a fresh black turtleneck, dark jeans, and crisp sneakers. He greeted Kiss and Onyx, welcoming them to his home.

"This shit is nice as hell, bro," Onyx complimented.

"Thank you. After dinner, I'll give y'all a tour."

When everyone sat down with plates piled high, conversation buzzed. At one point, Omari cleared his throat, tapping his glass with a fork.

"I just wanna say something real quick," he said, his voice carrying over the music. "This is just the start for me. I wanted y'all to be the first to see it, the first to celebrate with me. I got this place, and I want it to be a home for family. So, New Year's Eve? We bringing it in right – together."

The three of them clapped with OJ joining in. Tamika beamed, pride written all over her face. Kiss smiled too, warmth blooming in her chest. OJ clapped his little hands, not fully understanding but caught up in the excitement. After dinner, Omari showed Onyx the rest of the house, while Kiss sat on the couch, talking to Tamika over a glass of champagne. OJ was sitting on the far end of the sectional, playing with his toys, half asleep. The night was perfect, and Kiss couldn't help but smile at the way things had turned out. When Omari returned downstairs without Onyx, Kiss looked at him, confused.

"He upstairs in my room on the phone," Omari replied, already knowing what Kiss' look meant.

"Well, I'm about to go get him because it's almost midnight, and he can't miss the ball drop. Plus, we gotta kiss exactly at midnight."

Omari told Kiss where his room was, and she walked up the steps. Halfway down the hall, she could hear Onyx speaking in a low whisper but couldn't tell what he was saying. It wasn't until she got to the door that she heard him, and her heart sank.

"I know, baby, and I'm really gon' try. But it's gon' be after midnight. I told you my brother was having a dinner at his house, and I'm here with my family. Once I drop them off at home, I will come over."

Tears filled Kiss' eyes, as she listened to the conversation. Never in a million years would she have thought Onyx would ever cheat on her. They had been together since they were kids, and she thought they were happy. She rushed down the hall, not wanting to hear another word. She walked back down to the living room with a smile on her face as if nothing had happened. She poured herself another glass of champagne and took her seat on the couch.

Onyx appeared a few moments later, just in time to watch the ball drop. The moment the ball dropped, he turned to Kiss, kissing her on her lips. She kissed him back, but it was half-hearted, and Onyx noticed.

"You good?" he whispered.

"Yeah, I'm just tired."

"If you ready to go, we can leave. I gotta make a run anyway. Blue called me with some work," he lied.

Kiss knew he was lying, but she didn't push. Instead, she just nodded. Onyx told Omari and Tamika they were leaving, and they said their goodbyes. When they got home, Kiss took OJ to his room and tucked him in bed before getting in the shower. By the time she got out, Onyx was already gone.

Chapter Twenty-Seven

The water was hot, steam curling up around her face, carrying the faint scent of lavender from the bubbles that clung to her skin. Kiss sank deeper into the tub, the water hugging her body, but even its warmth couldn't loosen the knot in her chest. It had been months since she found out Onyx was cheating on her, and she still hadn't told him she knew. Every day when he left the house, Kiss wondered if he was going to see his other woman, whoever she was. Her mind kept circling back to the same thought, like a song stuck on repeat. *Onyx wanted someone else.*

She didn't know when the shift had happened, couldn't pinpoint the exact moment things went wrong. But ever since New Year's Eve, she'd noticed his phone buzzing at all hours of the night. Or the way he would tilt his phone away from her when he went through it. The excuses he gave for the early mornings or late nights were now just that, excuses. After all the years they'd been together, Kiss had never cheated on him, and she didn't think he had either – until now.

A tear slid down her cheek, vanishing into the foam. She swiped at her face quickly, frustration burning hotter than sadness. She was tired of doubting, tired of waiting in silence, while her gut screamed the truth she didn't want to face. Kiss sat up, letting the bubbles drip down her arms. She needed to get out the house and away from her thoughts. She reached for her phone, dialing her mother.

Sade picked up after two rings. "Hey, baby, what's up?"

Kiss bit her lip, forcing her voice steady. "Ma, can I use your car for a little while? I'll fill your tank."

There was a pause on the other end, long enough to make her stomach twist. Finally, Sade's voice came back, firm but soft. "You can. But only if you let OJ stay with me. I'll watch him while you're out."

Kiss nodded, even though her mother couldn't see her, relief curving in her chest. "Okay, Ma. Thank you."

When the call ended, Kiss drained the tub before rinsing off and stepping out. Wrapping a towel around her wet body, she stood in front of the mirror, water droplets tracing down her skin, her reflection staring back at her with tired eyes.

"You're stronger than this," she whispered to herself. "This shit can't break you."

She moved quickly, slipping into jeans and a fitted sweater, pulling her hair into a neat ponytail. She walked to OJ's room and took an outfit from his closet for him to wear.

"Where we going, Mommy?"

"To Grandma's," she replied with a smile. "You get to spend some time with her today."

He grinned, jumping up to help gather his toys into a small backpack. Kiss dressed him in a warm hoodie and jeans, wrapping his scarf around his neck before zipping up his coat. He leaned into her touch, and for a moment, her heart softened. Everything she did was for him. For his happiness. She couldn't let him grow up watching her drown in silence, watching her accept less than she deserved. She needed for him to know that his mama was a strong woman that didn't take shit from nobody. Not even his daddy.

With OJ ready, Kiss slung her purse over her shoulder just as Sade was pulling into her driveway. The house felt heavier than usual as she locked the door behind them, as if the walls themselves were trying to hold her back. The March air was crisp as they stepped outside. Although the sun was out, it was still cold as they rushed to the car.

"Grandma!" OJ squealed the moment he jumped into the car.

"Hey, Grandma big man, you ready to spend the day with me?"

"You know it. I brought some toys for us to play with. And do you have popcorn, so we can watch some movies?"

"Sure do and ice cream. And we can watch whatever movie you want."

"Yayyyy." OJ beamed.

"Thanks again, Ma. I really need this," Kiss voiced as she sat in the passenger's seat.

"You're welcome, but you need to get you a car, baby girl. Tell Onyx that y'all need two cars. You shouldn't have to be stuck in the house, while he's out running the streets or whatever he calls it."

"He's working, Ma."

"Right, working. If he works that much, he can afford to get a car for you to drive."

Kiss nodded her head, knowing what her mother was saying was true. However, she had too much on her mind to get into a conversation like this with her mother. So, she just nodded her head. When they pulled up to Sade's house, Kiss kissed OJ on the cheek before she watched them walk inside.

About fifteen minutes later, Kiss pulled up at a salon downtown. She walked inside, hoping someone would have room for her in their chair. She walked up to the desk and let the receptionist know that she wanted a silk press and a full set with a pedicure. The receptionist, a dark-skinned woman with hazel eyes and long hair, told Kiss to sign in then offered her a bottled water before telling her to take a seat.

About five minutes later, she was sitting in the chair, getting her hair washed. She closed her eyes, enjoying the feeling of the woman washing her scalp clean. Once she was washed and dried, the stylist pressed her hair out, parting it down the middle. Kiss smiled as she looked at herself in the mirror, feeling better already. Once her hair was done, she went and sat at the nail tech's booth. Her nails were a long coffin shape with white tips and gold and tan hand painted art. For her toes, she kept them a plain white. Kiss paid then walked out the salon, feeling twenty pounds lighter.

She called Sade when she left the salon, and Sade told her that she was having too much fun with OJ for Kiss to pick him up now. She told Kiss that he could spend the night and to just bring the car back in the morning. On the way home, she pulled into Walmart, deciding she wasn't ready to face the emptiness of the house just yet. She wandered the aisles slowly, cart rattling under her hands, letting herself choose without rushing.

She picked up a pair of pink satin pajamas with the words *sleep all day* written in white. She added fluffy socks and a cozy throw blanket she spotted on clearance. Then, she wheeled into the wine aisle, scanning labels, until she grabbed her favorite Moscato. In the snack aisle, she loaded the cart with salty chips, buttery popcorn, chocolate-covered pretzels, and OJ's favorite fruit snacks, already picturing his smile when she gave them to him tomorrow.

Kiss drove back home, bags secure in the passenger seat. She planned to take a shower and cuddle up in her new pajamas with her wine and snacks and watch a movie. The house would be quiet with OJ gone for the night, and Kiss planned to enjoy her alone time. She had turned down her block, rapping along to Cardi B, when she noticed the car parked in her driveway. Kiss slowed, frowning. She knew it wasn't Onyx's car and wondered whose car it was. She pulled in next to it, the tires crunching over the gravel. Her hands stayed gripping the wheel, her eyes locked on the other car. For a moment, neither door opened.

Finally, the driver's side door cracked open, and a woman stepped out. Kiss' breath caught in her throat. The woman looked to be about her age. She was bundled up in a thick coat until she unzipped it and exposed the curve of a pregnant belly. She looked to be about six months along, and Kiss was confused about why she was in her driveway. For a moment, they just stared at each other.

Kiss forced her door open, the weight of it heavier than it had ever been. Her heels clicked against the driveway, each step echoing. "Can I help you?" she asked, her tone clipped, sharper than she meant it to be.

The woman straightened her shoulders. "You Kiss, right?"

Something in her voice made Kiss' stomach twist. It wasn't a question. It was more like confirmation.

"Yeah," Kiss said cautiously. "And you are?"

The woman's lips curved into the faintest smile – not friendly, not mocking, just… knowing. "Aaliyah," she replied.

The name meant nothing to Kiss at first. She'd never heard anyone talk about a woman named Aaliyah. But the way she rubbed her stomach caught Kiss' attention.

Kiss' throat went dry. "Okay, Aaliyah, why are you in my driveway?"

Aaliyah's hand stroked her stomach absentmindedly. "We need to talk about Onyx."

The name landed like a blade. Kiss froze, the grocery bags forgotten in the car, her heartbeat thundering in her ears. She had imagined this moment in nightmares, in the quiet hours when suspicion crawled up her spine. But seeing it, seeing the woman standing here in her own driveway, staring at the proof wrapped in a stranger's body, was worse than anything she'd dreamed.

"You got the wrong house," Kiss said automatically, her voice brittle. "The wrong man."

Aaliyah shook her head slowly, pity softening her eyes. "But I don't, and you know it."

Silence stretched between them, thick and merciless. Kiss wanted to scream, to lunge at the woman for having the nerve to step to her at her house. She wanted to deny it and tell the woman that her man ain't have shit to do with her, but Kiss knew he did. So, instead, she folded her arms across her chest, tapping her foot, as she waited her Aaliyah to speak.

She thought of the late nights, the excuses, the way Onyx's phone lit up in the dark and he turned it face down. She thought of New Year's Eve and the conversation she'd overheard him having in Omari's room. Now here the woman was, standing right in front of her, and she was pregnant.

Kiss' laugh broke out, sharp and humorless. "You really came here? To my house? With this bullshit?" She gestured at Aaliyah's belly, her hand trembling. "Why the fuck are you here?"

Aaliyah didn't flinch. "You deserve to know. I don't know what he's been telling you, but…" She trailed off, her palm pressing firmer against her stomach. "This is his child."

The words hollowed Kiss' chest. She couldn't breathe. Couldn't think. The world narrowed to the woman in front of her, the swell of her belly, and the echo of her words ringing in her ears. For a split second, she wanted to break down and cry, but she wouldn't give Aaliyah the satisfaction of seeing her sweat.

"Look, bitch, I'm sure you don't know proper side bitch etiquette because you showed up at my fuckin' house, so let me give you some free game." Kiss stepped closer, eyes burning into Aaliyah. "You ain't supposed to step to wifey, ho. You are a secret, and you should have stayed that way. Now, after this, I can guarantee that you won't see him no more. I hope you saved up the money he been givin' you because after this, yo' ass ain't getting another dime."

Aaliyah's expression didn't change. "I didn't come to fight. I came so you know the truth. He can play both sides all he wants, but the baby won't let him hide forever."

Kiss' jaw clenched so tight it hurt. She wanted to scream and cry, and she knew that once Aaliyah left, she would. However, for right now, she had to keep her shit together.

"Bitch, you shouldn't have come here. And if you wasn't pregnant, I would be beating the shit out of you for even thinking you could come to my house and tell me anything about my man. You wanted to tell me Onyx got you pregnant? You said it. Now get the fuck out my driveway!"

"I'll go for now. But I have his baby, so I'm gon' always be around."

"Not after I tell Onyx to drop yo' bitch ass. He will be there for that baby, if it's even his, but you, bitch, you're done."

Kiss watched as Aaliyah nodded her head once before getting back into her car and pulling out the driveway. Kiss didn't remember deciding to drive. One minute, she was standing in her driveway, the cold air burning her cheeks. The next, she was gripping the steering wheel, headlights cutting through empty winter streets. Tears blurred her vision, streaking down her cheeks faster than she could wipe them away. The city lights smeared into hazy streaks of gold and white. She wasn't thinking about where she was going, just that she couldn't stay still. Couldn't go back into the house that smelled like Onyx's cologne and still held his lies in its walls.

By the time her thoughts caught up to her, she was parked in front of Omari's townhouse. Her chest tightened. She hadn't meant to come there, but she had. She got out the car and walked up to the door slowly, as if she knew she was walking into forbidden territory. Her knock was shaky but urgent. A beat later, the door opened, and Omari stood there in sweats and a fitted tee, confusion flashing across his face.

"Kiss?" he asked, his voice low. Then, his eyes dropped to

her tear-streaked face. His expression softened instantly. "What's wrong?"

The sight of him, the familiar lines of his face, the warmth in his gaze, all undid her. The words spilled out, broken and raw. "It's Onyx. He…" Her throat closed, the tears choking her. She pressed her hands to her face. "He got another woman pregnant."

Omari froze. For a moment, he didn't move. Then, he reached for her, pulling her inside, the door shutting softly behind them. His arms wrapped around her, holding her close. She pressed her face into his chest, the scent of him filling her nose. He didn't speak at first, just held her while she cried, his hand moving gently up and down her back.

"I'm so stupid," she whispered into his shirt. "I knew something was wrong. I just didn't want to believe it."

"You're not stupid," Omari murmured, his voice rough. "He's the one who messed up. Not you."

The words sank into her like seasoning, and for the first time all night, she let herself breathe. When she finally looked up, her eyes red and swollen, Omari was already watching her. His gaze was soft, but beneath it burned something else. Her heart pounded. The years between them melted away, and for a moment, she saw him not as the man standing in his townhouse but as the boy in her living room, asking her to be his girl. Without thinking, she leaned up and kissed him.

It started soft, her lips brushing his, tasting of salt from her tears. Omari hesitated only a moment before responding, his hand sliding to cradle her cheek. The kiss deepened, heat sparking between them, pulling at everything they'd buried. Kiss gasped against his mouth, her body pressed against his, the ache of betrayal blurring into the comfort of something familiar and forbidden.

Omari broke the kiss just long enough to whisper, "Kiss, you sure?"

Her answer was immediate. "I need you."

He picked her up, her legs wrapping around his waist, as he carried her up to his room, their lips still locked on one another's. He laid her on the bed gently before pulling off her pants and panties at the same time. She spread her legs, and Omari put his face between them. The first lick sent a moan from her lips. His tongue flickered, and she wrapped her legs around his shoulders.

Omari had dreamed about this moment every night when he was behind the wall, and the time had finally come. Her moans were like music to his ears, as he licked and sucked her softly. He felt her body trembling, and he knew she was close to cumming. She placed one hand on the back of his head, pushing him deeper into her. His tongue flickered once more, and she squirted into his mouth with him licking up every drop.

Kiss pulled him on top of her, her legs wrapping around him. Omari positioned himself at her opening before pushing his hardness inside of her. He groaned as he entered her, her tight wetness clenching down around him. He moaned her name as she moaned his. In that moment, he wasn't fucking his brother's girlfriend. He was making love to the love of his life. Everything else disappeared, and nothing mattered but the two of them. He'd told her that if they were meant to be, they would be, and deep down, Omari thought this was that moment. They made love for hours, neither of them wanting to let the other go.

When it was over, they both lay there in silence, tangled up in both the sheets and each other's arms. Kiss traced her fingertips over his chest, as she listened to his heartbeat. Then, as if the world dropped on her head, she sat up and looked at him.

"Oh, my God, Omari. What did we just do?"

"We did what we both wanted to do."

"Omari, you're his brother. I can't... Oh, my God. This is so fucked up. We have a son together, and I just fucked his brother."

Omari grabbed Kiss' hands, placing them into his. His eyes

met hers because he wanted her to know that he was serious. "He don't deserve you. You came here crying because he got another woman pregnant. I would never do that shit to you. Let me love you, Kiss, the way you deserve to be loved."

Chapter Twenty-Eight

iss woke up the next morning, wrapped in Omari's arms. Each time she'd tried to leave the night before, he'd stopped her, telling her how badly he wanted her to stay. She'd thought she'd feel much worse about the fact that she'd just slept with Onyx's brother, but the more she thought about Aaliyah's pregnant belly, the less guilt she felt. She looked over at the clock on Omari's nightstand and saw that it was a little after nine in the morning. She tried to sit up, but Omari pulled her closer.

"Where you going?" he asked, eyes still closed.

"I gotta go home, Omari. I gotta get OJ from my mama, and I've been gone all night. I'm sure Onyx is wondering where I am."

The very mention of Onyx's name made Omari scoff. He opened his eyes, raising his head from the pillow. "What you rushing back for? That nigga don't be rushing home to you, clearly, if he got a bitch coming to y'all house to tell you she pregnant by him." The words came out harsher than Omari meant them to, but it was the truth, nonetheless.

Kiss recoiled, pulling away from him and sliding out of bed. "Why would you say something like that?"

"I'm sorry, Kiss. I didn't mean for it to come out like that. I just don't want you to leave."

She didn't look at him as she pulled away and stood to her feet. "I can't stay here."

"Yes, you can." His voice carried quiet insistence. He sat all the way up now, the sheet slipping down to his waist. "Go get OJ from Sade and bring him here. We can spend the day here. We can cook or order in and maybe watch some movies together. It'll be fun."

The softness in his tone almost undid her. For a moment, she wanted to imagine it – herself, Omari, and OJ curled up on the couch, the townhouse filled with laughter, the smell of food in the air. It would be fun, but it would also be a lie, and she couldn't put her son in the middle of that.

She turned, meeting his gaze with glassy eyes. "I can't do that."

Omari frowned, confusion clouding his face. "Why not? You think I wouldn't take care of y'all? You think I don't want this?"

Kiss' chest ached. "That's not the point, Omari."

"Then what is?" His voice sharpened, frustration seeping in. "Because to me, the point is simple. You don't deserve what Onyx did to you. I'd never do no shit like that. I would love, honor, and cherish our family. I've loved you since I was thirteen years old. Everything I did in life was for you. Just let me show you, Kiss."

"Stop." She cut him off, her voice trembling. "Don't say that like it's easy. Don't act like one night erases everything that's happened over the years. Last night was amazing, but that doesn't change the fact that I'm with Onyx and that OJ is his."

Silence stretched between them, heavy with all the years of what-ifs. Kiss hugged herself, pacing slowly by the window. "Last night, I needed you. I won't lie about that. But this morning? I can't pretend we're something we're not. I can't wake up and play family with you just because Onyx betrayed me," she continued.

Omari stood, pulling on sweatpants, his face unreadable.

"This ain't just some rebound. We been meant to be since the day we met. You and Onyx on the other hand, y'all just happened."

Her throat tightened. "I'm the mother of his child, Omari. I'm his girl, and he's your brother. Your twin brother. We can't just do this to him."

Omari recoiled. He raked a hand down his face, exhaling hard. "You mean the same way y'all did it to me? It was fine when I was on the other end of the heartbreak, huh? It was cool when y'all made an entire life together, while I was locked away for trying to save you? Onyx gave me the gun that night, and I used it to protect you. Never said a word, just took that charge. Yet somehow, the two people I thought had my back were the ones holding the knife that stabbed me in it. But I guess that's fine as long as Onyx don't get hurt. Tell me something. Does Onyx know you his girl and the mother of his child? Because if you ask me, he not moving like it."

Kiss pressed her palms to the window, cold seeping through on her skin. "That's not fair, Omari, because that's not what I'm saying. I never meant to hurt you at all. And I had no idea where you got the gun from until now. You want me to go get my son, your nephew, and what? Pretend like we some big, happy family? I'm not doing that. That would confuse him. And you shouldn't want that either. I'm already drownin' in Onyx's lies. I can't drown in yours too."

His jaw clenched, his chest rising and falling with the force of words he didn't say. Finally, he crossed the room, his hand reaching for hers. "Kiss," his tone softened, "last night wasn't a mistake. Don't try to bury it like it was."

Tears burned her eyes again. "I'm not saying it was a mistake. I'm saying it can't be our beginning."

For a long moment, they just stood there, his hand wrapped around hers, both unwilling to let go. The air between them was thick with everything they wanted but couldn't claim.

Finally, she pulled free, gathering her purse. "I have to go home."

Omari's lips pressed into a thin line. He looked at her as if memorizing her, his eyes dark. "Then go. But don't forget what happened here."

Her chest clenched at the finality in his voice. She nodded once, her heart splintering, before walking to the door. The cold air outside slapped her cheeks, but it didn't numb the ache inside. She climbed into the car, gripping the steering wheel, staring at her reflection in the rearview mirror. Her eyes were swollen, her lips still bruised from Omari's kisses, her body humming with the memory of him. But the truth echoed louder. She wasn't ready to rewrite her life in one night. She wasn't ready to pretend she could erase Onyx, no matter how much he'd hurt her. She started the engine, the sound filling the silence, and pulled out of Omari's driveway.

The road stretched ahead, and with it, the weight of choices she didn't know how to make. She went to pick up OJ, and Sade drove them home. Onyx's car was in the driveway when they pulled up. She and OJ stepped out the car, and Onyx opened the door for them, as they walked up. Kiss' heart pounded in her chest because she knew Onyx had been waiting on them. She'd checked her phone in the car and saw several missed calls and texts from him.

OJ rushed inside, smiling, as he hugged Onyx. Onyx hugged him back before telling him to get an ice cream from the freezer and take it to his room.

"Really? I can eat in my room?"

"Yeah, just don't make a mess. I need to talk to Mommy for a minute. When I'm done, we can play some video games."

"Okay, Daddy," OJ cheered before running to the kitchen.

Seconds later, he was running back and up to his room. For a moment, Onyx just starred at Kiss, his eyes sharp. She could feel the anger through his gaze, but what he didn't know was that she was just as angry.

"Where were you, Kiss? And before you lie, I already know that OJ spent the night at Sade's house, and you didn't."

Kiss shook her head, looking Onyx directly in the eyes. "You right. I didn't. But the real question is where were you?"

"I was the fuck at home, waiting on you. I had brought food home and wanted us to have a chill little date night. But yo' ass was ghost, so where the fuck was you at?"

Kiss stepped closer. "I was here. And do you know why the fuck I wasn't here? Because when I got here, some bitch named Aaliyah was in my fucking driveway waiting on me to get home. Just so she could tell me that she was pregnant by yo' ass."

Onyx's eyes grew wide. "What?" he asked, confused.

"Nah, nigga, don't act confused now. You was just all in my face, wanting to know where the fuck I was. But who the fuck is Aaliyah? You got that bitch pregnant, huh?"

"Kiss, baby. I didn't…"

"You didn't what? You didn't mean to get caught? You didn't mean for that bitch to show up to my house and tell me that shit? How the fuck do that bitch even know where we stay?"

"I don't know," Onyx replied, defeated.

"I'm not about to be no step mama to no baby that you had on me. Now, either you get the fuck out or I do, but this shit right here," Kiss pointed between them, "this shit is over."

The words hit Onyx like a gut punch. He looked in her eyes, but her gaze didn't waver. Onyx dropped to his knees, pleading with Kiss not to leave him, not to break up their family, but she pushed him away.

"I've loved you since high school, and after all these years, this is what you do to me? How could you hurt me like this, Onyx?"

"Kiss, I'm sorry, baby. I'm so sorry. Please just let me fix it."

"You can't fix it. Just get out."

Chapter Twenty-Nine

The hotel room was nice, but it wasn't Onyx's home. The sheets were soft, there was a huge window overlooking the cold downtown streets, and a TV hummed softly in the background. But Onyx hated every second of being there. Kiss wasn't there, and neither was OJ. His family was at home, while he was alone in a hotel room surrounded by silence.

He sat on the edge of the bed, elbows on his knees, hands locked together so tight his knuckles turned white. Kiss had told him to leave, to get out the house they'd shared. She didn't want him there, and he couldn't even say he blamed her. He knew she was hurt and had known this was exactly what would happen if she found out about Aaliyah. Onyx rubbed his face, the sting of anger still burning behind his eyes.

His jaw clenched. He'd told Aaliyah to chill, told her he would handle things when the time was right. But she hadn't listened. Instead, she'd pulled up at the house, the house he shared with Kiss, and put everything in the open. The image of Kiss' face when she told him Aaliyah stopped by flashed in his head, and his stomach twisted. The betrayal in her eyes cut deeper than any blade.

"Damn, man," he muttered, leaning back against the headboard. "You really messed this up."

He missed them. As mad as he was at himself, at Aaliyah, and at the whole situation, the ache of not being home with Kiss and OJ gnawed at him. He'd built his hustle for them, stacked money for them, promised them more. Yet here he was, alone in a hotel room, while they were at home in the house he'd gotten for their family. He closed his eyes, exhaling hard. "I can't lose them," Onyx whispered to himself.

His phone buzzed on the nightstand. He glanced at the screen and saw it was Blue.

He hesitated before answering then pressed the phone to his ear. "What up doe?"

Blue's voice came sharp, getting straight to the point. "Meet me at the spot."

Onyx frowned. "For what?"

"Business," Blue said flatly. "Real money. Don't ask questions, just pull up. You need this. I know you do."

Onyx sat there for a second, his mind racing. He was still heated, still reeling from everything that happened with Kiss, but he knew better than to ignore Blue when he called like that.

"Alright," Onyx said finally. "Which spot?"

Blue chuckled low. "The one on Chene," he replied before the line went dead.

Onyx dropped the phone on the bed and stood, pulling on his jacket. His reflection in the mirror stopped him for a moment. He looked tired, and he was. He'd been running the streets for years to take care of his family, and now, he didn't even have his family. Onyx took a deep breath and walked out the door.

Onyx pulled up to the brick house and parked in the driveway. He killed the engine and sat for a beat, fingers tapping the steering wheel, listening to his heart beat under his ribs. Blue was already there, his black F150 parked in the driveway in front of Onyx's car. Onyx opened the door, stepping out the car slowly, and walked up the steps.

"What up doe, lil Blackwell?" Blue greeted the moment Onyx walked inside.

Onyx nodded, walking inside, and Blue motioned for him to have a seat.

"You know a nigga named Ocean?" Blue asked.

Omari shrugged. "I don't know the nigga personally, but I heard his name around the hood."

"That nigga is a problem for me and my business. That means he's a problem for you too. I need that problem handled. I'm offering fifty thousand for the hit. Twenty-five now, if you accept, then the other twenty-five when it's done."

Onyx's eyes widened when he heard the amount Blue was willing to pay. That money plus what he'd already saved up would be enough for him to get everything he needed. He could surprise Kiss with a bigger house and still have enough to help Aaliyah with what she needed for the baby. *If I got her a bigger house, she would forgive me and come back,* Onyx thought.

"This shit needs to be clean. No cops, no mistakes. This will be a little harder than any of the other jobs, so it pays more. But if anybody can handle this shit, you can," Blue continued.

Onyx nodded his head as he took in everything Blue was saying. He knew he needed the money, so whatever the job was, for fifty thousand, he was going to do it. He thought about Kiss and OJ sleeping alone in the house he'd gotten for their family – a house that Kiss no longer wanted him in. He thought about the hotel room he was forced to sleep in, and Aaliyah's face flashed before his eyes. She was the one decision that fucked up his entire life, and this job was about to help him fix it.

"Yeah, I know I can handle it," Onyx replied.

Blue nodded before standing up and leaving the room. He returned a few seconds later with an envelope in his hand that he handed over to Onyx. He opened it, thumbing through the bills inside. The cash was heavy in his palm, and a faint smile spread across his face.

"I need it done quick. Today if you can but tomorrow at the latest.

"I got you." Onyx nodded.

Blue handed Onyx a picture of Ocean, and he studied it, looking carefully at the features of his face, build, and hair. He stared at the picture in silence for about three minutes before placing it down on the coffee table in front of him. He nodded his head before standing to his feet. He slipped the envelope into his pocket, knowing that he'd make it work. He told himself that this money would be the way he got Kiss back.

"I'll call you when it's done," Onyx informed, walking out the house.

He walked back to his car with nothing but money on his mind. This money was about to buy his life back, and he knew it. He slid into the driver's seat, the envelope of cash resting in the pocket of his jacket. Onyx started the engine and drove back toward the hotel, knowing he wouldn't be there for long. He was going to get at Ocean tonight and have that fifty thousand in his pocket by sunrise.

Onyx left his hotel room at ten that night, ready to get the job done. Ocean wouldn't even see it coming until it was too late. Onyx was good at his job, one of the best, and everyone in Blue's crew knew it. The city lights blurred past Onyx as he drove, the engine humming low beneath him. His mind was locked on the job ahead, Blue's words still echoing as he told Onyx that Ocean was a problem for them all. His phone lit up on the passenger seat, and the name flashing across the screen made his grip on the wheel tighten. It was Aaliyah.

"What the hell you want?" he barked into the phone.

On the other end, her voice came quick, defensive. "Don't come at me like that, Onyx. We need to talk."

He laughed bitterly, shaking his head. "Talk? You already said everything you had to say when you showed up at my house. What the fuck was that, Aaliyah? Pulling up on Kiss like you had a right? Bitch, you on the side, and you knew that shit."

"You wasn't telling her!" Aaliyah snapped back, her tone sharp. "What was I supposed to do? Keep sitting around, waiting, while you played house with her like I don't exist? Like *our baby* don't exist?"

Onyx's knuckles whitened around the wheel. "That wasn't your call to make!" His voice was like thunder in the car, bouncing off the glass. "You ain't do that shit because you thought it was right. You did that shit to be fuckin' messy. You think if I'm not with Kiss, then I would be with you. Newsflash, bitch, if I wanted to be with you, I would, but the fact is I don't, and even if I did, after that messy shit you just did, I damn sure ain't fuckin' with you no more. You tried to ruin my family, bitch."

Her laugh came, harsh and bitter. "Family? You mean the one you lied to every damn night, while you were sliding into my bed? Don't talk to me about family when you couldn't even keep your zipper up long enough to protect the one you already had!"

"Bitch! You think I don't know that fuckin' a ho like you was a mistake? Believe me, I already know."

"You did that all by yourself," Aaliyah shot back. "Ain't nobody hold a gun to yo' head and tell you to fuck me raw. You was the one moanin' that you just wanted to put the tip in."

Onyx's chest heaved, his vision tunneling. He wanted to throw the phone, to end the call, and never hear her voice again, but he couldn't. Not with a child in the middle.

"I told you I'd handle it," he said finally, his voice low and dangerous. "But you didn't trust me. You had to blow it all up. Now look where we at."

There was a pause on the other end. When Aaliyah spoke again, her voice cracked, softer. "I just... I just wanted you to see me. To see us. I didn't want to feel like some dirty secret you could forget when you walk out my door. I don't want our child to be a secret either."

For a flicker of a second, guilt stabbed through his anger. Then, it hardened again, cold and sharp. "You wanted to be seen? Well, congratulations. Everybody see your ass now. And you made sure it cost me everything."

He ended the call before she could reply, tossing the phone onto the passenger seat. His heart pounded as the silence rushed back in. The anger didn't fade. It now burned even hotter, mixing with fear and with regret. He drove through the city streets on his way to a bar on the westside that he knew Ocean went to nightly. He pulled into the parking lot and saw the many cars parked inside. He didn't know which one was Ocean's, but he knew that he was there.

Onyx parked and got out the car. The bar was packed with people, and it took him a few minutes to spot Ocean and his crew. He sat at the bar where he had a clear view of Ocean's booth. Ocean sat with three other men that seemed to be in deep conversation, not even noticing that Onyx was watching them. For about an hour, Onyx nursed a glass of brown liquor as he watched the crew until they finally got up to leave.

He watched as they walked toward the door with Onyx slipping out behind them with another crowd of people. He walked to the parking lot, only a few steps behind them, without them even noticing. When Ocean got into his car, so did Onyx, following him out the parking lot. Onyx followed Ocean all the way to a house in Dearborn Heights. Onyx pulled onto the street, parking at the corner before turning his lights off.

He watched as Ocean pulled into the driveway of a house before walking inside. Onyx sat in his car for about an hour, just waiting. When he finally saw the lights go out in the house, he grabbed his gun from his center console and placed it in his waistline before getting out the car. He jogged around the back of the house, jimmying the lock on the back door, before walking inside.

The house was dark as Onyx carefully made his way through the downstairs, not seeing Ocean. When he walked upstairs, he could hear soft music playing. He crept inside the room the music was coming from, his gun leading the way. Ocean was in the shower, washing the day off. Onyx chuckled, walking into the bathroom and snatching back the curtain. Before Ocean could say anything, Onyx fired his gun twice, both bullets landing in Ocean's head, dropping him instantly.

As quick as Onyx came, he left, walking out the back door and jogging back to his car. He called Blue, as he pulled off down the street, letting him know the job was done and that he was on his way to pick up his money.

It had been a month since everything fell apart with Onyx, and the quiet in the house still felt strange to Kiss. No arguments echoing down the hallway. No Onyx sneaking in late at night with excuses already on his tongue. Just her and OJ, the soft hum of cartoons on Saturday mornings, the buzz of her phone lighting up with Omari's name instead of his brother's. The first week had been the hardest. OJ had asked where his daddy was, his little face scrunched in confusion when Kiss told him that Daddy was busy for a while. The question broke her in places she hadn't known were still fragile. But as the days stretched into weeks, OJ adjusted to Onyx not being there every day.

For Kiss, the ache lingered longer. She still caught herself listening for Onyx's keys in the door, still felt the ghost of his presence in the bedroom they'd once shared. But instead of drowning in it, she found herself at Omari's townhouse more often than not. At first, it had been once a week, when she got really lonely. But now, she was there at least three times a week, and when she was there, she didn't want to leave. Omari was sucking her back in, and she was allowing him to.

Omari's townhouse was nothing like the house she'd shared with Onyx. It was neat, almost minimal, with clean lines and warm touches that reflected his quiet nature. A cream colored sectional stretched across the living room, always draped with a blanket when she curled up to watch TV. His kitchen smelled faintly of spices and coffee, a scent that lingered even when nothing was cooking. The walls carried framed photographs, not of women or parties but of family, of him with Tamika, of childhood moments frozen in time. The space made Kiss feel safe, and she liked that.

Omari had a way of filling the silence without crowding Kiss. He cooked for her sometimes, nothing fancy, just pasta or fried catfish with cornbread on the side. Other nights, they ordered takeout and sprawled across the couch, OJ giggling between them, as they watched movies. When OJ wasn't there, the nights stretched longer, their conversations deeper, their laughter softer.

Kiss couldn't deny the way her heart reacted to Omari. It was complicated, layered with guilt, but the pull was undeniable. When she looked at him now, she didn't just see the boy who had once asked her to be his girlfriend or had walked her to the bus stop every day. She saw the man who had carried years of mistakes, who had faced consequences and walked back stronger. But the guilt was always there too, whispering in the back of her mind. Onyx was OJ's father. Their history was tangled, messy, and not easily erased. *Damn, this shit messy as hell, but I can't stop,* she thought one night after they were done having sex.

One Wednesday evening, Kiss found herself at Omari's place again. He'd cooked for her, baked chicken breast, rice, and fresh green beans. She smiled when she walked in and saw their plates sitting by candlelight at the dining room table.

"You didn't have to do all this," she whispered, smiling faintly, as she set her purse on the counter.

Omari shrugged, pulling a dish towel off his shoulder. "I wanted to. You deserve things like this, and I just want to show you that."

They ate together, the warm glow of the candlelight softening the edges of the room. OJ was with Sade that night, giving them time to themselves. Kiss caught herself watching him and smiling. Being with Omari was easier than being with Onyx. There was no yelling or miscommunication. Omari took his time with Kiss in everything they did, and Kiss felt appreciated. After dinner, Omari grabbed a bottle of wine and two glasses, and they went into the living room. Kiss set her glass down on the coffee table before turning to face Omari.

"Omari…" Her voice cracked slightly, and she had to take a breath before continuing. "I don't know what we're doing or what this is, but I don't want to let you go."

He looked at her steadily, no judgment in his eyes. "It's whatever you want it to be. And we ain't never gotta let it go."

"That's just it," she said, her fingers twisting in her lap. "I don't know what I want. But I know I want you in my life. I can't say that it'll be perfect because it won't be. This shit is messy as hell. I have an entire child with your twin brother. But when you kiss me, when you touch me, nothing else matters but us."

Omari leaned forward, resting his forearms on his knees. "Kiss, I'm not asking for perfect, just us. You and me. That's all I ever wanted. I'm not gonna hurt you the way he did. I would never do no shit like that. And I don't care about messy. I can handle Onyx."

Her chest tightened. "What if I can't give you all of me right now? What if I'm too broken?"

His hand reached out, covering hers. "You're not broken. But if you were, I would help put you back together piece by piece."

The room felt smaller, the silence between them charged. Kiss looked at him, really looked at him, and saw every piece of the boy she had once loved woven into the man sitting in front of her. She leaned forward, her lips brushing his in a kiss that started soft, almost questioning. Omari responded with the same gentleness, his hand sliding up to cradle her cheek. The kiss deepened slowly, carefully, like they both knew how much was at stake. Kiss felt warmth spread through her chest as she kissed him deeper.

When they finally pulled back, her breath came fast, her forehead resting against his. "I don't know where this is going," she whispered.

Omari's voice was steady, and sure. "Then let's just take it one step at a time. Together."

Omari grabbed her hand and led her up to his room. Kiss didn't object, wanting to feel him inside of her. They undressed each other before Kiss dropped to her knees. She put his manhood into her mouth, sucking it slowly, as she looked up at him. She watched as he bit his bottom lip before holding his head back. She listened to his moans as she sucked. A few minutes later, he pulled her back slowly, laying her on the bed and positioning himself between her legs. Kiss came twice before he crawled on top of her and put his already hard manhood inside of her wetness. They made love before falling asleep in each other's arms.

Onyx walked to his car smile he hadn't worn in weeks. For once, his life felt like it was tipping in the right direction. He'd sat across from his realtor, signing papers with steady hands, putting down a fat envelope of cash as the down payment on a four-bedroom, three-bathroom house. He'd toured it twice already, the fresh paint, polished floors, and a yard out back where OJ could run and play all he wanted. The kitchen had space for Kiss to cook Sunday dinners, sunlight streaming across the counters. Upstairs, one of the bedrooms had a little window seat; he pictured OJ curled there with books or toys, the sound of laughter filling the walls.

This was what he'd hustled for. What he'd risked everything

for. Stability for him and his family. A place his family could finally claim as their own. Onyx had left the office with the keys biting into his palm and a grin tugging at his mouth. For a moment, he forgot about Aaliyah. All he saw was his future with Kiss and OJ smiling in their new home.

He could've gone straight home. Could've saved the news for Kiss when he went to pick up OJ. But the excitement was too much to carry alone. And there was only one person he wanted to tell first – his brother.

Since Omari had come home, the brothers had gotten closer. Onyx couldn't wait to tell him about the house he'd gotten for his family. He knew this would be the glue that put them back together again. He pulled onto Omari's street, slowing as he neared the townhouse. The sight that greeted him made his stomach drop. Kiss stood on Omari's front porch, her purse slung over her shoulder, her hair catching the morning light. She leaned in close, too close. Omari bent down, pressing his lips to hers in a kiss that was not a goodbye between friends.

He slammed the car into park, flung the door open, and stormed across the street. "What the fuck is this?!" he roared, his voice carrying.

Kiss jerked back, eyes wide. Omari straightened, his expression tightening, but he didn't move away. Onyx's fists balled at his sides, rage vibrating through him.

"Is this what y'all do? Omari, you my fuckin' brother, and that's OJ's mother! This how the fuck y'all play me?"

Kiss stammered, her hands lifted as if to calm him. "Onyx, please…"

"Don't please me!" he snapped, eyes blazing. "How long has this shit been goin' on?"

Omari's jaw clenched, his voice low but steady. "It ain't like that, Onyx."

"Don't lie to me!" Onyx barked, stepping closer. "I just saw it with my own eyes! You couldn't wait, could you? Soon as I fucked up, soon as I slip, you right there, ready to take what's mine!"

Omari's nostrils flared, his fists curling. "She ain't yours, bro. Not anymore. You lost that when you couldn't be the man she needed."

The words were gasoline. Onyx lunged, shoving Omari hard in the chest. Omari staggered back a step then surged forward, meeting him with equal force. They collided, fists swinging wild, years of brotherhood curdling into violence. Onyx's knuckles cracked against Omari's jaw. Omari answered with a blow to Onyx's ribs, the thud echoing on the quiet street.

"Stop it! Please just stop!" Kiss screamed, grabbing at Onyx's arm, but he shook her off, too far gone.

Onyx landed a punch that split Omari's lip; Omari drove his shoulder into Onyx's chest, slamming him back against the porch railing. Breath tore from their lungs, sweat and fury mixing. This wasn't just about Kiss anymore. It was about everything – about how Omari had sacrificed, how he had suffered – and now, he'd finally been chosen.

Onyx roared as he swung again, catching Omari across the cheek. Blood spattered, but Omari didn't fall. He came back swinging, his fist connecting with Onyx's temple so hard stars burst across his vision. They tumbled to the ground, rolling across the concrete, their grunts and the crack of fists filling the air. Kiss' cries blurred into background noise.

Finally, they broke apart, both of them bruised, bloodied, and panting. Onyx wiped his mouth with the back of his hand, crimson streaking his skin. His chest rose and fell like a storm inside him.

Kiss stood on the porch, tears streaming down her face, her hands trembling. "Look at you two!" She sobbed. "Y'all are brothers, and y'all out here fighting like strangers in the street!"

Onyx's eyes locked on her, fury melting into something rawer, sharper. "I was out here thinking about you. About our son. I just put a down payment on a house, Kiss. Four bedrooms, three bathrooms with a yard. A real home. And this… this is what you do to me?"

Her face crumpled. "Onyx, I didn't ask you for a house. I asked you to be faithful. I asked for you to be honest with me, and instead, you let a woman come to my home and tell me shit about you."

The words gutted him. His dream of bringing her the keys, of watching her eyes light up, shattered at his feet.

Omari, bleeding from his lip, lifted his chin. "You don't get to blame her for your mistakes. You don't get to play victim when you're the one who put her through hell."

Onyx glared at him, his voice hoarse. "You always wanted her. Now, I guess you finally got what was mine," Onyx yelled before getting into his car. He didn't need an answer because he already knew what it was. Onyx pulled off down the street, not even looking back.

O mari sat slouched on the couch, one hand pressed against his nose, blood still dripping between his fingers. His chest rose and fell heavy, the aftermath of the fight still written in the tight lines of his shoulders. Kiss knelt beside him with tissues and a damp cloth, her hands gentle even as her own body trembled from what had just happened outside.

"Hold still," she murmured, dabbing carefully at the cut above his lip.

He winced but didn't pull away. "I'm fine."

"You're bleeding all over your damn face, Omari. That's not fine." She reached again, tilting his chin, so she could clean him properly.

Omari's voice was low, almost hoarse. "He came at me first."

Kiss' throat tightened. "You're brothers. You're supposed to protect each other, not hurt each other."

He looked at her, eyes dark. "What did you expect me to do? Let him talk to you like that? Let him act like he still owns you? He gave you up the moment he got that woman pregnant, and he needed to know that y'all were over."

Her hand froze, cloth hovering midair. She wanted to argue, to remind him that fighting Onyx only made things worse for them all, but the truth sat heavy between them. Omari had defended her. And deep down, a part of her ached because she knew she hadn't hated it. Even though fighting Onyx wasn't right, she couldn't help but to be turned on by the fact that Omari had fought in her honor.

Her phone buzzed on the coffee table. Once, twice, three times. The screen lit up with a name she didn't want to see. It was Onyx. Her stomach flipped. She reached for it, stared at it until it stopped ringing, then let it fall back with a dull thud. Omari's eyes flickered to the phone then back to her. He didn't say a word, but the tightness in his jaw said plenty.

Kiss swallowed hard. "I can't deal with him right now."

"Then don't," Omari said simply, leaning back against the cushions, a fresh tissue pressed to his face. "Fuck him, Kiss. He made his bed now let him lay in it. This was supposed to happen so that we could be together. We need each other, Kiss. This is the way it's supposed to be, me and you."

Kiss didn't say a word, just held the tissue to his nose until the bleeding stopped. Omari's face was bruised and starting to swell, and she could only imagine what Onyx's face looked like. Kiss cleaned up the bloody tissues and tossed them in the trash, her movements mechanical. She needed to breathe, to find some normalcy before she collapsed under the weight of it all.

"I should go," she spoke softly, grabbing her purse.

Omari stood, wincing, but didn't try to stop her. "Kiss…"

She turned, meeting his gaze. "I just… I need to clear my head. Be with OJ. That's all I know how to do right now."

He nodded slowly, lips pressed into a thin line. "Alright. Just call me when you're ready."

Kiss gave him a faint nod then slipped out the door, the air outside sharp against her flushed skin. The drive to Sade's house felt long, her thoughts circling like vultures. By the time she pulled up, she forced a smile onto her face. OJ ran out the door, arms open, his little voice carrying across the yard.

"Mommy!"

Kiss crouched low, scooping him into her arms, holding him tight enough to steady the cracks in her heart. "Hey, baby. I missed you so much. Come on. Let's go get some snacks, so we can cuddle up and watch some movies."

"Can we get popcorn and ice cream?"

"We sure can, baby boy. Whatever you want."

OJ cheered and got into the car. Sade came out and got into the driver's seat. She took Kiss to Kroger, so she could pick up the snacks OJ wanted before taking them home. The moment they walked inside the house, they both changed into their pajamas before meeting each other on the couch. They piled onto it together, her son tucked against her side, a bowl of popcorn balanced on her lap. The TV glowed with cartoons, the room filled with the sound of laughter that had nothing to do with her fractured love life.

OJ's little hand rested on hers, sticky with butter. "This is the best day, Mommy," he whispered sleepily halfway through the third movie.

Kiss kissed the top of his head, her throat tightening. "Yeah, baby. The best day."

For the rest of the night, she let the outside world disappear. No Omari, no Onyx, and no fights. Just her and her son, wrapped in a blanket, pretending life was simple. And for those few hours, it was.

Onyx sat in the living room of his brand-new house, the keys still laying on the table in front of him, their metallic glint catching the afternoon light. There were four bedrooms, three bathrooms of emptiness. There was fresh paint on the walls, brand-new carpet under his feet, a space that was supposed to mean new beginnings. It was everything he'd dreamed of, everything he'd broken his back for. And yet now, it meant nothing.

He leaned forward, elbows on his knees, staring at the blank walls like they might give him answers. All he saw was emptiness. No OJ playing with his toys all over the house. No Kiss humming in the kitchen while she prepared dinner. Just him and the weight of betrayal pressing down like a storm cloud that wouldn't break.

Omari's face wouldn't leave his head. The image replayed over and over in a cruel loop. Kiss leaning into him. Omari kissing her like it was the most natural thing in the world. The tenderness of it, the way she didn't pull away, seared itself into Onyx's chest until he thought it might cave in. Onyx's fists clenched tight, knuckles white. "My brother," he muttered bitterly to the empty room. "My own damn brother."

Onyx shook his head. They weren't kids anymore. Kiss was the mother of his child and someone Omari should not have touched. *This ain't no get back for what happened when we were kids. We grown now. That nigga foul as fuck for this,* Onyx thought.

It wasn't just about the kiss. It was everything that kiss represented. For years, he'd been the one to hold it down and provide for his family the way a man should. He'd never stopped hustling for them. Here Omari was, fresh out of lockup, and he had swooped in and took the one piece of happiness Onyx thought was untouchable. He'd given Kiss years, given her his loyalty in the only way he knew how. Sure, he'd made mistakes. Sure, he'd slipped with Aaliyah. But he was fixing it. He had this house and plans for their family. He was building them a future. Now, he was sitting in a house that wasn't a home.

Onyx tilted his head back, staring at the ceiling, and her face filled his mind. Kiss laughing at some dumb joke he cracked. Them curled up in bed, OJ tucked between them as they all slept. His gut twisted. Anger at Kiss tangled with love for her until he couldn't tell them apart. *How could she? After everything we've been through, after the child we made together, how could she look at Omari like that?* Onyx slammed a fist against the arm of the couch, the sound echoing through the empty house.

He thought about the way Omari had stolen his girl – the woman he wanted to marry, the only woman he'd ever truly loved. Onyx knew he'd gotten with Kiss when Omari liked her, but they were kids. At this point in their lives, Onyx felt that Omari should have known that Kiss was off limits to him. The thought of Omari's hands on her made Onyx's vision blur with rage. He could picture it too vividly. Omari kissing the same lips Onyx had kissed a thousand times, touching the same skin he'd memorized. The betrayal crawled under his skin, deeper than any wound the fight had left him with.

Onyx stood and walked the rooms, trying to shake the storm building inside. He ran his hand along the walls, imagining the home the house could have been. He knew there was no way he was just going to take this lying down. Onyx didn't give a fuck about Omari being his brother. He'd wronged him, and for that, he had to pay.

Chapter Thirty-Two

Kiss lay in bed, staring at the ceiling. The room was dark and quiet. She looked over at the clock that rested on her nightstand and saw that it was two in the morning. It had been days since Omari and Onyx had gotten into that fight, and she still hadn't slept. All she kept thinking about was how fucked up their situation was. She was with Omari first. He was her very first boyfriend, and it ended with him going to jail after protecting her. Then, she got with his twin, the first man she truly loved. She knew that no matter what, she would never love anyone as deeply as she loved Onyx.

However, when she thought about the way Omari touched her, the way he kissed her, it sent a fire through her body that she'd never felt before. He was so gentle and patient with her, unlike Onyx. Omari took his time and made sure Kiss received her pleasure first. As in love as she was with Onyx, he'd hurt her, and she wasn't sure if she could ever fully get over that. Still, her heart ached as her thoughts split down the middle.

Onyx, the boy who had turned into her first love. The father of her child. The one who knew her heart better than anyone else. With him, it had always been fire, passion, arguments, and apologies, the kind of love that sat your soul on fire even when it hurt. He was home in ways Kiss couldn't deny. But then, there was Omari. Her comfort, her anchor, the one who steadied her, learning her body inside and out.

Onyx has my heart, she thought miserably, *but Omari... Omari has my body.* It felt like a betrayal even to think of it that way, but it was the truth. She'd given herself to Omari in ways she hadn't expected, and yet when she closed her eyes, it was Onyx's face that her heart still yearned for. But Onyx had gotten another woman pregnant. *He let that bitch know where me and my son laid our head at.* To Kiss, that was unforgivable. Every time Kiss thought she could forgive Onyx for his mistakes, that memory slammed into her chest like a punch. It wasn't just cheating. It was a whole other life he'd built behind her back. A child she would have to share space with, a reminder of betrayal that would never go away.

Her stomach twisted. She could forgive many things, but not that. Not another woman swollen with his child while she was at home raising his son. That was why she hadn't answered his calls. That was why she'd chosen silence instead of letting him explain. Because no excuse in the world could erase the reality of Aaliyah's pregnancy. She closed her eyes, but all she saw was the fight. Onyx's face twisted in rage, a deep cut above his eye. Omari's lip split and bleeding, her own screams echoing uselessly in the street.

The sight of them swinging at each other still made her chest ache. She had been the wedge driven between a set of twin brothers. Yet she knew they had both also chosen. Omari had chosen to kiss her knowing what it meant. Onyx had chosen to betray her with another woman. Everyone had chosen in this situation. She turned onto her side, staring at the shadows stretching across the wall. For all the mess between her and the twins, one thing remained clear. She would always do what was best for OJ.

What would he think when he was old enough to understand? Would he hate her for the choices she made, for the men she let into his life? Or would he see the love she tried to give, the way she sacrificed so he could have stability? Tears pricked her eyes.

She pressed her face into the pillow, muffling the sob that threatened to escape.

She thought of Omari's townhouse, the smell of his cooking, the way his eyes softened when he looked at her. Her body still hummed with the memory of his touch, the way he had kissed her like she was something precious instead of broken. But her heart still pounded for Onyx, still remembered the nights of laughter, the sound of his voice promising her forever, the way he held their son like he was the greatest thing he'd ever made. That was the cruelest part. She wanted both, but the truth was she couldn't have either of them fully.

By the time the clock ticked closer to four, Kiss was still wide awake, staring at the ceiling. Her body ached for rest, but her mind wouldn't let go. All she could do was whisper into the dark, words no one else would hear.

"I don't know how to choose. I don't know how to forgive. And I don't know how to stop loving either of them." She spoke the words before finally falling asleep.

The sound of her phone buzzing dragged Kiss out of a restless sleep. She groaned, squinting at the screen glowing in the dim morning light. It was Omari.

Her thumb hesitated, hovering for a second, before she answered. "Hello?"

"Come outside." Omari's voice came through the phone, calm but insistent.

Kiss sat up, rubbing her eyes. "Outside? Omari, it's barely morning. What are you…"

"Just come out, Kiss," he interrupted softly. "Trust me."

She sighed, curiosity mixing with the heaviness that never seemed to leave her chest anymore. She pulled on a pair of gray sweatpants and a hoodie, slipped into her slides, and padded to the door. The cool air hit her as she stepped out onto the porch. Her eyes froze. Parked in the driveway was a sleek black Jeep, the morning sun bouncing off its polished surface. A giant red bow sat on the hood, bold and impossible to miss. For a second, Kiss thought she was dreaming.

Omari leaned against the Jeep, hands in his pockets, a small smile tugging at his lips. "Morning, beautiful."

Kiss blinked at him, then at the Jeep, then back at him again. "Omari, what is this?"

"It's yours," Omari uttered, pushing off the Jeep and walking toward her.

"Mine?" Her voice cracked. "Omari, don't play with me."

He chuckled, shaking his head. "I ain't playing. I know you been running around, depending on your mom's car, stressing about rides. You needed something that's yours. Something you can get my nephew around in, so here you go." Omari placed the fob into her hand, still smiling.

Kiss' hand flew to her mouth. "Omari…"

Tears welled up before she could stop them. She'd been holding herself together for weeks, juggling OJ, dodging Onyx's calls, trying to make sense of her life. And now, here was Omari, handing her not just a car but a piece of stability, a gift that screamed permanence. She walked slowly down the steps, fingertips brushing across the shiny hood.

"You didn't have to do this."

"I know," Omari spoke, watching her closely. "But I wanted to. You deserve more than struggling, Kiss. You deserve to have things come easy for once."

Her throat tightened. "This is too much."

"It's not enough," he countered softly.

Kiss turned, facing him fully now. The air between them felt thick, charged. "You can't keep doing things like this, Omari. Buying me cars. Fighting your brother for me. Acting like… like we're…"

"Like we're what?" he asked, stepping closer, eyes never leaving hers.

"Like we're building something real," she whispered, her voice trembling.

"Ain't we?" he asked, his tone steady but laced with emotion. "Kiss, I'm not doing this to play house. I want you for real. Same way I always have."

Her heart squeezed. She thought of Onyx, his laughter, his betrayal, the house he had bought that she hadn't even stepped foot in yet. Her chest was a battlefield, torn between the ghost of one love and the presence of another.

"Omari, are you sure you want to do this?"

"I've never been more sure of anything in my life. I love you, Kiss. Now, come on. Let's take your new car on a joy ride."

"I can't. OJ is in the house sleep."

"Come on. We'll just go around the block."

She nodded her head and slid into the driver's seat, inhaling the new car smell, her eyes darting across the dashboard. Omari climbed in on the passenger side, his presence steady and grounding. She pushed the start button, and the engine purred to life. For the first time in weeks, she felt a flicker of something that felt like pure happiness.

As they drove down the quiet street, Omari guided her gently. "See how smooth it is? Ain't nothing gonna stop you now."

Kiss laughed shakily, wiping at her tears. "You're crazy for this."

"Maybe," he said, smiling faintly. "But I'd rather be crazy for you than sane without you."

When they pulled back into her driveway, OJ was peeking out from the window, his little face lighting up at the sight of the Jeep. He burst out the front door in his pajamas, running toward them.

"Mommy! Is this ours?!"

Kiss scooped him up, pressing her face into his hair. "Yeah, baby. It's ours."

Omari stood beside them, watching them as he smiled. For a moment, it almost felt like they were a family already. Kiss and OJ smiling at something he'd provided for them made him feel more like a man than anything had ever done. Kiss walked OJ back into the house, and Omari followed them inside. He watched as she went to the kitchen and made OJ a bowl of cereal before walking into the living room to turn on cartoons.

"The TV is already on for you, so when you finish eating, come sit on the couch. I'm going to talk to Uncle Omari for a moment."

"Okay, Mommy," OJ replied, taking a spoonful of his cereal into his mouth.

Kiss took Omari's hand, leading him up to her bedroom before closing the door. She leaning in, kissing him passionately, her palms flattening against his chest, steadying her. Their tongues danced together as heat built between them. Kiss dragged her hands down Omari's chest, stopping at his belt. She unbuckled it, unzipping his pants and allowing them to fall to the floor. His manhood already stood at attention, and Kiss smiled before dropping down to her knees.

She took his hardness into her hands, spitting on the tip, before taking it into her mouth. Omari's soft moans filled the room as he grabbed Kiss' head gently. She swirled her tongue before sucking him deep.

"Shiiittt," Omari hissed, throwing his head back. He bit his bottom lip as his eyes rolled back in his head.

He pushed her back, unable to control himself. Bending her over the bed, he pulled her sweatpants down before sliding inside her. She moaned the moment he entered her. She clenched around him, and he thrust deeper. Kiss used her comforter to muffle the moans as they escaped. His thrusts were relentless as the sound of skin slapping together filled the air. Before he could even stop himself, Omari was spilling his seeds into Kiss.

Omari sat back in the cracked leather chair across from Blue, the dim light of the warehouse office making shadows dance across the walls. The air smelled faintly of smoke and oil, and the silver briefcase sitting on the desk between them gleamed under the single hanging bulb.

Blue leaned forward, his voice low and deliberate. "You handled that first job clean. That's why I like you, Omari. You think before you act."

Omari nodded, expression steady. "I had to learn that over the years. What's next though?"

Blue popped the briefcase open with a click. Inside were photos, glossy prints of another gallery's collection. He spread them across the desk like a hand of cards, each image showing priceless paintings under sterile museum light.

"These," Blue said, tapping one of the photos with a thick finger. "Worth millions on the market, but we ain't worried about the market. I got buyers who only care that they can hang 'em in a back room where nobody else can touch 'em."

Omari studied the photos, jaw tight. He knew he could do it. The other job had come easy. "How much you offering for each?"

"Twenty thousand a painting. These are some originals that buyers will pay five times that for."

Omari nodded, still looking at the photos. There were about fifteen different photos, each one with an address written on them, letting Omari know the location of each painting. Omari thumbed through the photos before picking them all up and telling Blue that he would start tonight. He tucked the photos safely into the pocket of his jacket. He pushed back his chair and stood, stretching the tension out of his shoulders.

"I'll keep it clean," he assured, nodding once.

"I already now you will," Blue replied.

Omari turned to leave just as the door opened. He froze when he saw Onyx walk in. He wore a dark hoodie, his jaw tight, his eyes colder than Omari remembered. For a split second, the brothers just stared at each other, silence so heavy it pressed against Omari's ribs. Omari's pulse spiked. He hadn't seen him since the fight outside his townhouse, since fists and blood were both flying through the air.

"Fuck you doin' here?" Onyx asked coldly.

"I'm here for work, same as you," Omari replied.

Omari could tell that Onyx wanted to say more. In fact, he challenged him to. But instead, Onyx walked past Omari and took his seat across from Blue. Omari kept walking out the door, ready to prepare for his job. On the drive home, he thought about all the money he was about to make. This next job was huge and would set him up with a nice stash. He already had money saved, and this new job would only add to it.

When he pulled up to his townhome, he went in and took a shower. He sat on his couch, looking through the photos he'd gotten from Blue. He found three paintings that were at the same gallery and decided they would be the ones that he took tonight. He placed the three photos on the coffee table in front of him before placing the others in the drawer of the same table. That night, Omari dressed in all black and broke into the gallery, taking the paintings and leaving before anyone even knew he was there.

Chapter Thirty-Three

For weeks, Onyx had slept alone in a brand-new house – a house that was supposed to be for his family. Instead, it was only him. He hadn't put any real furniture inside the home out of hopes that Kiss would come back and decorate. The only thing that was in the house was a king-sized bed, a couch, a small coffee table, and a TV.

Onyx lay, sound asleep one night, when his phone started buzzing. He groaned, swiping at it blindly, until the screen lit his face. It was Aaliyah. He almost ignored it, but something in his gut twisted. He answered, voice rough. "What?"

Her voice came fast, panicked. "Onyx, my water broke. I'm at the hospital. You gotta come now."

He shot upright, sleep evaporating in an instant. "Say what?"

"I'm in labor," she gasped. "It's happening now. Our baby is coming. Please hurry."

Onyx's chest clenched. He swung his legs out of bed, snatching his jeans from the chair. "I'm on my way. Hold tight, you hear me? Just hold on."

He sped through the city streets, headlights slicing the dark. His mind was a blur. Aaliyah's words rang over and over. *My water broke. She was about to have the baby, his baby, and he still didn't know how he felt about that.* A cocktail of emotions hit him at once – fear, adrenaline, and disbelief. He had been here before with Kiss, pacing hospital floors, watching his first-born take his first breath. But this was different. This wasn't the family he'd built his dreams on. This was the mistake that had blown everything apart.

By the time he pulled into the hospital lot, his hands were slick against the steering wheel. Inside, the harsh smell of antiseptic hit him. At the desk, a nurse asked for a name, and when he gave it, she pointed him down the hall. Onyx's shoes echoed against the linoleum as he walked, each step heavy with a weight he couldn't explain. When he reached the door, he pushed it open to find Aaliyah on the bed, her face contorted in pain, sweat dampening her hairline.

Her eyes found his instantly. "You came."

"Of course I came," he muttered, dragging a chair to her side. "What I look like letting you do this alone?"

She gripped his hand so hard his knuckles ached, but he didn't flinch. The contractions hit hard, and with each wave, Aaliyah's cries filled the room. Onyx leaned close, murmuring what little comfort he could find.

"Breathe, baby girl. You got this. In and out. Just focus on me."

He wiped her forehead with a cool cloth, adjusted her pillows, and squeezed her hand every time she begged for strength. He'd never seen her so raw, so stripped of the confident swagger she carried. In those hours, she was just a woman fighting through the fire of bringing life into the world. Every push brought Onyx closer to the fact that he was having a baby by a woman that wasn't Kiss.

The room erupted in chaos when the doctor finally said, "One more big push."

Onyx's pulse roared in his ears, as Aaliyah bore down, her grip crushing his hand. He shouted encouragement, his voice breaking. "Come on, you got it! Push! Push!"

A high-pitched cry split the air. Onyx's eyes stung as the doctor lifted a tiny, squirming body into view.

"It's a girl," the doctor announced.

Onyx's chest caved as he stared, wide-eyed, at the tiny baby being cleaned and wrapped. His daughter, his second child. When they placed her in his arms, he froze. The weight was feather-light, but it felt like he was carrying the world. Her face scrunched, lips puckered, eyes squeezed shut against the light. Something inside him cracked.

He traced a finger across her cheek, whispering hoarsely, "Damn, you perfect."

For the first time in weeks, the anger at Kiss and Omari slipped into the background. All he saw was her, his daughter. But the guilt followed close behind. Because while his arms cradled this child, his heart still ached for the family he'd already broken.

Aaliyah, exhausted but smiling faintly, whispered, "She's beautiful, isn't she?"

Onyx nodded, still staring down at the baby. "Yeah. She's everything."

He glanced at Aaliyah, and for a flicker of a second, he felt something like pride. She'd carried his daughter, fought through the pain, brought her here. Whatever else lay between them, he couldn't deny her strength. But in the same breath, his mind betrayed him with an image of Kiss in a hospital bed years ago, OJ's first cry echoing in his ears. Onyx was the one stuck in the middle, drowning between two families.

As the night deepened and the baby finally drifted to sleep in Aaliyah's arms, Onyx sat back in the chair, exhaustion dragging at his bones. He stared at them, mother and child, and wondered what kind of man he really was. Pride swelled in his chest, yes. But so did fear. Because he knew that when Kiss found out, whatever fragile thread still connected them would snap for good.

Onyx leaned forward, burying his face in his hands. "God help me," he muttered.

Aaliyah lay back against her pillows, exhausted but glowing, her daughter swaddled in her arms. Onyx sat in the chair beside the bed, elbows on his knees, staring at the baby with a mix of awe and unease. She was beautiful, no doubt about it. Tiny hands curled into fists, her skin smooth and soft, her face scrunched up in sleep. Onyx felt pride twist through his chest, but alongside it came the whisper of doubt. The streets had taught him to trust nothing at face value. And though Aaliyah had sworn up and down that the baby was his, Onyx knew too well how words could bend.

He shifted in his chair, jaw tight. "Aaliyah," he said finally, his voice low.

Her eyes fluttered open, tired but content. "Mm?"

"I need a DNA test."

The words landed heavy. Her smile faltered, confusion sliding across her face. "What?"

Onyx sat up straighter, locking his gaze on hers. "I need to know for sure that she's mine."

Her body stiffened, her grip on the baby tightening instinctively. "Onyx, how could you even ask me that? You know she's yours."

He exhaled hard through his nose, rubbing a hand across his face. "I know what you told me. But I need more than words, Aaliyah. I need facts. I need proof."

Her eyes flashed, wet with sudden tears. "You were right here with me, holding my hand. You saw her come into this world, and the first thing you say after is that you don't believe me?"

Onyx's chest tightened, but he didn't flinch. "It ain't about not believing. It's about making sure. Once that paper come back, I'll never question it again. But right now? My head won't rest until I know."

Aaliyah's voice broke, sharp with hurt. "You don't trust me at all, do you?"

Silence stretched between them, thick and suffocating. Onyx stared at the baby, guilt gnawing at him, but the knot in his stomach wouldn't let him back down.

The nurse returned to check vitals, and Onyx caught her before she left. "Ma'am, can we request a paternity test?"

The nurse's brows rose slightly, but she nodded. "We can draw samples before discharge. Results usually take about seventy-two hours."

Aaliyah turned her face to the wall, refusing to look at him, as the nurse explained the process.

Onyx stood tall, his voice steady even as the air between him and Aaliyah turned ice cold. "Set it up."

The nurse nodded and stepped out. When they were alone again, Aaliyah's whisper cut him sharper than any shout could. "You'll never know what it feels like to go through all that pain, to fight like I just did, and have the father of your baby doubt you in the first breath."

Onyx pinched the bridge of his nose, his chest heavy. "Don't do that. Don't make it about not respecting what you went through. I saw you fight. I saw you strong. That ain't what this is. This is about me needing to know without a doubt. My life's too messy, Aaliyah. I can't take chances, not even with this."

Her eyes filled, but she didn't answer. She just looked down at the baby, rocking her gently, shutting him out. Later, when Aaliyah drifted into an exhausted sleep, Onyx sat back in the chair, staring at the ceiling. The fluorescent lights buzzed faintly, a sound that grated on his nerves. Seventy-two hours. Three long days before he'd know for sure if the child in that bassinet was truly his.

His pride wrestled with his guilt. Part of him felt like a fool for doubting her, but another part clung stubbornly to the need for certainty. In his world, trust was a currency too easily spent, and he'd been burned enough to know better. Still, as he looked at the tiny bundle of life, a pang of fear cut through him. What if the test came back saying she wasn't his? What then? Would all of this have been for nothing? Onyx leaned forward, elbows on his knees, burying his face in his hands. "God," he muttered under his breath, "don't let me be wrong about this. Don't let me be wrong again."

The seventy-two hours went by slowly, but Onyx was at Aaliyah's house every day since they'd left the hospital, helping her with the baby. They had decided to name the baby Lyric, but Onyx had held off on signing the birth certificate until after the paternity test came back. He'd just gotten done laying Lyric in her crib when his phone rang. Swiping the talk button, he answered to find out it was the hospital letting him know the results were back.

"We gotta go back to the hospital. The results are in," Onyx informed

Onyx walked back into the hospital, holding Lyric's car seat with his jaw clenched. Aaliyah walked beside him, arms crossed tightly, her face set in stone. She hadn't forgiven him for asking for the test, not even close. The silence between them was heavier than any argument they'd ever had. At the desk, the nurse checked their IDs and then disappeared into the back. Onyx's heart slammed against his ribs. His palms were damp, fists clenching and unclenching at his sides.

The nurse returned with a sealed envelope. She held it out. "The results came in. These are for you."

Onyx stared at the envelope like it was a weapon. His chest rose and fell, breath sharp. Slowly, he reached out and took it.

Aaliyah's voice cut through the tension. "You don't need to open that. You should know she's yours."

Onyx's eyes flickered to her then back to the envelope. His voice was low, rough.

"Knowing and proving ain't the same thing."

The paper inside was crisp, clinical, full of numbers and medical jargon. But he didn't need to read it all. His eyes found the line that mattered, the bold letters that read: **Probability of Paternity: 0%.** The world tilted. His breath caught in his throat. His vision blurred. *Lyric's not mine?* He looked down at the car seat that was sitting on the floor next to him then back over at the paper.

He turned to Aaliyah, the paper trembling in his fist. "You lied to me."

Her face crumpled. "What? Onyx, I didn't…"

"Don't." His voice was a growl, low and dangerous. "You let me sit in that room, let me hold that baby and think she was mine. You let me believe she was mine. You let me ruin my whole life with my real family, all for nothing." His chest heaved. "You played me."

Tears welled in her eyes. "I thought she was yours. I swear I did. But there was… there was someone else. I just didn't think she was his."

The words made his vision go red. He slammed the paper down on the counter so hard the nurse jumped. "You knew. You knew there was a chance. And you let me stand there like a damn fool. Why the fuck would you tell Kiss that shit if you knew you was fuckin' somebody else? And how the fuck did you even know where I stayed?"

Aaliyah looked over at the nurse, who was still standing there, watching them. "Onyx, can we please talk about this in the car? This is a private matter."

"Bitch, these people in this hospital knew I wasn't the daddy before I did. You gon' answer my questions right here and now."

Aaliyah reached for him, her hand trembling. "Onyx, please. I just wanted you. I wanted us. When I was pregnant, you treated me like you cared, like we could be a real family." She walked closer to Onyx, placing her hand into his.

He jerked back. "Don't touch me."

Aaliyah sighed before she continued. "I wanted what you and Kiss had. I figured if Kiss knew I was pregnant, she would leave you, and you would come be with me and our baby. One day, I saw Kiss out Christmas shopping, and I followed her. I just wanted to know where and how y'all lived. So, when I realized you was trying to keep both of us, I went over there myself and told her."

"You crazy, jealous bitch. You wanted to hurt Kiss so bad that you would lie?"

"I wanted you, and Kiss don't deserve you. While you over there so worried about her, the whole city know that she fuckin' yo' brother. That nigga done bought her a car and everything."

"Bitch, shut yo' lyin' ass up. You think I'm gon' believe anything that comes out yo' mouth? Fuck outta here."

Onyx crumpled the paper in his fist, turned, and walked toward the exit without another word. Aaliyah's voice followed him down the hall, desperate and breaking.

"Onyx! Please don't leave us here. I didn't mean to hurt you!"

He didn't stop nor look back. When he walked outside, he sucked in a ragged breath, but it didn't ease the pressure in his chest. The anger was too much for him to bear. He'd ruined his relationship with Kiss – all for a lie that Aaliyah told. He didn't know who the father was nor did he care. All he knew was that now, he needed to fix things with Kiss before it was too late.

Chapter Thirty-Four

Kiss stood in her bathroom, looking at the two pink lines on the pregnancy test in front of her. She stepped back, feeling lightheaded. She took a seat on the toilet before looking at the test again. Her chest rose and fell unevenly, breath hitching as if the air had grown too heavy to carry. *Fuck, I'm pregnant,* she thought. She had known, deep down – the late period, the nausea in the mornings, the heaviness in her body. Still, seeing the proof spelled out in those bright lines made her stomach drop.

Kiss swallowed hard, her hands trembling. "Damn. This Omari's baby."

Her heart twisted at the thought. Omari had been good to her these past few months. He'd showed her that he truly loved her, and Kiss couldn't deny that. He gave her comfort, quiet strength, and a sense of safety she hadn't felt in years. Their nights together had been filled with laughter, with long talks, with touches that made her believe in something gentler than the chaos she was used to. But the weight of what this meant crushed her chest.

She already had OJ, Onyx's son. And now, this child growing inside her would belong to Omari. She would have two children by a set of twin brothers. Her children would be siblings and cousins. What would people say? What would their families think? The mess was already bad enough; now, she was adding another child to it all.

She pressed a hand to her stomach, tears stinging her eyes. Part of her heart swelled, the thought of carrying life again, of holding a newborn, of OJ having a sibling. She remembered the first time she'd held her son. *Oh, my God, OJ. What will I tell him? How will I tell him I'm having a baby by his uncle?* Kiss thought. The tears that were in her eyes now fell down her face. How would Onyx react when he found out? He'd already accused her of betraying him, already seen her kiss Omari with his own eyes. A baby would be the final blow. She imagined the rage in his face, the sharp words, the way his fists had swung at Omari outside the townhouse. She knew nothing good would come out of him finding out she was now pregnant.

Her chest tightened with fear. She thought of Sade, her mother, already skeptical of Omari. How would she take the news that her daughter was carrying his child? She thought of the whispers on the block, people talking about her and the things they would say. First, she was with one twin, now pregnant by the other. She could hear the judgment in their voices already, the way they'd pick her apart like she was nothing but a story to gossip about. The fear spread through her like wildfire. Fear of being judged. Fear of losing Onyx completely. Fear of failing OJ by dragging him deeper into their mess.

However, despite the fear, despite the shame, a small flicker of hope stirred in her chest. She thought of Omari holding her after long days, whispering that he wouldn't leave her, that he wasn't his brother. She thought of his steady hands, his quiet smile, the way he treated OJ like his very own son. Maybe this was fate's way of giving her a second chance. Maybe this baby wasn't a mistake but a new beginning.

Her tears spilled over, hot against her cheeks. She pressed her palm harder against her stomach. "It's you and me now," she whispered, her voice breaking. "You, me, and OJ."

Kiss walked out the bathroom and into OJ's room, finding

him laying in bed, watching cartoons. She smiled, crawling up into his bed next to him.

"Mommy, can I see my daddy today? I miss him."

Kiss looked down at her son. As much as she didn't want to see Onyx, she knew her son missed him.

"Yeah, I'll call him." Kiss got up and walked into her room to grab her phone from her nightstand. Her heart beat rapidly as she dialed Onyx's number. He picked up on the second ring.

"Kiss, I'm so glad you called. I've missed you so much, baby. I love…"

"OJ wants to see you," she spoke, cutting Onyx off midsentence.

"Okay, let me get dressed and I'll be there within the hour."

Before Onyx could say another word, Kiss ended the call. She told OJ that his dad was on his way before she got into the shower. She flat ironed her hair before putting on a pair of light wash jeans and fitted graphic tee, which she tied at the waist. She'd just sprayed Prada Candy all over her body when her doorbell rang. She'd locked the door on purpose so Onyx wouldn't be able to just walk right in. She already knew it was him, but she looked out the peephole anyway. Opening the door, she let him in before walking back up to her room.

"Kiss, can we talk please?' Onyx asked, standing in the doorway of the room he used to share with her.

"I asked you to come see your son. It's nothing that the two of us have to talk about," she replied, swinging her purse over her shoulder. "I'm about to go run some errands so that you can have some time alone with OJ."

With that, Kiss walked away, leaving Onyx standing there. She walked into OJ's room, kissing his forehead, before telling him that she would be back in a couple of hours. The sun was high in the sky when Kiss walked out the door. She'd kept it together while she was inside the house, but the moment she got inside her car, she broke down. She wanted to talk to Onyx, wanted to hear him out, but she was carrying Omari's baby. So, she didn't think anything he had to say would matter after that. Once he found out about the baby, there was no way he was going to want her anymore, and Kiss knew it.

Kiss' hands trembled as she gripped the steering wheel outside Omari's townhouse. The pregnancy test was in her purse. Her stomach turned as she killed the engine and sat there. She had practiced the words in her head a dozen times on the drive over. *Omari, I'm pregnant. Omari, we're having a baby.* But the closer she got, the harder they were to say. Finally, she forced herself out of the car and up the path. Before she could knock, the door opened. Omari stood there in a white tee and sweats, his hair still damp from the shower, eyes widening when he saw her.

"Kiss," he said, surprised but warm. "What you doing here so early?"

She bit her lip, fighting the urge to turn and run. "Can I come in? We need to talk."

"Yeah. Come on."

Inside, she perched on the edge of the couch, her hands folded tight in her lap. Omari sat beside her, searching her face.

"You okay?" he asked softly.

Kiss inhaled, exhaled, then met his eyes. "Omari, I'm pregnant."

For a moment, silence swallowed the room. His brows lifted, his mouth parting slightly. Then, his eyes softened, a slow smile spreading across his face.

"Pregnant?" he repeated, like he needed to taste the word.

She nodded, her throat tight.

His smile broke wide, his whole face lighting up. He laughed, not mocking but full of joy, his hands grabbing hers. "Baby, that's the best news I could ever get."

Kiss blinked, stunned. "You happy?"

"Happy?" he echoed. "Kiss, I'm over the moon. You serious right now? We're having a baby?"

Her tears broke loose, relief mingling with fear. "Yes. I took the test this morning."

Omari pulled her into his chest, his arms wrapping tight around her. "God, I can't believe it. This is real. This is everything I prayed for."

She buried her face against him, her heart racing. She'd had no clue how this conversation would go or what he would say, but as he sat beside her, smiling and holding her, she knew that everything was going to be okay.

When they pulled back, Omari's eyes were bright, full of determination. "Alright, first things first. You not stressing about shit 'cause I got you. We'll go to every doctor's appointment together. I'll set money aside, make sure we straight. You and OJ plus this baby? That's my family. And I'm gonna take care of y'all."

Kiss' lips parted, overwhelmed. "Omari…"

"I mean it," he cut in, his hand cupping her cheek. "I don't want you worrying about me being like him. I'm not Onyx. I won't hurt you. I want this. I want us."

Her heart cracked open, the words soaking into places she had tried to keep guarded. "It's not gonna be easy. People are gonna talk. Onyx is…"

Omari's jaw tightened, but he nodded. "Let 'em talk. Let him be mad. At the end of the day, you're with me. And this baby is ours. Nothing can change that. It was meant to be."

Kiss pressed a hand to her stomach, still flat. She whispered, "I just want this child to feel loved. No matter what."

Omari covered her hand with his. "And they will. I'll make sure of it. I'll be there for every moment, every step. I promise."

She studied him, searching for any flicker of doubt. But all she saw was conviction. For the first time since seeing those two pink lines, hope bloomed in her chest. They sat together on the couch, her hand in his, already talking about doctor visits, baby names, and the kind of life they could build. Somehow through all the chaos, Kiss felt safe with Omari.

Kiss returned home a few hours later, feeling ten times better than she did when she left. Her talk with Omari had made her feel better, and she now knew that things with him and the baby would be good. But when she walked in and saw Onyx sitting on the couch, playing video games with OJ, she knew that this was something that he wouldn't take well.

Onyx looked up at her, smiling. He told OJ he would be right back before standing to his feet and walking over to Kiss. "Can we talk please?"

Kiss nodded, her throat tight, as she led Onyx to the bedroom, her stomach in knots. She didn't know what Onyx wanted to talk to her about, but she knew what she had to say. They walked into the room, Kiss closing the door behind them before taking a seat on the bed. She looked up at Onyx, waiting on him to start the conversation.

"I got the DNA test back." He swallowed. "That baby, Aaliyah's baby, it ain't mine."

The words hit the air like a stone shattering glass. Kiss blinked, stunned. She wasn't sure what she expected him to say, but this wasn't it.

"I knew it," Onyx went on, voice raising with urgency. "I knew something was off. And now I got the proof. She lied to me, played me just because she didn't want us together. But it don't even matter no more. 'Cause now," his chest swelled, his eyes glistening, "now I can come back home to you and OJ. We can be the family we were always meant to be."

Onyx stepped closer, his voice trembling with conviction. "I already got us a spot, a brand-new house. It's big as hell too, four bedrooms, three baths. Big backyard for OJ to run around in. Been sitting on it, waiting for you to come back, waiting for us to do this right. I just need you to say the word, Kiss. Say you'll come home. We can fix this. We can be what we was always meant to be."

Tears pricked her eyes. She could see it in him, the boy she had loved, the father of her son, standing there with his heart wide open. His words painted pictures in her mind – OJ laughing in the yard, family dinners in the dining room, love rebuilt from the ashes. However, the truth was much heavier.

She turned away, dropping her head in her hands.

Onyx came up behind her, his voice breaking. "Kiss, say something please."

Her lips parted, but the words stuck like glass in her throat. How could she tell him? How could she take the dream in his eyes and smash it to pieces? Finally, she turned. Her tears spilled freely now, streaking down her cheeks.

"Onyx, I'm pregnant."

He froze. His face flickered with emotion – shock first then joy sparking in his eyes. "Pregnant? Baby, that's perfect! That's a sign. That's God telling us it's time to come back together."

She cut him off, her voice shaking. "It's not yours."

The words cracked through the room like thunder. Onyx's smile faltered, his eyes narrowing as if he hadn't heard right. "What you mean it's not mine? Whose baby is it then?"

Kiss' chest caved as she whispered, "It's Omari's."

Onyx staggered back a step, his mouth opening but no sound coming out. His hands curled into fists at his sides, his chest heaving like he'd been punched. Kiss pressed a hand to her stomach, sobbing.

"I didn't mean for it to happen like this. I never wanted to hurt you. But I can't change what it is. I'm carrying Omari's baby."

Onyx's face twisted – rage, grief, and betrayal all colliding at once. His voice came out low and dangerous. "My brother! My fuckin' brother? You sure do know how to keep it in the family, don't you?"

Kiss nodded, tears choking her. "Onyx, please."

He stormed across the room, pacing like a caged animal, running his hands over his head. "All this time." He shook his head. "All this time, I been holding on, thinking we'd get back together, thinking I'd fix everything, and you out here giving him what was supposed to be mine?"

Kiss cried harder, unable to look at him. She knew she was wrong, knew she'd crossed lines that shouldn't have been crossed, but the damage was already done.

Onyx slammed his fist into the wall, the sound reverberating. "I gave you everything, Kiss! I bled for us, hustled for us, built a whole damn house for us! And you telling me you carrying his child?"

Her sobs wracked her chest, but she forced herself to meet his eyes. "I know I broke you. I know I did. But I couldn't forgive you for Aaliyah. I couldn't. And Omari, he was there when I needed someone. He was steady. He didn't hurt me like you did. I knew it wasn't right, but at that moment, I didn't care."

Onyx's breathing grew ragged. He collapsed into a chair that sat by the window, burying his face in his hands. For the first time in years, he looked small and broken, just the way he felt. Kiss stood from the bed and stepped closer, her heart aching. She reached out for him, but he jerked away.

"Don't," he rasped. "Don't fuckin' touch me."

She froze, her tears falling faster. The silence stretched, broken only by the sound of his breathing, sharp and uneven. Finally, he looked up, eyes red, face streaked with sweat and rage.

"You killed me, Kiss. You killed what we had. And I swear I don't know if I'll ever forgive you."

Kiss pressed a trembling hand to her stomach, her tears soaking her lips. She whispered, "I'm sorry, Onyx."

Onyx stood to his feet and walked out the room, not saying another word. Moments later, she heard the front door slam. In that moment, Kiss did the only thing she could do. She laid across her bed and cried.

Onyx sat in the driver's seat of his car, staring out at nothing. His hands gripped the steering wheel so hard his knuckles turned white. The air inside the car was suffocating, thick with the heat of his rage. It had been a week since Kiss had told him the news, and it still felt like just yesterday. *Why the fuck would she go get pregnant by him out of all the niggas in the city?* He thought, hitting the steering wheel in frustration.

The words replayed in his head like a sick joke. He slammed his fist against the wheel, the horn blaring, echoing his fury. *How could she? How could they?* He'd been ready to forgive, ready to build again. He had the house and the future lined up. The dream of putting his family back together. And in one breath, Kiss had ripped it all away and turned it into a nightmare.

He thought back to the nights he'd held her in his arms. The early mornings with OJ climbing into their bed, waking them both before the sun was even out. The way Kiss' smile used to light up their home. They were his family, and his own twin was trying to take that away. Onyx's chest heaved, grief clawing at him from the inside. It wasn't just betrayal; it was humiliation. His brother had touched what was his, claimed what should never have been his to take.

"Damn, Aaliyah tried to tell me, but I ain't believe her ass. How the fuck did I let this shit happen? I can't let this nigga take my family."

It wasn't just about Kiss anymore. It was about pride, about his legacy, everything Onyx had built. He could lose money, cars, even friends to the streets, but not Kiss. Not the mother of his child, the only woman he'd ever loved. The thought of Omari raising a child with her twisted his gut into knots. He imagined Omari's hand on her stomach, Omari kissing her forehead, him standing in the delivery room where Onyx should have been. The image nearly drove him mad.

Onyx pressed his palms against his face, pulling at his hair. She'd said she couldn't forgive him for Aaliyah. She'd said Omari was there when she needed someone. But what about when he had been there for her? What about all the nights he'd hustled, breaking his back to keep a roof over their heads and food on the table? What about the house he bought for her and the sacrifices he made? None of that mattered to her now because all she saw was Omari.

The thought of his brother's face made Onyx's blood boil. They shared the same DNA, the same upbringing, the same struggles, even the same face. And yet Omari had chosen to stick a knife in his back. Onyx wanted to hurt him. He wanted to make him feel the way he felt now, hollowed out and raw. But even more than that, he wanted to take Kiss back. To prove that no matter what Omari gave her, it would never measure up to what Onyx could give. His chest rose and fell, breath ragged, as the war raged inside him. Part of him wanted to storm to Omari's townhouse and tear it apart brick by brick. Another part of him wanted to drop to his knees and beg Kiss not to throw him away.

The conflict ripped through him, pulling him apart. Love, hate, desire, and rage all tangled inside him. Onyx leaned back in the seat, his eyes burning with determination.

"She's mine," he whispered. "She'll always be mine. Omari can't take that from me."

Omari drove through the city streets with the windows rolled down as he felt the breeze. He couldn't help but smile at the way things had turned out for him. Life had done a one-eighty turn, and he was loving every minute of it. It had been a few months since Kiss had told him she was pregnant, and things were going great for them. Omari had also been working with Blue and stacking his money. In his hidden safe at home, he had almost two hundred thousand dollars, and the money was still rolling in with each job he took.

He pulled up at his townhouse, parking before walking up to his front door. He heard Kiss' laughter drifting from the kitchen the moment he stepped inside. He smiled, loving the thought of coming home to her. She and OJ had been at his house more than they'd been home since she'd told him she was pregnant. And Onari wouldn't have wanted it any other way.

When she came out, a glass of water in her hand and her other hand pressed absently against her growing stomach, Omari's heart swelled. The pregnancy had changed her, not just her body but her whole presence. She glowed in a way he couldn't explain. Her edges were softer, and her eyes were brighter.

"Hey, baby, just letting you know that I have another appointment next week." She reminded him with a teasing smile. "Don't you forget."

He grinned back. "I wouldn't miss it for the world."

And he meant it. He had been to every single one, sitting in those waiting rooms with her, hearing the doctor's words when she spoke. Each heartbeat they listened to together had carved itself into his soul, a rhythm that kept him grounded. Sometimes, he still couldn't believe it. He was about to be a father, not just to OJ but to his own child with Kiss. They had even started talking about marriage, casually at first but with more weight as time went on. Kiss would bring it up half-jokingly, testing the waters, and Omari would answer with all the seriousness she pretended not to expect.

"You already mine," he had told her one night, brushing her hair back as she lay on his chest. "But yeah, I want that. I want us married, making this shit official. I want the world to know."

He wasn't rushing her, but the thought of calling her his wife carried a peace he hadn't known before. He knew Kiss was the woman he was meant to be with, and he was happy that it had all finally came together. He hadn't talked to Onyx in months, and he didn't plan to. His brother's name was a wound he refused to touch.

The last time they'd spoken, fists had flown, blood had spilled, and words had cut deeper than knives. Omari didn't regret fighting for Kiss, but he did regret what it meant. It was the end of whatever bond had once tied them as twin brothers. Every now and then, he wondered how Onyx was living, whether he was sinking or climbing. But the thought never lingered long. Omari had chosen his lane, and he wasn't swerving back.

The air in Blue's back office was thick with cigar smoke, the scent clinging to the leather chairs and stacks of papers scattered across the desk. Omari sat across from Blue, steady despite the chaos around them. Blue was always moving, making calls, flipping through files, counting stacks of money, but when he finally turned to Omari, his eyes locked on him.

"You been making me proud," Blue spoke, voice low and gravelly. "You got discipline. That's why I trust you with this next one."

He pulled a silver briefcase from under the desk, popped it open, and slid five glossy photographs across the table. Each one showed a painting, some abstract, some classical, all worth more money than most people saw in a lifetime.

"These right here," Blue said, tapping a finger on the photos, "are sitting in a high-end gallery downtown. Security tight but not airtight. I need them gone from there and in my hands asap."

Omari studied each photos, memorizing the details, colors, frames, sizes.

"How much?" he asked.

Blue smirked. "Fifty large per painting. You bring 'em back to me tonight, you get half up front, half when they sell."

Omari didn't hesitate. "I'm on it."

That night, dressed in black from head to toe, Omari parked two blocks away from the gallery. His heart beat calm, steady, and his nerves were under control. He'd done harder jobs. But this one mattered. This money on top of what he already had saved would set him and his family up nice.

He checked his gear, gloves tight and ski mask folded in his pocket, his tools tucked into a small black bag. He was ready. The streets were quiet, as he approached the gallery. Its sleek glass windows reflected the night sky, the building standing like a jewelry box lit from within. Omari crouched low, circling to the side entrance. He had already studied the security layout Blue gave him. He knew about the two guards on rotation, the cameras in the corners, and the motion sensors inside. He also knew every blind spot.

He slipped a thin piece of metal into the lock, working it until the door clicked open. Inside, the air was cool, humming faintly with electricity. Shadows stretched across the gallery floor, broken by pools of light where the paintings hung like silent sentinels. Omari moved fast but careful, keeping to the shadows. His gloves brushed the frame of the first painting, an abstract swirl of reds and blacks. He unhooked it smoothly, sliding it into the padded bag.

He crossed to the second, ears tuned to every creak, every

shift of air. He worked with precision, each painting packed and stacked without a sound. By the time he reached the fifth, his adrenaline surged. The bag was heavy now, his shoulders burning, but his focus sharpened. He clipped the last frame free, wrapped it, and slid it in. He was done, had gotten every painting Blue wanted, and was now about to get his money.

Omari retraced his steps, heart pounding faster now. He slipped back through the side door, exhaling a breath he hadn't realized he was holding. But when his eyes adjusted to the street, his stomach dropped. Red and blue lights flashed across the dark, bouncing off the gallery's glass. Two squad cars idled at the curb, engines low, doors cracked open. A voice barked through a megaphone.

"Freeze! Detroit PD!"

Omari's chest tightened, his mind racing. He cursed under his breath, scanning quickly. Somebody had tipped them off. Maybe Blue hadn't told him everything. Maybe someone inside the gallery had tripped a silent alarm. Whatever it was, it didn't matter now. What mattered was the weight of the bag on his back, the millions worth of art inside it, and the fact that he wasn't about to let it end here. His muscles coiled, ready to run.

The officers stepped forward, guns drawn, voices sharp and commanding. "Put the bag down! Hands where we can see them!"

Omari's jaw clenched, eyes darting between the alley to his left and the flashing lights in front of him. His pulse thundered. This was the moment, the split second where his future with Kiss and the baby balanced on a knife's edge. And he knew whatever choice he made would change everything.

Omari went to take off running. But another police car pulled up, stopping him in his tracks. With nothing else to do, he dropped the bag to the ground, holding his hands in the air, before being placed in handcuffs.

Chapter
Thirty-Six

Kiss sat in her car in the parking lot of the 36th District Court. She didn't want to go inside, but she knew that she had to. She had to show her support for Omari. He had gone to jail again for her. However, this time, it was because he was trying to provide for their family. She opened the door to her Jeep slowly and stepped out the truck. The smell of Matiere Premiere's Vanilla Power hit her nose when the wind blew. She'd sprayed it on before she'd left the house, knowing it was Omari's favorite scent on her.

She walked into the courtroom, and the sterile air made Kiss' stomach twist even worse than it already did. She smoothed a hand over her round belly, as she walked through the heavy wooden doors, each step feeling heavier than the last. Kiss was six months pregnant, and she wished she wasn't coming to watch her child's father fight for his freedom.

Inside the courtroom, the benches were filled with people Kiss had never seen before. She spotted Tamika near the front, her shoulders stiff and her eyes dark with worry. Kiss slid into the seat beside her, gripping her hand without a word.

"You okay, baby?" Tamika asked quietly.

Kiss nodded, though her throat was tight. "Trying to be."

The bailiff's voice rang out, sharp and commanding. "All rise."

The judge entered, robe flowing, and the room shifted into

silence. Kiss' heart hammered as Omari was led in, shackled, in an orange jumpsuit that was given to him by the county jail. He looked older than he had just months ago, stress carved into his face. But when his eyes found hers, he straightened, as he lifted his chin. Kiss felt tears burn her eyes.

The prosecutor began, painting Omari as a career criminal, a thief who thought he could outsmart the law. They laid out the evidence – surveillance footage, and the stolen paintings recovered in Omari's bag. Each word stabbed at Kiss because she knew some of it was true, but she also knew Omari wasn't the monster they made him out to be. He was more than his mistakes. He was the man who held her belly at night, who whispered about baby names and their future together.

Omari's lawyer pushed back hard, arguing that the police had set him up, that Blue was the real mastermind pulling the strings. They spoke of Omari's attempts to turn his life around, about his steady relationship with Kiss, the child they had on the way, and his role in OJ's life.

"Mr. Blackwell is not a danger to society," the lawyer said firmly. "He is a young man trying to provide for his family. Yes, he made mistakes, but he does not deserve to lose years of his life for them."

Kiss squeezed her hands together, whispering silent prayers. When they called her to testify, her legs shook as she stood. Six months pregnant, her belly was impossible to hide. Murmurs rippled through the room, as she took the oath and sat in the witness chair. The prosecutor asked about her relationship with Omari, about his money, about whether she knew where it came from.

"I don't know about any of this," she said firmly. "Omari is a good man. He is a good partner and father. He was there for me when nobody else was. That's the Omari I know." Her voice broke on the last words, but she held her chin high.

When she returned to her seat, Omari's eyes followed her,

filled with a quiet gratitude that tore her heart apart. She wanted to run to him, to hold him in her arms and tell him everything would be okay, but she couldn't. The guards standing in the courtroom would surely stop her then put her out. So, instead, she sat there, waiting.

Hours had passed since the closing arguments ended. The jury had left the courtroom to deliberate. Kiss sat frozen beside Tamika, her hands clasped tight over her stomach, every minute stretching into eternity. Finally, the jury filed back in. The foreman stood, paper trembling slightly in his hands.

"We, the jury, find the defendant, Omari Blackwell… guilty."

The word slammed into Kiss like a blow. She gasped, clutching her belly, tears spilling down her cheeks. Tamika's arm wrapped around her, holding her steady. The judge's voice came through steady and unforgiving.

"Given the evidence presented, this court sentences you to three years in state prison."

Kiss' sobs shook her. Omari closed his eyes, his jaw growing tight. He opened his eyes and looked back at Kiss. He didn't cry or flinch, as he mouthed the words, *Take care of our baby.* Kiss pressed her hand to her lips, nodding through the blur of tears. The bailiff led him away in chains, and Kiss felt her heart shatter all over again. She was six months pregnant, carrying his child, and now, she would raise their baby alone, while he served his time. The courtroom emptied, but she stayed seated beside Tamika, unable to move, her hand on her stomach, whispering to the life inside her.

"We'll wait for him," she murmured. "It's only three years."

Onyx sat in the far back of the courtroom, hat pulled low, blending in with the rest of the people inside. He hadn't wanted anyone to know he was there – not Kiss, not Tamika, and definitely not Omari. This was his moment to watch quietly, to see how everything played out. The murmur of voices filled the room as the jury filed back in. Reporters shuffled papers, and spectators leaned forward. Onyx stayed still, eyes fixed on his twin at the front of the room.

Omari looked tense but strong, standing tall even in shackles. Onyx's jaw tightened. They were mirror images – same face, same blood – yet so different. Omari had taken what wasn't his. Kiss should have been off limits to him, but instead, she was having his baby, taking away whatever future Onyx believed belonged to him. Now, justice was being served.

From his seat, Onyx could see Kiss near the front, her hand resting protectively on her rounded belly. She was glowing even in her grief. Omari's child was growing inside her. The sight tore at him, a mixture of fury and longing burning in his chest. She should have been his. That baby should have been his. Instead, she cried for Omari as she waited for the verdict. Onyx's fists clenched in his lap. He forced himself to breathe slow, to keep his mask of calm in place.

The foreman spoke the word, "Guilty." The word echoed through the courtroom as gasps rippled. Kiss sobbed as Tamika held her. Omari bowed his head before turning to look at Kiss. Onyx felt the corners of his mouth twitch upward. He hid it quickly, leaning back into the bench.

The judge's voice carried: "Three years in state prison." And there it was. The gavel dropped, sealing Omari's fate.

As the bailiff led Omari away, Onyx's mind replayed the night of the heist. The phone call he'd made and that anonymous tip he'd given. The satisfaction of knowing the police would be waiting when Omari walked out with the paintings. His twin had thought he was slick, thought he could hustle for Blue and build a life with Kiss at the same time. But Onyx had made sure that wasn't going to last. The setup had been clean and untraceable. And Omari had walked right into it.

Some might have called it betrayal, turning on his own brother the way he did. But Onyx didn't see it that way. Omari had betrayed him first, stealing Kiss' love and planting his seed in her womb. All Onyx had done was restore balance. Put things back the way they were supposed to be. Now, Omari was gone and locked away for three years.

As the courtroom emptied, Onyx stayed seated, letting the crowd thin before he slipped out unnoticed. With Omari gone, he was one step closer – one step closer to Kiss, to OJ, to the family he believed should have been his all along. A cold smile touched his lips, knowing that this was only the beginning.

Chapter Thirty-Seven

The sky hung low and gray as Kiss steered her Jeep down the highway, the tires humming against the pavement. It had been two weeks since Omari was sentenced, and she couldn't believe this was happening again. Every mile she drove made her chest feel tighter, her nerves sparking in rhythm with her heartbeat. She adjusted the rearview mirror out of habit, catching a glimpse of herself. Her belly curved round and undeniable beneath the floral dress she wore. She sighed, resting one hand against it.

"You're gonna see your daddy today," she whispered. "And I'm gonna let him know that this time, everything will be okay."

But even as she said it, a lump formed in her throat. She hated the idea of her child knowing their father first through prison glass and correctional schedules. However, she knew there was nothing she could do about it. Omari was gone for the next three years, and this time, she planned to wait for him.

An hour and a half later, Kiss was pulling up to the prison. Tall fences coiled with barbed wire, and guard towers casted shadows over the yard. Kiss parked in the visitor lot, her hands trembling, as she cut the engine. She sat there for a moment, trying to steady herself, breathing in and out. She'd never visited anyone in a prison before, and she was nervous. Finally, she forced her body to move, grabbing her license and the small, clear purse they allowed her to bring inside.

At the entrance, officers checked her ID, patted her down, and scanned her bag. The cold professionalism in their eyes made her feel small, like her love for Omari was something criminal too. Still, she held her chin high, ready to see Omari.

The visiting room buzzed with noise – children running to hug parents, couples holding hands across scratched tables, and guards patrolling the edges like hawks. Kiss' stomach clenched as she scanned the rows, her eyes searching for Omari. Omari stepped through the door with the others, orange jumpsuit hanging loose on his frame, but his shoulders squared, his eyes alive the moment they locked with Kiss'. Her breath caught, and a smile spread across her face.

When he reached the table, Kiss stood, her tears already spilling. She wrapped her arms around his shoulders, hugging him tightly. He squeezed her, and she melted into his arms. She didn't want to let him go, but she knew the guards would break them apart soon if she didn't. They took their seats, Omari's hands reaching for hers across the table. When their fingers touched, it felt like the world stilled.

"Damn, I missed you," he informed, voice low but firm.

Kiss nodded, unable to speak at first. Finally, she whispered, "I missed you too."

For a moment, they just stared at each other, holding on, soaking in the presence they had been starved of.

Omari glanced down at her belly, his expression softening. "My baby growin' in there. You look beautiful."

Kiss laughed through her tears, rubbing her stomach. "The baby's been kicking like crazy. Probably ready to meet you already."

Omari's smile faltered, sorrow clouding his eyes. "I hate that I won't be there when you give birth. This was never in the plan, Kiss."

Kiss squeezed his hands tighter. "I know it wasn't. You were just trying to provide for us. And you will be there. Maybe not when I give birth, but we gonna come visit every week. And we gonna talk every day. I'm not going anywhere this time, Omari. This time, I'm going to wait for you. I promise."

Her words broke him. His eyes glossed, his jaw clenched, as he tried to stay strong, but she could see the cracks.

"You mean that?" he asked, voice rough.

"With everything in me."

Omari leaned forward, lowering his voice. "Then listen… you don't worry about me in here. I'll handle it. I'll do what I gotta do. But you? You take care of yourself, take care of our baby. That's all I need you to do. When I get out, it's gon' be like I never left."

Kiss nodded, tears falling freely. "I will. I promise."

He brushed his thumb over her hand, his eyes never leaving hers. "Three years ain't forever. When I get out, I'm coming home to you. And nothing, or no one, gon' stop me from being the man you and our kid deserve. I love you, Kiss."

"I love you too, Omari."

When the guard finally called time, Kiss' chest ached as she let his hands go. The sound of chains and keys echoed as Omari was led away, but his eyes stayed on hers until the last possible moment. Kiss sat there for a moment, tears rolling down her face. For three years, she would have to do everything alone, without the help of her child's father, and that scared her more than anything. She didn't have a job or any money saved up. Onyx gave her money every week, but that was used for bills and food. She knew if she was going to survive, she would need to find a way to make some money – fast.

***

The heavy clang of the steel door echoed down the tier, vibrating through the concrete walls, as Omari stepped back into his cell. The guard's keys rattled, the lock clicked, and then silence. He was alone again. The walls pressed in on him, a dull gray that was cold and lifeless. Just moments ago, he'd been sitting across from Kiss, her hands in his, her belly round with their child. For a brief moment, he'd felt alive again, felt like he still had something worth fighting for. Now, all that was stripped away, back to cinderblock walls, back to thin mattresses and bars between him and the life he wanted.

Omari sat down on the edge of the bunk, elbows resting on his knees, head in his hands. The regret came in waves, sharp and unforgiving. He had been so close to having everything he wanted. The townhouse, the money he was stacking, the plans he and Kiss made while they were lying next to each other. He'd had it all lined up, everything he thought he'd never have again. Then, one slip up had taken it all away.

He closed his eyes and saw her face, her tears, the way her voice trembled when she told him she'd wait. He wanted to believe her, and deep down, he did. This was his second chance to be with Kiss, and he knew it. Their love had stood every test. They had come back together because it was meant to be. So, if she said she would wait, then she would.

Still, the thought of her raising their baby without him by her side for the first three years tore at his chest. He wanted to be there, to hold her hand in the delivery room, to cut the cord, to hear that first cry. He wanted to see his child's first steps, hear their first words, first everything. But he wouldn't. Instead, he would hear about it in letters. Maybe see pictures if the guards allowed them through. That thought broke him.

The sadness weighed heavier than the chains on his wrists. Omari leaned back against the wall, staring up at the ceiling. He imagined Kiss at home, rubbing her stomach, talking to their unborn baby. He imagined OJ running through the house, asking questions about his new sibling that Kiss would have to answer alone. A tear slipped down his cheek before he could stop it. He wiped it away quickly, but the ache in his chest didn't ease.

He knew that once he was out, they would be a family again. Three years wasn't forever. He'd done seven before, so three would be nothing he couldn't survive. He would keep his head down, and when he got out, he would walk straight back to her and their family. And this time, he wouldn't let anything take it away from him.

As the prison went quiet for the night, Omari lay on the thin mattress, one hand on his chest. The sadness lingered, sharp and unrelenting. He felt as though he'd failed his family and hated himself for it. All he could do was pray that the next three years wouldn't break them.

Sunlight spilled through the thin curtains of Kiss' bedroom, painting golden streaks across the walls. The warmth of summer clung to the air even though it was barely morning. She stirred, blinking herself awake, one hand instinctively sliding over her round belly. The baby shifted beneath her palm, and she smiled softly.

"Good morning, little one," she whispered, her voice hushed in the quiet of the house.

She slipped out of bed, padding barefoot across the floor to the bathroom. Steam filled the small space as she turned on the water and stepped into the shower. The spray beat against her skin, washing away the night's rest and loosening the tension in her shoulders. She closed her eyes and let the water run down her body. For a moment, she imagined Omari's hands there, steady and grounding, the way he always rested them against her belly when they talked about the baby. By the time she stepped out, her head felt clearer, though the weight of everything still lingered.

It was hot already, so she kept her outfit simple but cute. A ribbed white tank top that clung comfortably to her figure and a pair of soft, high-waisted, denim shorts with stretchy sides that made room for her belly. On her feet, she slipped into fresh white Nike slides. She added small gold hoops to her ears, her anklet catching the light as she moved around. Her braids were neat, pulled back into a half-up ponytail, so they wouldn't cling to her neck in the heat.

On her dresser sat the fragrance she'd been spraying for the past week, Yara Candy. The sweet, sugary notes always lifted her mood, wrapping her in a candy-floss cloud that made her feel both pretty and powerful. She sprayed a mist across her neck and wrists then one last spritz into the air, walking through it with a satisfied smile. She checked herself in the mirror, turning side to side. The baby bump was front and center now, and she couldn't help but smile.

She picked up her phone and scrolled to Onyx's number. For a moment, she hesitated, biting her lip. Calling him always carried weight, always stirred something she wasn't sure she was ready for. But today was practical. She had a doctor's appointment, and someone had to keep OJ.

He picked up on the second ring, his voice low and rough like he'd just woken up. "What up doe, my baby?"

"Onyx," she said, trying to keep her tone even, "I got a doctor's appointment today. Can you watch OJ for me while I go?"

There was a pause on the other end, the sound of him exhaling. "Yeah," he said finally. "What time is your appointment? I can be there in about thirty minutes."

"Alright, thanks. It's at one," she replied, softer than she meant to.

When she hung up, her chest felt tight. No matter what had occurred between them, no matter how far apart they'd drifted, Onyx always showed up for his son. Kiss went into the kitchen and made a quick breakfast for OJ, while she waited on Onyx to arrive. She made waffles, eggs, and sausage, and by the time she was finished, Onyx was pulling up.

He walked into the house without knocking. Kiss couldn't be too mad because he was still paying the bills. However, she wanted him to know that this was her house now. Onyx greeted her before walking upstairs to wake OJ. She placed the breakfast she'd made on a plate and set it on the table before grabbing her purse and walking out the front door.

The doctor's office was cold when Kiss walked inside. It seemed as though they had the air on full blast, and she rubbed her hands over her arms, wishing she'd brought a sweater. She sat in the waiting room, flipping through a wrinkled magazine, her stomach rounding beneath her tank top. Other women sat around her, some holding newborns, others as pregnant as she was. Kiss tapped her foot nervously, wishing Omari could be sitting beside her. He had always been there before, hand on her leg, steady smile on his face.

The nurse called her name. "Kiss Johnson?"

Kiss stood and walked in the back. Inside, the exam room was small but bright. A chart of fetal development hung on the wall, colorful illustrations marking each stage of pregnancy. Kiss settled onto the table, the crinkle of paper beneath her.

The doctor entered with a warm smile, clipboard in hand. "Seven months, right? How are we feeling today?"

Kiss nodded. "Tired. He's been moving a lot."

The doctor chuckled. "That's a good sign."

The gel was cold against her belly, making her flinch. The wand pressed gently, and the machine hummed to life. The screen lit up with blurred gray and white, and then, there was her baby. Kiss' heart swelled as the image sharpened – a tiny body curled, tiny limbs shifting. She could hear the rhythmic thump of his heartbeat echoing in the room, steady and strong.

Her eyes filled with tears. "That's my baby in there, growing so big."

"Yes," the doctor replied softly. "Healthy heartbeat, measurements are right on track."

Kiss swallowed hard, remembering Omari's words during an earlier appointment: *I don't want to know the sex. I just want the surprise.* He had smiled, but she had seen the curiosity flicker in his eyes too. Kiss had always wanted to know. She needed to be able to dream, to plan, and to feel closer to the child she was carrying.

"Doctor Hampton," she asked quietly, her voice trembling, "can you tell me what it is?"

The doctor looked at her, as if making sure she was certain. Kiss nodded firmly.

The wand shifted, the doctor's gaze focused on the screen. After a moment, she smiled. "You're having another boy."

The words wrapped around Kiss like music. *A boy. Omari is going to be so happy.*

Her tears spilled freely now, sliding down her cheeks, as she stared at the grainy image. Joy and grief collided inside her chest. She thought of OJ, how excited he would be to have a little brother. She thought of Omari, locked away, who should have been here holding her hand as the words were spoken.

She laughed softly through her tears. "Omari… you gave me another son."

When the ultrasound ended, Doctor Hampton wiped the gel from her stomach and handed her a strip of black-and-white photos. Kiss held them gently as she smiled at what she and Omari had created. As she walked back through the waiting room, the sunlight spilling in through the glass doors, she whispered to herself again, "A boy. Omari will finally have his son."

The house was quiet when Kiss came back from her appointment, the faint smell of Onyx's cologne lingering in the air. She set her purse down, slipping out of her slides, and paused in the doorway. The living room was dim, sunlight filtering through half-closed blinds. Onyx sat on the couch, elbows on his knees, hands clasped. His head lifted when she walked in, his expression unreadable.

"Where's OJ?" she asked softly.

"He's upstairs, playing with his toys," he answered. His voice was calm, almost too calm. Then, he gestured toward the armchair. "Can we talk?"

Kiss hesitated. Her heart beat faster, not knowing where the conversation would lead. But she nodded and sat across from him. For a long moment, silence stretched between them. Onyx rubbed his palms together then finally looked at her. His eyes were dark and tired, but filled with something heavy.

"I still love you, Kiss," he spoke.

Her chest tightened as she looked into his eyes.

Onyx leaned forward, voice rough. "I know I messed up. I know I hurt you. But I never stopped loving you. Every day, even when I was with Aaliyah, even when we weren't talking, you were the only one on my mind. You and OJ, y'all my family. That's all I ever wanted."

Kiss swallowed hard, her throat dry. She thought of the baby kicking earlier during the ultrasound, the doctor's words still ringing in her ears. *You're having a boy.* She thought of Omari's face, how he would smile when he read her letter once Kiss gave birth.

Her voice came out soft but steady. "Onyx, I can't. I can't go back there. I can't be with you."

Pain flickered across his face. "Why not? You know what we had. So, you know what we still got."

Kiss shook her head, tears brimming. "Because I'm pregnant, Onyx. And the baby isn't yours. It's Omari's."

The words landed like a blow. Onyx sat back, his jaw tightening, hands balling into fists. He didn't look away, didn't blink, just stared at her as if trying to process the wound she had just reopened.

Finally, he exhaled sharply, shaking his head. "Omari can't be there like I can. He's locked up, Kiss. He ain't gonna be around when you need him most. But I will be."

Kiss pressed her hand to her belly, voice trembling. "That doesn't change who the father is. That doesn't change what I feel. Omari might be behind bars, but he's still here. We are still together."

Onyx leaned closer, desperation breaking through his anger. "And what about me? I'm right here, in front of you. I'm not in a cell. I can help with OJ. I can help with the baby. I can give you the life you want now. Why won't you let me?"

Tears spilled down her cheeks. "Because it's not about what you can give me anymore. It's about what's right. And this," she touched her belly, voice cracking, "this baby belongs to Omari. I can't betray him like that. Not again." Her words hung heavy in the room, final and unyielding.

Onyx sat back, his jaw clenched, pain and fury warring in his eyes. For a moment, she thought he might lash out, say something cruel. But instead, he stood abruptly, running a hand over his head.

"I hear you," he said finally, his voice low, almost a whisper. "But don't forget I'm still here. And I ain't going nowhere. I'm not givin' up on us, Kiss. We have a son and too much history for me to do that."

Without another word, he walked to the door, yanking it open and stepping out. The slam echoed through the house, rattling the frame. Kiss sat frozen, tears sliding silently down her face, one hand resting on her stomach. Onyx's words replayed in her mind, his voice sharp with longing and pain. She knew she had drawn her line. She had chosen Omari. But as the quiet settled over the house again, she couldn't shake the weight of Onyx's confession.

Chapter Thirty-Eight

The clang of gates echoed through Omari's chest as he stepped into the visitation room. The sound was as familiar now as his own heartbeat, but today, it felt softer, almost drowned out by the sight of Kiss waiting for him. She sat at their usual table, her belly round beneath the black sweater dress she wore. Her braids were long and hung down her back, and Omari couldn't help but smile at how beautiful she looked. When she saw him, her face lit up despite the tiredness etched in her eyes.

"Hey, baby," he greeted, sliding into the chair across from her.

"Hey yourself." Her voice was warm but weary, carrying the weight of everything she'd been carrying alone.

They started with the usual small talk. She told him about OJ, how he'd started asking more questions about when his uncle was coming home. How he'd drawn pictures of the baby in her stomach that he couldn't wait to meet. Omari chuckled, picturing his nephew's wide grin.

"Tell him I said I love him. And tell him I can't wait to meet the baby either."

Kiss nodded, her hand resting protectively on her belly. "He knows, Omari. I tell him all the time."

Omari told her about the yard, about how he'd started doing push-ups until his arms burned, about the card games with other inmates, and how he just wanted to stay out the way and do his time. He left out the darker parts – the tension, the fights. The man being murdered in the cell next to his.

Kiss sighed. "Omari… I probably won't be coming for a couple weeks."

His stomach tightened. "Why not?"

"I'm due next week," she informed. "Doctor thinks the baby could come any day now. Once the baby does come, I'll be busy, you know? Adjusting to having two children. Trying to manage OJ, the baby, everything else that's going on. It's just hard."

Her voice cracked, and the sight of tears glistening in her eyes cut him deeper than any blade ever could. Omari reached across the table, his hand covering hers.

"I know it's hard, baby. I know. And I hate that I can't be out there with you, that I can't be the one taking care of things." He hesitated, looking around the room, then leaned closer. His voice dropped low, meant only for her. "There's something I need to tell you. Something I been holding onto."

Her brows furrowed. "What is it?" she asked, leaning closer.

Omari glanced at her belly then back at her eyes. "In the townhouse, under the floorboard in the back closet, there's money. A lot of money. I put it away before everything went down."

Kiss' eyes widened, shock flashing across her face. "Money? How much?"

"More than enough, a couple hundred grand."

Her hand flew to her chest. "Omari, why didn't you tell me sooner?"

"Because it wasn't time. I wanted to hold onto it until I knew it was time to use it. And now, you need it. You got the baby coming, and you got OJ. You can't be stressing about bills or food or nothing like that. Not when I can take care of you, even from in here." He squeezed her hand, his eyes steady. "Listen to me. I want you to go there and get it. Don't tell nobody. Take fifty thousand out for you and keep the rest for me until I get out."

She opened her mouth to speak, but he cut her off. "I mean it, Kiss. That money is my lifeline. But you," his voice softened, breaking just slightly, "you can take fifty out. Just fifty. Use it to get what you need for the baby, for OJ, and for you. Don't be out here struggling when I got it sitting there."

Tears slid down her cheeks, but she nodded. "Omari, I don't even know what to say."

"Just say you'll do exactly what I said," he whispered.

"I'll do it."

Relief washed through him, loosening a knot that had been twisting in his chest for months. For the first time since stepping back inside a cell, he felt like he had some control again. Like he could still provide and protect.

"You don't know what this means to me," he said. "Knowing you and our baby will be straight, that's everything. I can breathe again."

The guard's voice called out, "Visitation ending in five minutes."

Omari's chest ached at the sound, but he leaned forward, locking eyes with Kiss. "Promise me you'll be careful. Promise me you'll keep it safe."

"I promise," she whispered.

When the guard came to lead him away, Omari stood tall, his hand slipping from hers reluctantly. He didn't look back until he was at the door. Kiss sat there, hands on her belly, eyes still on him. And in that moment, Omari knew. Three years or not, distance or not, they were bound together. By love, by loyalty, and by the family they were creating.

***

The sun had already started to sink behind the skyline when Kiss pulled out of her driveway, OJ strapped into the backseat, drowsy from a long day. She'd promised her mama she'd drop him off before "running errands", but the truth was heavier than errands. Tonight wasn't about groceries or baby clothes. Tonight was about going to get Omari's money. Her grip tightened on the steering wheel as she turned down the familiar streets. Every corner of the city held memories, some good, some painful. She hadn't been to Omari's townhouse since he'd went to jail, but tonight, she knew she had to do it.

When she arrived, Kiss parked down the street instead of directly out front. Paranoia clung to her like sweat. She glanced around before stepping out, keys trembling in her hand. She all but ran to the door, slowing down only when she got to the stairs. The townhouse door unlocked with a click that felt too loud. Kiss stepped inside quickly, closing the door behind her, her pulse racing. The air smelled faintly of dust and old cologne, Omari's cologne, and her eyes stung. The living room looked untouched, the couch still neat, the lamp still tilted slightly from the last time she'd been here with him.

Omari's words replayed in her mind. *Back closet. Under the floorboard.*

She moved through the townhouse quietly, as though afraid the walls might tell on her. Each step echoed. She reached the hallway, opening the door to Omari's bedroom, and walked into his closet. She dropped to her knees, running her hand over the hardwood. Her palms grew slick as she searched for seams in the boards. Her nails finally scraped over a groove. Her heart leapt. She pried at the edge, and with effort, the board lifted.

Beneath the floorboard was a black duffel bag. Kiss pulled it out, her breath catching in her throat. She unzipped it just enough to peek inside. Stacks of money, crisp bills bundled with rubber bands, were packed tight. Hundreds of thousands of dollars just sitting there in the dark. Her stomach turned. This wasn't just grocery money. This wasn't even rent money. This was life-changing money that she knew she needed. She couldn't believe Omari trusted her with all of it.

She zipped the bag, muscles straining as she lifted it. The weight shocked her, not just the physical heft but the metaphorical one. This bag didn't just carry cash. It carried Kiss' entire future. Kiss staggered as she carried it through the townhouse, heart hammering, ears straining for any sound outside. She walked back downstairs, bag in hand. She locked the door behind her and walked quickly to her car, forcing her breathing to stay steady even though her nerves screamed. She opened the trunk, placing the bag inside, before closing it quickly. Once she got into her truck, she started it and pulled off, picking up OJ before going back to her house.

Back home, the house was quiet. OJ went straight to his room to play with his toys. She carried the bag through the house, trying to find somewhere to hide it. *The basement*, she thought. That was the only place that made sense. She went downstairs, the concrete cool beneath her feet. In the far corner sat an old storage trunk, covered with blankets and boxes. Kiss dragged the duffel to it, opened the trunk, and lowered the money inside. She covered it with winter clothes, old books, anything she could find, then shut the lid tight.

When she finally straightened, sweat dampened her forehead, her chest heaving. She pressed her back against the wall, sliding down, until she sat on the cold floor. Her hands shook as she buried her face in them. She had the money now and knew that all her worries were lifted from her chest. She no longer had to worry about paying bills or getting what her children would need, and she owed it all to Omari. For the first time since Omari had been locked up, Kiss felt safe.

***

The morning light crept through Onyx's blinds, warm and unbothered, pulling him out of his sleep. For once, the city outside was quiet – no horns blaring, no voices carrying down the block, just the morning silence. He lay there for a few moments, staring at the ceiling, thinking about what he would do on this beautiful Saturday. He got out of bed and made himself a quick breakfast of eggs and toast. When he was done, Onyx headed up to the bathroom.

He showered quickly, dressing in fresh jeans and a white tee, and headed out. The city was already awake by the time he hit the streets of downtown. Stores buzzed with people, mothers tugging kids along, couples walking together hand in hand, and music coming from the cars on the streets. Onyx went straight to the kids' section at a department store. His hands brushed over tiny onesies, soft blankets, and miniature sneakers. He grabbed things for OJ too, a couple of new toys, a fresh pair of Jordans, shirts he knew his boy would love. By the time he left, his trunk was full of shopping bags for both OJ and the baby.

When he pulled up to Kiss' house, the first thing he noticed was how still it looked. There were no toys scattered in the yard, no movement in the window. He carried the bags up to the porch and knocked this time. The door opened slowly, and Kiss stood there. Immediately, Onyx's chest tightened. She didn't look right. Her face was pale, her hair clinging damply to her forehead, and her hand rested low on her belly.

"What's wrong?" he asked instantly, stepping forward.

Kiss swallowed hard. "I… I think I'm in labor."

Onyx's mind blanked for a second, the world narrowing to just her voice. "Labor? Right now?"

She nodded, wincing as another wave of pain seemed to hit. She gripped the doorframe, her knuckles white. Onyx dropped the bags without another thought, moving to her side. "Come on, we gotta go to the hospital. Where is OJ?"

"He's in his room."

Onyx rushed up to OJ's room, grabbing him, before running back down the stairs. He guided Kiss carefully, one arm around her waist, as she leaned into him, her breaths coming in sharp, uneven gasps. Every sound she made twisted at him. This was supposed to be a beautiful moment, but all he felt was terror. He helped her into the passenger seat of his car, buckling her in like she was fragile glass, before putting OJ into the car. Kiss clutched her belly, eyes shut tight, as another contraction rippled through her. Onyx's knuckles were white on the steering wheel as he pulled out, tires screeching against the pavement. His heart slammed in his chest, every red light feeling like a threat.

"It's okay, Kiss," he kept saying, though he wasn't sure who he was trying to convince, her or himself. "I got you. We almost there. Just breathe."

She nodded weakly, gripping the handle above the door, her breaths shallow. As soon as he pulled into the hospital lot, he reached for his phone. His voice was tight, urgent, as he dialed.

First, Sade. "It's me. Kiss is having the baby. We at the hospital now."

Her sharp inhale was audible through the line. "Lord have mercy. I'm on my way."

Next, Tamika. "Ma… it's happening. Kiss in labor. She at the hospital."

Tamika's voice trembled, a mix of worry and excitement. "I'll be there as soon as I can."

Onyx shoved the phone back into his pocket, his mind racing. Both mothers were on their way. He wasn't sure if that would bring peace or chaos, but right now, all he cared about was Kiss. Inside, nurses rushed her into labor and delivery. Onyx watched as they hooked her up to monitors, the steady beeping of the baby's heartbeat filling the room. Relief hit him hard. The sound was strong, steady, a promise that the child was fighting to come into the world. He didn't care that the baby wasn't his. All he cared about was that Kiss and the baby were safe.

Kiss turned her head toward him, her eyes glassy. "Don't leave me. Please, Onyx."

His throat closed. "I'm not going nowhere."

As the minutes stretched, Onyx couldn't stop the war in his head. The baby wasn't his, not this one. She was having his brother's baby. But watching Kiss fight through each contraction, holding her hand as she squeezed hard enough to break bone, he couldn't feel anything except love. Love for her. Love for the life she was bringing into the world. Love for the family he'd always wanted but never knew how to protect. This was Omari's child. But Onyx was the one here. The one watching and holding Kiss' hand through her pain. The one steadying her when she thought she couldn't do it herself. And part of him wondered if this was the universe's way of telling him something.

The door burst open, and Sade hurried in first, worry etched across her face. She rushed to Kiss' side, pressing a hand to her daughter's forehead.

"I'm here, baby," she whispered.

Tamika followed, her eyes flickering to Onyx before settling on Kiss. She looked both proud and pained, like she wanted to be everywhere at once. Together, Sade and Tamika took turns watching OJ in the waiting room, but Onyx stayed anchored at Kiss' side. He didn't flinch, didn't move. He was the wall she leaned on, the hand she held.

As the hours stretched deeper into the night, Onyx never left the room. Every cry, every breath, every squeeze of her hand rooted him there. Though the child coming into the world wasn't his, Onyx knew one thing with certainty. This moment would stay with him forever because on this day, in this hospital room, he was more than just the man who had messed up, more than just the twin living in his brother's shadow. He was present and needed, and this situation had proven that. At five fifty-two in the evening, Oryan Omari Blackwell was born, and Onyx was right by Kiss' side.

The hospital discharge papers crinkled in Kiss' lap as she settled into the backseat of Sade's car. The day was bright, but everything around her felt hazy, muffled, as though she were moving underwater.

Sade glanced at her as she started the engine. "You okay, baby?"

Kiss forced a nod. "Yeah. Just tired."

She sat next to Oryan, who was snuggled up in his car seat, sleeping peacefully. His tiny body was swaddled tight, and he wore the Jordan outfit that Onyx had bought for him. Beside him sat OJ, wide-eyed and fascinated, leaning over to peek at his little brother.

"That's your baby brother," Sade reminded him gently.

OJ grinned, nodding like he'd been handed the greatest gift in the world. Kiss' heart swelled then sank. She wanted to hold onto the sweetness of the moment, but fatigue, fear, and loneliness pressed in harder. She couldn't believe she was about to be a single mother for the next three years. When she had OJ, she didn't have to go through this. Onyx was there with her every step of the way. However, with Omari being in jail, she knew she would have nobody to help her when Oryan woke up for those 3 a.m. feedings.

When they pulled up to her house, Sade carried the diaper bag, while Kiss unbuckled Oryan. The car seat felt impossibly heavy for something so small. Inside, Sade helped her get settled, setting the bags on the couch. But after only a few minutes, Sade sighed.

"Baby, I hate to leave you like this, but I got to get to work. They short staffed today."

Kiss' chest tightened. She wanted to beg her mama to stay, but instead, she nodded. "It's okay, Ma. Go ahead."

Sade kissed her forehead, kissed OJ and Oryan, and then she was gone. The silence that followed felt deafening. Kiss set Oryan's car seat on the floor and sank onto the couch. Her body still ached from labor, stitches pulling, breasts sore, every movement a reminder of what she had just endured.

OJ plopped beside her, resting his head on her arm. "Mama, he so little," he whispered, eyes locked on the baby.

Kiss smiled faintly. "Yeah, he is."

She lifted Oryan gently, cradling him against her chest. His warmth soothed her, but the weight of reality pressed harder. She was home now. No nurses checking in, no one to call at the push of a button. Just her, her two boys, and the long stretch of night ahead. Her phone rang, and she balanced Oryan carefully as she answered it.

"Hello?"

"Baby?" It was Omari's voice.

Her chest squeezed. "Omari, I'm so glad to hear your voice."

"I been waiting all day to talk to you. How you feeling? You okay?" His voice was rough with concern.

Tears stung her eyes. "I had the baby. It's a boy, and his name is Oryan Omari Blackwell."

There was silence then a sound like a laugh choked with tears. "A boy… Damn, Kiss. We did it."

"Yeah," she whispered. "We did, and he's perfect."

They talked softly for a few minutes. Kiss told him about the labor and about OJ's excitement. But then, she broke the news. "I probably won't be able to come see you for a couple weeks. It's just a lot, and I gotta get used to this. Doing it on my own."

Omari went quiet for a moment, then he spoke low. "You ain't on your own. You got me, Kiss. Maybe not the way you want right now, but you got me. Don't forget that."

She closed her eyes, letting his words wash over her. "I won't."

When the call ended, she sat holding the phone, tears slipping down her cheeks, Oryan breathing softly against her chest. She wished he was here. Wished he could hold her at night and be the family they planned to be. But she knew they couldn't.

By evening, exhaustion hit her like a wall. Her body ached, and all she wanted to do was lay down and get some rest, but she knew she had to feed OJ and put him to bed. She was just getting ready to get up and find something to cook for him when there was a knock on her door. She got off the couch, slowly making her way to the door, as pain seared her lower body. She opened the door and smiled when she saw Onyx standing on the other side.

Onyx stepped in, carrying bags that smelled like food. His eyes scanned her instantly, concern flashing across his face. "You don't look good. You eat today?"

She shook her head weakly. "Nah, not yet. I was just about to get up and cook."

"Sit down," he ordered gently. "I got it."

He unpacked containers of fried chicken, mashed potatoes, greens, and cornbread. The smell filled the house, warm and comforting. He fixed a plate for her, set it on the coffee table, and nudged her until she picked up a fork. He then made a plate for OJ and sat him at the table.

She ate slowly, tears slipping down her cheeks, as the food touched her tongue. "Thank you," she whispered.

Onyx nodded. "You don't got to thank me. This what I'm

supposed to do. You are my son's mother. We will always be family, and family looks out for each other."

After dinner, Onyx took OJ's hand. "Come on, champ. Bath time."

Kiss watched as he led their son upstairs. She could hear the water running, OJ giggling as Onyx made silly voices and splashing noises. She was happy that Onyx was there to help her, even if he shouldn't be. By the time they came back down, OJ was in pajamas, smelling of soap, his hair damp. He ran over to Kiss and kissed her cheek, telling her that Onyx was going to read him a bedtime story. Kiss' chest ached again, but this time, it was from gratitude.

Onyx returned to the living room about twenty minutes later and sat next to her on the couch.

"Lil dude was out after the third page. He up there laid out like he just worked an eight-hour shift." Onyx laughed before picking the remote up from the coffee table. "Pick something."

She shook her head. "You pick."

They settled on an old comedy, *Boomerang*, which was one of Kiss' favorite movies. Kiss leaned back against the cushions, her body heavy, eyelids drooping. Onyx's arm rested along the back of the couch, and slowly, almost without thinking, she leaned into him. His warmth steadied her, his scent familiar. For the first time all day, she didn't feel alone. Sleep pulled at her, and she let it take her, her head resting against his chest, his arm tightening around her protectively.

Oryan's cry pierced the silence. Kiss stirred, but before she could move, Onyx was already up. He scooped the baby gently, murmuring softly. "Shhh, little man, I got you."

He warmed a bottle, fed Oryan slowly, rocking him in his arms until the cries quieted. The baby's tiny fingers curled around his pinky, and Onyx's chest swelled. When Oryan drifted back to sleep, Onyx laid him carefully in the bassinet then returned to the couch. Kiss was still asleep, her face soft, her breathing steady. He sat beside her, staring at her for a long time, the weight of everything heavy in his chest. He wasn't supposed to be here. This wasn't supposed to be his moment. But right now, it was.

As dawn crept through the curtains, Onyx was still awake, Oryan and OJ sleeping soundly, Kiss curled against him. He closed his eyes finally, whispering to himself, "I'll always be here for you," before drifting off to sleep.

***

Omari hadn't slept. He tossed and turned on the thin prison mattress all night, staring at the ceiling, his stomach tight with anticipation. It had been three months since Kiss had given birth to their son, and today was the day he would finally see them. He talked to her on the phone every other day, but it was nothing like seeing her face to face. He needed to see her, hug her, and hold her hand. She could tell him that she was fine over the phone, but she wouldn't be able to lie to him if he was looking at her. He needed to make sure that she and their son were both doing good. Today was the day that he would finally be able to meet his son, and he was more excited about that than anything.

Every thought made him restless, giddy even. He felt like a little boy waiting on Christmas morning, waiting for the sound of wrapping paper tearing, for the gift he'd been dreaming of all year. Only this wasn't a toy; this was his family. He'd traded a whole pack of cigarettes to get one of the older guys in the block to line him up the night before. Now, his hair was sharp, his face was clean, and he looked like himself again. When he glanced in the cloudy metal mirror, he actually smiled. *Yeah. Kiss gonna see me lookin' right.*

Visitation days always stretched like rubber bands – slow, tense, and loud with guards barking orders and the shuffle of men waiting to hear their names. Omari sat stiff on the hard bench, his leg bouncing. His palms itched with nerves. Every time a guard's voice boomed, he sat straighter, hoping and praying that he would be called next.

Hours passed, and the anticipation built so high it made his stomach ache. He pictured Kiss looking good in whatever she put on, OJ tugging at her hand, the car seat cradling little Oryan. He imagined their faces lighting up when they spotted him.

Finally, a guard called his name. "Blackwell! You got a visitor."

Omari's chest swelled, his heart pounding as he stood. His feet carried him fast down the corridor, every step echoing like a drumbeat of hope. The visitation room was buzzing with voices and laughter, the scrape of chairs against concrete, the familiar sting of disinfectant mixed with the faint scent of food. Omari's eyes scanned the room, searching, already smiling. His pulse kicked harder, ready for the sight of Kiss' face. But the smile slipped when he realized the visitor he had wasn't Kiss. At the table where he expected to see her, OJ, and the baby, sat Blue, dressed sharp in a black suit. Omari froze mid-step, his heart dropping into his stomach.

For a moment, he thought maybe there'd been a mistake. Maybe Kiss was late. Maybe she was still on the way. But Blue lifted his chin, his eyes locking on Omari's, and gestured casually at the chair across from him. The guard behind Omari nudged him forward. Omari's jaw clenched as he forced his legs to move. Each step toward that table felt heavier, the lightness of his anticipation replaced with suspicion and dread. He pulled the chair back slowly and lowered himself onto it, his eyes never leaving Blue's.

The chair's legs scraped against the floor as Omari sat, his body tight, his eyes locked on Blue. The room buzzed around them, other men talking, families reuniting, and kids giggling, but all Omari thought about was the fact that he was sitting across from Blue instead of Kiss and his son.

Omari leaned forward, his voice low, sharp. "What you doing here, Blue? You were not who I was expecting."

Blue smiled, not warm or kind but the sly grin of a man who carried information like a loaded gun. He folded his hands on the table. "That's exactly what I came to talk to you about. The reason why you here."

Omari's chest went tight. "What you talking 'bout? We know why I'm here."

Blue leaned in, his tone casual but cutting. "You ever wonder how the cops just so happened to be waiting for you that night at the gallery?"

Omari's jaw clenched. The memory hit like a fist – the sirens flashing, cold metal cuffs biting his wrists, paintings still in his bag. "What you sayin', Blue?"

Blue tapped the table with one finger, slow and deliberate. "I'm saying it wasn't cause they was lucky. Somebody tipped them off. And you wanna know who?"

Omari's heart thudded hard, his fists balling beneath the table. "Say it."

Blue's grin widened. "Onyx."

The word landed like a blade. Omari froze, staring, searching Blue's face for a lie, a crack, anything. But Blue's eyes were flat, certain.

"That's a damn lie," Omari hissed, though the back of his neck burned.

Blue shook his head slowly. "Ain't no lie. One of the cops on my payroll played me the tape himself. The voice that sent them to the gallery? Your brother's. Clear as day."

Omari's stomach flipped, bile rising in his throat. His own brother, his twin? The one that had put him in the game had turned snitch? Omari couldn't believe it. He'd known Onyx was mad at him about being with Kiss, but he never thought that he would snitch on him.

Blue kept talking, his voice almost bored. "I tried to line him up since then, put him down myself. But every time I send some-body, he's with his girl and the kids. Ain't trying to spray no family, you feel me?"

Omari blinked, his mind catching on one word. "Kids?"

Blue's gaze sharpened, enjoying the twist of the knife. "Yeah. Kiss and Onyx just had a baby a few months ago. He always with her and them kids. That nigga done became a real family man."

The room tilted. Omari gripped the table to steady himself, rage and grief flooding his chest. *That's my baby, not his,* Omari thought. He thought of Kiss' swollen belly during visits, her hand on it, the soft glow in her eyes when she spoke of their child. His child. And if the streets thought Onyx was the father, that meant Onyx was there – at her side, playing the role that belonged to Omari. Heat blurred Omari's vision. He wanted to flip the table, wanted to scream, wanted to claw through the walls until he was outside and in front of his brother. But all he could do was sit, the fury vibrating through his bones.

Blue leaned back, satisfied. "So, now you know. Your brother a dirty ass snitch, and you know what they say about snitches."

Omari's teeth clenched so hard his jaw ached. His chest rose and fell like he'd just run miles. He didn't trust his voice not to crack, didn't trust himself not to roar across the room. All he could do was sit there, staring at Blue, the truth burning hotter with every heartbeat. He listened to Blue talk for twenty more minutes, but all he could think about was the way Kiss and his brother had played him. He wondered if Kiss knew that Onyx had called the police on him. For the second time in his life, he felt like the two people he should have been able to trust had fucked him over.

***

Kiss had just finished packing the last of OJ's clothes, and Onyx took the box to the U-Haul that was attached to Kiss' Jeep.

She'd told Omari that she would bring the baby to see him today, but instead, she and her family were moving. Since the day she'd gotten home after having Oryan, Onyx had been there. They'd gotten back together, and although she'd told Omari she would wait for him, Kiss let it all go to finally be with Onyx forever. They had gone and eloped just a week ago, and Kiss and Onyx had even bought a house together in Ohio.

They wanted to get out of Detroit and raise their children in a better neighborhood. Onyx had sold the house he'd bought, and Kiss had taken the money Omari told her to hold. In her eyes, he was gone for three years and wouldn't need the money anyway. *By the time that nigga gets out, we'll be long gone,* she thought. Kiss used half of the money to open a clothing store, and her grand opening was just two weeks away. Kiss took one last look at the house that had been her home for the past five years before walking out the door.

***

The SUV slowed as it turned onto the quiet cul-de-sac, tires crunching over the smooth pavement. Kiss sat in the passenger seat, Oryan cooing in his car seat behind her, OJ's face pressed to the window with wide eyes. The house came into view, and Kiss couldn't help but smile. The six-bedroom estate stretched wide and proud, its red brick exterior trimmed with clean white shutters. Black iron railings lined the wraparound porch, and two tall oaks shaded the manicured lawn. A three-car garage gleamed to the side, and every window reflected the soft Ohio sunlight.

It wasn't Detroit. It wasn't cramped, loud streets and sirens at night. This was space that her family needed. It was proof of their come up, and Kiss was ready to start her new life. Onyx pulled into the long driveway, cutting the engine.

"Welcome home, Mrs. Blackwell," he said, his voice low with pride.

Kiss smiled and stepped out, her shoes clicking against the concrete. The porch stretched across the front like something out of a dream, wide enough for rocking chairs, a porch swing, and maybe even a line of potted plants she could see herself arranging come spring. Two stone steps led to the black double doors with frosted glass panels etched in elegant swirls.

OJ hopped out the back, spinning in a circle. "It's huge, Mama!" he yelled.

Kiss laughed softly, tears brimming in her eyes. "Yes, it is, baby. And it's all ours."

Inside, the house smelled faintly of new paint and polished wood. The foyer opened into a wide hallway with high ceilings, a crystal chandelier glittering overhead. Light poured through the arched windows, bouncing off gleaming hardwood floors. To the left, a sunken living room stretched wide with built-in bookshelves and a fireplace framed in stone. To the right, a formal dining room stood ready, its crown molding crisp and white, its bay window overlooking the front lawn.

Farther back, the kitchen was every bit the dream Kiss never thought she'd touch. There were marble countertops, stainless steel appliances, and a massive island with stools tucked neatly beneath it. French doors led out to a fenced backyard with a stone patio big enough for cookouts, family gatherings, and other celebrations.

Upstairs, six bedrooms waited. The master suite had vaulted ceilings, a fireplace of its own, and a walk-in closet bigger than the bedroom Kiss had grown up in. The bathroom gleamed with a deep soaking tub and a glass shower, twin sinks sitting beneath a wall-to-wall mirror.

Each child had their own room now, painted in warm colors, sunlight spilling across new carpet. Kiss walked slowly through it all, Oryan nestled in her arms, her free hand brushing walls and doorknobs like she had to touch everything to believe it. This wasn't temporary. This wasn't someone else's apartment or her mama's house. This was theirs, their forever home. Her chest ached with gratitude and relief. For the first time in years, she felt like she could breathe without waiting for the floor to collapse beneath her. She glanced at Onyx, who was watching her, pride written all over his face. He'd hustled for this. He'd bled and sweated for it. And now, they had something no one could take away.

As she laid Oryan gently in the crib Onyx had set up in the nursery, Kiss let her thoughts drift to Omari, locked away, waiting on her. She knew what it looked like. That she'd played him. Twice. That she'd given him promises she couldn't keep. But when she looked at OJ, already racing from room to room with joy, Oryan, peaceful in his crib, and Onyx, steady and strong at her side, she knew where her heart belonged. It belonged here – with her husband.

Chapter Forty

Onyx woke before the sun, the Ohio air still cool and clean compared to the heavy, restless mornings back in Detroit. He stretched in the wide bed, the ceiling fan humming above him, and glanced to his side. Kiss lay there, her face relaxed in sleep, her hair spilled across the pillow, one hand resting lightly on his chest. Even in her rest, she grounded him. She was his wife, his forever, and Onyx still couldn't believe that they'd made it. Over the years, they had been through everything that should have broken them apart, and here they were, happily married.

The move had been the right call. No more eyes on them, no more feeling like every corner held a trap. In Ohio, in their six-bedroom home tucked into a quiet neighborhood, it felt like he could finally exhale. Yet a sliver of tension never left him. He knew that Blue wanted him dead, and if he ever found him, he would be.

Onyx sat up slowly, careful not to wake Kiss. He walked to the window, pulling the curtains back just enough to see the front lawn – perfectly cut grass, the cul-de-sac empty, peaceful. Onyx smiled, but he knew the truth. Blue had found out that Onyx had made the call that got Omari locked up. That secret had been heavy, and now, it was exposed. Blue had made moves already, tried to line him up, but every time, Onyx had OJ or Oryan with him, Kiss by his side. Blue wasn't reckless enough to hit an entire family. That was the real reason they left Michigan. Onyx wanted peace for his wife and kids, wanted space where Blue's reach didn't stretch.

Still, standing in the quiet of his new home, Onyx felt proud. He'd done this. He'd given Kiss the life she deserved – a house big enough for their kids to grow, safe streets where OJ could ride his bike, schools that didn't feel like warzones. And Kiss had blossomed into a beautiful and successful woman. He thought of the small shop she'd opened downtown, a boutique filled with clothes she'd handpicked, racks neat and mannequins styled with her vision. The grand opening had been crowded, the ribbon cut by Kiss herself, Oryan in her arms and OJ tugging at her dress. Onyx had stood behind her the whole time, his chest swelling with pride.

Onyx walked back to the bed, sliding under the covers again, his mind already spinning with plans. Kiss' birthday was coming up in a few weeks, and he wanted it to be perfect, not just a dinner with flowers and gifts. Even though that was something he still might do, he wanted to take her on a trip as well. She'd mentioned once, late at night, how she'd always dreamed of seeing the ocean – not just the Detroit River or Lake Erie but the real ocean. Clear water, white sand, and sun so bright it kissed the skin golden.

They had money stacked away, and even if Onyx never got back on the block again, they would be straight. *Maybe I'll take her to Miami or the Caribbean,* he thought, somewhere she could breathe, relax, and smile the way she used to before the weight of everything pressed down on her. He pictured her in a sundress, her laughter carried by ocean wind, their kids building sandcastles while he wrapped his arm around her waist.

A small cry stirred from the baby monitor on the nightstand, breaking his thoughts – Oryan's tiny voice, hungry and insistent.

Onyx was up before Kiss could move. "I got him, baby," he murmured.

He padded down the hall to the nursery, the soft blue walls glowing in the nightlight's glow. Oryan kicked in his crib, fists waving, his face scrunched in a cry.

Onyx scooped him up, rocking him gently. "Shhh, lil' man. Daddy here."

Since Omari was locked up when Kiss had Oryan, Onyx had been the one to sign the birth certificate. By law and by love, Oryan was his, and Onyx wouldn't have wanted it any other way. He fed him, burped him, and laid him back down, watching his tiny chest rise and fall until sleep claimed him again.

Onyx walked back to his bedroom as the house settled back into the quiet. Onyx lay awake, thoughts turning heavy again. He had gone from a gangsta to a family man, and there was no other place he would have rather been. He knew that no matter what, he would protect his family at all costs. No matter what skeletons came out the closets over the years, Onyx would make sure he protected his family from them.

***

Kiss stirred before her alarm went off, her body used to the rhythm of motherhood now. Oryan was already fussing over the monitor, and Kiss knew that meant he was ready to eat. She got out of bed, slipping into her house shoes, before making her way to his room. She smiled at him as she saw him lying on his stomach, his little fists clenched like he was mad. Kiss scooped him up, pressing his warm cheek to hers.

"Good morning, my little man," she whispered.

She walked down to the kitchen and placed Oryan in his highchair before quickly preparing him a bowl of oatmeal. She fed him and placed apple juice into his bottle. She'd just placed Oryan into his playpen when OJ came running down the stairs in his race car pajamas.

"Mama, can I have pancakes?" he asked, his eyes bright.

Kiss laughed. "You always want pancakes."

"That's because they my favorite."

"Yeah, I can whip up some pancakes right quick. But you have to go take your shower and get ready for school while I cook."

"Okay, Mommy." OJ beamed, running out of the kitchen and up to his room. She took eggs and sausage from the fridge before taking the pancake mix out of the pantry. She moved through the kitchen with ease, flipping pancakes, cracking eggs, and placing sausages into the pan. OJ came back down about thirty minutes later, fully dressed. He sat at the table, and Kiss placed his plate in front of him.

Onyx walked into the kitchen a few moments after OJ. "Mmm," he said, sniffing the air. "My wife really spoiling us, huh?"

"It's just breakfast, babe." Kiss leaned in and kissed Onyx before making him a plate.

After breakfast, Kiss headed upstairs to shower and get dressed for the day. She wanted to look good. It was Friday, and she knew she would have a lot of customers coming in and out of the boutique, and she wanted to look like the businesswoman she now was. She slipped into a cream-colored romper that cinched at the waist, showing off her curves while still airy enough for the summer heat. The shorts brushed her thighs, her skin glowing against the light fabric. On her feet, she chose nude sandals with gold straps.

She styled her sleek knotless braids into a half ponytail at the top of her head, letting the rest fall down her back in a neat cascade. For jewelry, she kept it simple – gold hoops, a thin chain with her nameplate, and her wedding ring catching the light. Last came the finishing touch, her fragrance of the day. She picked up the frosted pink bottle of Burberry Her Blossom. With a few spritzes at her neck and wrists, the scent of soft florals and fruit wrapped around her like confidence. She checked herself in the mirror, smiling at the woman staring back. Kiss wasn't the scared little girl anymore. She'd grown into a woman that she could be proud of.

She packed OJ's lunch, kissed Oryan's forehead, and scooped her keys from the counter. Onyx had Oryan in his arms now, rocking him gently.

"I shouldn't be home too late. I'm thinking about closing the store around six, so I would need for you to pick OJ up from school," Kiss spoke.

"Okay, I'll be there. Have a good day, Mrs. Blackwell." Onyx smiled.

OJ hugged Onyx and kissed Oryan on the forehead before he walked out the door with Kiss. She dropped him off at school, telling him she loved him before he got out the car. She watched, waiting on OJ to go into the school, before she pulled off, ready to start her day.

Her boutique sat on a corner in downtown Columbus, the glass windows polished until they gleamed. The sign above read "Kiss'd By Style", scripted in bold, gold letters that caught the sunlight. Inside, the space was airy and chic – white walls, light wood floors, gold racks lined with dresses, tops, jeans, and accessories Kiss had handpicked herself. A chandelier sparkled above the checkout counter, and full-length mirrors reflected every angle of her customers. Mannequins stood near the front window, styled in summer looks – floral maxi dresses, cropped denim jackets, and statement heels. Along one wall, shelves displayed candles, handbags, and perfumes curated by Kiss herself. It was everything she'd imagined it would be.

The bell over the door chimed as a young woman walked in, her eyes wide. "This place is beautiful," she breathed.

"Thank you." Kiss smiled, her voice warm as she approached. "Looking for something special today?"

The woman nodded shyly. "I got a date tonight. Wanted to find something cute to wear."

Kiss smiled, her instincts kicking in. She walked her through options, pulling dresses off racks, holding them against her frame, offering honest opinions. By the time the woman left, she carried a bag in one hand and gratitude in her eyes.

"You really got an eye for this," another customer told Kiss later that day. "I'll be back for sure."

Each interaction lit something inside of her. This wasn't just selling clothes. It was giving women confidence and making them feel seen. As she rang up another sale, Kiss thought about the money that had made it all possible. The duffel bag that she had hidden in her basement. Omari's voice telling her to only take fifty thousand. However, she didn't just take fifty. She had taken it all. She didn't regret it one bit. That money had given her a freedom she'd never had before.

They had moved out of state, and nobody knew exactly where they were. They hadn't even let their mothers come visit them yet. So, she knew that whenever Omari did get out of prison, he wouldn't be able to find them. Onyx didn't know she'd taken Omari's money, and in Kiss' eyes, he never would. That was a secret that Kiss was going to take to her grave.

By afternoon, the boutique buzzed with women laughing and trying on outfits, while music floated through the speakers. Kiss moved between them, confident and graceful, her perfume mixing with the smell of new fabric and fresh flowers in vases by the register. She was happy, genuinely happy. For the first time in a long time, she wasn't wondering what would go wrong because she knew that it was only up from there. Her life was going great, and she couldn't wait to see what was next.

***

Omari stared at the phone on the wall of the cellblock, the dial tone buzzing in his ear. He'd already punched in Kiss' number three times this week, each time praying for her voice, for the sound of her breathing, for even just a whisper of the life they'd built in his head. But each time, the call rang into nothing – no answer, no voicemail, just silence.

He pressed his forehead against the cool wall by the phone, his fist tight around the receiver. "Come on, Kiss, just pick up." His voice cracked.

Two months had turned into three and then four. The baby had been born months ago, and she had promised to wait on him. Promised they would be a family. But since the last time he'd seen her swollen belly walking into visitation, she hadn't come back. He tried to tell himself she was just tired, over-whelmed, caught up in the storm of being a newly single mama. But deep down, the ache grew sharper. Blue's words clawed at him. *She's back with Onyx. They even got a baby together.*

Omari had laughed it off in the moment, angered by the suggestion. But now, every unanswered call, every empty chair at visitation, made that voice harder to ignore.

The guard's bark jolted him out of his daze. "Blackwell! You got a visit."

Omari's heart leapt. He scrubbed his hands against his pants, straightened his jumpsuit, forcing himself to look alive. Maybe she'd finally come. Maybe she brought the baby to finally meet his daddy. But when he stepped into the visitation room, it wasn't Kiss he saw. It was Tamika. His mother sat stiffly in the chair, her hands folded tightly in her lap. Her eyes were tired but warm when they found him.

"Mama," he spoke softly, sliding into the chair. He forced a smile. "Good to see you. How's everything? How's Kiss? How's my boys? I've been trying to call her a lot lately. I know it must be hard for her raising the two boys by herself, but I want to be there for her, even if it is from here."

Tamika's lips pressed together. "Omari…"

His chest tightened. "What? What is it?"

"I don't want to be the one to tell you this," she spoke carefully.

Anger flared in him, sudden and hot. "Tell me what?"

"Son, Kiss is married now."

The words hit harder than any punch he'd ever taken. He blinked, the room spinning. "What? Nah. That-that can't be true, Ma. Why would you say that?"

Tamika's eyes watered. "Because it is true, baby. She married your brother."

Omari sat, frozen. His hands clenched into fists against the cold metal table, veins straining in his arms. His mouth dropped open, and he looked at his mother, trying to find the lie in what she said. When he couldn't find one, he finally spoke.

"She married Onyx?" His voice was raw, broken. "While I'm in here? She told me she would wait on me. She has my son."

Tamika reached for him, but he pulled his hands back, hurt stinging his eyes.

"She played me again," he whispered, more to himself than to her. "First time, I let it slide. Said maybe life just pushed her that way. But twice? Twice is too much. She made me trust her, told me shit was different, and I believed her."

His chest heaved, the betrayal cutting deeper than steel. He thought of the promises, the letters, the way she'd cried, telling him she'd wait. He thought of the baby, his baby, growing up in another man's arms – his own brother's arms. It hollowed him out, taking everything he had left.

Tamika's voice trembled. "I didn't want you to hear it from the streets. I wanted you to hear it from them, but I knew they wasn't going to tell you. So, I had to. I'm so sorry, son."

Omari sat back slowly, staring at the ceiling, willing the tears not to fall. But they did anyway, hot and relentless. Tamika tried to hold his hand, but he pulled away, not wanting to be touched.

His heart was crushed, and this was a heartbreak that he didn't ever think he was going to get over.

***

The weeks that followed were a blur. He stopped calling her number. Stopped expecting to see her walk-through visitation. Instead, he threw himself into workouts, doing push-ups until his arms gave out and laps around the yard until his lungs burned, anything to keep from drowning in his thoughts. At night, though, when his cellblock went quiet, the ache gnawed at him. He thought of Oryan's first smile, first words, and first steps, moments he would never see, stolen from him and handed to Onyx. Sometimes, rage kept him awake. Sometimes, grief did the same. Either way, he thought about how he'd been replaced.

One day, Omari woke up to talks around the prison. COVID was what they called it, some virus out there, spreading faster than anyone could stop. It crept into the prison through guards, through new intakes. Men coughed in their bunks, fevers spiking, and cells locked down tighter than ever. The place was overcrowded, packed beyond what it could handle. Quarantine was impossible. Tension turned into riots, fights breaking out over masks and soap. Omari stayed sharp, knowing he needed to keep his head on a swivel. Then came the announcement over the loud speaker. Certain inmates were being released early – overcrowding, risk, and compassionate measures was what they called it.

When the guard slid open his cell and called him to pack up, Omari's heart thudded in disbelief. He was finally leaving. The walls that had caged him for years of his life opened wide, and the air outside hit different. But his freedom was laced with fury, knowing that he wasn't coming home to Kiss and their son. Kiss had chosen Onyx and married him to show Omari that it was real. She'd played him again, and this time, Omari knew that he could never forgive her.

Omari's shoes hit the familiar pavement outside his old townhouse, each step echoing with memories. The building looked the same, brick exterior, same cracks in the walkway, the porch light still tilted slightly. But as he pushed open the door, his chest hollowed. The air inside was stale, thick with dust and abandonment. His furniture was there, the walls unchanged, but the life he'd left behind had gone cold. He checked the stash spots beneath the floorboards in the closet automatically. His jaw clenched. He knew he'd told her to get it, but he told her to only take fifty grand. He'd thought that when she married Onyx, Kiss would have taken the money back. However, she hadn't.

That evening, Omari found himself in a dimly lit bar on the eastside. Blue was already there, a heavy presence in a corner booth, a cigar smoldering between his fingers.

Omari slid into the seat across from him. "Where Kiss at?" His voice was flat, stripped of patience. "She with Onyx, so if you know where he is, you know where she is."

Blue studied him for a long moment before smirking. "Straight to it, huh? Thought you'd want a drink first."

"I ain't here to play no games."

Blue leaned back, exhaling smoke. "They ain't in the city no more. Your brother was smart enough to get them out of here. Moved to Ohio. Some big ass house in a quiet neighborhood."

Omari's chest tightened. "Where?"

Blue shrugged. "That I don't know. But I do know this. She got a boutique in downtown Columbus. Nice spot, shiny windows, gold letters. *Kiss'd By Style.*"

Omari's teeth ground together at the sound of her success dripping off Blue's tongue. He left the bar with his mind made up. His townhouse was empty of money, his heart was empty of loyalty, and he was empty of everything. In the back bedroom closet, beneath a false panel in the wall, sat a steel safe he'd had installed years ago. His fingers moved through the familiar combination, the click echoing like a heartbeat. Inside lay two pistols, wrapped in cloth, oiled and waiting. He lifted them one by one, the weight both familiar and foreign after years without holding them. He checked the chambers and the magazines before he slid them into his duffel bag.

By nightfall, Omari was behind the wheel of a borrowed car, the interstate stretching ahead of him. The hum of the tires was the only sound he heard steady and relentless. His mind replayed everything – Kiss' promises, Onyx's betrayal, the image of his son growing up calling another man Daddy. It was all too much for him to handle.

Hours later, he rolled into Columbus. The city lights glowed against the dark sky, unfamiliar streets winding toward downtown. He parked across from the boutique Blue had described, the gold letters gleaming even in the night. *Kiss'd By Style.* Omari killed the engine and sat back, his eyes locked on the glass windows of the shop. He was done being forgotten, and soon, Kiss would know just that.

Omari hadn't slept. He'd been parked down the block since before dawn, engine off, his body stiff in the driver's seat. Every nerve in him was alive, tuned to the storefront across the street. A few hours after the sun came up, he saw her – Kiss – unlocking the boutique doors with a jangle of keys, her braids swaying as she pushed the glass open. For a moment, Omari just stared, breath caught in his throat. She looked the same and yet different. She was now more polished and confident, smiling at the first customer who walked in.

He stayed the entire day – watched her greet women with hugs, style mannequins in the window, and ring up sales. He stayed there all day, watching Kiss' every move, and she didn't even realize she was being watched. By late afternoon, the boutique lights dimmed. Kiss walked out the front door, locking it behind her. She slid into her car, not the Jeep that Omari had gotten for her a couple years ago. She had now upgraded to a Range Rover.

Omari followed at a distance, his hands tight on the wheel. He trailed her to OJ's school, watched her hug the boy, as he came running into her arms. Omari's heart twisted painfully as he watched his nephew. He followed again as she drove through quiet Ohio streets, pulling into the driveway of a sprawling house. *This must be that six-bedroom house Blue was telling me about,* he thought. Omari parked in the shadows and killed the engine. He sat there for hours, just watching.

The house came alive in the evening, lights glowing in the kitchen, shadows moving across curtains, the faint sound of laughter when the windows opened. Omari lit no cigarettes, made no noise. He just watched, not wanting anyone to know he was there. One by one, the rooms went dark – the kids' lights first then the downstairs lights. Finally, after what seemed like hours, the one light that was on upstairs went off. Omari figured that was the master bedroom where Kiss and Onyx were.

Omari's pulse quickened as he pulled his guns from the duffle bag and placed them both in his waistline. The house loomed ahead, pristine white shutters and manicured bushes framing the porch. Omari's footsteps were silent on the drive-way. He slipped around the side and found the back door. The lock was newer but not strong. A little pressure, a twist of his knife, and it gave way with a muted click.

Omari walked inside the house, gun leading the way. He walked directly upstairs, looking for the room that belonged to Kiss and Onyx. The smell of laundry detergent mixed with cologne drifted out to him. The first door he came to was not the master. It must have been a guest room because no one was inside. It was the same for the next room he walked into. Finally, he opened the door to a room that made his heart jump.

There, lying sound asleep in his crib, was his son –the son he'd never even seen before. He walked inside the room quietly, not wanting to wake him. Omari touched his chest, feeling his small heartbeat, and Oryan stirred just a little. Omari stood there, just watching his son sleep, for about five minutes before walking out the room.

He heard the soft music as he walked down the hall. He figured the room it came from had to be the master. Omari crept up slowly, opening the door with his gun still in his hand. He stepped in to see Onyx with his head between Kiss' legs, her soft moans filling the air. Omari flicked on the light, startling both Kiss and Onyx at the same time.

"So, y'all muthafuckas think I'm somebody to be played with, huh? Think because I gave y'all a pass when we was kids that I'm some kinda bitch, huh?"

"Omari, what the hell are you doing here?" Kiss screamed, quickly covering herself with the comforter.

Onyx stood up, jaw tight, as he looked Omari in the eye. "Nigga, you should put that gun down now, while you still have a chance."

Without a word, Omari busted Onyx in the face with the gun, causing him to fall to the floor. Kiss screamed, jumping up and rushing to Onyx. Tears ran down her face as she saw the blood pouring from Onyx's nose.

"Omari, why are you…"

"Bitch, where the fuck is my money?" Omari asked, cutting her off.

"Fuck you talkin' bout, nigga? She ain't got no money from you. I take care of my family. She don't need yo' ass as you can see," Onyx shot, blood and spittle flying from his mouth. He stood to his feet, looking Omari directly in the eyes. Letting him know he wasn't scared of him.

"Omari, please just put the gun down. My kids are asleep in their bedrooms." Kiss looked up at Omari with pleading eyes. However, Omari didn't give a damn.

"I'm going to ask you one more time. Where the fuck is my money?" This time, Omari aimed the gun directly at Kiss' head.

"Get that fuckin' gun off…"

However, before Onyx could finish his sentence, Kiss blurted out, "I don't have it anymore."

Onyx heard the words when she spoke them, but at that moment, the only thing he thought about was keepin' his family safe.

Omari shook his head, gun still on Kiss. "I should have known. That was probably all yo' snake ass wanted anyway. Fuckin' ho. Did you tell my brother the way you sucked my dick for that Jeep I got you?"

Onyx's chest rose in anger. "Look, Omari, Kiss is my wife. This my house and my family. You think I give a fuck about that gun you got in yo' hand? I'll beat the fuck out of you then shoot you with yo' own gun. I'd suggest you leave before you make me do some shit I don't want to do." Onyx stood strong, not giving a damn about the gun in Omari's hand. He pushed Kiss behind him as he looked Omari in the eyes. "You should go."

"I spent my entire life loving both of y'all, and in the end, y'all were the ones to hurt me the most. I went to jail for you twice, Kiss. But you ain't give a shit. Now you got this nigga raising my baby like he's his. And you," Omari turned the gun to Onyx, "you my twin, my first best friend, and you take the only woman I ever loved. You gave me that gun that night I shot Darren, but I never said shit. Then, you turn around and snitch on me and sent me to jail just so you could marry my girl and raise my child? With twins like you, who the fuck would ever need an enemy? Tell me something, Onyx. How did you know I was going to be there?"

"You think I don't know every job Blue sent you on? I brought you into this shit. I knew about the job before you did."

Onyx opened his mouth to say something else, but Omari didn't want to hear anymore of Onyx's bullshit. So, before Onyx could say another word, Omari pulled the trigger, sending one bullet straight into Onyx's head, dropping him instantly. Kiss screamed, dropping to the floor beside Onyx.

"Omari! What did you do? Oh, my God! Onyx, baby, please get up. Please, baby."

Omari chuckled sinisterly as he looked down at Kiss cradling Onyx's lifeless body in her arms. "You callin' that nigga baby when I been the one that loved you since I was thirteen. I sacrificed my entire life for you. Kept you safe when nobody else did. Now you over there crying about my brother. It's til death do y'all part, right? Then you can die with that nigga, bitch."

Omari pulled the trigger three more times, bullets ripping into Kiss' chest. She slumped over Onyx, her body lifeless. For a moment, Omari just stood there, looking at them. They were both dead, and Omari had finally gotten his revenge on the two people that hurt him the most. For a few seconds, Omari felt good. Felt that he'd finally gotten his lick back. Then, he thought about the two innocent children, one of which was his. They would be the ones to find their bodies, and Omari didn't want that.

He also thought about prison, a place he knew he couldn't go. This would be his third strike, so he knew that would mean life. He knew he couldn't do any more time in prison. *Fuckk!* he thought as he hit his head with his palm. He grabbed his phone and called Tamika. She answered on the fourth ring, voice thick with sleep.

"Mama, I just shot Onyx and Kiss. They both dead."

"What?! Omari, this is not funny. Don't even fuckin' play like that," Tamika ordered.

"Listen to me, Mama. This is not a joke. They dead, and I killed them. The kids are still in the house. You need to call the police and come to Ohio and get them. I don't want them to be the ones to find the bodies in the morning. The address is 645 Brooklane. Call the police and come now."

Tamika's sobs shot through the phone, damn near ripping Omari in half.

"Mari, no. Please tell me you didn't. Please, Mari."

"Just come to the address, Mama. Get the kids and keep them safe. I love you."

Before Tamika could say a word, Omari hung up. He sat on the floor next to Kiss and took her hand. He thought about how his love for her had taken him to a point of no return. Because of her, he'd done things he never thought he would. Placing the gun to his own head, he looked over at Kiss before pulling the trigger.

The End.

DID YOU ENJOY?

Did you enjoy the read?
Let us know how much by leaving us a
review on Amazon and Goodreads.

OTHER BOOKS BY
URBAN AINT DEAD

Tales 4rm Da Dale

The Hottest Summer Ever

Hittin' Licks For The Holidays: Atlanta

Wet Dreams On Lockdown: The Nurse

How To Publish A Book From Prison

How To Invest In The Stock Market From Prison

First Summer Out With My Prison Bae

By **Elijah R. Freeman**

Despite The Odds

Despite The Odds 2

By **Juhnell Morgan**

Hittaz

Hittaz 2

Hittaz 3

Hittaz 4

Hittaz 5

Hittaz 6

Coldhearted

Coldhearted 2

Coldhearted 3

By **Lou Garden Price, Sr.**

A YN'S Muse For The Summer

Wizdom: Forever Your Gangsta

Charge It To The Game

Charge It To The Game 2

Charge It To The Game 3

A Summer To Remember With My Hitta

Snatched Up By A Hitta

Santa Sent Me A Real One For Christmas

Wet Dreams On Lockdown: The Unit Manager

Thug Me The Right Way 2

Thug Me The Right Way 3

Seizing A Gangsta's Heart For The Summer

Yours For The Taking

Wrapped Up In A Hitta's Love For Christmas

By **Nai**

A Set Up For Revenge

A Set Up For Revenge 2

Wet Dreams On Lockdown: The Librarian

By **Ashley Williams**

Trickin' On A Heaux For Christmas

Homie Hoppin' For The Holidays

Wet Dreams On Lockdown: The Female C.O

Letters Of His Love

By **Telia Teanna**

The State's Witness

The State's Witness 2

The State's Witness 3

This Time Won't You Save Me

This Time Won't You Save Me 2

His Summer Side Piece

A Holiday Heist

Healing The Heart Of A Detroit Gangsta

Summer Vows With A Detroit Gangsta

The Promissory

The Promissory 2

By **Kyiris Ashley**

Stuck In The Trenches

Stuck In The Trenches 2

By **Huff Tha Great**

Melted The Heart Of A Menace

Wet Dreams On Lockdown: Lieutenant Grace

By **P. Wise**

Merry Trapmas

By **Mia Sky**

Thug Me The Right Way

By **DiamondATL & Nai**

Wet Dreams On Lockdown: The Counselor

By **Paris Iman**

Wet Dreams On Lockdown: The Male C.O

By **Tamyra Griffin**

Wet Dreams On Lockdown: The Captain

By **TN Jones**

Wet Dreams On Lockdown: The Warden

By **Shawnice**

Atlantastan

Atlantastan 2

By **Chris Green**

IN The Streetz

IN The Streetz 2

IN The Streetz 3

IN The Streetz 4

IN The Streetz 5

By **Tron Hill**

Hittin' Licks For The Holidays: New York

Bandemic

By **Freshh Moneyy**

Coming Soon From
URBAN AINT DEAD

Drill
The Hottest Summer Ever 2
THE G-CODE
Tales 4rm Da Dale 2
How To Build Your Credit From Prison
By **Elijah R. Freeman**

Despite The Odds 3
By **Juhnell Morgan**

A Felon's Promise
By **Nai**

Atlantastan 3
By **Chris Green**

IN The Streetz 6
By **Tron Hill**

Bandemic 2
By **Freshh Moneyy**

www.ingramcontent.com/pod-product-compliance
Lightning Source LLC
Chambersburg PA
CBHW070651010826
48975CB00013B/468